June 14, 1992

Happy Birthday, Daddy !

D1231078

The Rise and Fall
of
César Birotteau

HONORÉ DE
BALZAC

The
Rise and Fall
of
César Birotteau

Translated by Ellen Marriage

Carroll & Graf Publishers, Inc.
New York

First Carroll & Graf edition 1989

Carroll & Graf Publishers, Inc.
260 Fifth Avenue
New York, NY 10001

ISBN: 0-88184-448-9

Manufactured in the United States of America

THE RISE AND FALL OF CESAR BIROTTEAU

Retail Perfumer,
Deputy-Mayor of the Second Arrondissement, Paris, Chevalier of the Legion of Honor, etc.

To Monsieur Alphonse de Lamartine,
from his admirer,

De Balzac.

I.

CESAR'S APOGEE

THERE is but one brief interval of silence during a winter night in the Rue Saint-Honoré; for to the sounds of carriages rolling home from balls and theatres succeeds the rumbling of market gardeners' carts on their way to the Great Market. During this pause in the great symphony of uproar sent up by the streets of Paris, this cessation of traffic towards one o'clock in the morning, the wife of M. César Birotteau, of the retail perfumery establishment near the Place Vendôme, dreamed a frightful dream, and awoke with a start.

She had met her double. She had appeared to herself, clad in rags, laying a meagre, shriveled hand on her own shop-door handle. She had been at once in her chair at the cash desk and on the threshold; she had heard herself begging; she had heard two selves speaking in fact, the one from the desk, the other from the doorstep. She turned and stretched out her hand for her husband, and found his place cold. At that her terror grew to such a pitch that she could not move her head, her neck seemed stiffened to stone, the walls of her throat were glued together, her voice failed her; she sat up rigid and motionless, staring before her with wide eyes.   Her hair rose with a painful sensation, strange sounds rang in her ears, something clutched at her heart though it beat hard, she was covered with perspiration, and yet shuddering with cold in the alcove behind the two open folding doors.

Fear, with its partially morbific effects, is an emotion which puts so violent a strain upon the human mechanism, that the mental faculties are either suddenly stimulated by it to the highest degree of activity, or reduced to the last extremity of disorganization.   Physiology has long been puzzled to account for a phenomenon which upsets its theories and stultifies its hypotheses, although it is simply and solely a shock brought about spontaneously, but, like all electrical phenomena, erratic and unaccountable in its manifestations.   This explanation will become a commonplace when men of science will recognize the great part played by electricity in human thinking power.

Mme. Birotteau was just then enduring the pangs which bring about a certain mental lucidity consequent on those terrible discharges when the will is contracted or expanded by a mysterious mechanism.   So that, during a lapse of time, exceedingly short if measured by the tickings of a clock, but incommensurable by reason of the infinite rapid impressions which it brought, the poor woman had the prodigious power of uttering more thoughts and of calling up more memories than would have arisen in her mind in its normal state in the course of a whole day.   Her soliloquy during this vivid and painful experience may be resumed in a few words she uttered, incongruous and nonsensical as they were :—

"There is no reason whatever why Birotteau should be out of bed.—He ate so much veal; perhaps it disagreed with him. —But if he had been taken ill, he would have waked me up. —These nineteen years that we have slept here together under this roof, he has never got up in the middle of the night without telling me, poor dear!—He has never slept out except when he was on guard.—Did he go to bed when I did?   Why, yes.   Dear me! how stupid I am!"

She glanced over the bed. There lay her husband's night-cap, moulded to the almost conical shape of his head. "Can he be dead?—Can he have made away with himself?—Why should he?" she thought. "Since they made him deputy-mayor two years ago, I haven't known what to make of him.—To get mixed up with public affairs, on the word of an honest woman, isn't it enough to make you feel sorry for a man?—The business is doing well.—He has just given me a shawl.—Perhaps it is doing badly!—Pshaw! I should know of it if it were.—But is there any knowing what is in the bottom of a man's mind? Or a woman's either? There is no harm in that.—Haven't sales amounted to five thousand francs this very day!—And then a deputy-mayor is not likely to kill himself; he knows the law too well for that.—But where can he be?"

She had no power to turn her head; she could not stretch out a hand to the bell-rope, which would have set in motion a general servant, three shopmen, and the errand boy. The nightmare that lasted on into her waking moments was so strong upon her that she forgot her daughter, peacefully sleeping in the next room, beyond the door which opened at the foot of the bed.

"Birotteau!" She received no answer. She fancied that she had called aloud, but, as a matter of fact, she had only spoken in her thoughts.

"Suppose he should have a mistress? But he has not wit enough for that," she thought, "and then he is too fond of me.—Didn't he tell Mme. Roguin that he had never been unfaithful to me, even in thought?—Why, the man is honesty itself!—If any one deserves to go to heaven, he does.—What he finds to say to his confessor, I don't know. He tells him make-believes.—For a Royalist as he is (without any reason to give for it, by the by), he does not make much of a puff of his religion.—Poor dear, he slips out to mass at eight o'clock as if he were running off to amuse himself on the sly. It is the fear of God that he has before his eyes; he does not trouble himself much about hell. How should he have a mistress? He keeps so close to my apron-strings that I get tired of it. He loves me like the apple of his eye; he would put out his eyes for me.—All these nineteen years he has never spoken a harsh word to myself.—I come before his daughter with him.—Why, Césarine is there . . . (Césarine! Césarine!)—Birotteau never has a thought that he does not tell me.—It was a true word he said when he came to the sign of the *Little Sailor* and told me that it would take time to know him. And he's gone! . . . that is the extraordinary thing!"

She turned her head with an effort, and peered into the darkness. Night filled the room with picturesque effects, the despair of language, the exclusive province of the painter of genre. What words could reproduce the whimsical shapes that the curtains took as the draught swelled them, or the startling zigzag shadows that they cast? The dim night-light flickered over the red cotton folds; the brass rosette of the curtain-rest reflected the crimson gleams from a central boss, bloodshot like a robber's eyes; a ghostly gown was kneeling there; the room was filled, in fact, with all the strange, unfamiliar appearances which appall the imagination at a time when it can only see horrors and exaggerate them.

Mme. Birotteau fancied that she saw a bright light in the next room, and a thought of fire flashed across her; but she caught sight of a red bandana handkerchief, which looked to her like a pool of blood, and in another moment she discovered traces of a struggle in the arrangement of the furniture, and could think of nothing but burglars. She remembered that there was a sum of money in the safe, and a generous fear extinguished the cold ague of nightmare. Thoroughly alarmed, she sprang out on to the floor in her night-dress, to go to the assistance of the husband whom she fancied as engaged in a hand-to-hand conflict with assassins.

"Birotteau! Birotteau!" she cried in a voice of anguish.

The retail perfumer was standing in the middle of the adjacent room, apparently engaged in measuring the air with a yard stick. His dressing-gown (of green cotton, with chocolate-colored spots) covered him so ill that his bare legs were red with the cold, but he did not seem to notice this.

When César turned round with a "Well, what is it, Constance?" he looked as a man absorbed by his schemes is apt to look—so ludicrously foolish, that Mme. Birotteau began to laugh.

"Dear me, César, how queer you look!" said she. "What made you leave me alone without saying anything? I nearly died of fright. I did not know what to think. What are you after, open to every wind that blows? You will catch your death of cold. Birotteau! do you hear?"

"Yes, wife; here I am," and the perfumer returned to the bedroom.

"There, come along and warm yourself, and tell me what crotchet you have in your head," returned Mme. Birotteau, raking among the ashes, which she hastily tried to rekindle. "I am frozen. How stupid it was of me to get up in my night-dress! But I really thought you were being murdered."

The merchant set down the bedroom candlestick on the chimney-piece, huddled himself in his dressing-gown, and looked about in an absent fashion for his wife's flannel petticoat.

"Here, pussie, just put this on," said he. "Twenty-two by eighteen——" he added, continuing his soliloquy. "We could have a magnificent drawing-room."

"Look here! Birotteau, you seem to be in a fair way to lose your wits. Are you dreaming?"

"No; I am thinking, wife."

"Then you might wait; your follies will keep till daylight at any rate," cried she, and, fastening her petticoat under her sleeping jacket, she went to open the door of their daughter's room.

"Césarine is fast asleep. She will not hear a word. Come, Birotteau, tell me about it. What is it?"

"We can give the ball."

"Give a ball! *We* give a ball! My dear! on the word of an honest woman, you are dreaming!"

"Dreaming? not a bit of it, darling.

"Listen; you should always do your duty according to your station in life. Now the Government has brought me into prominence, I belong to the Government, and it is incumbent upon us to study its spirit and to forward its aims by developing them. The Duc de Richelieu has just put an end to the occupation of the Allied troops. According to M. de la Billardière, official functionaries who represent the city of Paris ought to regard it as a duty—each in his own sphere of influence—to celebrate the liberation of French soil. Let us establish beyond proof a genuine patriotism which shall put those accursed schemers that call themselves Liberals to the blush, eh? Do you think that I do not love my country? I mean to show the Liberals and my enemies that to love the King is to love France!"

"Then do you think that you have enemies, my poor Birotteau?"

"Why, yes, we have enemies, wife. And half our friends in the quarter are among them. They all say, 'Birotteau has such luck; Birotteau was once a nobody, and look at him now! He is deputy-mayor; everything has prospered with him.' Very well; there is a nice disappointment still in store for them. You should be the first to hear that I am a Chevalier of the Legion of Honor; the King signed the patent yesterday!"

"Oh! well then, dear, we must give the ball," cried Mme. Birotteau, greatly excited. "But what can you have done so great as to have the Cross?"

Birotteau was embarrassed.

"When M. de la Billardière told me about it yesterday," said he, "I asked myself, just as you did, what claim I had to it. But, after thinking it over, I saw that I deserved it, and ended by approving the action of the Government. To begin with, I am a Royalist, and I was wounded at Saint-Roch in Vendémiaire; it is something, isn't it, to have borne arms for the good cause in those times? Then some of the merchants think that the way I discharged my duties as arbitrator at the Consular Tribunal had given general satisfaction; and lastly, I am a deputy-mayor, and the King is distributing four Crosses among the municipal authorities in the city of Paris. After they had gone into the claims of the deputy-mayors for a decoration, the Prefect put me down at the top of the list. The King, too, is sure to know my name; thanks to old Ragon, I supply him with the only hair powder he will use; no one else has the recipe for the powder the late Queen used to wear, poor dear august victim! The Mayor backed me up with all his might. What was I to do? If the King gives me the Cross when I don't ask him for it, it looks to me as if I could not decline it without failing in respect. Was it my doing that I was made a deputy-mayor? So as we have the wind in our sails, wife, as your uncle Pillerault says when he is in a joking humor, I have made up my mind that we must live up to our high position. If I am to be somebody, I will have a try at being whatever Providence meant me to be; a sub-prefect, if such is my destiny. And you make a great mistake, wife, when you imagine that a citizen has discharged all the duty he owes his country when he has supplied his customers with scent across the counter for a score of years. If the State demands the co-operation of our intelligence, we are as much bound to give it, as to pay succession duty, or the door and window tax, *et cetera*. Do you want to sit at your desk all your life? You have been there a pretty long time (God be thanked). The ball will be a private fête of our own. No more of the shop; for *you,* that is. I shall burn the signboard *The Queen of Roses,* and the words CESAR BIROTTEAU (LATE RAGON), RETAIL PERFUMER, shall be painted out on the shop-front. I shall simply put up PERFUMERY in big gold letters instead. There will be room on the mezzanine floor for a cash desk and the safe, and a nice little room for you. I shall make the back-shop and the present dining-room and kitchen into a warehouse. Then I mean to take the first floor next door, and make a way into it through the wall. The staircase must be altered so that we can walk on the level out of one house and into the

other. We shall have a fine set of rooms then, furnished
up to the nines.

"Yes. I will have your room done up, and contrive a
boudoir for you, and Césarine shall have a pretty room.
You must engage a young lady for the shop, and she and
the assistant and your waiting-maid (yes, madame, you
shall have a waiting-maid) shall have rooms on the second
floor. The kitchen must be on the third floor. The cook
and the errand-boy shall be lodged up there, and we will
keep the stock of bottles, and flasks and china on the fourth.
The workrooms can be in the attics, so when people come
in they will not see bottles being filled and stoppered and
labeled, nor sachets being made. That sort of thing is all
very well for the Rue Saint-Denis, but it won't do in the
Rue Saint-Honoré! Bad style. Our shop ought to be as
snug as a drawing-room. Just tell me this: are we the only
perfumers who have come in for honors? Aren't there
vinegar makers and mustard manufacturers who have a
command in the National Guard, and are well looked on at
the Tuileries? Let us do as they do, and extend the business, at the same time making our way in society."

"One moment, Birotteau. Do you know what I think
while I hear you talk? Well, to me, it is just as if a man
was starting out on a wild-goose chase. Don't you remember what I told you when there was talk of your being made
mayor? A quiet life before all things, I said; you are about
as fit for public life as my arm for a windmill sail. Grand
doings will be the ruin of you.

"You did not listen to me; and here the ruin has come
upon us. If you are going to take part in politics, you must
have money; and have we money? What! you mean to burn
the signboard that cost six hundred francs, and give up the
Queen of Roses and your real glory? Leave ambition to
other people. If you put your hand in the fire, you get
singed, don't you? Politics are very hot nowadays. We
have a hundred thousand francs good money invested outside the business, the stock, and the factory, have we? **If**

you have a mind to increase it, do now as you did in 1793. The funds are at seventy-two, buy *rentes;* you would have ten thousand livres a year coming in without drawing anything out of the business. Then take advantage of the transfer to marry our Césarine, sell the business, and let us go and live in your part of the world. Why, any time for these fifteen years you have talked of buying the Treasury Farm, that nice little place near Chinon, with streams, and meadows, and woods, and vineyards, and crofts. It would bring you in a thousand crowns a year, and we both of us like the house. It is still to be had for sixty thousand crowns, and my gentleman must meddle and make in politics, must he?

"Just remember what we are—we are perfumers. Sixteen years ago, before you thought of the Superfine Pâte des Sultanes and the Carminative Toilet Lotion, if any one had come and said to you, 'You will have money enough to buy the Treasury Farm,' wouldn't you have been wild with joy? Very well; and now, when you can buy the property which you wanted so much that you talked of nothing else every time that you opened your mouth, you begin to talk of squandering the money that we have earned by the sweat of our brows, *ours* I may say, for all along I have sat there at the desk like a dog in a kennel. Now, instead of turning five halfpence into six farthings, and six farthings into nothing at all, wouldn't it be better to have a daughter married to a notary in Paris, and a house that you can stay at, and to spend eight months in the year at Chinon?

"Wait till the funds rise. You can give your daughter eight thousand livres a year; we will keep two thousand for ourselves, and the sale of the business will pay for the Treasury Farm. We will take the furniture down into the country, dear, it is quite worth while, and there we can live like princes, while here one must have at least a million to cut a figure."

"That is just what I expected," said César Birotteau.

"Oh! you think I am very foolish, no doubt, but I am not so foolish but that I have looked at the thing all round. Attend to what I am going to say. Alexandre Crottat is a son-in-law that would suit us to a T, and he will have Roguin's practice; but do you imagine that he would be satisfied with a hundred thousand francs? (always supposing that we pay down all our ready money when we marry our daughter; and I am of that way of thinking, for I would have nothing but dry bread for the rest of my days to see her as happy as a queen and the wife of a Paris notary, as you say.) Very well, but a hundred thousand francs down, or even eight thousand francs of *rentes*, would go no way towards buying Roguin's practice.

"Young Xandrot (as we call him) thinks, like everybody else, that we are a great deal richer than we are. If that father of his, a rich farmer who sticks to his property like a leech, does not sell something like a hundred thousand francs worth of land, Xandrot will not be a notary, for Roguin's practice is worth four or five hundred thousand francs. If Crottat does not pay half the money down, how will he manage the business? Césarine ought to have a portion of two hundred thousand francs, and we should retire like decent citizens of Paris on fifteen thousand livres a year in the funds; that is what I should like. If I could make you see all this as clear as daylight, you would have nothing left to say for yourself, eh?"

"Oh! if you have the wealth of the Indies——"

"So I have, darling. Yes," he put his arm round his wife's waist, and tapped her gently with his fingers, impelled by the joy that shone from every feature of his face. "I did not want to say a word about this to you till the thing was ripe, but, faith! to-morrow perhaps it will be settled. This it is.

"Roguin has been proposing a business speculation to me, so safe that he and one or two of his clients, and Ragon, and your uncle Pillerault, are going into it. We are to buy some building land near the Madeleine. Roguin thinks that we can buy it now for a quarter of the price it will fetch in three years' time when the leases will be out, and we shall be free to exploit it. There are six of us; each agrees to take so much; I am finding three hundred thousand francs for the purchase of three-eighths. If any of us are short of money, Roguin will advance it, taking a mortgage on the share of the land as security. Pillerault, old Ragon, and I are going to take half of it among us; but I want to have it registered in my name, so as to keep hold of the handle of the pan and see how the fish are frying. Roguin himself, under the name of M. Charles Claparon, will be joint-owner with me; he will give a guarantee to each of his partners, and I shall do the same with mine. The deeds of purchase will be private deeds until we have all the lands in our hands. Roguin will look into it, and see which of the purchases must be completed, for he is not sure that we can dispense with intermediary registration, and yet transfer a separate title to the buyers when we break up the estate into separate lots; but it would take too long to explain it to you.

"When the building land has been paid for, we shall have nothing to do but fold our arms, and in three years' time we shall have a million. Césarine will be twenty years old, we shall have sold the business, and then, God willing, we will go modestly toward greatness."

"Well, but where are the three hundred thousand francs to come from?" asked Mme. Birotteau.

"My dear little woman, you know nothing of business. There are the hundred thousand francs in Roguin's hands; I will pay them down. Then I shall borrow forty thousand francs on the buildings and the land that our factory stands on, over in the Faubourg du Temple, and we have twenty thousand francs in bills and acceptances in the portfolio—altogether that makes a hundred and sixty thousand francs. There remain a hundred and forty-thousand francs to be raised; I will draw bills to the order of M. Charles Claparon the banker; he will advance the money, less the discount. And there are our three hundred thousand

francs; and you don't owe an account until it is due. When
the bills fall due, we shall be ready for them, with the profits
of the business. If we should find any difficulty in meeting
them, Roguin would lend me the money at five per cent on a
mortgage on my share of the building land. But there is
no need to borrow. I have discovered a specific for making
the hair grow, a Comagen oil. Livingston has put up a
hydraulic press for me down yonder for the hazel-nuts; all
the oil should be squeezed out at once under such strong
pressure. In a year's time the probabilities are that I shall
have made a hundred thousand francs at least. I am thinking
about a placard with *Down with Wigs!* for a heading. It
would make a prodigious sensation. *You* don't notice how
I lie awake. These three months past Macassar Oil has not
let me sleep. I mean to do for Macassar!"

"So these are the fine plans that have been running in
your head for a couple of months, and not a word to me
about them. And I have just seen myself begging at my
own door; what a warning from Heaven! There will be
nothing left to us after a while except our eyes to cry with
over our troubles. Never shall you do it so long as I am
alive; do you hear, César? There is some underhand work
somewhere that you do not see; you are so straightforward
and honest that you don't suspect others of cheating. What
makes them come to offer you millions? You are giving
bills; you are going beyond your means; and how if the Oil
does not take? Suppose that the money does not come in,
—suppose that you do not sell the building lots, how are you
going to meet the bills? With the hazel-nut shells? You
want to rise in the world; you don't intend to have your
name over your own shop-door any longer; you mean to
take down the sign—the *Queen of Roses*—and yet you are
making up rigmaroles of prospectuses and placards, and
César Birotteau's name will be posted up at every street-
corner, and all over the hoardings, wherever there is building going on."

"Oh, no such thing! I shall open a branch business

under the name of Popinot. I shall take a shop somewhere
near the Rue des Lombards, and put in young Anselme
Popinot to look after it. I shall pay a debt of gratitude
which we owe to M. and Mme. Ragon by starting their
nephew in a business that may make his fortune. The poor
Ragons have looked very seedy for some time past, I have
thought."

"There! those people are after your money."

"Why, what people, my charmer? Your own uncle, who
loves us like his own life, and comes to dine here every Sunday? Then there is that kind old Ragon, our predecessor,
who plays boston with us; old Ragon, with a record of forty
years of fair dealing. And lastly, do you mean Roguin, a
notary of Paris, a man of fifty, who has been in practice for
twenty-five years? A notary of Paris would be the best of
the bunch if all honest folk were not equally good. My
partners will help me out at a pinch. Where is the plot,.
darling?—Look here, I must give you a piece of my mind.
On my word as an honest man, it weighs upon me.—You
have always been as suspicious as a cat! As soon as we had
two pennyworth of goods in the shop, you began to think
that the customers were thieves.—A man has to go down
on his knees to beg and pray of you to allow your fortune
to be made. For a daughter of Paris, you have scarcely any
ambition! If it were not for your eternal fears, there
would not be a happier man than I am.—If I had listened
to you, I should never have made the Pâte des Sultanes nor
the Carminative Toilet Lotion. We have made a living out
of the shop, but it was those two discoveries and our soaps
that brought in the hundred and sixty thousand francs
which we have over and above the business!—But for my
genius, for I have talent as a perfumer, we should be petty
shopkeepers, hard put to it to make both ends meet, and I
should not be one of the notable merchants who elect the
judges at the Tribunal of Commerce; I should neither have
been a judge nor a deputy-mayor. Do you know what I
should have been? A shopkeeper like old Ragon,—no

offence to him, for I respect shops; a shop has been the making of us. After selling perfumery for forty years, we should have had three thousand livres a year, as he has; and as prices go now, when things are twice as dear as they used to be, we too should have had hardly enough to live upon. (Day after day, it goes to my heart more and more to think of that old couple. I must come at the truth; I will have it out of Popinot to-morrow.)—Yes, if I had taken advice of you, of you that are afraid of your own luck, and are always asking if you will have to-morrow what you hold to-day, I should have no credit, nor the Cross of the Legion of Honor, and I should not be looked on as a man who knows what he is about. Oh, you may shake your head; if this succeeds, I may be deputy for Paris some day. Aha! I was not named César for nothing; everything has succeeded with me.—This is inconceivable! Everybody out of my own house admits that I have some capacity; but here at home, the one person that I want so much to please, and I toil and moil to make her happy, is just the very one who takes me for a fool."

There was such a depth of real and constant affection in these phrases, divided up by eloquent pauses and hurled forth like cannon balls (as is the wont of those who take up a recriminating attitude), that Mme. Birotteau in her secret heart felt touched, but, wife-like, she took advantage of the love she inspired to gain her own ends.

"Very well, Birotteau," said she, "if you love me, let me be happy in my own way. Neither you nor I have had any education; we do not know how to talk, nor how to flatter like worldly-wise people, and how can you expect that we should succeed in office under Government? I myself should be quite happy at the Treasury Farm. I have always been fond of animals and birds, and I could spend my time quite well in looking after the poultry, and living like a farmer's wife. Let us sell the business, marry our Césarine, and let your *Imogen* alone. We will pass the winters in Paris in our son-in-law's house, and we shall be happy; nothing in politics nor in business could change our ways. Why should you try to eclipse other people? Is not our fortune enough for us? When you are a millionaire, will you be able to eat two dinners a day? Do you want another wife? Look at uncle Pillerault! He is wisely satisfied with what he has, and spends his life in doing good. What does HE want with fine furniture? For I know you have been ordering furniture; I saw Braschon in the shop, and he was not here to buy scent."

"Well, yes, darling, there is some furniture ordered for you. The workmen will begin to-morrow under an architect recommended by M. de la Billardière."

"Good Lord, have mercy upon us!"

"Why, you are unreasonable, pet. Do you think that, fresh and pretty as you are, you can go and bury yourself at thirty-seven at Chinon? I myself, thank the Lord, am only thirty-nine. Chance has opened up a fine career to me, and I am going to enter upon it. If I manage wisely, I can found a house famous among Paris citizens, as people used to do, build up a business, and the Birotteaus shall be like Roguin, Cochin, Guillaume, Le Bas, Nucingen, Saillard, Popinot, and Matifat, all of whom are making, or have made, their mark in their quarter. Come! come! if this speculation were not as safe as gold ingots——"

"Safe!"

"Yes, safe. I have been reckoning it out these two months. Without appearing to do so, I have been making inquiries as to building, at the Hôtel de Ville, and of architects and contractors. M. Grindot, the young architect who is to remodel our place, is in despair because he has no capital to invest in our speculation."

"He knows that there will be houses to build; he is urging you on so as to gobble you up."

"Can people like Pillerault, like Charles Claparon, and Roguin be taken in? The gain is as certain as the profits on the *Pâte*, you see."

"But why should Roguin want to speculate, dear, when

he has bought his practice and made his fortune? I see him go by sometimes; he looks as thoughtful as a minister; he has an underhand look that I do not like; he has secret cares. In five years he has come to look like an old rake. Whose word have you for it that he will not take to his heels as soon as your money is in his hands? Such things have been known. Do we know much about him? It is true that we have been acquainted for fifteen years, but he is not one that I would put my hand into the fire for. I have it! he has ozæna; he does not live with his wife; he has mistresses no doubt, and they are ruining him; there is no other reason for his low spirits that I see. As I dress in the morning, I look through the blinds, and I see him going home on foot. Where does he come from? Nobody knows. It looks to me as if he had another establishment somewhere in town, and he spends one way, and madame another.

"Is that a life for a notary? If they make fifty thousand francs and get through sixty thousand, there will be an end of the money; in twenty years time they would be as bare as shorn lambs; but if a man is used to shine, he will plunder his friends without mercy. Charity should properly begin at home. The little rascal du Tillet, who used to be with us, is one of his cronies, and I see nothing good in that friendship. If he could not find out du Tillet, he is very blind; and if he knows him, why does he make so much of him? You will say that there is something between Roguin's wife and du Tillet. Very well; I look for no good from a man who has no sense of honor where his wife is concerned. And in any case, aren't the owners of the building lots very stupid to sell the worth of a hundred francs for a hundred sous? If you were to meet a child who did not know what a louis was worth, would you not tell him? Your stroke of business looks to me myself very much like a robbery, no offence to you."

"Dear me! what queer things women are sometimes, and how they mix up their ideas! If Roguin had never meddled in the matter, you would have said, 'Stay, César, stop

a bit; you are acting without consulting Roguin, it will come
to no good.' In this present instance he is pledged as it
were, and you tell me——"

"No; it is a M. Claparon."

"But a notary's name cannot appear in a speculation."

"Then why should he do something against the law?
What do you say to *that,* you who are such a stickler for
the law?"

"Just let me go on. Roguin is going into it himself, and
you tell me that it will come to no good. Is that sensible?
Again you say, 'He is doing something against the law.'
But his name will appear in it if necessary. And now you
tell me that 'he is rich.' Might not people say as much of
me? Ragon and Pillerault might just as well say of me,
'Why are you going into this when you are wallowing in
riches?'"

"A tradesman is one thing and a notary another," ob-
jected Mme. Birotteau.

"In short, my conscience is quite clear," César went on.
"People who sell, sell because they cannot help it; we are
no more robbing them than we rob fund-holders when we
buy at seventy-five. To-day you buy building lots at to-
day's prices; in two years time it will be different, just as
it is with *rentes.* You may be quite sure, Constance-Barbe-
Joséphine Pillerault, that you will never catch César Birotteau doing anything that is against the law, nor against his
conscience, nor unscrupulous, or not strictly just and fair.
That a man who has been in business eighteen years should
be suspected in his own family of cheating!"

"Come, César, be pacified! A wife who has known you
all that time knows the depths of your soul. You are the
master after all. You made the money, didn't you? It is
yours; you can spend it. We might be brought to the lowest
depths of poverty, but neither your daughter nor I would
ever say a single word of reproach. But listen. When you
invented the Pâte des Sultanes and the Carminative Toilet
Lotion, what risk did you run? Five or six thousand

francs perhaps. To-day you are risking all you have on a single stake, and you are not the only player in this game, and some of the others may turn out sharper than you are.

"You could give this ball and have the rooms redecorated, and spend a thousand francs over it—a useless expense, but not ruinous—but as to the Madeleine affair, I am against it, once and for all. You are a perfumer; be a perfumer, and not a speculator in building land. We women have an instinct that does not lead us astray. I have warned you; now act on your own ideas. You have been a judge at the Tribunal of Commerce, you know the law, you have steered your boat wisely, and I will follow you, César! But I shall have misgivings until I see our fortune on a sound basis and Césarine well married. God send that my dream was not prophetic!"

This meekness was annoying to Birotteau. He had recourse to a simple stratagem, which he found useful on such occasions.

"Listen, Constance; I have not really given my word, though it is as good as if I had."

"Oh! César, there is nothing more to be said, so let us say no more about it. Honor before riches. Come, get into bed, dear; there is no firewood left. Besides, it is easier to talk in bed if it amuses you.—Oh! the bad dream I had! Good Lord, to see *yourself!* Why, it was fearful! . . . Césarine and I will make a pretty number of *neuvaines* for the success of the land."

"Of course, the help of God would do us no harm," Birotteau said gravely, "but the essence of hazel-nuts is a power likewise, wife. I discovered this, like the Pâte des Sultanes, by accident; the first time it was by opening a book, but it was an engraving of *Hero and Leander* that suggested this new idea to me. A woman, you know, pouring oil on her lover's head; isn't it nice? The most certain speculations are those that are based on vanity, self-love, or a regard for appearances. Those sentiments will never be extinct."

"Alas, I see that clearly."

"At a certain age," pursued Birotteau, "men will do anything to grow hair on their heads when they have none. Hairdressers have told me for some time past that they are selling hair-dyes and all sorts of drugs that are said to promote the growth of the hair as well as Macassar Oil. Since the peace, men live more among women, and women do not like bald heads, eh! eh! *mimi!* So the demand for that class of article can be explained by the political situation.

"A composition which would keep your hair in good condition would sell like bread, and all the more so because the essence will doubtless be approved by the Académie des Sciences. Perhaps kind M. Vauquelin will do me another good turn. I shall go to submit my notion to him to-morrow, and ask him to accept that engraving which I have found at last after inquiring for it for two years in Germany. M. Vauquelin is engaged in analyzing hair, precisely the subject, so Chiffreville (who is associated with him in the production of chemicals) tells me. If my discovery concurs with his, my essence will be bought by both sexes. There is a fortune in my idea, I repeat. Good Heavens! I cannot sleep for it. Eh! luckily, little Popinot has the finest head of hair in the world. With a young lady in the shop whose hair should reach to the ground, and who should say (if the thing is possible without sinning against God or your neighbor) that the Comagen Oil (for it is decidedly an oil) counts for something in bringing that about; all the grizzled heads will be down upon it like poverty upon the world. And I say, dearie, how about your ball? I am not spiteful, but I really should like to have that little rogue of a du Tillet, who swaggers about and never sees me on 'Change. He knows that I know something that is not pretty about him. Perhaps I let him off too easily. How funny it is, wife, that one should always be punished for good actions; here below, of course! I have been like a father to him; you do not know all that I have done for him."

"Simply to hear you talk of him makes my flesh creep.

If you had known what he intended to do to you, you would
not have kept the theft of three thousand francs so quiet (for
I have guessed how the thing was arranged). If you had
put him in the police court, perhaps you might have done a
good many people a service."

"What did he mean to do to me?"

"Nothing. Birotteau, if you were inclined to listen to
me to-night, I would give you a bit of sound advice, and that
is to let du Tillet alone."

"Would not people think it very strange if I were to forbid an old assistant my house after I had been his surety
for twenty thousand francs when he first started in business
for himself. There, let us do good for its own sake. And
perhaps du Tillet has mended his ways."

"Everything must be put topsy-turvy here!"

"What is this about topsy-turvy? Why, it will all be
ruled like a sheet of music. So you have forgotten already
what I have just told you about the staircase, and how I
have arranged with Cayron, the umbrella merchant next
door, to take part of his house! He and I must go together
in the morning to see his landlord, M. Molineux. I have
as much business on hand to-morrow as a Minister."

"You have made me dizzy with your plans," said Constance; "I am muddled with them; and besides, Birotteau,
I am sleepy."

"Good-morning," returned her husband. "Just listen—
I say good-morning, because it is morning now, *mimi!* Ah,
she has dropped off to sleep, dear child! There! you shall
be the richest of the rich, or my name will not be César any
longer," and a few minutes later Constance and César were
peacefully snoring.

A rapid glance over the previous history of this household will confirm the impression which should have been
conveyed by the friendly dispute between the two principal
personages in this *Scène,* in which the lives of a retail shopkeeper and his wife are depicted. This sketch will explain,

moreover, the strange chances by which César Birotteau became a perfumer, a deputy-mayor, an ex-officer of the National Guard, and a Chevalier of the Legion of Honor. By
laying bare the depths of his character and the springs of
his greatness, it will be possible to comprehend how it is that
the vicissitudes of commerce, which strong heads turn to
their advantage, become irreparable catastrophes for weaker
spirits. Events are never absolute; their consequences depend entirely upon the individual. The misfortune which
is a stepping-stone for genius, becomes a piscina for the
Christian, a treasure for a quick-witted man, and for weaklings an abyss.

A cotter, Jacques Birotteau by name, living near Chinon,
took unto himself a wife, a domestic servant in the house of a
lady, who employed him in her vineyard. Three sons were
born to them; his wife died at the birth of the third, and
the poor fellow did not long survive her. Then the mistress,
out of affection for her maid, adopted the oldest of the cotter's boys; she brought him up with her own son, and placed
him in a seminary. This François Birotteau took orders,
and during the Revolution led the wandering life of priests
who would not take the oath, hiding from those who hunted
them down like wild beasts, lucky to meet with no worse fate
than the guillotine. At the time when this story begins he
was a priest of the cathedral at Tours, and had but once left
that city to see his brother César. On that occasion the
traffic in the streets of Paris so bewildered the good man
that he dared not leave his room; he called the cabs "half-
coaches," and was astonished at everything. He stayed one
week, and then went back to Tours, promising himself that
he would never revisit the capital.
The vinedresser's second son, Jean Birotteau, was drawn
by the army, and during the early wars of the Revolution
promptly became a captain. At the battle of the Trebbia,
Macdonald called for volunteers to storm a battery, and
Captain Jean Birotteau charged with his company and fell.

It appeared to be the destiny of the Birotteaus that other
men should supplant them, or that events should be too
strong for them wherever they might be.

The youngest son is the chief actor in this *Scène*. When
César was fourteen years old, and could read, write, and
cipher, he left the district, and with one louis in his pocket
set out on foot for Paris to make his fortune. On the recommendation of an apothecary in Tours, M. and Mme.
Ragon, retail perfumers, took him as errand boy. César
at that time was possessed of a pair of hobnailed shoes, a
pair of breeches, blue stockings, a sprigged waistcoat, a
countryman's jacket, three ample shirts of good linen, and
a stout walking-stick. His hair might be clipped like a
chorister's, but he was a solidly-built Tourangeau; and any
tendency to the laziness rampant in his district was coun-
teracted in him by a strong desire to make his way in the
world. Perhaps he was lacking somewhat in brains as in
education, but he had inherited upright instincts and scrupu-
lous integrity from his mother, who had "a heart of gold,"
as they say in Touraine.

César was paid six francs a month by way of wages. He
boarded in the house, and slept on a truckle-bed in the attics
next to the servant's room. The shopmen showed him how
to fetch and carry and tie up parcels, to sweep out the shop
and the pavement before it, and made a butt of him, breaking him in to business after the manner of their kind, and
contriving to blend a good deal of amusement (for themselves) with his instruction. M. and Mme. Ragon spoke to
him as if he were a dog. Nobody cared how tired the ap-
prentice might be, and he was often very tired and footsore
of a night after tramping over the pavements, and his
shoulders often ached. The principle "each for himself,"
that gospel of great cities, put in application, made César's
life in Paris a very hard one. He used to cry sometimes
when the day was over, and he thought of Touraine, where
the peasant works leisurely, and the mason takes his time
about laying a stone, and toil is judiciously tempered by

idleness; but he usually fell asleep before he reached the
point of thinking of running away, for his morning's round
of work awaited him, and he did his duty with the instinctive obedience of a yard dog. If he happened to complain,
the first shopman would smile jocosely. "Ah, my boy," said
he, "life is not all roses at the *Queen of Roses,* and larks
don't drop ready roasted into your mouth; first catch your
lark, and then you want the other things before you cook it."

The cook, a stout Picarde, kept the best morsels for herself, and never spoke to César but to complain of M. and
Mme. Ragon, who left her nothing to purloin. On one
Sunday at the end of every month she was obliged to stop
in the house, and then she broke ground with César. Ursule, scoured for Sunday, was a charming creature in the
eyes of the poor errand boy, who, but for a chance, was
about to make shipwreck on the first sunken reef in his
career. Like all human beings who have no one to care for
them, he fell in love with the first woman who gave him a
kind glance. The cook took César under her wing, and
secret love passages followed, at which the assistants jeered
unmercifully. Luckily, two years later, the cook threw
over César for a young runaway from the army, a fellow-
countryman of hers who was hiding in Paris; and the
Picard, a land-owner to the extent of several acres, allowed
himself to be drawn into a marriage with Ursule.

But during those two years the cook fed her lad César
well, and explained to him the seamy side of not a few of
the mysteries of Paris. Motives of jealousy led her to instil
into him a perfect horror of low haunts, whose perils seemingly were not unknown to her. In 1792 César, the basely
deserted, had grown accustomed to his life; his feet were
used to the pavements, his shoulders accommodated to pack-
ing-cases, his wits to what he called the *humbug* of Paris.
So, when Ursule threw him over, he promptly took comfort,
for she had not realized any of his intuitive ideas as to sentiments. Lascivious, bad-tempered, fawning, and rapacious,
a selfish woman, given to drink, she had jarred on Birot-

teau's unsophisticated nature, and had opened out no fair future to him. At times the poor boy saw with dismay that he was bound by the strongest of ties for a simple heart to a creature with whom he had no sympathy. By the time that he was set free he had developed, and had reached the age of sixteen. His wits had been sharpened by Ursule and by the shopmen's jokes; he set himself to learn the business. Intelligence was hidden beneath his simplicity. He watched the customers with shrewd eyes. In his spare moments he asked for explanations concerning the goods; he remembered where everything was kept; one fine day he knew the goods, prices, and quantities in stock better than the newer comers, and thenceforward M. and Mme. Ragon looked on him as a settled institution.

When the Requisition of the terrible year II. made a clean sweep of Citizen Ragon's house, César Birotteau, promoted to be second assistant, improved his position, received a salary of fifty livres per month, and seated himself at the Ragons' table with joy unspeakable. The second assistant at the sign of the *Queen of Roses* had by this time saved six hundred francs, and he now had a room filled with furniture such as he had for a long time coveted, in which he could keep the belongings which he had accumulated under lock and key. On Décadis, dressed after the fashion of an epoch which affected rough and homely ways, the quiet, humble peasant lad looked at least the equal of other young citizens, and in this way he overleapt the social barriers which in domestic life would, in different times, have been raised between the peasant and the trading classes. Towards the end of that year his honesty won for him the control of the till. The awe-inspiring Citoyenne Ragon saw to his linen, and husband and wife treated him like one of the family.

In Vendémiaire 1794 César Birotteau, being possessed of one hundred gold louis, exchanged them for six thousand francs in assignats, bought *rentes* therewith at thirty francs, paid for them when depreciated prices ruled on the Exchange, and hoarded his stock-receipt with unspeakable delight. From that day forward he followed the rise and fall of the funds and the course of events with a secret anxiety that made his heart beat fast at the tidings of every victory or defeat which marked the history of that period.

At this critical period M. Ragon, sometime purveyor of perfumes to Her Majesty Queen Marie-Antoinette, confided to César Birotteau his attachment to the fallen tyrants. This confidence was an event of capital importance in César's life. The Tourangeau was transformed into a fanatical adherent of Royalty in the course of evening conversations after the shutters were put up, the books posted, and the streets quiet without. César was simply obeying his natural instincts. His imagination kindled at the tale of the virtuous deeds of Louis XVI., followed by anecdotes told by husband and wife of the good qualities of the Queen whom they extolled. His tender heart was revolted by the horrible fate of the two crowned heads, struck off but a few paces from the shop door, and he conceived a hatred for a system of government which poured forth innocent blood that cost nothing to shed.

Commercial instincts made him quick to see the death of trade in the law of maximum prices, and in political storms, which always bode ill to business. In his quality of perfumer, moreover, he loathed a Revolution that forbade powder, and was responsible for the fashion of wearing the hair *à la Titus.* The tranquillity secured to the nation by an absolute monarchy seemed to be the one possible condition in which life and property would be safe, so he waxed zealous for a monarchy.

M. Ragon, finding so apt a disciple, made him his assistant in the shop, and initiated him into the secrets of the *Queen of Roses.* Some of the customers were the most active and devoted of the secret agents of the Bourbons, and kept up a correspondence between Paris and the West. Carried away by youthful enthusiasm, electrified by contact with such men as Georges, La Billardière, Montauran, Bauvan, Longuy, Manda, Bernier, du Guénic, and Fontaine, César flung himself into the conspiracy of the 13th Vendémiaire, when Royalists and Terrorists combined against the dying Convention. César had the honor of warring against Napoleon on the steps of the Church of Saint-Roch, and was wounded at the beginning of the action. Every one knows the result of this attempt. The obscurity from which Barras' aide-de-camp then emerged was Birotteau's salvation. A few friends carried the bellicose counter-hand home to the *Queen of Roses,* where he lay in hiding in the garret, nursed by Mme. Ragon, and lucky to be forgotten. César's military courage had been nothing but a flash. During his month of convalescence he came to some sound conclusions as to the ludicrous alliance of politics and perfumery. If a Royalist he remained, he made up his mind that he would be simply and solely a Royalist perfumer, that he would never compromise himself again, and he threw himself body and soul into his calling.

After the 18th Brumaire, M. and Mme. Ragon, despairing of the Royalist cause, determined to retire from the perfumery trade, to live like respectable private citizens, and to cease to meddle in politics. If they were to receive the full value of their business, it behoved them to find a man who had more honesty than ambition, and more homely sense than brilliancy, so Ragon broached the matter to his first assistant. Birotteau hesitated. He was twenty years old, with a thousand francs a year invested in the public funds; it was his ambition to go to live near Chinon as soon as he should have fifteen hundred francs a year, and the First Consul, after consolidating his position at the Tuileries, should have consolidated the national debt. He asked himself why he should risk his little honestly-earned independence in business. He had never expected to make so much wealth; it was entirely owing to chances which are only embraced in youth; and now he was thinking of taking a wife in Touraine, a woman who should have an equal fortune, so that he might buy and cultivate a little property called the Treasury Farm, a bit of land on which he had set longing eyes since he had come to man's estate. He dreamed of adding more land to the Treasury Farm, of making a thousand crowns a year, of leading a happy and obscure life there. He was on the point of refusing the perfumer's offer, when love suddenly altered his resolutions and multiplied the total of his ambitions by ten.

Since Ursule's base desertion, César had led a steady life; this was partly a consequence of hard work, partly a dread of the risks run in pursuit of pleasure in Paris. Desire that remains unsatisfied becomes a craving, and marriage for the lower middle classes becomes a fixed idea, for it is the one way open to them of winning and appropriating a woman. César Birotteau was in this case. The first assistant was the responsible person at the *Queen of Roses;* he had not a moment to spare for amusement. In such a life the craving is still more imperatively felt; so it happened that the apparition of a handsome girl, to whom a dissipated young fellow would scarcely have given a thought, was bound to make the greatest impression upon the steady César.

One fine June day, as he was about to cross the Pont Marie to the Ile Saint-Louis, he saw a girl standing in the doorway of a corner shop on the Quai d'Anjou. Constance Pillerault was a forewoman in a linen-drapery establishment, at the sign of the *Little Sailor,* a pioneer instance of a kind of shop which has since spread all over Paris, with painted signboards more or less in evidence, flying flags, much display. Shawls are suspended in the windows, and piles of cravats erected like card castles, together with countless devices to attract custom, ribbon streamers, showcards, notices of fixed prices; optical illusions and effects carried to the pitch of perfection which has made of shop windows the fairyland of commerce.

The low prices asked at the sign of the *Little Sailor* for the goods described as "novelties" had brought this shop, in one of the quietest and least fashionable quarters of Paris, an unheard-of influx of custom.

The aforesaid young lady behind the counter was as cele-

brated for her beauty as La belle Limonadière of the Café
des Milles Colonnes at a later day, and not a few others whose
unfortunate lot it has been to attract faces young and old,
more numerous than the paving stones of Paris, to the windows of milliners' shops and cafés. The first assistant from
the *Queen of Roses,* whose life was spent between Saint-Roch
and the Rue de la Sourdière, in the daily routine of the perfumery business, did not so much as suspect the existence of
the *Little Sailor,* for retailers in Paris know very little of
each other.

César was so violently smitten with the beautiful Constance
that he hurried tempestuously into the *Little Sailor* to bargain for half-a-dozen linen shirts. Long did he haggle over
the price, bale after bale of linen was displayed for his inspection; he behaved exactly like an Englishwoman in a humor
for shopping. The young lady condescended to interest herself in César's purchase; perceiving, by certain signs which
women understand, that he had come to the shop more for
the sake of the saleswoman than for her goods. He gave his
name and address to the young lady, who became quite indifferent to the customer's admiration as soon as he had made
his purchase. The poor assistant had done but little to gain
Ursule's good graces; if he had been sheepish then, love now
made him more sheepish still; he did not dare to say a syl-
lable, and was, moreover, too much dazzled to note the indifference which succeeded to the smiles of this siren of commerce.

Every evening for a week he took up his post before the
Little Sailor, hanging about for a glance as a dog waits for
a bone at a kitchen door; regardless of the jibes in which the
shopmen and saleswomen indulged at his expense; making
way meekly for customers or passers-by, watchful of every
little change that took place in the shop. A few days later,
he again entered the paradise where his angel dwelt, not so
much to purchase pocket-handkerchiefs of her as with a view
of communicating a luminous idea to the angel's mind.

"If you should require any perfumery, mademoiselle," he

remarked, as he paid the bill, "I could supply you in the same way."

Constance Pillerault daily received brilliant proposals, in which there was never any mention of marriage; and though her heart was as pure as her white forehead, it was not until the indefatigable César had proved his love by six months of strategical operations, that she deigned to receive his attentions. Even then she would not commit herself. Prudence had been demanded of her by the multitudinous number of her admirers—wholesale wine merchants, well-to-do bar-keepers, and others, who made eyes at her. The lover found a supporter in her guardian, M. Claude-Joseph Pillerault, an ironmonger on the Quai de la Ferraille, a discovery made by the secret espionage which is pre-eminently a lover's shift.

In this rapid sketch, it is impossible to describe the delights of this harmless Parisian love-intrigue; the little extravagances characteristic of the shopman—the first melons of the season, the little dinners at Vénua's, followed by the theatre, the drives into the country in a cab on Sunday—must be passed over in silence. César was not a positively handsome young fellow, but there was nothing in his appearance to repel love. Life in Paris and days spent in a dark shop had toned down the high color natural to the peasant lad. His thick black hair, his Norman breadth of shoulder, his sturdy limbs, his simple straightforward look, all contributed to prepossess people in his favor. Uncle Pillerault, the responsible guardian of his brother's child, made various inquiries about the Tourangeau, and gave his consent; and in the fair month of May 1800, Mlle. Pillerault promised to marry César Birotteau. He nearly fainted with joy when Constance-Barbe-Joséphine accepted him as her husband under a lime-tree at Sceaux.

"You will have a good husband, my little girl," said M. Pillerault. "He has a warm heart and sentiments of honor. He is as straight as a line, and as good as the Child Jesus; he is a king of men, in short."

Constance put away once and for all the dreams of a brilliant future, which, like most shop girls, she had sometimes indulged. She meant to be a faithful wife and a good mother, and took up this life in accordance with the religious programme of the middle classes. After all, this part suited her ideas much better than the dangerous vanities tempting to a youthful Parisian imagination. Constance's intelligence was a narrow one; she was the typical small tradesman's wife, who always grumbles a little over her work, who refuses a thing at the outset, and is vexed when she is taken at her word; whose restless activity takes all things, from cash-box to kitchen, as its province, and supervises everything, from the weightiest business transactions down to almost invisible darns in the household linen. Such a woman scolds while she loves, and can only conceive ideas of the very simplest; only the small change, as it were, of thought passes current with her; she argues about everything, lives in chronic fear of the unknown, makes constant forecasts, and is always thinking of the future. Her statuesque yet girlish beauty, her engaging looks, her freshness, prevented César from thinking of her shortcomings; and, moreover, she made up for them by a woman's sensitive conscientiousness, an excessive thrift, by her fanatical love of work, and genius as a saleswoman.

Constance was just eighteen years old, and the possessor of eleven thousand francs. César, in whom love had developed the most unbounded ambition, bought the perfumery business, and transplanted the *Queen of Roses* to a handsome shop near the Place Vendôme. He was only twenty-one years of age, married to a beautiful and adored wife, and almost the owner of his establishment, for he had paid three-fourths of the amount. He saw (how should he have seen otherwise?) the future in fair colors, which seemed fairer still as he measured his career from its starting-point.

Roguin (Ragon's notary) drew up the marriage-contract, and gave sage counsels to the young perfumer; he it was who interfered when the latter was about to complete the purchase of the business with his wife's money. "Just keep the money by you, my boy; ready money is sometimes a handy thing in a business," he had said.

Birotteau gazed at the notary in admiration, fell into the habit of consulting him, and made a friend of Roguin. Like Ragon and Pillerault, he had so much faith in notaries as a class, that he placed himself in Roguin's hands without admitting a doubt of him. Thanks to this advice, César started business with the eleven thousand francs brought him by Constance; and would not have "changed places" with the First Consul, however brilliant Napoleon's lot might seem to be.

At first the Birotteau establishment had but one servant-maid. They lodged on the mezzanine floor above the shop. In this sort of den, passably furnished by an upholsterer, the newly-wedded pair entered upon a perennial honeymoon. Mme. César at her cash desk was a marvel to see. Her famous beauty exercised an enormous influence on the sales; the dandies of the Empire talked of nothing but the lovely Mme. Birotteau. If César's political principles were tainted with Royalism, it was acknowledged that his business principles were above suspicion; and if some of his fellow-tradesmen envied him his luck, he was believed to deserve it. That shot on the steps of the Church of Saint-Roch had gained him a certain reputation—he was looked upon as a brave man, and a man deep in political secrets; though he had nothing of a soldier's courage in his composition, and not even a rudimentary political notion in his head.

On these data the good folk of the Arrondissement made him a Captain of the National Guard, but he was cashiered by Napoleon (according to Birotteau, that matter of Vendémiaire still rankled in the First Consul's mind), and thenceforward César was invested with a certain halo of martyrdom, cheaply acquired, which made him interesting to opponents, and gave him a certain importance.

Here, in brief, is the history of this household, so happy in itself, and disturbed by none but business cares.

During the first year, César instructed his wife in all the ins and outs of the perfumery business, which she was admirably quick to grasp; she might have been brought into the world for that sole purpose, so well did she adapt herself to her customers. The result of the stocktaking at the end of the year alarmed the ambitious perfumer. After deducting all expenses, he might perhaps hope, in twenty years' time, to make the modest sum of a hundred thousand francs, the price of his felicity. He determined then and there to find some speedier road to fortune, and, by way of a beginning, to be a manufacturer as well as a retailer.

Acting against his wife's counsel, he took the lease of a shed on some building land in the Faubourg du Temple, and painted up thereon, in huge letters, CÉSAR BIROTTEAU's FACTORY. He enticed a workman from Grasse, and with him began to manufacture several kinds of soap, essences, and eau-de-cologne, on the system of half profits. The partnership only lasted six months, and ended in a loss, which he had to sustain alone; but Birotteau did not lose heart. He meant to obtain a result at any price, if it were only to escape a scolding from his wife; and, indeed, he confessed to her afterwards that, in those days of despair, his head used to boil like a pot on the fire, and that many a time, but for religious principles, he would have thrown himself into the Seine.

One day, depressed by several unsuccessful experiments, he was sauntering home to dinner along the boulevards (the lounger in. Paris is a man in despair quite as often as a genuine idler), when a book among a hamperful at six sous apiece caught his attention; his eyes were attracted by the yellow dusty title-page, *Abdeker,* so it ran, *or the Art of Preserving Beauty.*

Birotteau took up the work. It claimed to be a translation from the Arabic, but in reality it was a sort of romance written by a physician in the previous century. César happened to stumble upon a passage therein which treated of perfumes, and with his back against a tree in the boulevard, he turned the pages over till he reached a footnote, wherein the learned author discoursed of the nature of the dermis and epidermis. The writer showed conclusively that such and such an unguent or soap often produced an effect exactly opposite to that intended, and the ointment, or the soap, acted as a tonic upon a skin that required a lenitive treatment, or *vice versâ.*

Birotteau saw a fortune in the book, and bought it. Yet, feeling little confidence in his unaided lights, he went to Vauquelin, the celebrated chemist, and in all simplicity asked him how to compose a double cosmetic which should produce the required effect upon the human epidermis in either case. The really learned—men so truly great in this sense that they can never receive in their lifetime all the fame that should reward vast labors like theirs—are almost always helpful and kindly to the poor in intellect. So it was with Vauquelin. He came to the assistance of the perfumer, gave him a formula for a paste to whiten the hands, and allowed him to style himself its inventor. It was this cosmetic that Birotteau called the Superfine Pâte des Sultanes. The more thoroughly to accomplish his purpose, he used the recipe for the paste for a wash for the complexion, which he called the Carminative Toilet Lotion.

He took a hint from the *Little Sailor,* and was the first among perfumers to make the lavish use of placards, handbills, and divers kinds of advertisement, which, perhaps not undeservedly, are called quackery. The Pâte des Sultanes and the Carminative Toilet Lotion were introduced to the polite world and to commerce by gorgeous placards, with the words *Approved by the Institute* at the head. The effect of this formula, employed thus for the first time, was magical. Not France only, but the face of Europe was covered with flaming proclamations, yellow, scarlet, and blue, which informed the world that the sovereign lord of the *Queen of Roses* manufactured, kept in stock, and supplied everything in his line of business at moderate charges.

At a time when the East was the one topic of conversation, in a country where every man has a natural turn for the part

of a sultan, and every woman is no less minded to become a
sultana, the idea of giving to any cosmetic such a name as
the Pâte des Sultanes might have occurred to any ordinary
man, it needed no cleverness to foresee its fascination; but
the public always judges by results, and Birotteau's reputation for business ability but grew the more when he indited a
prospectus, and the very absurdity of its language contributed
to its success. In France we only laugh at men and things
who are talked about, and those who fail to make any mark
are not talked about. So although Birotteau's stupidity was
real and not feigned, people gave him credit for playing the
fool on purpose.

A copy of the prospectus has been procured, not without
difficulty, by the house of Popinot & Co., druggists in the Rue
des Lombards. In a more elevated connection this curious
piece of rhetoric would be styled an historical document, and
valued for the light that it sheds on contemporary manners.
Here, therefore, it is given:—

César Birotteau's

SUPERFINE PÂTE DES SULTANES

AND

CARMINATIVE TOILET LOTION.

A Marvelous Discovery!

Approved by the Institute.

" For some time past a preparation for the hands, and a toilet
lotion more efficacious than Eau-de-Cologne, have been generally
desired by both sexes throughout Europe. After devoting long
nights to the study of the dermis and epidermis of both sexes—for
both attach, and with reason, the greatest importance to the soft-
ness, suppleness, bloom, and delicate surface of the skin—M. Birotteau, a perfumer of high standing, and well known in the capital
and abroad, has invented two preparations, which from their first
appearance have been deservedly called 'marvelous' by people of

the highest fashion in Paris. Both preparations possess astonishing properties, and act upon the skin without bringing about premature wrinkles, the inevitable result of the rash use of the drugs hitherto compounded by ignorance and cupidity.

"These inventions are based upon the difference of temperaments, which are divided into two great classes, are indicated by the difference of color in the pâte and the lotion; the rose-colored preparations being intended for the dermis and epidermis of persons of lymphatic constitution, and the white for those endowed with a sanguine temperament.

"The pâte is called the 'Pâte des Sultanes,' because the specific was in the first instance invented for the Seraglio by an Arab physician. It has been approved by the Institute on the report of our illustrious chemist Vauquelin, and the lotion, likewise approved, is compounded upon the same principles.

"The Pâte des Sultanes, an invaluable preparation, which exhales the sweetest fragrance, dissipates the most obstinate freckles, whitens the skin in the most stubborn cases, and represses the perspiration of the hand from which women suffer no less than men.

"The 'Carminative Toilet Lotion' removes the slight pimples which sometimes appear inopportunely on ladies' faces, and contravene their projects for the ball; it refreshes and revives the color by opening or closing the pores of the skin in accordance with the exigencies of the temperament, while its efficacy in arresting the ravages of time is so well known already that many ladies, out of gratitude, call it the 'Friend of Beauty.'

"Eau-de-Cologne is purely and simply an ordinary perfume without special efficacy, while the Superfine Pâte des Sultanes and the Carminative Toilet Lotion are two active remedies, powerful agents, perfectly harmless in their operation of seconding the efforts of nature; their perfumes, essentially balsamic and exhilarating, admirably refresh the animal spirits, and charm and revive ideas. Their merits are as marvelous as their simplicity; in short, to woman they offer an added charm, while a means of attraction is put within the reach of man.

"The daily use of the Carminative Toilet Lotion allays the smarting sensation caused by shaving, while it keeps the lips red and smooth, and prevents chapping; it gradually dissipates freckles by natural means; and finally, it restores tone to the complexion. These results are the signs of that perfect equilibrium of the humors of the body, which ensures immunity from the migraine to those who are subject to that distressing complaint.   In short, the Carminative Toilet Lotion, which may be used in all the operations of the toilet, is a preventive of cutaneous affections, by permitting free transpiration through the tissues, while imparting a permanent bloom to the skin.

"All communications should be prepaid, and addressed to M. César Birotteau (late Ragon), Perfumer to her late Majesty, Queen Marie-Antoinette, at the 'Queen of Roses,' Rue Saint-Honoré, near the Place Vendôme, Paris.

"The price of the Pâte is three livres per tablet, and of the Toilet Lotion, six livres per bottle.

"To prevent fradulent imitations, M. Birotteau warns the public that the wrapper of every tablet bears his signature, and that his name is stamped on every bottle of the Toilet Lotion.'"

The success of this scheme was due, as a matter of fact (though César did not suspect it), to Constance, who proposed that they should send sample cases of the Carminative Toilet Lotion and the Superfine Pâte des Sultanes to every perfumer in France or abroad, offering, at the same time, a discount of thirty per cent as an inducement to take a gross of either article at a time.

The Pâte and the Lotion were really better than similar cosmetics, and the simple were attracted by that distinction made between the two temperaments.   The discount was tempting to hundreds of perfumers all over France, and each would take annually three hundred gross or more of both preparations; and if the profits on each article were small, the demand was great, and the output enormous.   César was able to buy the sheds and the plot of land in the Faubourg du Temple.   He built a large factory there, and had the *Queen of Roses* magnificently decorated.   The household began to feel the small comforts of an easier existence, and the wife quaked less than heretofore.

In 1810 Mme. César predicted a rise in house rents.   At her instance her husband took the lease of the whole house above the shop, and they removed from the mezzanine floor (where they had begun housekeeping together) to the first floor. A piece of luck which befell them about this time decided Constance to shut her eyes to Birotteau's follies in the matter of decorating a room for her. The perfumer was made a judge of the Tribunal of Commerce. It was his character for integrity and conscientiousness, together with the esteem in which he was held, that gained this dignity for him; thenceforward he must be considered as a notable among the tradesmen of Paris.

He used to rise at five o'clock in the morning to read handbooks on jurisprudence and works which treated of commercial law. With his instinct for fair dealing, his uprightness, his readiness to take trouble—all qualities essential for the appreciation of the knotty points submitted to arbitration—he was one of the most highly esteemed judges in the Tribunal. His faults contributed no less to his reputation. César was so conscious of his inferiority that he was ready and willing to take his colleagues' opinion, and they were flattered by the attention with which he listened to them. Some of them thought a good deal of the silent approbation of such a listener, reputed to be a hard-headed man; others were delighted with his amiability and modesty, and extolled him on those grounds. Those amenable to his jurisdiction lauded his benevolence and conciliatory spirit, and he was often called in to act as arbitrator in disputes wherein his homely sense suggested to him a kind of Cadi's justice.

He managed to invent and use throughout his term of office a style of his own; it was stuffed with platitudes, interspersed with trite sayings, and pieces of reasoning rounded into phrases which came out without effort, and sounded like eloquence in the ears of shallow people. In this way he commended himself to the naturally mediocre majority, condemned to penal servitude for life and to views of the earth earthy.

César lost so much time at the Tribunal that his wife put pressure upon him, and thenceforward he declined the costly honor.

In the year 1813 this household, thanks to its constant unity, after plodding along through life in a humdrum fashion, entered upon an era of prosperity which nothing seemingly ought to check.

M. and Mme. Ragon (their predecessors), Uncle Pillerault, Roguin the notary, the Matifats (druggists in the Rue des Lombards who supplied the *Queen of Roses*), Joseph Lebas (a retail draper, a leading light in the Rue Saint-Denis, successor to Guillaume at the *Cat and Racket*), Judge Popinot (Mme. Ragon's brother), Chiffreville (of the firm of Protez & Chiffreville), M. Cochin (a clerk of the Treasury, and a sleeping partner in Matifat's business), his wife, Mme. Cochin, and the Abbé Loraux (confessor and director of the devout among this little circle) made up, with one or two others, the number of their acquaintance. César Birotteau might be a Royalist, but public opinion at that time was in his favor; and though he had scarcely a hundred thousand francs beside his business, was looked upon as a very wealthy man. His steady-going ways, his punctuality, his habit of paying ready money for everything, of never discounting bills, while he would take paper to oblige a customer of whom he was sure,—all these things, together with his readiness to oblige, had brought him a great reputation. And not only so; he had really made a good deal of money, but the building of his factories had absorbed most of it, and he paid nearly twenty thousand francs a year in rent. The education of their only daughter, whom Constance and César both idolized, had been a heavy expense. Neither the husband nor the wife thought of money where Césarine's pleasure was concerned, and they had never brought themselves to part with her.

Imagine the delight of the poor peasant-parvenu when he heard his charming Césarine play a sonata by Steibelt or sing a ballad; when he saw her writing French correctly, or making sepia drawings of landscape, or listened while she read aloud from the Racines, father and son, and explained the beauties of the poetry. What happiness it was for him to live again in this fair, innocent flower, not yet plucked from the parent stem; this angel, over whose growing graces and earliest development they had watched with such passionate tenderness; this only child, incapable of despising her father or of laughing at his want of education, so much was she his little daughter.

When César came to Paris, he had known how to read, write, and cipher, and at that point his education had been arrested. There had been no opportunity in his hard-working life of acquiring new ideas and information beyond the perfumery trade. He had spent his time among folk to whom science and literature were matters of indifference, and whose knowledge was of a limited and special kind; he himself, having no time to spare for loftier studies, became perforce a practical man. He adopted (how should he have done otherwise?) the language, errors, and opinions of the Parisian tradesman who admires Molière, Voltaire, and Rousseau on hearsay, and buys their works, but never opens them; who will have it that the proper way to pronounce *armoire* is *ormoire*: *or* means gold, and *moire* means silk, and women's dresses used almost always to be made of silk, and in their cupboards they locked up silk and gold—therefore, *ormoire* is right and *armoire* is an innovation. Potier, Talma, Mlle. Mars, and other actors and actresses were millionaires ten times over, and did not live like ordinary mortals; the great tragedian lived on raw meat, and Mlle. Mars would have a fricassee of pearls now and then—an idea she had taken from some celebrated Egyptian actress. As to the Emperor, his waistcoat pockets were lined with leather, so that he could take a handful of snuff at a time; he used to ride at full gallop up the staircase of the orangery at Versailles. Authors and artists ended in the workhouse, the natural close to their eccentric careers; they were, every one of them, atheists into the bargain, so that you had to be very careful not to admit anybody of that sort into your house. Joseph Lebas used to advert with horror to the story of his sister-in-law Augustine who married the artist Sommervieux. Astronomers lived on spiders. These bright examples of the attitude of the bour-

geois mind towards philology, the drama, politics, and science
will throw light upon its breadth of view and powers of com-
prehension.

Let a poet pass along the Rue des Lombards, and some stray
sweet scent shall set him dreaming of the East; for him,
with the odor of the Khuskus grass, would come a vision of
Nautch girls in an Eastern bath. The brilliant red lac would
call up thoughts of Vedic hymns, of alien creeds and castes;
and at a chance contact with an ivory tusk, he would mount
an elephant and make love, like the king of Lahore, in a
muslin-curtained howdah.

But the petty tradesman does not so much as know whence
the raw materials of his business are brought. Of natural
history or of chemistry, Birotteau the perfumer, for instance,
knew nothing whatever. It is true that he regarded Vauquelin as a great man, but Vauquelin was an exception. César
himself was about on a par with the retired grocer, who summed up a discussion on the ways of growing tea by announc-
ing with a knowing air that "there are only two ways of
obtaining tea—from Havre or by the overland route." And
Birotteau thought that aloes and opium were only to be found
in the Rue des Lombards. People told you that attar of
roses came from Constantinople, but, like eau-de-cologne, it
was made in Paris. These names of foreign places were
humbug; they had been invented to amuse the French nation,
who cannot abide anything that is made in France. A French
merchant has to call his discovery an English invention, or
people will not buy it; it is just the same in England, the
druggists there tell you that things come from France.

Yet César was not altogether a fool or a dunce; an honest
and kind heart shed a lustre over everything that he did and
made his a worthy life, and a kindly deed absolves all possible
forms of ignorance. His unvarying success gave him assurance; and, in Paris, assurance, the sign of power, is taken
for power itself.

César's wife, who had learned to know her husband's character during the early years of their marriage, led a life of

perpetual terror; she represented sound sense and foresight in the partnership; she was doubt, opposition, and fear, while César represented boldness, ambition, activity, the element of chance and undreamed-of good luck. In spite of appearances, the merchant was the weaker vessel, and it was the wife who really had the patience and courage. So it had come to pass that a timid mediocrity, without education, knowledge, or strength of character, a being who could in nowise have succeeded in the world's slipperiest places, was taken for a remarkable man, a man of spirit and resolution, thanks to his instinctive uprightness and sense of justice, to the goodness of a truly Christian soul, and love for the one woman who had been his.

The public only see results. Of all César's circle, only Pillerault and Judge Popinot saw beneath the surface; none of the rest could pronounce on his character. Those twenty or thirty friends, moreover, who met at one another's houses, retailed the same platitudes, repeated the same stale commonplaces, and each one among them regarded himself as superior to his company. There was a rivalry among the women in dinners and dress; each one summed up her husband in some contemptuous word.

Mme. Birotteau alone had the good sense to show respect and deference to her husband in public. She saw in him the man who, in spite of his private weaknesses, had made the wealth and earned the esteem which she shared along with him; though she sometimes privately wondered if all men who were spoken of as superior intellects were like her husband. This attitude of hers contributed not a little to maintain the respect and esteem shown by others to the merchant, in a country where wives are quick-witted enough to belittle their husbands and to complain of them.

The first days of the year 1814, so fatal to Imperial France, were memorable in the Birotteau household for two events, which would have passed almost unnoticed anywhere else; but they were of a kind to leave a deep impression on simple souls like César and his wife, who, looking back upon their past, found no painful memories.

They had engaged a young man of two-and-twenty, Ferdinand du Tillet by name, as first assistant. The lad had come to them from another house in the perfumery trade, where they had declined to give him a percentage of the profits. He was thought to be a genius, and he had been very anxious to go to the *Queen of Roses,* knowing the place, and the people, and their ways. Birotteau had engaged him at a salary of a thousand francs, meaning that du Tillet should be his successor. This Ferdinand du Tillet was destined to exercise so great an influence over the family fortunes, that a few words must be said about him.

He had begun life simply on his Christian name of Ferdinand. There was an immense advantage in anonymity, he thought, at a time when Napoleon was pressing the young men of every family into the army; but if he had no name, he had been born somewhere, and owed his birth to some cruel or voluptuous fancy. Here, in brief, are the few facts known as to his name and designation.

In 1793 a poor girl of Tillet, a little hamlet near the Andelys, bore a child one night in the curé's garden at Tillet, tapped on the shutters, and then drowned herself. The good man received the child, named him after the saint of that day in the calendar, and reared him as if he had been his own son. In 1804 the curé died, and the little property that he left was insufficient to complete the education thus begun. Ferdinand, thrown upon Paris, there led the life of a freebooter, amid chances that might bring him to the scaffold or to fortune, to the bar, the army, commerce, or private life. Ferdinand, compelled to live like a very Figaro, first became a commercial traveler, then, after traveling round France, and seeing life, became a perfumer's assistant, with a fixed determination to make his way at all costs. In 1813 he considered is expedient to ascertain his age, and to acquire a status as a citizen; he therefore petitioned the Tribunal of the Andelys to transfer the entry of his baptism from the church records to the mayor's register; and, further, he asked that they should insert the surname of du Tillet, which he had assumed, on the ground of his exposure at birth in the commune of that name.

He had neither father nor mother; he had no guardian save the procureur-impérial; he was alone in the world, and owed no account of himself to any one; society was to him a harsh stepdame, and he showed no mercy in his dealings with society, knew no guide but his own interests, found all means of success permissible. The Norman, armed with these dangerous capacities, combined with his desire to succeed the crabbed faults for which the natives of his province are, rightly or wrongly, blamed. Beneath his insinuating manner there was a contentious spirit; he was a most formidable antagonist—a blustering litigant, disputing another's least rights audaciously, while he never yielded a point himself. He had time on his side, and wearied out his opponent by his inflexible pertinacity. His principal merits were those of the Scapins of old comedy; he possessed their fertility of resource, their skill in sailing near the wind, their itch to seize on what seems good to have and hold. Indeed, he meant to apply to his poverty a motto which the Abbé Terray applied in statecraft; he would make a clean record by turning honest later on.

He was endowed with strenuous energy, with the military intrepidity which demands good deeds or bad indifferently of everybody, justifying his demand by the theory of personal interest; he was bound to succeed; he had too great a scorn of human nature; he believed too firmly that all men have their price; he was too little troubled by scruples as to the choice of means, when all were alike permissible; his eyes were too fixedly set upon the success and wealth that should purchase absolution for a system of morals which worked thus not to be successful.

Such a man, between the convict's prison on the one hand, and millions upon the other, must of necessity become vindictive, domineering, swift in his decisions, a dissembling Cromwell scheming to cut off the head of probity. A light, mocking wit concealed the depth of his character; mere shopman though he was, his ambition knew no bounds; he had comprehended society in one glance of hatred, and said to himself, "You are in my power." He had vowed that he would not marry before he was forty years old. He kept his word with himself.

As to Ferdinand's outward appearance, he was a slim, well-shaped young fellow, with adaptable manners that enabled him at need to take any tone through the whole gamut of society. At first sight his weasel face was not displeasing; but after more observation, you detected the strange expressions which are visible on the surface of those who are not at peace with themselves, or who hear at times the warning voice of conscience. His hard high color glowed under the soft Norman skin. There was a furtive look in the wall-eyes, lined with silver leaf, which grew terrible when they were fixed full on his victim. His voice was husky, as if he had been speaking for long. The thin lips were not unpleasing, but the sharply-pointed nose and slightly rounded forehead revealed a defect of race. Indeed, the coloring of his hair, which looked as if it had been dyed black, indicated the social half-breed, who had his cleverness from a dissolute great lord, his low ideas from the peasant girl, the victim of seduction; who owed his knowledge to an incomplete education; whose vices were those of the waif and stray.

Birotteau learned, to his unbounded amazement, that his assistant went out very elegantly arrayed, came in very late, and went to balls at bankers' and notaries' houses. These habits found no favor with César. To his way of thinking, a shopman should study the ledgers, and think of nothing but the business. The perfumer had no patience with folly. He spoke gently to du Tillet about wearing such fine linen, about visiting cards, which bore the name *F. du Tillet*—manners and customs which, according to his commercial jurisprudence, should be confined to the fashionable world.

But Ferdinand had established himself in this house to play Tartuffe to Birotteau's Orgon; he paid court to Mme. César, tried to seduce her, and gauging his employer with appalling quickness, judged him as his wife had previously judged. Du Tillet only said what he meant to say, and was both reserved and discreet; but he unveiled opinions of mankind and views of life in a fashion that dismayed a timorous, conscientious woman, who thought it a sin to do the slightest wrong to her neighbor. In spite of the tact which Mme. Birotteau employed, du Tillet felt her contempt for him; and Constance, to whom Ferdinand had written several amorous epistles, soon noticed a change in the manners of her assistant. He began to behave presumptuously, to give others the impression that there was an understanding between them. Without informing her husband of her private reasons, she recommended him to dismiss the man, and Birotteau was of his wife's opinion on this head. Du Tillet's dismissal was resolved upon; but one evening, on the Saturday before he gave notice, Birotteau balanced his books, as he was wont to do every month, and found that he was three thousand francs short. He was in terrible consternation. It was not so much the actual loss that affected him as the suspicion that hung over his three assistants and the servant, the errand-boy, and the workmen. On whom was he to lay the blame? Mme. Birotteau was never away from the cash desk. The book-keeper, who lodged in the house, was a young man of eighteen, Popinot by name, a nephew of M. Ragon, and honesty itself. Indeed, on Popinot's own showing, the money was missing, for the cash did not agree with the balance. Husband and wife agreed to say nothing, and to watch every one in the house.

Monday came, and their friends came to spend the evening. Every family in this set entertained in turn. While they played at *bouillotte,* Roguin the notary put down on the table some old louis-d'or which Mme. César had taken some days before of a bride, Mme. d'Espart.

"Have you been robbing the poor-box?" asked the perfumer, laughing.

Roguin said that he had won the money of du Tillet at a banker's house on the previous evening, and du Tillet bore him out in this without a blush. As for the perfumer, he turned crimson. When the visitors had gone, and Ferdinand was about to go to bed, Birotteau called him down into the shop, on pretence of business to discuss.

"We are three thousand francs short in the cash, du Tillet," the good man said, "and I cannot suspect anybody. The matter of the old louis-d'or seems to be too much against you to be passed over entirely, so we will not go to bed till we have found out the mistake, for, after all, it can be nothing but a mistake. Very likely you took the louis on account of your salary."

Du Tillet owned to having taken the louis. The perfumer thereupon opened the ledger; the assistant's account had not yet been debited with the sum.

"I was in a hurry. I ought to have asked Popinot to enter it," said Ferdinand.

"Quite true," said Birotteau, disconcerted by this off-hand coolness. The Norman had taken the measure of the good folk among whom he had come with a view to making his fortune.

The perfumer and his assistant spent the night in checking the books, the worthy merchant knowing all the while that it was trouble thrown away. As he came and went he slipped three banknotes of a thousand francs each into the safe, pressing them between the side of the drawer and the groove in the safe; then he pretended to be tired out, seemed to be fast asleep, and snored. Du Tillet awakened him in triumph, and showed exaggerated delight over the discovery of the mistake.

The next morning Birotteau scolded little Popinot and Mme. César in public, and waxed wrathful over their carelessness.

A fortnight later, Ferdinand du Tillet entered a stockbroker's office. The perfumery trade did not suit him, he said; he wanted to study banking. At the same time, he spoke of Mme. César in a way that gave the impression that motives of jealousy had procured his dismissal.

A few months later du Tillet came to see his late employer, and asked him to be his surety for twenty thousand francs, to complete the guarantees required in a matter which was to put him in the way of making his fortune. Seeing Birotteau's surprise at this piece of effrontery, du Tillet scowled and asked the perfumer whether he had no confidence in him. Matifat and two men with whom Birotteau did business were there at the time; his indignation did not escape them, though he controlled his anger in their presence. Perhaps du Tillet had returned to honesty; a gambling debt or some woman in distress might have been at the root of that error of his; and the fact that an honest man publicly declined to have anything to do with him might launch a man, still young, and perhaps penitent, on a career of crime and misfortune. The angel of mercy took up the pen and set his signature on du Tillet's papers, saying as he did so that he was heartily glad to do a small service for a lad who had been very useful to him. The color came into the good man's face as he told that kindly lie. Du Tillet could not meet his eyes, and doubtless at that moment vowed an eternal enmity, the truceless hate that the angels of darkness bear the angels of light.

Du Tillet kept his balance so skilfully upon the tight rope of speculation, that he was always fashionably dressed, and was apparently rich long before he was rich in reality. When he set up a cabriolet he never put it down again; he held his own in the lofty spheres where pleasure and business are mingled, among the Turcarets of the epoch for whom the crush-room of the Opéra is a branch of the Stock Exchange.

Thanks to Mme. Roguin, whom he had met among the Birotteaus' circle, he became rapidly known in high financial regions. Ferdinand du Tillet had attained a prosperity in nowise delusive; he was on an excellent footing with the firm of Nucingen, to whom Roguin had introduced him; and he had not been slow to secure the Keller connection, and to make friends among the upper banking world. Nobody knew where the young fellow found the vast capital which he could command, but they set down his luck to his intelligence and honesty.

The Restoration made a personage of César Birotteau, and, in the vortex of political crises, he not unnaturally forgot these two cross events in his household. The tenacity with which he had held to his opinions—for though since his wound it had been a strictly passive tenacity, he still held to his principles for decency's sake—had brought him patronage in high quarters, precisely because he had asked for nothing. He received an appointment as major in the National Guard, though he did not so much as know a single word of command.

In 1815 Napoleon, inimical as ever to Birotteau, ejected him from his post. During the Hundred Days, Birotteau became the *bête noire* of the Liberals in his quarter; for party feeling began to run high in that year among the commercial class, who hitherto had been unanimous in voting for peace for business reasons.

After the second Restoration, the Royalist Government found it necessary to manipulate the municipal body. The prefect wanted to transform Birotteau. into a mayor, but, thanks to his wife, the perfumer accepted the less conspicuous position of deputy-mayor. His modesty added not a little to his reputation, and brought him the friendship of the mayor, M. Flamet de la Billardière. Birotteau, who had seen him at the *Queen of Roses* in the days when Royalist plotters used to meet at Ragon's shop, suggested his name to the Prefect of the Seine, who consulted the perfumer on the choice. M. and Mme. Birotteau were never forgotten in the mayor's invitations, and Mme. Birotteau often asked for charitable subscriptions at Saint-Roch in good society.

La Billardière warmly supported Birotteau when it was proposed to distribute the Crosses awarded to the municipal body; when names were being weighed, he laid stress upon César's wound received at Saint-Roch, on his attachment to the Bourbons, and on the respect in which Birotteau was held. So the minister, who, while he endeavored to undo the work

of Napoleon, was wishful to make creatures of his own, and
to secure partisans for the Bourbons from the ranks of commerce, and among men of art and science, included Birotteau
in the list of those to be distinguished.

This favor, together with the glory which César already
shed around him in his Arrondissement, put him in a position that was bound to magnify the ideas of a man who had
met hitherto with nothing but success; and when the mayor
told him of the approaching distinction, it was the final argument which urged the perfumer into the speculation which
he had just disclosed to his wife; for it opened up a way of
quitting the perfumery trade, and of rising to the upper
ranks of the Parisian bourgeoisie.

César was forty years old. Hard work at his factory had
set one or two premature wrinkles in his face, and slightly
silvered the long bushy hair, on which the constant pressure of
his hat had impressed a glossy ring. The outlines of his hair
described five points on his forehead, which told a story of
simplicity of life. There was nothing alarming about the
bushy eyebrows, for the blue eyes, with their clear, straightforward expression, were in keeping with the honest man's
brow. His nose, broken at his birth, and blunt at the tip,
gave him the astonished look of the typical Parisian cockney.
His lips were very thick, his chin heavy and straight. It
was a high-colored face with square outlines, and a peculiar
disposition of the wrinkles,—altogether it was of the ingenuous, shrewd peasant type; and his evident physical strength,
his sturdy limbs, broad shoulders, and big feet, all denoted
the countryman transported to Paris. The large hands,
covered with hair, the creases in the plump finger-joints,
and broad, square-shaped nails at the tips, would alone have
attested his origin if there had not been signs of it about his
whole person.

He always wore the bland smile with which a shopkeeper
welcomes a customer; but this smile, assumed for business
purposes in his case, was the outward and visible expression
of inward content, and reflected the serenity of a kindly soul.

His distrust of his species was strictly confined to the business; he parted company with his shrewdness as he came away from the Exchange or shut his ledger. Suspicion for him was one of the exigencies of business, like his printed bill-heads.

There was a comical mixture of assurance, fatuity, and good-nature in his face, which gave it a certain character of its own, and redeemed it, to some extent, from the vapid uniformity of Parisian bourgeois countenances. But for the expression of artless wonder and trustfulness, people would have stood too much in awe of him; it was thus that he paid his quota of absurdity that put him on a footing of equality with his kind.

It was a habit of his to cross his hands behind him while speaking; and when he meant to say something particularly civil or striking, he gradually raised himself on tiptoe once or twice, and came down heavily upon his heels, as if to emphasize his remark. Sometimes in the height of a discussion he would suddenly swing himself round, take a step or two as if in search of objections, and then turn abruptly upon his opponent. He never interrupted anybody, and not seldom fell a victim to his finer punctilious observance of good manners, for others did not scruple to take the words out of his mouth, and when the worthy man came away he had been unable to put in a word.

In his wide experience of business he had acquired habits which others sometimes described as a mania. For instance, if a bill had not been met, he would put it in the hands of the process-server, and give himself no further trouble about it, save to receive the capital, interest, and court expenses. The matter might drive the customer into bankruptcy, and then César went no further. He never attended a meeting of creditors; his name never appeared in any list; he kept his claims. This system, together with an implacable contempt for bankrupts, had been handed down to him by old M. Ragon, who, after a long commercial experience, had come to the conclusion that the meagre and uncertain dividend paid under the circumstances was a very poor return for the time wasted in law proceedings, and held that he could spend his time to better purpose than in running about after excuses for dishonesty.

"If the bankrupt is an honest man, and makes his way again, he will pay you," M. Ragon was wont to say. "If he has nothing, and is simply unfortunate, what is the good of tormenting him? And if he is a rogue, you will get nothing in any case. If you have a name for being hard on people, they will not try to make terms with you; and so long as they can pay at all, you are the man whom they will pay."

César kept his appointments punctually; he would wait for ten minutes, and nothing would induce him to stay any longer, a characteristic which was a cause of punctuality in others who had to do with him.

His dress was in keeping with his appearance and habits. No power on earth would have induced him to resign the white lawn neck-cloths with drooping ends, embroidered by his wife or daughter. His white drill waistcoats, adorned with a double row of buttons, descended low upon his prominent abdomen, for Birotteau was inclined to corpulence. He wore blue breeches, black silk stockings, and walking-shoes adorned with ribbon bows that were apt to come unfastened. Out of doors his too ample green overcoat and broad-brimmed hat gave him a somewhat Quakerly appearance. On Sunday evenings he wore a coat of chestnut-brown cloth, with long tails and ample skirts, and black silk breeches; the corners of the inevitable waistcoat were turned down a little to display the pleated shirt-front beneath, and there were gold buckles on his shoes. Until the year 1819 his person was further adorned by two parallel lines of watch-chain, but he only wore the second when in full dress.

Such was César Birotteau—a worthy soul, from whom the mysterious powers that preside at the making of man had withheld the faculty of seeing life or politics as a whole, and the capacity of rising above the social level of the lower middle class; in all things he was destined to follow in the ruts of the old road; he had caught his opinions like an infection, and he put them in practice without examining into them. But if he was blind, he was a good man; if he was not very clever, he was deeply religious, and his heart was pure. In that heart there shone but one love, the light of his life and its motive power; for his desire to rise in the world, like the meagre knowledge that he had learned in it, had its source in his love for his wife and daughter.

As for Mme. César, at that time, at the age of thirty-seven, she so exactly resembled the Venus of Milo, that when the Duc de Rivière sent the beautiful statue to France, all her acquaintance recognized the likeness. A few short months, and trouble so swiftly spread its sallow tinge over the dazzling fairness of her face, so ruthlessly darkened and hollowed the blue-veined circles in which the beautiful hazel eyes were set, that she came to look like an aged Madonna; for in the wreck of her beauty she never lost her sweet ingenuousness, though there was a sad expression in the clear eyes; and it was impossible not to see in her a still beautiful woman, staid in her demeanor, and full of dignity. Moreover, during this ball of César's planning, her beauty was to shine forth radiantly for the last time to the admiration of beholders.

Every life has its apogee; there is a time in every existence when active causes bring about exactly proportionate results. This high noon of life, when the vital forces are evenly balanced and put forth in all the glory of their strength, is common not only to organic life; you will find it even in the history of cities and nations and institutions and ideas, in commerce, and in every kind of human effort, for, like noble families and dynasties, these too have their birth and rise and fall.

How comes it that this argument of waxing and waning is applied so inexorably to everything throughout the system of things?—to death as to life; for in times of pestilence, death runs his course, abates, returns again, lies dormant. Who knows but that our globe itself is a rocket somewhat longer lived than other fireworks?

History, telling over and over again the reasons of the rise and fall of all that has been in the world in the past, might be a warning to man that there is a moment when the active play of all his faculties must cease; but neither conquerors, nor actors, nor women, nor writers heed the wholesome admonition. César Birotteau, who should have looked upon himself as having reached the apogee of his career, mistook the summit for the starting-point. He did not know the reason of the downfalls of which history is full; nay, neither kings nor peoples have made any effort to engrave in imperishable characters the causes of the catastrophes of which the history of royal and of commercial houses affords such conspicuous examples. Why should not pyramids be reared anew to put us constantly in mind of the immutable law which should govern the affairs of nations as well as of individuals: *When the effect produced is no longer in direct relation with nor in exact proportion to the cause, disorganization sets in?* And yet—these monuments are all about us—in legends, in the stones that cry out to us of a past, and bear perpetual record to the freaks of a stubborn Fate whose hand sweeps away our illusions, and makes it clear to us that the greatest events resolve themselves at last into an Idea, and the "Tale of Troy" and the "Story of Napoleon" are poems and nothing more.

Would that this story might be the Epic of the Bourgeoisie; there are dealings of Fate with man which inspire no voice, because they lack grandeur, yet are even for that very reason immense: for this is not the story of an isolated soul, but of a whole nation of sorrows.

César as he dropped off to sleep feared that his wife might bring forward some peremptory objection in the morning, and laid it upon himself to wake betimes and settle everything. As soon as it grew light, he rose noiselessly, leaving his wife asleep, dressed quickly, and went down into the shop just as the boy was taking down the numbered shutters. Birotteau, finding himself in solitary possession, stood waiting in the doorway for the assistants, watching critically meanwhile the way in which Raguet the errand boy discharged his duties, for Birotteau was an old hand. The weather was magnificent in spite of the cold.

"Popinot, fetch your hat and your walking shoes, and tell M. Célestin to come down; you and I will go to the Tuileries and have a little talk together," said he, when Anselme came.

Popinot, that admirable foil to du Tillet, whom one of those happy chances which induce a belief in a protecting Providence had established in César's household, will play so great a part in this story, that it is necessary to give a sketch of him here.

Mme. Ragon's maiden name was Popinot. She had two brothers. One of them, the youngest of the family, was at the present time a judge in the Tribunal of First Instance of the Seine. The older had gone into the wool-trade, had lost his patrimony, and died, leaving his only son to the Ragons and his brother the judge, who had no children. The child's mother had died at his birth.

Mme. Ragon had found this situation for her nephew, and hoped to see him succeed to Birotteau. Anselme Popinot (for that was his name) was short and club-footed, a dispensation common to Byron, Sir Walter Scott, and Talleyrand, lest others thus afflicted should be too much discouraged. He had the brilliant complexion covered with freckles which usually distinguishes red-haired people; but a clear forehead, eyes like agates streaked with gray, a pretty mouth, a pale face, the charm of youthful diffidence, and a want of confidence in himself, due to his physical deformity, aroused a kindly feeling towards him in others. We love the weak, and people felt interested in Popinot.

Little Popinot, as everybody called him, took after his family. They were people essentially religious, whose virtues were informed by intelligence, whose quiet lives were full of good deeds. So the child, brought up by his uncle the judge, united all the qualities pleasing in youth; he was a good and affectionate boy, a little bashful, but full of enthusiasm; docile as a lamb, but hard-working, faithful, and steady, endowed with all the virtues of a Christian in the early days of the Church.

When Popinot heard of the proposed walk to the Tuileries, the most unlooked-for remark that his awe-inspiring employer could have made at that time of day, his thoughts went to his own settlement in life, and thence all at once to Césarine, the real queen of roses, the living sign of the house. He had fallen in love on his very first day in the shop, two months before du Tillet's departure. He was obliged to stop more than once on his way upstairs, his heart so swelled, and his pulses beat so hard.

In another moment he came down, followed by Célestin, the first assistant. Then Anselme and his employer set out without a word for the Tuileries.

Anselme Popinot was just twenty-one years of age; Birotteau had married at one-and-twenty, so Anselme saw no hindrance to his marriage with Césarine on that score. It was her beauty and her father's wealth that set enormous obstacles in the way of such ambitious wishes as his, but love grows with every up-leaping of hope; the wilder the hopes, the more he clung to them, and his longings grew the stronger for the distance between him and his love. Happy boy, who in a time when all and sundry are brought down to the same level, when every head is crowned with a precisely similar hat, can still contrive to create a distance between a perfumer's daughter and himself—the scion of an old Parisian family! And he was happy, in spite of his doubts and fears; every day of his life he sat next to Césarine at dinner; he set about his business with a zeal and enthusiasm that left no element of drudgery in his work; he did everything in the name of Césarine, and never wearied. At one-and-twenty devotion is food sufficient for love.

"He will be a merchant some of these days; he will get on," César would say, speaking of Anselme to Mme. Ragon, and he would praise Anselme's activity in the filling-out department, extolling his quickness at comprehending the mysteries of the craft, relating how that, when goods were to be sent

off in a hurry, Anselme would roll up his sleeves and work
bare-armed at packing the cases and nailing down the lids,
and the lame lad would do more than all the rest of them
put together.

There was another serious obstacle in the way of the orphan's success. It was a well-known and recognized fact that
Alexandre Crottat, Roguin's head-clerk, the son of a rich
farmer of la Brie, hoped to marry Césarine; and there were
other difficulties yet more formidable. In the depths of
Popinot's heart there lay buried sad secrets which set a yet
wider gulf between him and Césarine. The Ragons, on whom
he might have counted, were in difficulties; the orphan boy
was happy to take them his scanty salary to help them to eke
out a living. But in spite of all these things, he hoped to
succeed! More than once he had caught a glance from
Césarine, and beneath her apparent pride he had dared to
read a secret thought full of tender hopes in the depths of her
blue eyes. So he worked on, set in a ferment by that gleam of
hope, tremulous and mute, like all young men in a like case
when life is breaking into blossom.

"Popinot," the good man began, "is your aunt quite well?"

"Yes, sir."

"Somehow she has seemed to me to have an anxious look
for some time past; can something have gone askew with
them? Look here, my boy, you must not make a stranger of
me, that am almost like one of the family, for I have known
your Uncle Ragon these five-and-twenty years. When I first
came to him, I was fresh from the country, and wore a pair of
hobnailed boots. They call the place the Treasury Farm,
but all I brought away with me was one gold louis which my
godmother gave me, Madame the late Marquise d'Uxelles,
who was related to le Duc and Mme. la Duchesse de Lenoncourt, who are among our patrons. So I always say a prayer
every Sunday for her and all the family; and her niece, Mme.
de Mortsauf, in Touraine, has all her perfumery from us.
Customers are always coming to me through them. There is
M. de Vandenesse, for example, who spends twelve hundred

francs with us every year. One ought to be grateful from
prudence, if one is not grateful by nature; but I am a well-
wisher to you, without an afterthought, and for your own
sake."

"Ah, sir, if you will allow me to say so, you had a level
head."

"No, my boy, no; that won't do everything. I don't say
that my headpiece isn't as good as another's, but I stuck to
honesty through thick and thin; I was steady, and I never
loved any one but my wife. Love is a fine *vehicle,* a neat expression of M. de Villèle's yesterday at the Tribune."

"Love!" cried Popinot. "Oh! sir, do you——?"

"Stop a bit, stop a bit! There is old Roguin coming along
the further side of the Place Louis XV. at eight o'clock in the
morning. What can the old boy be about?" said César to
himself, and he forgot Anselme Popinot and the hazel-nut oil.

His wife's theories came up in his memory, and instead
of turning into the garden of the Tuileries, he walked on to
meet the notary. Anselme followed at a distance, quite at a
loss to explain the sudden interest which Birotteau appeared
to take in a matter so unimportant; but very happy in the
encouragement which he derived from his employer's little
speech about hobnailed boots, and louis-d'or, and love.

Roguin, a tall, burly man, with a pimpled face, an almost
bald forehead, and black hair, had not formerly been lacking
in comeliness; and he had been young and ambitious once
too, and from a mere clerk had come to be a notary; but now
a keen observer would have read in his face the exhaustion
and fatigue of a jaded seeker after pleasure. When a man
plunges into the mire of excess, his face hardly escapes without a splash, and the lines engraved on Roguin's countenance
and its florid color were alike ignoble. Instead of the pure
glow which suffuses the tissues of men of temperate life and
imparts a bloom of health, there was visible in Roguin the
tainted blood inflamed by a strain against which the body
rebelled. His nose was meanly turned up at the end, as is apt
to be the case with those in whom humors taking this channel

induce an internal affection, which a virtuous Queen of France innocently believed to be a misfortune common to the species, never having approached any man but the King sufficiently closely to discover her mistake. Roguin's efforts to disguise his infirmity by taking quantities of Spanish snuff served rather to aggravate the troublesome symptoms, which had been the principal cause of his misfortunes.

Is it not carrying flattery of society somewhat too far to paint individuals always in false colors, to conceal in certain cases the real causes of their vicissitudes, so often brought about by disease? Physical ills, in their moral aspects and the influences that they bring to bear on the mechanism of life, have perhaps been too much neglected hitherto by the historian of manners. Mme. César had rightly guessed the secret of Roguin's married life.

His wife, a charming girl, the only daughter of Chevrel, the banker, felt an unconquerable repugnance for the poor notary, which dated from the night of her marriage, and had been determined to demand an immediate divorce. But Roguin, too happy to have a wife who brought him five hundred thousand francs, to say nothing of her expectations, had implored her not to enter her plea, leaving her her liberty, and accepting all the consequences of such a compact. Mme. Roguin, mistress of the situation, treated her husband as a courtesan treats an elderly adorer. Roguin soon found his wife too dear, and, like many another Parisian, had a second establishment in the town. At first the expenditure did not exceed a moderate limit.

For a while Roguin found, at no great outlay, grisettes who were too glad of his protection; but at the end of three years he fell a prey to a violent sexagenarian passion for one of the most magnificent creatures of the time, known as *La belle Hollandaise* in the calendars of prostitution, for she shortly afterwards fell back into that gulf, which her death made illustrious. One of Roguin's clients had formerly brought her to Paris from Bruges; and when, in 1815, political considerations forced him to fly, he made her over to the notary.

Roguin had taken a little house in the Champs-Élysées for his enchantress; he had furnished it handsomely, and had allowed himself to be led by her, until he had squandered away his fortune to satisfy her extravagant whims.

The gloomy expression, which vanished from Roguin's countenance at the sight of his client, was connected with mysterious events, wherein lay the secret of du Tillet's rapid success. While du Tillet was still under Birotteau's roof, on the first Sunday which gave him an opportunity of observing how M. and Mme. Roguin were situated with regard to each other, his plans had undergone a change. His designs upon Mme. César had been subordinated to another purpose; he had meant to compel an offer of Césarine's hand as compensation for repulsed advances; but it cost him the less to give up this marriage since he had discovered that César was not rich, as he had believed. Then du Tillet played the spy on the notary, insinuated himself into his confidence, obtained an introduction to *La belle Hollandaise,* ascertained the terms on which she stood with Roguin, and learned that she was threatening to dismiss her adorer if he curtailed her extravagance. *La belle Hollandaise* was one of those scatter-brained creatures who take money without disturbing themselves as to how it was made, or how they come by it; women who would give a banquet with a parricide's crowns. She took no thought for the morrow, and was careless of yesterday. The future for her meant after dinner, and eternity lay between the present moment and the end of the month, even when she had bills to fall due. Du Tillet was delighted to find a first lever to his hand, and began his campaign by obtaining a reduction from *La belle Hollandaise,* who agreed to solace Roguin's existence for thirty thousand francs instead of fifty thousand, a kind of service which sexagenarian passion rarely forgets.

At length, one night after deep potations, Roguin opened out his financial position to du Tillet in an after-supper confidence. His real estate was mortgaged to its full value under his wife's marriage settlement, and in his infatuation he had appropriated moneys deposited with him by his clients; more than half the value of his practice had been embezzled in this way. When he had run through the rest, the unfortunate Roguin would blow his brains out, for he thought he should diminish the scandal of his failure by exciting the pity of the public. Du Tillet, listening, beheld success, rapid and assured, gleaming like a flash of lightning through the obscurity of drunkenness. He reassured Roguin, and repaid his confidence by persuading him to fire his pistols into the air.

"When a man of your calibre takes such risks upon himself," said he, "he ought not to flounder about like a fool; he should set to work boldly."

Du Tillet counseled Roguin to help himself to a large sum of money, and to intrust it to him (du Tillet) to speculate boldly with it on the Stock Exchange, or in some other enterprise among the hundreds that were being started at that speculative epoch. If the stroke was successful, the two of them should found a bank, speculate with the deposits, and with the profits the notary should satisfy his cravings. If the luck went against them, Roguin should go abroad, instead of killing himself, for his devoted du Tillet would be faithful to the last penny. It was a rope flung out to a drowning man, and Roguin did not see that the perfumer's salesman was fastening it round his neck.

Du Tillet, master of Roguin's secret, used it to establish his power over the wife, the husband, and the mistress. Mme. Roguin, to whom he gave warning of a disaster, which she was far from suspecting, accepted du Tillet's assiduities, and then it was that the latter left the perfumer's shop, feeling that his future was secure. It was not difficult to persuade the mistress to risk a sum of money that in case of need she might not be obliged to go on the street. The wife looked into her affairs, and accumulated a small amount of capital, which she handed over to the man in whom her husband placed confidence, for at the outset the notary put a hundred thousand francs into the hands of his accomplice. Brought in this way into close contact with Mme. Roguin, du Tillet contrived to transform interest into affection, and to inspire a violent passion in that handsome woman. In his speculations on the Stock Exchange he naturally shared in the profits of his three associates, but this was not enough for him; he had the audacity to come to an understanding with an opponent, who refunded to him the amount of fictitious losses, for he played for his own hand as well as for his clients.

As soon as he had fifty thousand francs, he was sure of making a large fortune. He watched with the eagle's eye that was one of his characteristics, over the phases of political life in France; he speculated for a fall in the Funds during the campaign of France, and for a rise when the Bourbons came back.

Two months after the return of Louis XVIII., Mme. Roguin possessed two hundred thousand francs, and du Tillet a hundred thousand crowns. In the notary's eyes this young man was an angel; he had restored order in his affairs. But *La belle Hollandaise* fell a victim to a wasting complaint which nothing could cure, a virulent cancer called Maxime de Trailles, one of the late Emperor's pages. Du Tillet discovered the woman's real name from her signature to a document. It was Sarah Gobseck. Then he remembered that he had heard of a money-lender of the name of Gobseck; and, struck by the coincidence, paid a visit to that aged discounter of bills, and providence of young men with prospects, to find out how this female relative's credit stood with him. The bill-broking Brutus proved inexorable where his grand-niece was concerned, but du Tillet himself managed to find favor in his eyes by posing as Sarah's banker with capital to invest. The Norman and the money-lender found each other congenial.

Gobseck wanted a clever young fellow who could look after a bit of business abroad for him just then. The return of the Bourbons had taken a State auditor by surprise. To this financier, wishful to stand well at Court, it had occurred that he might buy up the debts contracted by the Princes in Ger-

many during the emigration. He offered the profits of the
affair, which for him was purely a matter of policy, to any
one who would advance the necessary money. Old Gobseck
had no mind to disburse moneys over and above the market
value of the debts, into which a shrewd representative must
first examine. Money-lenders trust nobody; they must always
have a guarantee; the occasion is omnipotent with them;
they are ice when they have no need of a man, affable and
obliging when he is likely to be useful. Du Tillet knew the
immense part played, below the surface, in the Paris money
market by Werbrust and Gigonnet, discount brokers of the
Rue Saint-Denis and Rue Saint-Martin, and by Palma, a
banker in the Faubourg Poissonnière, who was almost always
associated with Gobseck. He therefore offered to pay down
caution money, requiring on his own side a share in the
profits of the transaction, and asking that these gentlemen
should employ in the money-lending business the capital
which he should deposit with them. In this way he secured
supporters. Then he accompanied M. Clément Chardin des
Lupeaulx on a trip to Germany during the Hundred Days,
and came back with the Second Restoration, with some added
knowledge that should lead to success rather than with actual
wealth. He had had an initiation into the secrets of one of
the cleverest schemers in Paris; he had won the goodwill of
the man whom he had been set to watch; a dexterous juggler
had laid bare for him the springs of political intrigue and the
rules of the game.

Du Tillet's intelligence was of the order which understands
at half a word; this journey formed him. On his return he
found Mme. Roguin still faithful; but the poor notary was
expecting Ferdinand with quite as much impatience as his
wife. *La belle Hollandaise* had ruined him again!

Du Tillet, questioning *La belle Hollandaise,* could not
elicit from her an account that represented all the money
which she had squandered. And then it was that he discovered the secret so carefully kept from him—Sarah Gobseck's
infatuation for Maxime de Trailles, known at the very outset

of his career of vice and debauchery for a political hanger-on of a kind indispensable to all good government, and for an insatiable gambler. After this discovery du Tillet understood old Gobseck's indifference to his grand-niece.

At this critical juncture, du Tillet the banker (for by this time he was a banker) strongly recommended Roguin to put by something for a rainy day; to engage some of his richest clients in a business speculation, and then to keep back considerable sums out of the money paid over to him, in case he should be compelled to become a bankrupt in the course of a second career of speculation. After various rises and falls in the price of stocks, which brought luck only to du Tillet and Mme. Roguin, the notary's hour struck. He was insolvent, and thereupon, in his extremity, his closest friend exploited him, and du Tillet discovered that speculation in building land in the neighborhood of the Madeleine. Naturally, one hundred thousand francs which Birotteau had deposited with Roguin until an investment should be found for them, were paid over to du Tillet, who, bent upon compassing the perfumer's ruin, made Roguin understand that he ran less risk by ensnaring his own intimate friends in his toils.

"A friend," said du Tillet, "will not go all lengths even in anger."

There are not many people at this present day who know how little land was worth per foot in the district of the Madeleine at this time; but the building lots must necessarily shortly be sold for more than their momentary depreciation, caused by the necessity of finding purchasers who would profit by the opportunity. Now it was du Tillet's idea to reap the benefit without keeping his money locked up in a lengthy speculation. In other words, he meant to kill the affair, so that a corpse which he knew how to resuscitate might be knocked down to him.

In such emergencies as this, the Gobsecks, Palmas, Werbrusts, and Gigonnets all lent each other a hand, but du Tillet did not know them well enough to ask them to help

him; and, besides, he meant to hide his action in the matter
so thoroughly that, while he steered the whole business, he
might receive all the profits and none of the disgrace of the
robbery. So he saw the necessity of one of those animated
lay figures termed *men of straw* in commercial phrase. The
man who had once before acted the part of a stock-jobber
for him seemed to be a suitable tool to his hand, and he in-
fringed the Divine rights by creating a man. Of a former
commercial traveler, without a farthing on this earth, with
no ability, no capacity save for empty rambling talk on all
sorts of subjects, and but just sufficient wit to suffer himself
to be drilled in a part and to play it without compromising
the piece, and yet endowed with the rarest sense of honor—
that is to say, a faculty for silently accepting the dishonor
of his principal—of him, du Tillet made a banker, the originator and promoter of commercial enterprises on the largest
scale; him he metamorphosed into the head of the firm of
Claparon.

Should the exigencies of du Tillet's affairs at any time
demand a bankruptcy, it was to be Charles Claparon's fate to
be delivered over to Jews and Pharisees, and Claparon knew
it. Still, for the present, the scraps and pickings that fell
to his share were an El Dorado for a poor devil who, when
his chum du Tillet came across him, was sauntering along
the Boulevards with no prospects beyond the two-franc piece
in his pockets; so his friendship for and devotion to du Tillet,
swelled by a gratitude that did not look to the future, and
stimulated by the cravings of a dissolute and disreputable
life, led him to say *Amen* to everything.

When he had once sold his honor, he saw that it was risked
with so much prudence, that at length he came to have a
sort of dog-like attachment for his old comrade du Tillet.
Claparon was a very ugly performing poodle, but he was
ready at any moment to make the leap of Curtius for his
master.

In the present scheme Claparon was to represent one-half
of the purchasers of the lots, as Birotteau represented the

other half. Then the bills which Claparon would receive
from Birotteau should be discounted by some money-lender,
whose name du Tillet would borrow; so that when Roguin
absconded with the rest of the purchase-money, Birotteau
would be left on the brink of ruin. Du Tillet meant to direct
the action of the assignees; there should be a forced sale of
the building land, and du Tillet meant to be the purchaser;
he would buy it for about half its value, and pay for it with
Roguin's money and the dividend of the bankruptcy; so
under different names he was in possession of the money paid
down by the perfumer and his creditor to boot.

It was a prospect of a goodly share of the spoils that led
Roguin to meddle in this scheme; but he had practically surrendered himself at discretion to a man who could and did
take the lion's part. It was impossible to bring du Tillet
into a court of law, and the notary in a remote part of
Switzerland, where he found beauties of a less expensive
kind, was lucky to have a bone flung to him once a month
or so.

The ugly scheme was no deliberate invention, no outcome
of the broodings of a tragedian weaving a plot, but the result
of circumstances. Hatred, unaccompanied by a desire for revenge, is as seed sown upon the granite rock: du Tillet swore
to be revenged upon César Birotteau, and the prompting was
one of the most natural things in the world; if it had been
otherwise, there had been no quarrel between angels of darkness and the angels of light.

Du Tillet could not, without great inconvenience, murder
the one man in Paris who knew that he had been guilty of
petty theft; but he could sully his old master's name and
crush him until his testimony was no longer admissible. For
a long time past the thought of vengeance had been germi-
nating in his mind; but it had come to nothing. The rush
of life in Paris is so swift, and so full of stir, chance counts
for so much in it, that even the most energetic haters do not
look very far ahead; yet, on the other hand, if the constant
ebb and flow is unfavorable to premeditated action, it affords

excellent opportunities for carrying out projects that lurk in
politic brains, clever enough to lie in wait for the chances
that come with the tide. Du Tillet had had a dim inkling
of the possibility of ruining César from the moment when
Roguin first opened out his case to him; and he had not mis-
calculated.

Roguin, meanwhile, on the point of leaving his idol,
drained the rest of the philtre from the broken cup, going
daily to the Champs-Élysées, and returning home in the small
hours. There were grounds, therefore, for Mme. César's
suspicious theories. When a man has made up his mind to
play such a part as du Tillet had assigned to Roguin, he
perforce acquires the talents of a great actor; he has the eyes
of a lynx and the penetration of a seer; he finds ways of
magnetizing his dupe, so the notary had seen Birotteau long
before Birotteau set eyes on him; and when he saw that he
was recognized, he held out a hand while he was still at some
distance.

"I have just been making the will of a great person who
has not a week to live," said he, with the most natural air
in the world, "but they have treated me like a village doctor
—sent a carriage to fetch me, and let me go home afoot."

A slight cloud of suspicion which had darkened the perfumer's brows cleared away at these words; but Roguin had
noticed it, and took good care not to be the first to speak
about the building land, for he meant to give his victim the
finishing stroke.

"After a will come marriage-contracts," said Birotteau;
"such is life. Ah! by the by, Roguin, old fellow, when do
we make a match of it with the Madeleine, eh?" and he tapped
the other on the chest. Among men, the best-conducted
bourgeois will try to appear a bit of a rogue with the women.

"Well, it is to-day or never," returned the notary with a
diplomatic look. "We are afraid that the affair will get
noised abroad; already two of my richest clients want to go
into the speculation, and are very keen about it. So you

can take it or leave it. After twelve o'clock this morning
I shall draw up the deeds, and until one o'clock it is open to
you to join us if you choose. Good-bye. Xandrot made a rough
draft of the documents for me last night, and I am about
to read them through this very minute."

"All right, the thing is settled, you have my word," cried
Birotteau, hurrying after the notary, and striking hands upon
it. "Take the hundred thousand francs that were to have
been my daughter's portion."

"Good," said Roguin, as he walked away.

In the brief interval as Birotteau returned to young
Popinot he felt a sensation of feverish heat run through
him, his diaphragm contracted, sounds rang in his ears.

"What is the matter, sir?" asked the assistant, looking at
his employer's pale face.

"Ah, my boy, I have just concluded a big piece of business
with a single word. No one in such a position can help feeling some emotion. You know all about it, however; and besides, I brought you here so that we could talk comfortably
where no one will listen to us. Your aunt is pinched; what
did she lose her money in? Tell me about it."

"My uncle and aunt put their capital into M. Nucingen's
bank, and were obliged to take over shares in the Worstchin
mines in settlement of their claims; no dividends have been
paid on them as yet, and at their time of life it is difficult
to live on hope."

"Then how do they live?"

"They have been so good as to accept my salary."

"Good, Anselme, good," said the perfumer, looking up
with a tear in his eyes; "you are worthy of the attachment I
feel for you. And you shall be well rewarded for your application in my service."

As he spoke, the merchant grew greater in his own es-
timation as well as in Popinot's eyes; a sense of his ad-
ventitious superiority was artlessly revealed in his homely
and paternal way of speaking.

"What! Can you have guessed my passion for——?"

"For whom?" asked the perfumer.

"For Mademoiselle Césarine."

"Boy!" cried Birotteau, "you are very bold. But keep your secret carefully; I promise to forget it, and you shall go out of the house to-morrow. I don't blame you; the devil no! In your place I should have done just the same. She is so pretty."

"Ah, sir!" cried the assistant, in such a perspiration that his shirt felt damp.

"This cannot be settled in a day, my boy. Césarine is her own mistress, and her mother has her ideas. So keep yourself to yourself, wipe your eyes, hold your heart well in hand, and we will say no more about it. I should not blush to have you for a son-in-law. As the nephew of M. Popinot, judge of a Tribunal of First Instance, and as the Ragons' nephew, you have as good a right to make your way as another, but there are *ifs* and *buts* and *ands!* What a devil of a notion you have sprung upon me in the middle of a talk about business! There, sit you down on that bench, and business first and love affairs after.—Now, Popinot, is there mettle in you?" said Birotteau, looking at his assistant. "Do you feel that you have courage enough to wrestle with those that are stronger than you? for a hand-to-hand fight, eh?"

"Yes, sir."

"To keep up a long and dangerous combat?——"

"What is it?"

"To drive Macassar Oil from the field!" cried Birotteau, drawing himself up like one of Plutarch's heroes. "We must not undervalue the enemy; he is strong, well intrenched, and formidable. Macassar Oil has been well pushed. It is a clever idea, and the shape of the bottles is out of the common. I had thoughts of a triangular bottle for this plan of mine, but after mature reflection, I am inclined for little blown glass flasks covered with wicker work; they would look mysterious, and the public like anything that tickles their curiosity."

"It would cost a good deal," said Popinot. "Everything

ught to be on the cheapest possible footing, so as to allow a heavy discount to the trade."

"Right, my boy; those are sound principles of business. Bear in mind that Macassar Oil will show fight! 'Tis a specious thing; the name is attractive. It is put before the public as a foreign importation, and we, unluckily, are in our own country. Look here, Popinot, do you feel strong enough to do for Macassar? To begin with, you will oust it from the export trade; it seems that Macassar really does come from the Indies, so it is more natural to send French goods to the Indians than to ship them back the stuff that they are supposed to send to us. So there's the export trade for you! But it will have to be fought out abroad, and all over the country; and Macassar Oil has been so well advertised, that it is no use blinking the fact that it has a hold; it is pushed everywhere, and the public are familiar with it."

"I will do for it!" cried Popinot, with eyes on fire.

"And how?" returned Birotteau. "It is like the impetuosity of these young people! Just hear me out."

Anselme looked like a soldier presenting arms to a Marshal of France.

"I have invented an oil, Popinot, an oil which invigorates the scalp, stimulates the growth of the hair, and preserves its color—an oil for both sexes. The essence should have no less success than the Pâte and the Lotion, but I do not want to exploit the secret by myself; I am thinking of retiring from business. I want *you*, my boy, to bring out the *Comagen* —from the Latin word *coma,* which means hair (so M. Alibert, physician to the King, told me). In *Bérénice,* Racine's tragedy too, there is a king of Comagène, a lover of the beautiful queen who was so famous for her hair; no doubt it was out of compliment to her that he called his kingdom Comagène. How clever these great men of genius are! they descend to the smallest details."

Little Popinot listened to these incongruities, evidently meant for his benefit, who had had some education, and yet kept his countenance.

"Anselme," continued Birotteau, "I have cast my eyes on you as the founder of a wholesale druggist's business in the Rue des Lombards. I will be a sleeping-partner, and find you the capital to start it with. When we have begun with the Comagen, we will try essence of vanilla and essence of peppermint. In short, by degrees we will go into the drug trade and revolutionize it, by selling articles in a concentrated form instead of the raw products. Are you satisfied, ambitious young man?"

Anselme was so overcome that he could not reply, but his tear-filled eyes made answer for him. It seemed to him that this offer was the outcome of a fatherly indulgence which said, "Deserve Césarine by earning wealth and respect."

"I too will succeed, sir," he said at last, taking Birotteau's emotion for astonishment.

"Just what I was at your age," cried the perfumer; "those were just the very words I used! Whether you have my daughter or no, at any rate you will have a fortune. Well, my boy, what has come to you?"

"Let me hope that by gaining the one I may win the other."

"I do not forbid you to hope, my dear fellow," said Birotteau, touched by Anselme's tone.

"Very well, sir; may I begin to look out at once for a shop, so as to begin as soon as possible?"

"Yes, my boy. To-morrow we will shut ourselves up in the factory. You might look in at Livingston's on your way to the Rue des Lombards, and see if my hydraulic press will be in working order by to-morrow. To-night, at dinner-time, we will go to see that great man, kind M. Vauquelin, and ask him about this. He has been investigating the composition of hair quite lately, trying to find out its coloring matter, and where it comes from, and what hair is made of.—It all lies in that, Popinot. You shall know my secret, and all that remains to do is to exploit it intelligently.—Look in at Pieri Bérard's before you go round to Livingston.—My boy, M. Vauquelin's disinterestedness is one of the great troubles of my life. You cannot get him to accept anything. Luckily, I found out from Chiffreville that he wanted a Madonna at Dresden, engraved by one Müller, and after two years of inquiry for it in Germany, Bérard has found a copy at last—a proof before letters on India paper; it cost fifteen hundred francs, my boy. And now to-day our benefactor shall see it in the ante-chamber when he comes to the door with us; framed, of course, you will make sure of that. So in that way we shall recall ourselves to his memory, my wife and I; for as to gratitude, we have put his name in our prayers every day these sixteen years. For my part, I shall never forget him; but, you know, Popinot, these men of science are so deep in their work, that they forget everything, wife and children, and those they have done a good turn to. As for the like of us, our little intelligence permits us to have warm hearts at any rate. That is some comfort for not being a great man. These gentlemen at the Institute are all brain, as you will see; you will never come across one of them in a church. There is M. Vauquelin, always in his study when he isn't in his laboratory; I like to believe though that he thinks of God while he analyzes His works.—This is the understanding: I am to find the capital, I will put you in possession of my secret, and we will divide the profits equally, so there will be no need to draw up a deed. Good success to us both! We will tune our pipes. Off with you, my boy; I have affairs of my own to see after. One moment, Popinot; in three weeks' time I am going to give a grand ball, have a suit of clothes made, and come to it like a merchant already in a good way of business——"

This last piece of kindness touched Popinot so much that he grasped César's large hand in his and kissed it. The good man's confidence had flattered the lover, and a man in love is capable of anything.

"Poor fellow!" said Birotteau, as he watched his assistant hurrying across the gardens of the Tuileries, "if Césarine only cared about him! But he limps, his hair is the color of a basin, and girls are such queer things! I can scarcely be-

lieve that Césarine . . . And then her mother would like
to see her a notary's wife. Alexandre Crottat would make her
a rich woman; money makes anything endurable, while there
is no happiness that will stand the test of poverty. After
all, I have made up my mind that my girl shall be mistress
of herself, so that she stops short of folly."

Birotteau's next-door neighbor, Cayron by name, was a
dealer in umbrellas, sunshades, and walking sticks. He came
from Languedoc, his business was not doing well, and César
had helped him several times. Cayron asked nothing better
than to contract his limits, and to effect a proportionate saving in house rent by giving up two first-floor rooms to the
wealthy perfumer.

"Well, neighbor," said Birotteau familiarly as he entered
the umbrella shop, "my wife consents to the enlargement of
our place. If you like, we will go round and see M. Molineux at eleven o'clock."

"My dear M. Birotteau," returned he of the umbrella shop,
"I have never asked anything for the concession on my part,
but you know that a good man of business ought to turn everything to money."

"The deuce!" cried the perfumer; "I have no money to
throw away, and I am waiting to know if my architect thinks
the thing feasible. 'Before you settle anything,' so he said,
'we must know whether the floors are on a level; and then we
must have M. Molineux's leave to make an opening in the
wall, and is it a party wall?' And after that I shall have to
turn the staircase in my house, so as to alter the landing and
have the whole place level from end to end. There will be a
lot of expense, and I don't want to ruin myself."

"Ah, sir," cried the Languedocien, "when *you* are ruined,
heaven and earth will come together and have a family."

Birotteau stroked his chin, raised himself on tiptoe, and
came down again.

"Besides," Cayron went on, "I only ask you to take this
paper of me——" and he held out a little statement for five
thousand francs and sixteen bills.

"Ah!" said the perfumer, turning them over, "all for small amounts, at two months and three months——"

"Take them of me, and don't charge me more than six per cent," pleaded the umbrella dealer humbly.

"Am I a Jew?" asked the perfumer reproachfully.

"Goodness, sir, I took them to du Tillet that used to be your assistant, and he would not have them at any price; he wanted to know how much I would consent to lose, no doubt."

"I know none of these signatures," said the perfumer.

"Well, we have funny names in the cane and umbrella trade; they are hawkers."

"Well, well; I do not say that I will take the lot, but I might manage to take all at the shortest dates."

"Don't leave me to run after those horse-leeches that drain us of the best part of the profits, for a thousand francs at four months; take the lot, sir! I do so little discounting, that no one gives me credit; that is the death of us poor retailers in a small way."

"Well, well, I will take your little bills. Célestin shall settle it with you. Be ready at eleven.—Here comes my architect, M. Grindot," added the perfumer, as he saw the young man whom he had met by appointment at M. de la Billardière's house on the previous evening.—"Unlike most men of talent, you are punctual, sir," said César, in his most genteel manner.

"If punctuality—in the phrase of a king who was a clever man as well as a great statesman—is the courtesy of kings, it is no less the fortune of architects. Time—time is money; most of all for you artists. Architecture combines all the other arts, I permit myself to say. We will not go through the shop," he added, as he showed the way to the sham carriage entrance.

Four years ago M. Grindot had taken the *Grand Prix d' Architecture;* and now, he had just returned from a three years' sojourn in Rome at the expense of the State. While he was in Italy the young artist had thought of his art; in

Paris he turned his attention to money-making. Governments alone can give the necessary millions to erect public
buildings and monuments to an architect's enduring fame;
and it is so natural, when fresh from Rome, to take one's self
for a Fontaine or a Percier, that every ambitious young architect has a leaning towards Ministerialism; so the subsidized
Liberal, metamorphosed into a Royalist, sought to find patrons in power; and when a *Grand Prix* conducts himself after
this fashion, his comrades call him a sycophant.

Two courses lay open to the youthful architect—he might
serve the perfumer or make as much as he could out of him.
But Birotteau the deputy-mayor; Birotteau, the future possessor of half that building estate near the Madeleine, where
a quarter full of handsome houses was sure to be built sooner
or later, was a man worth humoring, so Grindot sacrificed
present gain to future opportunities. Patiently he listened
to the plans, ideas, and vain repetitions of this shopkeeping
Philistine, the artist's butt and laughing-stock, and the particular object of his scorn, and followed the perfumer about
his house, bowing respectfully to his ideas. When Birotteau
had said all that he had to say, the young architect tried to
give a summary of his own views.

"You have three windows looking out upon the street in
your own house," he said, "as well as the window that is
wasted on the stairs and required for the landing. To these
four windows you add two on the same floor in the next house,
by turning the staircase so that you can walk on level from
one end to the other on the side nearest the street."

"You have understood me exactly," said the amazed perfumer.

"To carry out your plan, we shall have to light the new
staircase from above, and contrive a porter's lodge in the
plinth."

"Plinth?"

"Yes; the part of the wall under the——"

"I see, sir."

"As to your rooms, and their arrangement, and decoration,

give me *carte-blanche.* I should like to make them worthy——"

"Worthy! You have said the very word, sir."

"How long can you give me to carry out this scheme of decoration?"

"Twenty days."

"What are you prepared to put down for the workmen?"

"Well, what are the repairs likely to mount up to?"

"An architect can estimate the cost of a new building almost to a centime," said the other; "but as I have not undertaken a *bourgeois* job as yet (pardon me, sir, the word slipped out), I ought to tell you beforehand that it is impossible for me to give estimates for alterations and repairs. In a week's time I might be able to make a rough guess. Put your confidence in me; you shall have a charming staircase lighted from above, and a pretty vestibule, and in the plinth——"

"The plinth again!"

"Do not be anxious. I will find room for a little porter's lodge. The alteration and decoration of your rooms will be a labor of love. Yes, sir, I am thinking of art and not of making money. Above all things, if I am to succeed, I must be talked about, must I not? So, in my opinion, the best way is not to haggle with tradesmen, but to obtain a good effect cheaply."

"With such ideas, young man," Birotteau said patronizingly, "you will succeed."

"So you will yourself arrange with the bricklayers, painters, locksmiths, carpenters, and cabinet-makers; and I, for my part, undertake to check their accounts. You will simply agree to pay me a fee of two thousand francs; it will be money well laid out. Put the whole place into my hands by twelve o'clock to-morrow, and tell me whom you mean to employ."

"What is it likely to cost at first sight?" asked Birotteau.

"Ten to twelve thousand francs," said Grindot, "without counting the furniture; for, of course, you will refurnish the rooms. Will you give me the address of your carpet manufacturer? I ought to come to an understanding with him about the colors, so as to have a harmonious unity."

"M. Braschon in the Rue Saint-Antoine has my order," said the perfumer, assuming a ducal air.

The architect made a note of the address on one of those little tablets which are unmistakably a pretty woman's gift.

"Well," said Birotteau, "I leave it all to you, sir. Still, wait until I have arranged to take over the lease of the two rooms next door, and obtained permission to make an opening through the wall."

"Send me a note this evening," said the architect. "I must spend the night in drawing plans. We architects would rather work for a city merchant than for the King of Prussia, that is to say, as far as our own taste is concerned. In any case, I will set about taking measurements, the height of the rooms, the dimensions of the door and window embrasures, and the size of the windows."

"It must be finished by the date I have given, or it is no good."

"It certainly must," returned the architect. "The men shall work day and night, and we will employ processes for drying the paint; but do not let the builders swindle you, make them quote beforehand, and have the agreement in writing."

"Paris is the only place in the world where one can make such strokes of the wand," said Birotteau, indulging in a flourish worthy of some Asiatic potentate in the *Arabian Nights.*—"Do me the honor of coming to my ball, sir. All men of talent do not feel the contempt for trade which some heap upon it; and I expect you will meet one scientific man of the highest rank—M. Vauquelin of the Institute!—besides M. de la Billardière, M. le Comte de Fontaine, M. Lebas a judge, and President of the Tribunal of Commerce; and several magistrates, M. le Comte de Granville of the Court Royal, and M. Popinot of the Court of First Instance, M. Camusot of the Tribunal of Commerce, and his father-in-law M. Cardot. . . . Perhaps, even M. le Duc de Lenoncourt, first Gentleman of the Bedchamber. It is a gathering of my friends, quite as much in honor of—er—the liberation

of the soil—as to celebrate my—promotion to the Order of
the Legion of Honor."

Grindot's gesture was peculiar.

"Possibly—I have deserved this—signal mark of royal—
favor by the discharge of my functions at the Consular
Tribunal, and by fighting for the Bourbons on the steps of
Saint-Roch's Church on the 13th Vendémiaire, when I was
wounded by Napoleon. These claims to——"

Constance, in morning dress, came out of Césarine's bedroom, where she had been dressing; her first glance stopped
her husband's fervid eloquence; he cast about for some every-
day phrase which should modestly convey the tidings of the
glory awaiting him on the morrow.

"Here, *mimi,* this is M. *de* Grindot, a distinguished young
man of great talent.—This gentleman is the architect whom
M. de la Billardière recommended; he will superintend our
little alterations here."

The perfumer placed himself so that his wife could not
see him, and put his finger on his lips as he uttered the word
little. The architect understood.

"Constance, this gentleman will take the dimensions of the
rooms.—Let him do it, dear," said Birotteau, and he whisked
out into the street.

"Will it cost a great deal?" Constance asked the architect.

"No, madame; six thousand francs, roughly speaking——"

"Roughly speaking!" cried Mme. Birotteau. "Sir, I beg
of you not to begin without an estimate, and to do nothing
until a contract has been signed. I know the way of those
gentlemen the builders—six thousand means twenty thousand. We are not in a position to squander money. I beg of
you, sir, although my husband is certainly master in his own
house, to leave him time to think this over."

"Monsieur told me, madame, that he must have the rooms
finished in twenty days; if we make a delay, you may incur
the expense without obtaining the result."

"There is expense and expense," said the fair mistress of
the *Queen of Roses.*

"Eh! madame; is it so very glorious, do you think, for an architect who would like to erect public monuments to super-intend alterations in a private house? I only undertook the little commission to oblige M. de la Billardière, and if you are alarmed——"

He made as if he would withdraw.

"Well, well, sir," said Constance, going back to her room. Once there she hid her head on her daughter's shoulder.— "My child," she cried, "your father is ruining himself! He has engaged an architect who wears moustaches and a *royale* on his chin, and talks about erecting public monuments! He will fling the house out of the windows to build us a Louvre. César is always in a hurry when there is anything crazy to be done; he only told me about the plan last night, and he is setting about it this morning."

"Bah! mamma, never mind papa; Providence has always taken care of you," said Césarine, putting her arms about her mother. Then she went to the piano, to show the architect that a perfumer's daughter was no stranger to the fine arts.

When the architect came into the room, he was surprised by Césarine's beauty, and stood almost dumfounded. For the artist saw before him Césarine just come from her little room, in her loose morning-gown, fresh and blooming with the fresh-ness and the bloom of eighteen years, blue-eyed, and slender, and fair-haired. Youth gave the elasticity (so rare in Paris) which lends firmness to the most delicate tissues; youth tinted the blue network of veins throbbing beneath the transparent skin with the color adored by painters. For though she lived in the relaxing atmosphere of a Parisian shop, where the fresh air can scarcely penetrate, and the sunlight seldom comes, the outdoor life of Roman Trasteverine could not have been a more successful beautifier than Césarine's manner of living. Her thick hair grew erect like her father's, and being dressed high, afforded a view of a well-set neck among a shower of curls—the elaborate coiffure of the damsels of the counter, in whom a desire to shine inspires a more than English atten-tion to trifling details in matters of the toilette.

Césarine's beauty was neither that of an English court lady nor of a French duchess, but the plump and auburn-haired comeliness of Rubens' Flemish women. She had inherited her father's turned-up nose, but its delicacy of outline gave a sprightly charm to a face, of the essentially French type so well rendered by Largillière. The rich silken tissue of the skin indicated the abundant vitality of girlhood. Her mother's broad brow was lighted by a girlish serenity, untroubled by care, and there was a tender grace in the expression of the blue liquid eyes of the happy-hearted, fair-haired maid. If happiness had taken from her face the romantic interest which painters inevitably give to their compositions by an expression somewhat too pensive, the vague, wistful instincts of the young girl who has never left her mother's wing made an approach to this ideal. With all her apparent slenderness, she was strongly made. Her feet indicated her father's peasant origin, a racial defect, like the redness of her hands—the sign-manual of a purely bourgeois descent. Sooner or later she was sure to grow stout. Occasionally young and fashionable women had come within her ken; and in course of time she had acquired from them the instinct of dress, certain ways of carrying her head, and manners of speaking and moving, thus copied, which turned the heads of the assistants and other young men; in their eyes she seemed to have a distinguished air.

Popinot had vowed to himself that no woman but Césarine should be his wife. This mobile blonde, whom a glance seemed to read, who seemed ready to melt into tears at a harsh word, was the one woman in whose presence he could feel conscious of masculine superiority. The charming girl inspired love, without leaving time to consider whether or no she had sufficient *ésprit* to ensure that the love should be lasting; but what need is there for what we in Paris call *ésprit*, in a class where the essential elements of happiness are good sense and virtue?

In character, Césarine was a second edition of her mother, slightly improved by an education which had taught her

superfluous accomplishments.   She was fond of music, and
had made a crayon drawing of the *Madonna of the Chair;*
she perused the works of Mesdames Cottin and Riccoboni,
and the writings of Fénelon, Racine, and Bernardin de Saint-
Pierre. She never appeared at her mother's side at the cash-
desk save for a few moments before dinner, or when, on rare
occasions, she took her place.   Her father and mother, like
all self-made people, who hasten to plant the seeds of ingratitude in their children by putting the younger generation on
a higher level, delighted to make an idol of Césarine, who,
happily, possessed the good qualities of her class, and did not
take advantage of their weakness.

Mme. Birotteau followed the architect's movements with
earnest, anxious eyes; looking on in consternation, calling her
daughter's attention to the strange gyrations of the footrule,
as Grindot took his measurements after the manner of architects and builders.   For her, each one of those strokes of the
wand seemed to lay the place under an evil enchantment, and
boded ill to the house; she would fain have had the walls less
lofty and the rooms smaller, and dared not put any questions
to the young man as to the results of this sorcery.

"Be easy, madame," he said, with a smile; "I shall not carry
anything away."

Césarine could not help laughing.

"Sir," pleaded Constance, who did not so much as notice
the architect's quip, "aim at economy; some day we may be
able to make you a return——"

Before César went to M. Molineux, the landlord of the
next house, he asked Roguin for the transfer of the lease
which Alexandre Crottat was to have drawn up.   As he came
away from the notary's house, he saw du Tillet at Roguin's
study window.   Although the *liaison* between his sometime
assistant and Mme. Roguin was a sufficient explanation of du
Tillet's presence in the house at a time when the negotiations
for the building land were impending, Birotteau, trustful
though he was, felt uncomfortable.   Du Tillet's animated
face suggested that a discussion was going on.

"Suppose that he should be in the business?" he asked himself, in an access of his commercial prudence.

The suspicion flashed like lightning across his mind. He turned again and saw Mme. Roguin at the window; and then the banker's presence no longer looked so suspicious.

"Still, how if Constance was right?" he asked himself. "How stupid I am to pay any attention to a woman's notions! However, I will talk it over this morning with our uncle. It is only a step from the Cour Batave, where M. Molineux lives, to the Rue des Bourdonnais."

A suspicious onlooker, a man of business with some experience of rogues, would have been warned; but Birotteau's previous career, together with his lack of mental grasp (for he was but little fitted for retracing a chain of inductions, a process by which an able man arrives at a cause), all led to his ruin. He found the umbrella dealer dressed in his best, and was starting away with him to the landlord, when Virginie, the servant, caught her master by the arm.

"The mistress hopes you will not go out again, sir——"

"Come!" cried Birotteau; "some more women's notions!"

"Without taking your cup of coffee. It is ready for you."

"Oh! all right. I have so many things in my head, neighbor," said Birotteau, turning to Cayron, "that I do not listen to my stomach. Be so good as to walk on; we shall meet each other at M. Molineux's door, unless you go up and explain the matter to him first. We should save time that way."

M. Molineux was an eccentric person of independent means, a specimen of a kind of humanity which you will no more find out of Paris than you will find Iceland moss growing anywhere out of Iceland. The comparison is but so much the more apt, for that the man in question belonged to that doubtful borderland between the animal and vegetable kingdoms which awaits the Mercier, who shall classify the various *cryptogamia* which strike root, thrive, or die among the plaster walls of the strange unwholesome old houses affected by the species.

This particular human plant was an umbellifer, to judge

by the blue tubular cap which crowned a stem sheathed in a pair of greenish-colored breeches, and terminated by bulbous roots enveloped in list slippers. At first sight the plant seems harmless and colorless enough; there is certainly nothing to suggest poison in its appearance. In this strange freak of nature you would have recognized the typical shareholder, who believes in all the news which the daily press baptizes with printer's ink, whose "Look at the paper" is a final appeal to authority; this (you would have thought) was the bourgeois, essentially a lover of order, always (in theory) in rebellion against the powers that be, to whom in practice he punctually yields obedience; a ferocious creature, take him singly, who grows tame in a crowd of his like. The man who is obdurate as a bailiff where his dues are concerned, gives fresh groundsel to his birds, and saves the fish-bones for the cat; he looks up in the middle of making out a receipt to whistle to the canary; he is suspicious as a turnkey, but will hurry to invest his money in some doubtful undertaking, and then try to recover his losses by the most sordid meanness. The noxious qualities of this hybrid growth are only discovered by use; its nauseous bitterness requires the coction of some piece of business wherein its interests are mingled with those of men.

Like all Parisians, Molineux felt a need to make his power felt. He craved that particular privilege of a sovereignty more or less exercised by every creature, down to the very porter, over a larger or smaller number of victims—a woman, a child, a clerk, or lodger, a horse, a dog, or monkey—that part of domination which consists in handing on to another the mortifications received by an aspirant to higher spheres. The tiresome little old person in question, having neither wife, nor child, nor niece, nor nephew, treated his charwoman so harshly that she gave him no opportunity of venting his spleen upon her, and avoided all collision with him by a rigorous discharge of her duties.

So his appetite for domestic tyranny being thus balked, he was fain to find other ways of satisfying it. He had made

a patient study of the law of landlord and tenant, and of
the legal aspects of the party-wall; he had fathomed the mysteries of jurisprudence with regard to house-property in Paris,
and was learned in its infinitely minute intricacies with regard to boundaries and abutments, easements, rates, charges,
regulations for the cleansing of the street, hangings for Fête-
Dieu processions, waste-pipes, lights, projections over the
public way, and the near proximity of insanitary dwellings.
All his mental and physical energies, all his intelligence was
devoted to maintaining his authority as a landlord with a
high hand; he had made a hobby of his occupation, and the
hobby was becoming a mania.

He loved to protect citizens against encroachments on their
rights, but opportunities occurred so seldom that his thwarted
passion expended itself upon his tenants. A tenant became
his enemy, his inferior, his subject, his vassal. He felt that
their homage was a due, and regarded those who passed him
without a salutation on the stairs as boors. He made out
his receipts himself, and sent them at noon on the quarter
day; and those who were behindhand received a summons by
a certain hour. Then followed a distraint and costs, and all
the cavalry of the law came into the field with the celerity
of "the machine," as the headsman calls his instrument of
execution. Molineux gave no grace and no delay; his heart
was indurated on the side of rents.

"I will lend you the money if you want it," he would say
to a solvent tenant, "but pay me my rent; any getting behindhand with the rent means a loss of interest for which the
law provides no remedy."

After a prolonged study of the skittish humors of successive tenants who conformed to no standard and, like successive dynasties, nor more nor less, invariably overturned the
institutions of their predecessors, Molineux had promulgated
a charter, which he observed religiously. By virtue of it,
the good man never did any repairs; none of his chimneys
smoked, his staircases were always in order, his ceilings white,
his cornices above reproach, his floors held securely to the

joists, and there was no fault to find with the paint. All the
locks had been put in within the last three years, every window
pane was whole, and as for cracks in the walls, they did not
exist; he could see no broken tiles in the floors till the
tenants were leaving the house. He usually appeared upon
the scene to receive the incoming tenants with a locksmith and
a painter and glazier, very handy fellows, he said. The
tenant was doubtless at liberty to make improvements; but if
the thriftless creature redecorated his rooms, old Molineux
set his wits to work, and pondered night and day how to dis-
lodge him and let the newly papered and painted abode to
another comer. He set his snares, bided his time, and began
the whole series of his unhallowed devices. There was no
subtlety in the regulations of Paris with regard to leases that
he did not know. He indited polite and amiable communications to his victims; but beneath the manner, as beneath the
harmless and obliging expression of the pettifogging scribbler
himself, lurked the spirit of a Shylock.

He must always be paid six months in advance, to be de-
ducted from the last half-year's rent, subject to a host of
thorny conditions of his own invention. He assured himself that the value of the tenant's furniture was sufficient
to cover the rent, and reconnoitered every new tenant like a
detective when he came in. There were some occupations
which he did not like, and the least sound of a hammer
frightened him. When the time came for handing over a
lease, he kept it back for a week, conning it over for fear it
should contain what he denominated *notary's et ceteras.*

Apart from his character of landlord, Jean-Baptiste
Molineux was apparently good-natured and obliging. He
could play a game of boston without complaining of being
badly seconded by his partner; his stock subjects for conversation were of the ordinary bourgeois kind, and he found
the same things laughable—the arbitrary acts of bakers
(the rascals), who give short weights, which are winked at
by the police, the heroic seventeen deputies of the Left. He
read the Curé Meslier's *Bon Sens,* yet went to mass, halting

between Deism and Christianity; but he subscribed nothing for sacramental bread, under the plea that you must resist the encroachments of the priesthood. The indefatigable redresser of grievances would write to this effect to the newspapers, though the newspapers neither inserted his letters nor replied to them. Molineux was, in short, in many respects the ordinary estimable citizen who burns a yule log at Christmas, draws for king on Twelfth Night, plays tricks on the 1st of April, makes the round of the boulevards when the weather is fine, goes to watch the skating; and on days when there are to be fireworks in the Place Louis XV., will take his place there at two o'clock in the afternoon with a piece of bread in his pocket, so as to be "in the front row."

The Cour Batave, where the little old man lived, is a result of one of those freaks of the speculative builder which cannot be explained after they have taken substantial form. It is a cloister-like building with its freestone arcading, its covered galleries surrounding the court with a fountain in the middle—a thirsty fountain with its lion jaws agape, not to supply, but to ask for water of every passer-by. Possibly it was intended for a sort of Palais-Royal to adorn the Faubourg Saint-Denis. There is a little light and stir of life during the day in the unwholesome pile shut in on all four sides by tall houses; it lies in the centre of a labyrinth of dank alleys, where the rheumatism lurks for the hurrying foot-passenger, a maze of dark narrow passages which converge here and connect the Quartier des Halles and the Quartier Saint-Martin by the famous Rue Quincampoix; but at night there is no spot in Paris more deserted, and these little slums might be called the catacombs of commerce. It is the sink of several industries; and if there are few natives of Batavia proper, there are plenty of small tradesmen.

Naturally, all the suites of rooms in this merchant's palace have but one outlook—into the central courtyard—and for this and other reasons the rents asked are of the lowest. M. Molineux inhabited one of the angles of the building. Considerations of health had prompted the choice of a sixth-floor lodging; for fresh air was only to be had at a height of seventy feet from the ground. From the leads, where the worthy owner of house-property was wont to take exercise, he enjoyed a charming view of the windmills of Montmartre. He grew flowers up there too, in defiance of police regulations against these hanging-gardens of the modern Babylon. His sixth floor establishment consisted of four rooms, without counting the water-closets on the floor above, a valuable property to which his claim was incontestable; he had the key, he had established them. On a first entrance, an indecent bareness at once revealed the miserly nature of the man. Half-a-dozen straw-bottomed chairs stood in the lobby; there was a glazed earthenware stove; and on the walls, covered with a bottle-green paper, hung four prints bought at sales. In the dining-room you beheld a couple of sideboards, two cages full of birds, a table covered with oilcloth, a weather-glass, mahogany chairs with horsehair cushions, and through a French window a view of the aforesaid hanging-gardens. Short, antiquated green silk curtains adorned the sitting-room, and the white painted wooden furniture was upholstered in green Utrecht velvet. As for the furniture of the old bachelor's room, it was of the period of Louis XV.; disfigured by prolonged wear, and so dirty that a woman in a white gown would have shrunk from contact with it. The chimney-piece boasted a clock; the dial, between two columns, served as a pediment beneath a statuette of Pallas brandishing a lance—a fabulous personage of antiquity. The tiled floor was so littered over with plates full of scraps for the cats, that it was scarcely possible to move about without setting a foot in one of them. Above the rosewood chest of drawers hung a pastel—Molineux in his youth. Add a few books, tables covered with shabby green card-board boxes, a case full of the stuffed forms of some departed canaries on a console table, and, to complete the list, a bed so chilly-looking that it might have been a rebuke to a Carmelite.

César Birotteau was charmed with Molineux's exquisite

politeness. He found the latter in his gray flannel dressing-gown, keeping an eye on the milk set on a little cast-iron plate warmer, in a corner of the hearth, while he poured the contents of a brown earthen pipkin, in which he had been boiling coffee grounds, into his *cafétière* by spoonfuls at a time. The umbrella dealer had opened the door, lest his landlord should be disturbed in this occupation; but Molineux, holding mayors and deputy-mayors ("our municipal officers," as he called them) in great veneration, rose at first sight of the magistrate, and stood cap in hand until the great Birotteau should be seated.

"No, sir . . . Yes, sir . . . Ah, sir, if I had known that I was to have the honor of housing a member of the municipal government of Paris amid my humble Penates, pray believe that I should have made it my business to repair to your house; although I am your landlord, or—on the point —of—being——"

Here Birotteau by a gesture entreated him to put on his cap.

"I shall do nothing of the kind; I shall remain bareheaded until you are seated, and have put on your hat if you have a cold. My room is rather chilly; my narrow means do not permit—God bless you, Mr. Deputy-mayor!"

Birotteau had sneezed while fumbling for his papers. He held them out, not without remarking that to save any delay he had had them made out at his own expense by M. Roguin his notary.

"I do not call M. Roguin's knowledge in question; 'tis an old name, well known in the Parisian notariat; but I have my little ways of doing things, and I look after my affairs myself, a hobby excusable enough; and my notary is——"

"But this is such a simple matter," said the perfumer, accustomed to prompt decisions on the part of buyers and sellers.

"*Simple!*" echoed Molineux. "Nothing is simple where house property is concerned. Ah! you are not a landlord, sir; so much the happier you! If you but knew the lengths to which a tenant will push ingratitude, and what precautions we have to take! Now just listen to this, sir: I have a tenant——" and for fifteen minutes Molineux held forth, relating how that M. Gendrin, a draughtsman, had eluded the vigilance of the caretaker in the Rue Saint-Honoré. M. Gendrin had perpetrated scandals worthy of a Marat, obscene drawings! and the police tolerated it, nay, they were made with the connivance of the police! Then this Gendrin, an artist of thoroughly immoral character, had gone back to the house with loose women, and made it impossible to go up and down the stairs, a prank worthy of a man who drew caricatures to ridicule the Government. And why all these misdeeds? . . . Because he was asked to pay his rent on the 15th! Gendrin and Molineux were about to go to law about it; for while the artist did not pay, he insisted on occupying the empty rooms. Molineux received anonymous letters—from Gendrin no doubt—threatening to murder him some night in the alleys about the Cour Batave.

"Things have arrived at such a pitch, sir," he went on, "that the Prefect of Police, to whom in confidence I related my difficulty (at the same time, I took the opportunity of saying a word or two touching the alterations that ought to be made in the provisions of the law for such cases), gave me an authorization to carry firearms in self-defence."

The little old man got up to look for his pistols.

"Here they are, sir!" cried he.

"But you have nothing of that kind to fear from me, sir," said Birotteau, glancing at Cayron with a smile that plainly expressed his pity for such a man.

Molineux caught the glance, and was shocked to see such a look on the countenance of a "municipal officer," whose duty it was to see to the safety of those in his district. He could have forgiven it in anybody else, but in Birotteau it was unpardonable.

"Sir," Molineux answered dryly, "one of the most highly respected judges in the Consular Tribune, a deputy-mayor, and an honorable merchant, would not condescend to such baseness, for baseness it is! But in this particular case you want the consent of your landlord, M. le Comte de Granville, before you make a hole in the wall, and stipulations must be made in the agreement touching the restoration of the wall on the expiration of the lease. As a matter of fact, too, the rent is a great deal lower than it will be; rents will go up all about the Place Vendôme; they are going up already! The Rue Castiglione is about to be built. I am binding myself down—I am binding—myself——"

"Let us have done with it," said Birotteau. "What do you want? I have had enough experience of business to guess that your reasonings can be silenced by the great argument—money! Well, how much do you want?"

"Nothing but what is fair, sir. How long has your lease to run?"

"Seven years," answered Birotteau.

"What may not my first floor be worth in seven years' time?" cried Molineux. "What will two furnished rooms let for over in your quarter? More than two hundred francs a month very likely! I am binding myself; binding myself down by a lease. So we will set down the rent at fifteen hundred francs. At that figure I will consent to receive you as a tenant for the two rooms instead of M. Cayron here," giving the dealer a sly wink, "and let you have them on lease for seven consecutive years. The opening in the wall you will make at your own charges, subject to your bringing to me proof that M. le Comte de Granville sanctions it and waives all his rights in the matter. Whatever happens in consequence of the small opening, the responsibility will rest upon you; but you shall be in nowise bound to reinstate the wall so far as I am concerned; you shall pay me down five hundred francs now instead; we never can tell what may happen; and I don't want to run about after anybody to put up my wall again for me."

"The conditions seem to me scarcely fair," put in Birotteau.

"Then you must pay me down seven hundred and fifty

francs *hic et nunc,* to be carried forward till the last six months of possession; the lease will be a sufficient discharge. Oh! I will take bills of exchange for value received in rent, at any date you please, so that I have my guarantee. I am a plain-dealing man, and go straight to the point in business. We will stipulate that you shall wall up the door on my staircase, where you have no right of way . . . at your own expense . . . in brick and mortar. Reassure yourself, I shall not call upon you to make it good when the lease expires; I shall regard the five hundred francs as an indemnity. You will always find me reasonable, sir."

"We in business are not so particular," said the perfumer; "if we had all these formalities, we should do no business at all."

"Oh, in business, that is quite another thing, especially in the perfumery line, where everything slips off and on like a glove," said the little old man, with a sour smile. "But with house property in Paris, sir, you cannot be too particular. Why, I had a tenant in the Rue Montorgueil——"

"I should be very sorry to delay your breakfast, sir," said Birotteau; "here are the deeds, set them right, all that you ask me is agreed to; let us sign the documents to-morrow, and give our promises by word of mouth to-day, for to-morrow my architect must be put in possession of the place."

Molineux looked again at the umbrella-dealer. "There is part of the term expired, sir; M. Cayron has no mind to pay for it; we will add the amount to the little bills, so that the agreement will run from January to January. That will be more business-like."

"So be it," said Birotteau.

"There is the halfpenny in the shilling for the porter——"

"Why, you are not allowing me to use the staircase and the doorway; it is not right that——"

"Oh! but you are a tenant!" cried little Molineux in peremptory tones, up in arms for the principle involved. "You must pay door and window taxes and your share of the rates. If once we clearly understand each other, sir, there will be no difficulties hereafter.—Is your business rapidly increasing, sir; are you doing well?"

"Yes," said Birotteau, "but that is not my reason. I am inviting a few of my friends, partly to celebrate the evacuation of the foreign troops, partly on the occasion of my own promotion to the Legion of Honor——"

"Aha!" cried Molineux, "a well-deserved honor."

"Yes," said Birotteau. "It may be that I have shown myself not unworthy of this signal mark of royal favor by acting in my capacity at the Consular Tribunal, and by fighting for the Bourbons on the steps of Saint-Roch, on the 13th of Vendémiaire, where I was wounded by Napoleon; these claims——"

"Equal those of our heroes in the late army. The ribbon is red, because it has been dyed in blood shed for France."

At these words, a quotation from the *Constitutionnel*, Birotteau could not resist the impulse to invite little Molineux, who grew quite incoherent in his thanks, and was almost ready to forgive the slight which had been put upon him. The old man went as far as the stairhead with his new tenant, overwhelming him with civilities.

As soon as they were outside in the Cour Batave, Birotteau looked at Cayron with an amused expression.

"I did not think that there was such a weak-minded creature in existence," he said; "idiot" had been on the tip of his tongue, but he suppressed it in time.

"Ah, sir!" said Cayron, "everybody is not as clever as you are."

Birotteau might be excused for thinking himself a clever man compared with Molineux; the umbrella-dealer's reply drew a pleasant smile from him; he took leave of his companion with a regal air.

"Here am I at the Market," he said to himself; "let us arrange about the hazel-nuts."

After an hour spent in making inquiries, the market-woman referred Birotteau to the Rue des Lombards, the headquarters of the trade in nuts for confectionery, and

there his friends the Matifats informed him that the only
wholesale dealer in hazel-nuts was one Mme. Angélique
Madou, resident in the Rue Perrin-Gasselin; and that this
was the one house in the trade for genuine Provençal filberts
and white Alpine hazel-nuts.

The Rue Perrin-Gasselin lies in a quadrangle bounded
by the Quay, the Rue Saint-Denis, the Rue de la Ferronnerie,
and the Rue de la Monnaie, a labyrinth of slums which are,
as it were, the entrails of Paris. Here countless numbers
of heterogeneous and nondescript industries are carried on;
evil-smelling trades, and the manufacture of the daintiest
finery, herrings and lawn, silk and honey, butter and tulle,
jostle each other in its squalid precincts. Here are the headquarters of those multitudinous small trades which Paris no
more suspects in its midst than a man surmises the functions
performed by the pancreas in the human economy. In this
congested district, in which one Bidault of the Rue Grenétat
(otherwise known as Gigonnet the pawnbroker) played the
part of leech, the whole stock of goods sold in the Great
Market is kept. The ancient mews are warehouses where tons
of oil are stored; the old coach-houses hold thousands of
pairs of cotton stockings.

Mme. Madou, sometime a fish-wife, had gone into the
"dry-fruit line" some ten years before this present year of
grace, on her entrance into a partnership with the late owner
of the business, who had an old-established connection among
the ladies of the Great Market. Her beauty, of a vigorous
and provocative order, had disappeared in excessive stout-
ness. She lived on the ground floor of a yellow dilapidated
house, held together by iron cramps at every story. The
departed dealer in dry fruit had succeeded in ridding himself of competitors, and had secured a monopoly of the trade;
so that in spite of some slight defects of education, his successor could continue in the same groove, and came and went
in her warehouses, old out-buildings, stables, and workshops,
where she waged war against insect life with some success.

Mme. Angélique Madou dispensed with counting-house,

safe, and book-keeping (for she could neither read nor write), and answered a letter by blows of the fist, for she looked upon it as an insult. In other respects she was a good-natured soul, with a high-colored countenance, and a bandana handkerchief tied about her head beneath her cap, and a trumpet voice which won the respect of the carmen who brought goods to the Rue Perrin-Gasselin, and whose "rows" with her usually ended in a bottle of *petit blanc*. She could not well have any trouble with the growers who supplied her, for she always paid cash on delivery, the only way of carrying on such a business as hers, and Mother Madou went into the country to see them in the summer-time.

Birotteau found this shrewish saleswoman among her sacks of hazel-nuts, chestnuts, and walnuts.

"Good day, my dear lady," said Birotteau flippantly.

"*You dear!*" returned she. "So you have pleasant recollections of your dealings with me, have you? Have we met each other at Court?"

"I am a perfumer, and what is more, deputy-mayor of the Second Arrondissement of Paris, and I have a right to ex-pect a different tone from you."

"I marry when I have a mind," said the virago; "I am no customer at the mayor's office, and don't trouble deputy-mayors much. And as for my customers, they adore me, and I talk to 'em as I please. If they don't like it, they may take themselves somewhere else."

"See what comes of a monopoly," muttered Birotteau.

"Popole? that's my godson; he has been up to some foolery perhaps; have you come for him, your worship?" she asked, in milder tones.

"No. I have the honor to inform you that I come to you as a customer."

"All right. What is your name, my lad? I haven't seen you here before."

"If that is the way you talk, you ought to sell your nuts cheap," said Birotteau, and he mentioned his name and designation.

"Oh! you are the famous Birotteau with the handsome wife.
Well, and what weight do you want of these little dears of
hazel-nuts, honey?"

"Six thousand pounds weight."

"It is as much as I have," said the saleswoman, with a
voice like a cracked flute. "You are not in the do-nothing
line, marrying the girls, and making scent for them. Lord,
bless you! you do a trade, you do! Sorry I have so little for
you! You will be a fine customer, and your name will be
written on the heart of the woman that I love best in the
world——"

"Who may that be?"

"Who but dear Madame Madou."

"What do you want for the nuts?"

"Twenty-five francs the hundred-weight to you, mister,
if you take the lot."

"Twenty-five francs," said Birotteau. "That is fifteen
hundred francs! And I shall very likely take a hundred
thousand pounds weight in a year!"

"But just look at the quality; no husks!" cried she, plung-
ing a red arm into a sack of filberts. "Sound kernels, my
dear sir. Just think, now, the grocers sell their mixed dessert
fruits at twenty-four sous the pound, and in every four pounds
they put more than a pound of hazel-nuts. Am I to lose
money on the goods to please you? You are a nice man, but
I don't care enough about you yet to do that. As you are
taking such a quantity, we might let you have them at twenty
francs, for it won't do to send away a deputy-mayor; it would
bring bad luck to the young couples! A good article; just
feel the weight of them! They wouldn't go fifty to the
pound! Sound nuts they are, not a maggot among them!"

"Well, send six thousand pounds weight early to-morrow
morning to my factory in the Rue Faubourg-du-Temple, for
two thousand francs at ninety days."

"They shall be punctual as a bride at a wedding. Well,
good-bye, M. le Maire; we part good friends. But if it is
all the same to you," she added, following Birotteau into the

court, "I would rather have a bill at forty days, for I have let you have them too cheap, and I can't afford to lose the interest on the money too. For all his sentimental ways, old Gigonnet sucks the life out of us, as a spider sucks a fly."

"Very well, yes, fifty days. But I'll have the nuts by weight, so as not to lose on the hollow ones. They must be weighed or I'll have nothing to do with them."

"Oh, the fox; he knows that dodge, does he?" said Mme. Madou; "you can't catch him napping. Those beggars in the Rue des Lombards put him up to that! Those great wolves yonder are all in a league to devour us poor lambs."

The lamb was five feet high and three feet round; she had not a vestige of a waist, and looked like a post in a striped cotton gown.

As he went along the Rue Saint-Honoré, the perfumer, lost in his schemes, meditated on his duel with Macassar Oil. He designed the labels, decided on the shape of the bottles, the quality of the corks, the color of the placards. And people say that there is no poetry in business! Newton did not make more calculations over the discovery of the famous binomial theorem than Birotteau made for the "Comagen Essence" (for it was an essence now; the words oil and essence possessed no definite meaning for him, and he went from the one to the other). All these combinations were seething in his head, and he mistook the ferment of an empty brain for the germination of an idea. So absorbed was he in his meditations, that he went past the Rue des Bourdonnais, and bethinking himself of his uncle, was obliged to retrace his steps.

Claude-Joseph Pillerault, formerly a retail ironmonger at the sign of the *Golden Bell,* was one of those human beings whose exterior is the outward and visible expression of a beautiful nature; and heart and brain, language and thought, his manner and the clothes that he wore, were all in harmony. He was the only relation that Mme. Birotteau had in the world, and upon her and on Césarine Pillerault had centered all his affections; for in the course of his business career

he had lost his wife and his son, and a boy whom he had
adopted, the son of his cook.

These cruel bereavements had given to the good man's
thoughts a cast of Christian stoicism, a lofty doctrine which
was the informing spirit of his life, and shed the radiance
of a winter sunset over his last years, a glow that brings no
warmth. There was a tinge of asceticism about the thin,
worn face, where sallow and swarthy tones were harmoni-
ously blended; you saw in it a striking resemblance to typical presentments of Time; but the every-day cares of a retail
business had touched this face, there was less of the monu-
mental quality, less of the grimness insisted upon by painters,
sculptors, and designers of bronze figures for clocks.

Pillerault was of middle height, and thick-set rather than
stout. Nature had fashioned him for hard work and a long
life; he was strongly built, as his square shoulders indicated;
a man of phlegmatic temper, whose feelings, though he could
feel, did not lie on the surface. His quiet manner and resolute face indicated that he was little given to the expression
of his emotions; but reserved and undemonstrative though
he was, there were depths of tenderness in Pillerault's nature.
The principal characteristic of the hazel eyes, with dark
specks in them, was their unvarying clearness. There were
deep furrows in a forehead sallowed by time, narrow, contracted, and stern, and covered with gray hair, cut so short
that it looked like felt. Prudence, not avarice, was expressed
in the lines of the thin lips. The brightness of the eyes told
of a temperate life; and, indeed, sincerity, a sense of duty,
and a real humility glorified his features and set off his face,
as health does.

For sixty years he had led a hard and dreary existence,
a constant struggle for a livelihood. It was the same story
as César's own, with César's luck omitted. Pillerault had
remained an assistant till he was thirty years old; he had
embarked his capital in business at an age when César was
investing his savings in *rentes;* then the law of the maximum
had hit him hard, and his pickaxes and spades had been

requisitioned. His taciturn wisdom, his foresight, and logical clear-headedness had had their effect on his "ways of doing business." His bargains were concluded as a rule by word of mouth and difficulties seldom arose. Like most meditative people, he was an observer; he said little, and studied those who talked; often he had declined good bargains of which his neighbors had availed themselves, and subsequently repented, and vowed that Pillerault could smell out a rogue. He preferred sure gains, if of the smallest, to bold strokes of business involving heavy sums.

His stock of hardware consisted of grates, gridirons, cast-iron fire-dogs, boilers, and copper caldrons, hoes, and such agricultural implements as laborers use, somewhat unremunerative branches of a business that involves continual drudgery. Hardware is ponderous, awkward to handle, and difficult to store, and the profits are not heavy in proportion; so Pillerault had nailed up many a case, sent off many packages, and unloaded many vans. Never had a competence been more honorably earned, more thoroughly deserved, more to the credit of the man who had made it. He had never asked too much, had never run after business. Towards the end of the time, you might have seen him smoking his pipe in the doorway and watching his assistants at work. In 1814, when he retired, his actual capital at first consisted of seventy thousand francs, which he invested in Government stock, that brought him in five thousand and some odd hundred francs a year, with a further forty thousand francs due in five years' time, when the assistant to whom he had sold the business was to pay for it. On this amount, meanwhile, no interest was paid. For thirty years he had annually made seven per cent on a turn-over of a hundred thousand francs, and had lived on half his income. Such was his balance-sheet.

His neighbors, but little jealous of this by no means brilliant success, extolled his wisdom without·comprehending it.

At the corner of the Rue de la Monnaie and the Rue Saint-Honoré stands the Café David, where a few retired tradesmen such as Pillerault, congregate of an evening to take their coffee. At one time, Pillerault's adoption of his cook's son had occasioned a few jokes among its frequenters, such jokes as are addressed to a man looked up to among his fellows, for the ironmonger received a respect for which he had not sought; his own self-respect sufficed him. So when Pillerault lost the poor young fellow, there were more than two hundred people at the funeral who followed his adopted child to the grave. He behaved heroically in those days, making no parade of his grief, bearing it as a brave man bears sorrow. This increased the sympathy felt in the quarter for the "good man," as they called him, and the accent in which the words were spoken gave the words a wider and ennobled meaning when they were applied to Pillerault.

Claude Pillerault had become so accustomed to the sober even tenor of his life, that when he retired from business and entered upon the time of leisure, which hangs so heavily on many a Parisian tradesman's hands, he could not unbend and divert himself with the amusements of an idle life; he made no change in his housekeeping; and his old age was enlivened by his political opinions, which, let us admit it at once, were those of the extreme Left.

Pillerault belonged to the artisan class, which the Revolution had brought into co-operation with the small shopkeepers. The one blot on his character was the importance which he attached to the victory of his principles; he dwelt fondly on his rights, on liberty, on the great results of the Revolution; he firmly believed that his political freedom and existence were being undermined by the Jesuits, whose underhand power the Liberals discovered, and threatened by the ideas with which the *Constitutionnel* credited Monsieur the King's brother. He was, however, consistent in his life and in his ideas; there was nothing narrow in his political views; he never abused his adversaries, he held courtiers in suspicion, and believed in Republican virtues. He imagined that Manuel was guiltless of any excesses, that General Foy was a great man, and Casimir Périer without ambition; to his thinking, Lafayette was a political prophet, Courier a good man. In short, he beheld noble chimerical visions.

The good man was domestic in his habits; he made part of the family circle in which his niece lived—the Ragons, Judge Popinot, Joseph Lebas, and the Matifats. Fifteen hundred francs a year supplied his needs; the rest of his income was spent in charitable deeds and in presents to his grand-niece; four times a year he gave a dinner to his friends at Roland's in the Rue du Hasard, and took them afterwards to the play. He played the part of the old bachelor friend on whom married women draw bills at sight for their fancies; for a country excursion, a party for the Opéra or the Montagnes-Beaujon; and Pillerault would be very happy at such times in the pleasure he was giving, and felt the gladness in other hearts.

If Molineux's character was written at large in his queer furniture, Pillerault's pure heart and simple life were no less revealed by his surroundings. His abode consisted of a lobby, a sitting-room, and bedroom. But for the difference in size, it might have been a Carthusian's cell. The lobby, floored with red tiles, which were beeswaxed, boasted but one window, hung with dimity curtains edged with scarlet; mahogany chairs with red leather cushions, and studded with brass nails, stood against the wall, which was covered with an olive-green paper, and adorned with pictures—a *Declaration of Independence,* a portrait of Bonaparte as First Consul, and a *Battle of Austerlitz.* The furniture of the sitting-room, doubtless left to the upholsterer, was yellow, and covered with a flowered pattern; there was a carpet on the floor; the bronze ornaments on the chimney-piece were not gilded. There was a painted fire-screen before the grate; a vase of artificial flowers under a glass shade stood on a console, and a liqueur stand on a round table covered with a cloth. It was evident trom the unused look of the room that it was a concession to convention on the part of the retired ironmonger, who rarely received visitors.

His own room was as bare as that of a monk or an old soldier, the two men who make the truest estimate of life. In the alcove a holy-water stoup caught the eye, a profoundly touching confession of faith in a Republican stoic.

An old woman came in to do the work of the establishment, but so great was Pillerault's reverence for womankind, that he would not allow her to clean his shoes, and made an arrangement with a shoeblack.

His costume was plain, and never varied. He always wore a coat and breeches of blue cloth, a cotton waistcoat, a white cravat, and very low walking-shoes; and on high days and holidays a coat with metal buttons. He rose, breakfasted, went out, dined, and returned home when the evening was over with the strictest regularity, for a methodical life conduces to health and length of days. César, the Ragons, and the Abbé Loraux always avoided the subject of politics; those of his own circle knew better than to court attack by trying to convert him. Like his nephew and the Ragons, he put great faith in Roguin; for him a notary of Paris was always a being to be venerated, and probity incarnate. In the matter of the building land, Pillerault had examined it so thoroughly, that the remembrance of his investigations had given César moral support in the combat with his wife's forebodings.

As César climbed the seventy-two steps of the stairs which led to the brown doorway of his uncle's rooms, he thought within himself that the old man must be very hale to go up and down them daily without a murmur. He found the coat and breeches hanging on a peg outside, and Mme. Vaillant busy rubbing and brushing them; while the philosopher himself, in his gray flannel dressing-gown, was breakfasting by the fireside, and conning the reports of parliamentary debates in the *Constitutionnel* or the *Journal du Commerce*.

"The affair is settled, uncle," said César; "they are just about to draft the documents; but if you have any doubts or regret about it, there is still time to cry off."

"Why should I cry off? It is a good piece of business, but it takes some time to realize, like everything that is safe. My fifty thousand francs are lying at the bank; the last instalment of five thousand francs for my business was paid in yesterday. As for the Ragons, they are putting all that they have into it."

"Why, how do they live?"

"Never mind; they live, at all events."

"I understand you, uncle," said Birotteau, deeply touched, and he grasped the austere old man's hands tightly in his.

"What are you going to do about this business?" Pillerault asked abruptly.

"I shall take three-eighths; you and the Ragons will take an eighth between you; I shall credit you with the amount in my books until they decide the question of the deeds."

"Good! Are you so very rich, my boy, that you pay down three hundred thousand francs? It looks to me as though you were risking a good deal of money outside your business; won't the business suffer? After all, it is your own affair. If you are pulled up, here are the funds at ninety; I could sell out two thousand francs in consols. Take care, though, my boy; if you come to me, you will be laying hands on your girl's fortune."

"Uncle, you say the kindest of things as if they were a matter of course; it goes to my heart to hear you."

"General Foy touched me after another fashion just now! There, at all events, it is settled. The building lots won't fly away; we shall have them for half their value; and even if we should have to wait six years, there will still be something in the way of interest; timber-yards would pay rent, so we cannot lose. There is only one thing, and that is impossible—Roguin will not run away with our capital——"

"But that is what my wife said last night; she is afraid——"

"That Roguin will run off with our money," said Pillerault, laughing; "and why?"

"Well, she says she doesn't like the cut of his features; and, like all men who cannot have women, he is frantic for——"

An incredulous smile stole over Pillerault's face; he tore a leaf out of a little book, filled in the amount, and signed his name.

"Here, this is an order on the bank for a hundred thousand francs, for Ragon's share and mine. Those poor people, though, to make up the money, sold out their fifteen shares in the Wortschin mines to your worthless rogue of a du Tillet. Good people in sore straits; it goes to one's heart to see it. And such good people they are, such noble people, the flower of the old-fashioned bourgeoisie, in fact! Their brother Popinot, the judge, knows nothing about it; they are hiding their affairs from him, lest they should hinder him from giving free course to his benevolence. People who have worked as I did for thirty years——"

"God grant that the Comagen Oil succeeds!" cried Birotteau, "and I shall be doubly pleased. Good-day, uncle; you are coming to dine with us on Sunday with the Ragons and Roguin, and M. Claparon is coming, for we are all going to sign the papers the day after to-morrow; to-morrow will be Friday, and I don't want to do bus——"

"Do you really believe in those superstitions?"

"I shall never believe that the day when the Son of God was put to death by men can be a lucky day, uncle. Why? —people stop all business even on the 21st of January."

"Good-bye till Sunday," said Pillerault abruptly.

"If it weren't for his political opinions," said Birotteau to himself, as he went downstairs again, "I do not know where they would find his equal here below. What are politics to him? He would get on very nicely without thinking of them at all. His infatuation shows that no one is perfect.—Three o'clock already!" said César, as he entered his shop.

"Are you going to take these bills, sir?" asked Célestin, holding out the umbrella-dealer's collection of bills.

"Yes, at six per cent, no commission.—Wife, put out all my things ready for me; I am going to call on M. Vauquelin, you know why. Above all things, a white cravat."

Birotteau gave some orders to his assistants; he did not see Popinot, guessed that his future partner had gone to dress for the visit, and went up at once to his own room, where the Dresden Madonna met his eyes in a magnificent frame, according to his orders.

"Well, it looks fine, doesn't it?"

"Why, papa, say it is beautiful, or people will laugh at you."

"Here is a girl for you that scolds her father! . . . Well, for my own part, I like *Hero and Leander* quite as much. The *Madonna* is a religious subject, which could be hung up in an oratory; but *Hero and Leander!* Ah! I will buy it, for the flask of oil suggested some ideas to me."

"But I don't understand, papa."

"Virginie, call a cab!" shouted César, in a voice that rang through the house. He had finished shaving, and the shy Anselme Popinot appeared, dragging his feet, for he thought of Césarine. He had not discovered as yet that he was not lame in the eyes of his lady-love, a sweet proof of love, which only those to whom fate has given some bodily deformity can receive.

"The press will be in working order to-morrow, sir," he said.

"Very well. What is the matter, Popinot?" asked César, seeing Anselme's flushed face.

"I am so glad, sir; I have found a place, a front and back shop, and a kitchen, and the rooms above, and a store-room, all for twelve hundred francs a year, in the Rue des Cinq-Diamants."

"We must have an eighteen years' lease of it," said Birotteau. "But let us go to M. Vauquelin, and we can talk on the way," and César and Popinot drove away under the eyes of the assistants, who were at a loss what to think of such magnificent attire, and so unusual a portent as a cab, igno-

rant as they were of the mighty matters that occupied the
owner of the *Queen of Roses.*

"So we shall soon know the truth about the hazel-nuts!"
said the perfumer.

"Hazel-nuts?" queried Popinot.

"You have my secret, Popinot," said the perfumer; "I
let slip the word 'hazel-nuts,' and that tells everything.
Hazel-nut oil is the only oil which produces any effect on
the hair; no other house has thought of it. When I saw the
print of *Hero and Leander,* I said to myself, 'If the
ancients put so much oil on their heads, there must have
been some reason for it,' for the ancients are the ancients!
In spite of modern pretensions, I am of Boileau's opinion
about the ancients. From that I came to the idea of hazel-
nuts, thanks to young Bianchon, the medical student, your
relative; he told me that the students at the École put hazel-
nut oil on their moustaches and whiskers to make them
grow. All we want now is the illustrious M. Vauquelin's
approval. Enlightened by him, we shall not deceive the
public. Only just now I was over in the Market buying the
raw material of a saleswoman there; and in another moment I shall be in the presence of one of the greatest scientific men in France for the quintessence of the matter.
There's sense in proverbs—extremes meet. Trade is the
intermediary between vegetable products and science, you
see, my boy! Angélique Madou collects the material, M.
Vauquelin distils it, and we sell an essence. Hazel-nuts
are worth five sous the pound, M. Vauquelin will increase
their value a hundred-fold, and we shall perhaps do a service to humanity; for if vanity is a plague of man, a good
cosmetic is a benefit."

The devout admiration with which Popinot listened to
the father of his Césarine stimulated Birotteau's eloquence;
he indulged in the crudest rhetorical display that a philistine's brain can devise.

"Be reverent, Anselme," he said, as they reached the
street in which Vauquelin lived; "we are about to enter

the sanctuary of science. Put the *Madonna* in evidence, but without making a parade of it, on a chair in the dining-room. If only I can manage to say what I want to say without making a muddle of it!" cried Birotteau artlessly. "Popinot, that man produces a chemical effect on me, the sound of his voice makes me quite hot inside, and even gives me a slight colic. He is my benefactor, Anselme, and in a few minutes he will be your benefactor too."

Popinot turned cold at the words, set down his feet as if he were treading on eggs, and looked uneasily round the room.

M. Vauquelin was in his study when Birotteau was announced. The man of science knew that the perfumer was a deputy-mayor and in high favor; he received his visitor.

"So you do not forget me now that you are so high up in the world," he said; "well, between a chemist and a perfumer there is but a hand's-breadth."

"Alas! there is a great distance between your genius and a plain man like me, sir; and as for what you call 'being high up in the world,' it is all owing to you, and I shall never forget it in this world or the next."

"Oh! in the next we shall all be equal they say, cobblers and kings."

"That is to say, those kings and cobblers who have lived piously," remarked Birotteau.

"Is this your son?" asked Vauquelin, looking at little Popinot, who was beyond expression amazed to find nothing extraordinary in the study. He had expected to see prodigious marvels, giant engines, vivified substances, and metals flying about.

"No, sir; but he is a young man in whom I am very much interested, and he has come to entreat your goodness, which is equal to your talent, and is it not infinite?" remarked Birotteau diplomatically. "We have come, after an interval of sixteen years, to consult you a second time on a matter of importance, concerning which I am as ignorant as a perfumer."

"Let us hear about it. What is it?"

"I know that the subject of hair occupies your nights, and that you are devoting yourself to the analysis of the substance! While you have been thinking for glory, I have been thinking too for trade."

"Dear M. Birotteau, what do you want of me—an analysis of hair?"

He took up a loose sheet.

"I am about to read a paper before the Académie des Sciences," he went on. "Hair is composed of a somewhat large proportion of mucus, a little colorless oil, a larger proportion of dark-greenish oil, and iron; I find a certain amount of oxide of manganese, and of phosphate of lime, and traces of carbonate of lime, and silica; sulphur enters largely into its composition. The proportions in which these different substances are present vary, and so cause the different colorings of hair. Red hair, for example, on analysis yields much more of the dark green oil than the other kinds give."

César and Popinot opened their eyes ludicrously wide.

"Nine things," cried Birotteau. "What, are there metals and oils in hair? It takes the word of a man like you, whom I venerate, to make me believe it. How extraordinary! . . . God is great, M. Vauquelin."

"Hair is produced by a follicular organ," the great chemist continued; "a follicle is a sort of bag open at both ends; at the one end it is connected with nerves and blood-vessels, and the hair issues from the other. According to some of our learned associates, one of whom is M. de Blainville, the hair is dead matter expelled from the sac or secreting gland, which is full of a pulpy tissue."

"It is like perspiration in sticks, as you might say," cried Popinot, for which the perfumer promptly kicked his shins.

Vauquelin smiled at Popinot's notion. On this, "He has capacity, hasn't he?" said César, looking at Popinot. "But if hair is dead, to begin with, sir, you can't possibly restore it, and it is all over with us! the prospectus is nonsense! You don't know how funny the public is; you can't go and tell people——"

"That there is a rubbish heap on their heads," said Popinot, trying to make Vauquelin laugh again.

"An aërial catacomb," returned the chemist, keeping up the joke.

"And the nuts that are bought!" cried Birotteau, with a lively sense of the pecuniary loss. "But why do they sell——?"

"Reassure yourself," said Vauquelin, smiling. "I see; some secret for preventing the hair from falling out or turning gray is the matter in question. Listen; here are my conclusions after all my researches."

Popinot pricked up his ears at this like a startled leveret.

"The blanching of the fibres, dead or alive, is, in my opinion, produced by an interruption of the secretion of the coloring matter; this theory would explain the fact that some fur-bearing animals in cold climates turn white or some lighter color at the beginning of winter."

"Hm! Popinot."

"It is evident," Vauquelin continued, "that the change of color is due to sudden change in the temperature of the circumambient air——"

"Circumambient, Popinot—mind that! mind that!" cried César.

"Yes," said Vauquelin, "to alternations of cold and heat, or to interior phenomena, which produce the same effect. So, in all probability, headaches and other local affections dissipate the fluid or derange the secretions. The inside of the head is the doctor's province. As for the outside, put on your cosmetics by all means."

"Well, sir," said Birotteau, "now I can breathe again after what you say. I thought of selling the oil of hazel-nuts, remembering the use the ancients made of oil for their hair; and the ancients are the ancients, I am of Boileau's opinion. Why did wrestlers oil themselves——?"

"Olive-oil would do quite as well as oil of hazel-nuts, said Vauquelin, who had paid no attention to Birotteau's remarks. "Any oil will do to protect the hair bulbs from outside influences injurious to the substances which it contains in process of formation; in course of deposit, we chemists would say. Perhaps you are right; the essential oil of hazel-nuts is an irritant, so Dupuytren once told me. I will try to find out the difference between walnut and beech-nut oils, colza, olive, and so forth."

"Then I am not mistaken," Birotteau exclaimed triumphantly, "and a great man bears me out in my opinion. Macassar is done for! Macassar, sir, is a cosmetic they give you, that is, sell you, and sell very dear, to make your hair grow."

"My dear M. Birotteau," said Vauquelin, "there are not two ounces of oil of Macassar in Europe. Oil of Macassar produces not the slightest effect on hair. The Malays will pay its weight in gold for it, because of its supposed preservative action on the hair, not knowing that whale oil is quite as good. No power chemical or divine——"

"Oh! divine—do not say that, M. Vauquelin."

"Why, my dear sir, God's first law is conformity with Himself; without unity there is no power——"

"Oh, looked at in that way——"

"No power whatever can make the hair grow on a bald head, and you cannot dye white or red hair without danger; but you will do no harm, and there will be no fraud in extolling your oil, and I think that those who use it might preserve their hair."

"Do you think that the Royal Academy of Science would approve it?"

"Oh! it is no discovery," said M. Vauquelin. "And besides, quacks have taken the name of the Academy in vain so often, that it would not help you at all. My conscience will not allow me to look on oil of hazel-nuts as a prodigy."

"What would be the best way of extracting it, by pressure or by decoction?" asked Birotteau.

"You will obtain the most oil by pressure between two hot

plates; but if the plates are cold, it will be of better quality. It ought to be applied to the skin itself, and not rubbed into the hair," continued Vauquelin good-naturedly, "or the effect will be lost."

"Mind you remember this, Popinot," said Birotteau, as his face flushed up with enthusiasm.—"You see in him, sir, a young man who will reckon this day among the great days of his life. He knew and revered you before he had seen you. Ah! we often talk of you at home; a name that is always in the heart comes often to the lips. We pray every day for you, my wife and daughter and I, as we ought to do for our benefactor."

"It is too much for so little," said Vauquelin, embarrassed by the perfumer's voluble gratitude.

"Tut, tut, tut!" said Birotteau. "You cannot hinder us from loving you, you who will accept nothing from me. You are like the sun; you shed light around you, and those on whom it shines can do nothing for you in return."

The man of science rose, smiling, to his feet; Birotteau and Anselme Popinot rose also.

"Look round, Anselme; take a good look at this study. If you will allow him, sir? Your time is so valuable, perhaps he will never come here again."

"Well, are you satisfied with your business?" asked Vauquelin, turning to Birotteau; "for, after all, we are both of us men of business——"

"Pretty well, sir," said Birotteau, going towards the dining-room, whither Vauquelin followed him; "but it will take a great deal of capital to start this oil under the name of Comagen Essence——"

" 'Essence' and 'Comagen' are two words that clash. Call your cosmetic Birotteau's Oil; or if you have no mind to blaze your name abroad, take another——Why, there is the Dresden Madonna. . . . Ah! M. Birotteau, you mean us to fall out at parting."

"M. Vauquelin," said the perfumer, taking both the chemist's hands in his, "the scarce print has no value save for the persistent efforts which I have made to find it; all Germany has been ransacked for a proof before letters on India paper; I knew you wished to have it, you were too busy to procure it yourself, so I have taken it upon myself to be your agent. Please accept, not a paltry print, but the earnest efforts, the care, and pains which prove a boundless devotion. I should have been glad if you had wanted some substances that could only be found in the depths of an abyss, that I might come to tell you, 'Here they are!' We have so many chances to be forgotten, let me put myself, my wife, and daughter, and the son-in-law whom I shall have one day, all before your eyes; and say to yourself when you see the Madonna, 'There are honest folk who think of me.'"

"I accept it," said Vauquelin.

Popinot and Birotteau wiped their eyes, so much moved were they by the kind tone in which the chemist spoke.

"Will you carry your kindness yet further?" asked the perfumer.

"What is it?" asked Vauquelin.

"I am inviting a few of my friends—(here he raised himself on tiptoe, but his face assumed a humble expression)—partly to celebrate the liberation of the soil, and partly on the occasion of my own promotion to the Legion of Honor."

"Aha!" said Vauquelin in astonishment.

"It may be that I have shown myself worthy of this signal mark of royal favor, by discharging my functions at the Consular Tribunal, and by fighting for the Bourbons on the steps of Saint-Roch's Church on the 13th of Vendémiaire, when I was wounded by Napoleon. . . . My wife is giving a ball on Sunday in twenty days' time; will you come to it, sir? Do us the honor of dining with us on that day; and for my own part, it will be as if they had given me the Cross twice. I will write to you in good time."

"Very well, yes," said Vauquelin.

"My heart is swelling with pleasure," cried the perfumer when they were in the street. "He will come to my house! I am afraid that I have forgotten what he said about hair; do you remember it, Popinot?"

"Yes, sir, and in twenty years' time I shall still remember it."

"A great man, that he is! What insight and what penetration!" exclaimed Birotteau. "He went straight to the point, he read our thoughts at once, and showed us how to make a clean sweep of Macassar Oil. Ah! nothing can make hair grow, Macassar, so that is a lie! Popinot, there is a fortune within our grasp. So let us be at the factory by seven o'clock to-morrow morning, the nuts will come in, and we will make the oil. There is no use in his saying that any oil will do; it would be all over with us if the public knew that. If there were not a little hazel-nut oil and scent in this composition of ours, what excuse should we have for selling it at three or four francs for as many ounces?"

"And you are to be decorated, sir!" said Popinot. "What glory for——"

"For commerce, isn't it, my boy?"

César Birotteau, sure of a fortune, looked so triumphant, that the assistants noticed his expression, and made signs to each other; for the appearance of a cab, and the fact that their employer and his cashier had changed their clothes, had given rise to the wildest imaginings. The very evident satisfaction of the pair, revealed by the diplomatic glances exchanged between them, and the hopeful eyes that Popinot turned once or twice on Césarine, announced that some important event was imminent, and confirmed the assistants' suspicions. The smallest chance events in their busy and almost monastic lives were as interesting to them as to any prisoner in solitary confinement. Mme. César's face (for she responded doubtfully to the Olympian looks her husband turned on her) portended some new development in the business, for at any other time Mme. César would have been serenely content,—Mme. César, who was so blithe over a good day, and to-day the takings had amounted to the extraordinary sum of six thousand francs; some old outstanding accounts had been paid.

The dining-room and the kitchen were both on the mezzanine floor, where César and Constance had lived during the first years of their married life. This dining-room, where their honeymoon had been spent, looked like a little drawing-room. The kitchen windows looked out into a little yard; a passage separated the two rooms, and gave access to the staircase, contrived in a corner of the back-shop.

Raguet the errand boy looked after the shop while they sat at dinner; but when dessert appeared, the assistants went downstairs again, and left César and his wife and daughter to finish their meal by the fireside. This tradition had been handed down from the days of the Ragons, who had kept up all the old-fashioned customs and usages in full vigor, and set the same enormous distance between themselves and the assistants that formerly existed between masters and apprentices. Césarine or Constance would then prepare the cup of coffee, which the perfumer took in a low chair by the fire. It was the hour when César told his wife all the small news of the day; he would tell her anything that he had seen in Paris, or what they were doing in the Faubourg du Temple, and about the difficulties that arose there.

"This is certainly one of the most memorable days in our lives, wife!" he began, when the assistants had gone downstairs. "The hazel-nuts have been bought, the hydraulic press will be ready for work to-morrow, the matter of the building lands has been concluded. And, while I think of it, just put away this order on the bank," he went on, handing over to her Pillerault's draft. "The redecoration of the rooms, our new rooms, has been settled.—Dear me! I saw a very queer man to-day in the Cour Batave!"

And he told the women about M. Molineux.

"I see," his wife broke in, in the middle of a tirade, "that you will have to pay two hundred thousand francs!"

"True, my wife," said the perfumer, with mock humility. "Good Lord! and how are we to pay it? for the building lands near the Madeleine, that will be the finest quarter in Paris some day, must be taken as worth nothing."

"Some day, César."

"Dear, dear!"—he continued his joke—"my three-eighths will only be worth a million in six years' time. And how shall we pay two hundred thousand francs?" asked César, making as though he were aghast. "Well, we will pay it with this," and he drew from his pocket one of Mme. Madou's hazel-nuts, which he had carefully kept.

He held it up between his thumb and finger. Constance said nothing; but Césarine, whose curiosity was tickled, brought her father his cup of coffee with a "Come, now, papa, are you joking?"

The perfumer, like his assistants, had noticed the glances Popinot had given Césarine during dinner; he meant to clear up his suspicions.

"Well, little girl, this hazel-nut is to work a revolution in the house. There will be one less under our roof after to-night."

Césarine looked straight at her father, as who should say, "What is that to me?"

"Popinot is going away."

Although César was a poor observer, although his remark had been meant to prepare the way for the announcement of the new firm of A. Popinot and Company, as well as for a trap for his daughter, his father's tenderness told him the secret of the vague emotions which sprang up in the girl's heart, and blossomed in red upon her cheek and brow, brightening her eyes before they fell. César thought at once that some word had been exchanged between Césarine and Popinot. Nothing of the kind had happened; the boy and girl understood each other, after the fashion of shy young lovers, without a word.

There are moralists who hold that love is the most involuntary, the most disinterested and least calculating of all passions, a mother's love always excepted, a doctrine which contains a gross error. The larger part of mankind may be ignorant of their motives; but any sympathy, physical or mental, is none the less based upon calculations made by brain or heart or animal instincts. Love is essentially an egoistical affection, and egoism implies profound calculation. For the order of mind which is only impressed by outward and visible results, it may seem an improbable or unusual thing that a poor, lame, red-haired lad should find favor in the eyes of a beautiful girl like Césarine; and yet it was only what might be expected from the workings of the bourgeois mind in matters of sentiment. The explanation would account for other marriages that are a constant source of amazement to onlookers, between tall or beautiful women and insignificant men, or when some well-grown stripling marries some ugly little creature.

For a man affected with any physical deformity, be it a club foot, lameness, a hunch-back, excessive ugliness, spot, blemish, or disfigurement, Roguin's infirmity, or other anomalous affection for which his progenitors are not responsible, there are but two courses open; he must either make himself feared, or cultivate an exquisite goodness—he cannot afford to steer an undecided middle course between the two extremes like the rest of humanity. The first alternative requires talent, genius, or force of character; for a man can only inspire terror by his power to do harm, impose respect by his genius, or compel fear by his prodigious wit. In the second he studies to be adored; he lends himself admirably to feminine tyranny, and is wiser in love than others of irreproachable physical proportions.

Anselme Popinot had been brought up by the good Ragons, upright citizens of the best type, and by his uncle the judge —a course of training which, with his ingenuous and religious nature, had led him to redeem his slight deformity by the perfection of his character. Constance and César, struck by a disposition which makes youth so attractive, had often praised Anselme in Césarine's hearing. With all their narrowness in other respects, this shopkeeper and his wife possessed nobility of soul and hearts that were quick to comprehend. Their praises found an echo in the girl's own heart; in spite of her inexperience, she read in Anselme's frank eyes a passion that is always flattering, no matter what the age, rank, or figure of the lover may be.

Little Popinot, not being a well-shaped man, had all the more reasons for loving a woman. Should she be fair, he would be her lover till his dying day; love would give him ambition; he would work himself to death to make his wife happy; he would suffer her to be the sovereign mistress of his home; and her empire over him would be boundless.

This, crudely stated, is perhaps what Césarine thought, unconsciously within herself; she had had a bird's-eye glimpse of the harvests of love, and she had drawn her own inferences; her mother's happiness was under her eyes, she wished no other life for herself; instinctively she discerned in Anselme another César, polished by education, as she herself had been. In her dreams, Popinot was the mayor of an arrondissement, and she liked to imagine herself asking for subscriptions to charities in her district, as her own mother did in the parish of Saint-Roch. And so at length she forgot that one of Popinot's legs was shorter than the other, and would have been quite capable of asking, "Does he really limp?" She liked the clear eyes; she liked to see the change that came over them when, at a glance from her, they lighted up at once with a flash of timid love, and then fell despondently again.

Roguin's head clerk, Alexandre Crottat, gifted with a precocious knowledge of the world, acquired by professional experience, disgusted Césarine with his half-cynical, half-good-natured air, after putting her out of patience with his commonplace talk. Popinot's silence revealed a gentle nature; she liked to watch the half-sad smile with which he endured meaningless trivialities; the babble which made him smile always roused a feeling of annoyance in her; they smiled or looked condolence at each other.

Anselme's mental superiority did not prevent him from working hard with his hands; the way in which he threw himself into everything that he did also pleased Césarine; she guessed that while all the other assistants said, "Césarine is going to be married to M. Roguin's head clerk," Anselme, lame and poor and red-haired, did not despair of winning her. The strength of a hope proves the strength of a love.

"Where is he going?" Césarine asked, trying to look indifferent.

"He is going to set up for himself in the Rue des Cinq-Diamants! And, upon my word, by the grace of God!——" But neither his wife nor daughter understood the ejaculation. When Birotteau's mind encountered any difficulty, he behaved like an insect that encounters an obstacle, he swerved to left or right; so now he changed the subject, promising himself to speak of Césarine to his wife.

"I told uncle your notions about Roguin and your fears; he began to laugh," he went on, addressing Constance.

"You ought never to repeat things that we say between ourselves," she cried. "Poor Roguin! he may be the most honest man in the world; he is fifty-eight years old, and I expect he no more thinks——"

She too broke off; she saw that Césarine was listening, and warned César of that fact by a glance.

"So I did well to strike the bargain."

"Why, you are the master," returned she.

César took both his wife's hands in his, and kissed her on the forehead. That answer had always been her passive form of assent to her husband's projects. And with that, Birotteau went downstairs into the shop.

"Come!" he cried, speaking to the assistants, "we will put up the shutters at ten o'clock. We must do a stroke of work, gentlemen! We must set about moving all the furniture from the first floor to the second to-night! We shall have to put the little pots into the big ones, as the saying is, so as to give my architect elbow-room to-morrow.—Popinot has gone out without leave," said César, looking round. "Oh! I forgot, he does not sleep here.—He is gone to see about the shop, or else he is putting down M. Vauquelin's ideas," he thought.

"We know why the furniture is being moved, sir," said Célestin, spokesman for the two assistants and Raguet, who stood by him. "May we be allowed to congratulate you on an honor which reflects glory on the whole establishment? . . . Popinot told us——"

"Well, boys, it can't be helped; I have been decorated. So we are inviting a few friends, partly to celebrate the liberation of the soil, and partly on the occasion of my own promotion to the Legion of Honor. It may be that I have shown myself worthy of this signal mark of royal favor by the discharge of my functions at the Consular Tribunal, and by fighting for the Royalist cause—when I was your age, on the steps of Saint-Roch, on the 13th of Vendémiaire; and, on my word, Napoleon the Emperor, as they called him, gave me my wound. For I was wounded, and on the thigh, what is more, and Mme. Ragon nursed me. Be brave, and you will be rewarded! So there, you see, my children, that a mishap is never all loss."

"People don't fight in the streets nowadays," said Célestin.

"Well, we must hope," said César, and thereupon he took occasion to read his assistants a little homily, which he rounded off with an invitation.

The prospect of a dance put new life into the three assistants; under the stimulus of the excitement, the three, with Virginie and Raguet, performed acrobatic feats. They came and went up and down the stairs with their loads, and nothing was broken, nothing was upset. By two o'clock in the morning the removal was accomplished; César and his wife slept on the second floor, Célestin and the second assistant occupied Popinot's room. The third floor was converted, for the time being, into a furniture warehouse.

When the assistants had gone down into the shop after dinner, Popinot, usually so quiet and equable, had been as fidgety as a racehorse just arrived upon the course. A burning desire to do something great was upon him, induced by a superabundance of nervous fluid, which turns the diaphragm of the lover or the man of restless ambition into a furnace.

"What can be the matter with you?" Célestin had asked.

"What a day! I am setting up for myself, my dear fellow,"

he whispered in Célestin's ear, "and M. César is to be decorated.":

"You are very lucky; the governor is helping you," exclaimed the assistant.

Popinot gave him no answer; he vanished, whirled away by the wind—the wind of success.

"Oh, as to lucky!" said an assistant, as he sorted gloves in dozens, to his neighbor, who was busy checking the prices on the tickets. "The governor has seen the eyes that Popinot has been making at Mlle. Césarine; he is a shrewd one, the governor, so he is getting rid of Anselme; it would be difficult to refuse outright, because of the relatives. Célestin takes the trick for generosity."

Anselme Popinot meanwhile had turned down the Rue Saint-Honoré and hurried along the Rue des Deux-Écus to secure some one in whom his commercial second-sight beheld the principal instrument of success. Judge Popinot had once done a service to this young man, the cleverest commercial traveler in Paris, whose activity and triumphant gift of the gab was to earn for him at a later day the title of "The Illustrious." At this time the great commercial traveler was devoting his energies to the hat trade and the "fancy-goods line"; he was simply Gaudissart as yet, without the prefix, but at the age of twenty-two he had already distinguished himself; his magnetic influence upon customers was beginning to be recognized. He was thin and bright-eyed at that time; he had an eloquent face, an indefatigable memory, a quick perception of the taste of those with whom he came in contact; he deserved to be, what he afterwards became— the king of commercial travelers, the Frenchman *par excellence*.

Popinot had come across Gaudissart some days previously, and the latter had announced that he was about to go on a journey; the hope of finding him still in Paris had sent Popinot flying down the Rue des Deux-Écus. At the coach-office he learned that the commercial traveler had taken his place. Gaudissart's leave-taking of his beloved city had taken the shape of an evening at the Vaudeville, where there was a new play. Popinot resolved to wait for him. To confide the agency of the hazel-nut oil to this invaluable launcher of commercial enterprises, already courted and cherished by the best houses, was like drawing a bill of exchange on fortune! Popinot had claims on Gaudissart. The commercial traveler, so skilled in the art of entangling that froward race, the petty country shopkeepers, in his toils, had once allowed himself to become entangled in a political web, in the first conspiracy against the Bourbons after the Hundred Days; and Gaudissart, to whom open air was a vital necessity, found himself in prison with a capital charge hanging over him. Judge Popinot, the examining magistrate, saw that it was a piece of youthful folly that implicated Gaudissart in the affair, and set him at liberty; but if the young man had chanced upon a magistrate eager to commend himself to the authorities, or upon a rabid Royalist, the luckless pioneer of commerce might have mounted the scaffold. Gaudissart, who knew that he owed his life to the judge, was in despair, because a barren gratitude was all the return he could make; and as it was impossible to thank a judge for doing justice, he had betaken himself to the Ragons, and there sworn fealty to the family of Popinot.

While Popinot waited, he naturally spent the time in going to see his shop in the Rue des Cinq-Diamants once more. He asked for the landlord's address, so as to come to terms with him about the lease. Then, wandering through the murky labyrinth about the Great Market, with his thoughts full of ways and means of making a rapid fortune, Popinot came into the Rue Aubry-le-Boucher, and there met with a wonderful and auspicious opportunity, with which César's heart should be gladdened on the morrow. Then he took up his post at the door of the Hôtel du Commerce at the end of the Rue des Deux-Écus; and towards midnight heard, afar off, a voice uplifted in the Rue de Grenelle; it was Gaudissart singing a bit of the last song in the piece, to the accompaniment of the sound of a walking-stick, trailed with expression upon the pavement.

"Sir," cried Anselme, suddenly emerging from the doorway, "can I have a couple of words with you?"

"Eleven, if you like," said the other, raising a loaded cane.

"I am Popinot," said poor Anselme.

"Right," said Gaudissart, recognizing his friend. "What do you want? Money? Absent on leave, but there is some somewhere. An arm for a duel? I am at your service from heel to head.

> "You see him where he stands—
> Every inch a Frenchman and a soldier!"

"Come and have ten minutes' talk with me, not in your room, we might be overheard, but on the Quai de l'Horloge; there is nobody there at this time of night," said Popinot, "it is a question of the greatest importance."

"You are in a hurry, are you? Come along!"

Ten minutes later, Gaudissart, now put in possession of Popinot's secrets, recognized the importance of the matter.

"Approach, ye hairdressers and retail perfumers," cried Gaudissart, mimicking Lafon in the Cid. "I will get hold of all the perfumers of France and Navarre. Oh! I have it! I was going away, but I shall stop here now and take agencies from the Parisian perfumery trade."

"Why?"

"To choke off your competitors, innocent! By taking on their agencies, I can make their perfidious cosmetics drink to their own confusion in your oil, for I shall talk of nothing else and push no other kind. A fine commercial traveler's dodge! Aha! we are the diplomatists of commerce. Famous! As for your prospectus I will see to it. I have known Andoche Finot since we were boys; his father is a hatter in the Rue du Coq, the old fellow started me; it was through him that I began to travel in the hat line. Andoche is a very clever fellow; he has the cleverness of all the heads that his father ever fitted with hats. He is in the literary line; he does the minor theatres for the *Courrier des Spectacles*. His father, an old fox, has abundant reason for not liking cleverness; he doesn't believe in cleverness; it is impossible to make him see that cleverness will sell, and that a young man of spirit can make a fortune by his wits; indeed, as to spirit, the only spirit he approves of is proof-spirit. Old Finot is reducing young Finot by famine. Andoche can do anything, and he is my friend, moreover, and I don't rub against fools (except in the way of business). Finot does mottoes for the *Fidèle Berger,* which pays him, while the newspapers, for which he works like a galley slave, snub him right and left. How jealous they are in that line! It is just like it is in the fancy article trade.

"Finot wrote a splendid one-act comedy for Mlle. Mars, the greatest of the great. (Ah! there's a woman that I admire!) Well, and to see it put on the stage at all, he had to take it to the Gaîté. Andoche understands prospectuses; he enters into a man's ideas about business, he is not proud, he will block out our prospectus *gratis.* Goodness! we will treat him to a bowl of punch and little cakes; for, no nonsense, Popinot; I will travel for you without commission or expenses; your competitors shall pay me, I will bamboozle them. Let us understand each other clearly. The success of this thing is a point of honor with me; my reward shall be to be best-man at your wedding! I will go to Italy, Germany, and England! I will take placards in every language with me, and have them posted up everywhere, in the villages, at church doors, and in all the good situations that I know in country towns! The oil shall make a blaze; it shall be on every head! Ah! your marriage will not be a marriage in water-colors; it shall be done in oils! You shall have your Césarine, or I am not 'The Illustrious,' a nickname old Finot gave me because I made a success of his gray hats. I shall be sticking to my own line, too, the human head; oil and hats, as is well known, are meant to preserve the hair of the public."

Popinot went to his aunt's house, where he was to spend the night, in such a fever, brought on by visions of success, that the streets seemed to him to be rivers of oil. He scarcely slept at all, dreamed that his hair was growing at a furious rate, and beheld two angels, who unrolled above his head a scroll (as in a pantomime), whereon the words *Cesarian Oil* were written; and he awoke, but remembered his dream, and determined to give the name to the oil of hazel-nuts. He saw the will of heaven revealed in this fancy.

César and Popinot were both at the factory in the Faubourg du Temple long before the hazel-nuts arrived. While they waited for Mme. Madou's porters, Popinot in high glee told the history of his treaty of alliance with Gaudissart.

"We have the illustrious Gaudissart for us; we shall be millionaires!" cried the perfumer, holding out a hand to his cashier, with the air of a Louis XIV. receiving a Maréchal de Villars after Denain.

"And yet another thing," said the happy assistant, drawing a bottle from his pocket, a gourd-shaped flask, flattened so as to present several sides. "I have found ten thousand bottles like this one, ready made and washed, at four sous and six months' credit."

"Anselme," said Birotteau, beholding this marvel, "yesterday (here his voice grew solemn), yesterday, in the garden of the Tuileries—yes, no longer ago than yesterday, your words to me were, 'I shall succeed.' To-day, I myself say to you, 'You will succeed!' Four sous! Six months! An entirely new shape! Macassar is shaking in his shoes; what a deathblow for Macassar! What a good thing that I have bought up all the nuts I could lay my hands on in Paris! But where did you find these bottles?"

"I was waiting to speak to Gaudissart, and sauntering about——"

"Just as I once did," exclaimed Birotteau.

"And as I went down the Rue Aubry-le-Boucher, I saw a wholesale glass merchant's place, a dealer in bell-glasses and glass shades, who has a very large stock; I saw this bottle—— Oh! it stared me in the face like a flash of light; something said, 'Here is the thing for you!'"

"A born merchant! He shall have my daughter," muttered César.

"In I went, and saw thousands of the bottles standing there in boxes."

"Did you ask him about them?"

"You do not think me such a ninny!" cried Anselme, grieved at the thought.

"Born merchant!" repeated Birotteau.

"I went in to ask for glass shades for little wax statuettes. While I was bargaining for the glass shades, I found fault with the shape of these bottles. That led to a general confession; my bottle merchant went from one thing to another, and told me that Faille and Bouchot, who failed lately, were about to bring out a cosmetic, and wanted an out-of-the-way shape. He distrusted them; he wanted half the money down; Faille and Bouchot, hoping for a success, parted with the money, and the failure came out while the bottles were being made. When they put in a claim to the trustees for the rest, the trustees compromised the matter by leaving them with all the bottles and half the money that had been paid, as an indemnity for goods which they said were absurdly shaped, and impossible to dispose of. The bottles cost him eight sous, and he would be glad to let any one have them for four. He might have them on his hands for Heaven knew how long; there was no sale for such a shape. 'Will you engage to supply ten thousand at four sous? I can take the bottles off your hands; I am M. Birotteau's assistant.' And so I opened up the subject, and drew him out, led him on, and put pressure on my man, and he is ours."

"Four sous!" said Birotteau. "Do you know that we can bring out the oil at three francs, and make thirty sous, leaving twenty to the retailers?"

"The Cesarian Oil!" cried Popinot.

"Cesarian Oil? . . . Ah, master lover, you have a mind to flatter father and daughter. Very well; let it be Cesarian Oil if you like. The Cæsars conquered the world; they must have had famous heads of hair."

"Cæsar was bald," said Popinot.

"Because he did not use our oil, people will say. The Cesarian Oil at three francs; Macassar Oil costs twice as much. Gaudissart is in it; we shall make a hundred thousand francs a year, for we will set down all heads that respect themselves for a dozen bottles every twelve-month; eighteen francs of profit! Say there are eighteen thousand heads—a hundred and forty-four thousand francs. We shall be millionaires."

When the hazel-nuts arrived, Raguet and the work-people, with Popinot and César, cracked the shells, and a sufficient quantity was pressed. In four hours' time they had several pounds' weight of oil. Popinot took some of it to Vauquelin, who presented him with a formula for diluting the essential oil with a less expensive medium and for perfuming it. Popinot straightway took steps for taking out a patent for the invention and the improvement. It was Popinot's ambition to pay his share of the expense of starting the enterprise, and the devoted Gaudissart lent the money for the deposit.

Prosperity has an intoxicating effect, which always turns weak heads. One result of this uplifted state of mind is readily foreseen. Grindot came. He brought with him a sketch in water-colors of a charming interior, the design for the future rooms when furnished. Birotteau was carried away with it. He agreed to everything, and the workmen began at once; every stroke of the pickaxe drew groans from the house, and from Constance. The painter, M. Lourdois, a very wealthy contractor, who engaged to leave nothing undone, talked of gilding the drawing-room. Constance interposed at this.

"M. Lourdois," said she, "you have thirty thousand francs a year of your own; you live in your own house, and you can do what you like in it; but for people like us——"

"Madame, commerce ought to shine; it should not suffer itself to be eclipsed by the aristocracy. Besides, here is M. Birotteau in the Government; he is a public man——"

"Yes, but he is still in the shop," said Constance aloud, before the assistants and her five auditors; "neither he, nor I, nor his friends, nor his enemies will forget that."

Birotteau raised himself on tiptoe several times, with his hands clasped behind his back.

"My wife is right," said he. "We will be modest in prosperity. Besides, so long as a man is in business, he ought to be careful of his expenses, and to keep them within bounds; indeed, he is bound by law not to indulge in 'excessive expenditure.' If the enlargement of my premises, and the amount spent on the alterations, exceeds a certain limit, it would be imprudent in me to go beyond it; you yourself would blame me, Lourdois. The quarter has its eyes upon me; successful people are looked upon jealously and envied.—Ah! you will soon know that, young man," he said, addressing Grindot; "if they slander us, at any rate let us give them no cause to say evil of us."

"Neither slander nor spite can touch you," said Lourdois; "your position makes an exception of you; and you have had such a great experience of business, that you know how to keep your affairs within due limits. You are shrewd."

"I have had some experience of business, it is true; do you know the reason why we are enlarging our house? If I exact a heavy penalty to secure punctuality it is——"

"No."

"Well, then, my wife and I are inviting a few friends, partly to celebrate the liberation of the soil, partly on the occasion of my promotion to the Order of the Legion of Honor."

"What, what?" cried Lourdois. "Have they given you the Cross?"

"Yes. It may be that I have shown myself worthy of this signal mark of Royal favor by discharging my functions at the Consular Tribunal, and by fighting for the Royalist cause on the 13th of Vendémiaire at Saint-Roch, when I was wounded by Napoleon. Will you come and bring your wife and your young lady—— ?"

"Enchanted by the honor you condescend to bestow upon me," said Lourdois, a Liberal. "But you are a droll fellow, Birotteau; you mean to make sure that I shall keep my word, and that is why you ask me to come. Well, well; I will set

my best workmen on to it; we will have roaring fires to dry
the paint and use drying processes, for it will not do to dance
in a room full of steam from the damp plaster. The surface
shall be varnished, so that there shall be no smell."

Three days later, the announcement of Birotteau's forthcoming ball created a flutter in the commercial world of that
quarter. And not only so, every one could see for himself
the timber props, necessitated by the hurried alteration of the
staircase, and the square wooden shaft holes, through which
the rubbish was shot into the carts beneath. The men in their
haste worked by torchlight, for they had a night-and-day shift,
and this collected idlers and inquisitive gazers in the street.
On such preparations as these, the gossip of the neighborhood
reared sumptuous fabrics of conjecture.

On the Sunday, when the documents relative to the building
land were to be signed, M. and Mme. Ragon, and uncle Pillerault, came at four o'clock, after vespers. César said that as
the house was so much pulled to pieces, he could only ask
Charles Claparon, Roguin, and Crottat for that day. The
notary brought a copy of the *Journal des Débats,* in which M.
de la Billardière had inserted the following paragraph:—

"We hear that the liberation of the soil will be celebrated
with enthusiasm throughout France; but, in Paris, the mem-
bers of the municipal administration have felt that the time
had come for reviving the splendor of the capital, which has
been eclipsed during the foreign occupation, from a feeling
of patriotism. Each of the mayors and deputy-mayors pro-
poses to give a ball, so that the winter season promises to be a
very brilliant one, and the National movement will be followed up. Among the many fêtes about to take place is the
much-talked-of ball to be given by M. Birotteau, recently
nominated for the Legion of Honor, and so widely known for
his devotion to the Royalist cause. M. Birotteau, wounded in
the affair of Saint-Roch on the 13th of Vendémiaire, and one
of the most highly respected judges of the Consular Tribunal,
has doubly deserved this distinction."

"How well they write nowadays!" exclaimed César.—"They are talking about us in the paper," he added, turning to Pillerault.

"Well, and what of that?" returned the uncle, who particularly detested the *Journal des Débats.*

"Perhaps the paragraph may sell some of the Pâte des Sultanes and the Toilet Lotion," said Mme. César in a low voice to Mme. Ragon. Mme. Birotteau did not share her husband's exhilaration.

Mme. Ragon, a tall, thin woman, with a sharp nose and thin lips, looked a very fair imitation of a marquise of the *ancien régime.* A somewhat wide margin of red encircled her eyes, as sometimes happens with aged women who have known many troubles. Her fine austere face, in spite of its kindliness, was dignified, and there was moreover a quaint something about her which struck beholders, yet did not excite a smile, a something interpreted by her manner and her dress. She wore mittens; she carried in all weathers a cane umbrella, such as Marie Antoinette used at the Trianon; her favorite color was that particular pale shade of brown known as *feuille-morte;* her skirts hung from her waist in folds, which will never be seen again, for the dowager ladies of a bygone day have taken their secret with them. Mme. Ragon had not given up the black mantilla bordered with square-meshed black lace; the ornaments in her old-fashioned caps reminded you of the filagree work on old picture-frames. She took snuff with the dainty neatness and the little gestures which a younger generation may recall, if they have been so fortunate as to see their great-aunt or grandmother solemnly set her gold snuff-box on the table beside her, and shake the stray grains from her fichu.

The Sieur Ragon was a little man, five feet high at the most, with a countenance of the nutcracker type. Two eyes were visible, two prominent cheek-bones, a nose, and a chin. As he had lost his teeth, he mumbled half his words, but he talked like a brook, politely, somewhat pompously, and always with a smile—the same smile with which he had greeted the fair ladies of quality whom one chance or another brought to his shop. His hair, tightly scraped back from his forehead and powdered, described a snowy half-moon on his head, with a pair of "pigeon's wings" on either side of a neat queue tied with ribbon. He wore a cornflower-blue coat, a white waistcoat, silk breeches and stockings, black silk gloves, and shoes with gold buckles to them. The most peculiar thing about him was his habit of walking out in the street hat in hand. He looked rather like a messenger of the Chamber of Peers, or some usher-in-waiting at the palace—one of those attendant satellites of some great power, which shine with a reflected glory, and remain intrinsically insignificant.

"Well, Birotteau," he remarked, and from his tone he might have been addressing an assistant, "are you sorry now, my boy, that you took our advice in those days? Did we ever doubt the gratitude of our beloved royal family?"

"You must be very happy, my dear," said Mme. Ragon, addressing Mme. Birotteau.

"Yes, indeed," returned the fair Constance, who always fell under the charm of that cane umbrella, those butterfly caps, those tight-fitting sleeves, and the ample fichu à la Julie that Mme. Ragon wore.

"Césarine looks charming.—Come here, pretty child," said Mme. Ragon. She spoke in a patronizing manner, and with a high head-voice.

"Shall we settle the business before dinner?" asked uncle Pillerault.

"We are waiting for M. Claparon," said Roguin; "he was dressing when I left him."

"M. Roguin," César began, "does he quite understand that we are to dine in a wretched little *entresol*——"

("Sixteen years ago he thought it magnificent," murmured Constance.)

"Among the rubbish, and with all the workmen about?"

"Pooh! you will find him a good fellow, and not hard to please," said Roguin.

"I have left Raguet to look after the shop; we cannot come

in and out of our own door now; as you have seen, it has all
been pulled down," César returned.

"Why did you not bring your nephew?" asked Pillerault
of Mme. Ragon.

"Shall we see him later?" suggested Césarine.

"No, darling," said Mme. Ragon. "Anselme, dear boy, is
working himself to death. I am afraid of that close street
where the sun never shines, that vile-smelling Rue des Cinq-
Diamants; the gutter is always black or blue or green. I
am afraid he may die there. But when young people set
their minds upon anything——!" she said, turning to Césarine with a gesture that interpreted "mind" as "heart."

"Then, has the lease been signed?" asked César.

"Yesterday, before a notary," Ragon replied. "He has
taken the place for eighteen years, but he pays the rent six
months in advance."

"Well, M. Ragon, are you satisfied with me?" Birotteau
asked. "I have given him the secret of a new discovery—
in fact!"

"We know you by heart, César," said little Ragon, taking
César's hands, and pressing them with devout friendliness.

Roguin meanwhile was not without inward qualms. Claparon was about to appear on the scene, and his habits and
manner of talking might be something of a shock to these
respectable citizens. He thought it necessary to prepare their
minds, and spoke, addressing Ragon, Pillerault, and the
women.

"You will see an eccentric character," he said; "he hides
his talents beneath shocking bad manners; his ideas have
raised him from a very low position. No doubt he will
acquire better tastes in the society of bankers. You might
come across him slouching half-fuddled along the boulevard,
or in a café playing at billiards; he looks like a great hulking
idiot.—But nothing of the kind; he is thinking all the time,
pondering how to put life into trade by new ideas."

"I can understand that," said Birotteau; "my best ideas
came to me while I was sauntering about, didn't they, dear?"

"Claparon makes up for lost time at night, after spending the daytime in meditating over business combinations. All these very clever people lead queer inexplicable lives," Roguin continued. "Well, with all his desultory ways, he gains his end, as I can testify. He made all the owners of our building land give way at last; they were not willing, they demurred at this and that; he mystified them—tired them out; day after day he went to see them, and this time the lots are ours."

A peculiar sounding *broum! broum!* characteristic of drinkers of strong waters and spirits, announced the arrival of the most grotesque personage in this story—who was in the future to enact the part of the arbiter of César's destinies. The perfumer hurried down the narrow, dark staircase, partly to tell Raguet to close the shop, partly to make his excuses for receiving Claparon in the dining-room.

"Eh, what? Oh, it will do very well for stowing the vict——, I mean for doing business in."

In spite of Roguin's skilful opening, the entrance of the sham great banker at once produced an unpleasant impression upon those well-bred citizens, M. and Mme. Ragon, upon the observant Pillerault, and upon Césarine and her mother.

At the age of twenty-eight, or thereabouts, the former commercial traveler had not a hair on his head, and wore a wig of corkscrew curls. Such a manner of dressing the hair demands a girlish freshness, a milk-white skin, and the daintiest feminine charm; so it brought out all the vulgarity of a pimpled countenance, a dark-red complexion, flushed like that of a stage coachman, and covered with premature wrinkles and deeply cut grotesque lines which told of a dissolute life; its ill effects could be read only too plainly in the bad state of his teeth and the black specks dotted over the shriveled skin.

There was something about Claparon that suggested the provincial actor who frequents fairs, and is prepared to play any and every part, to whose worn, shrunken cheeks and flabby lips the paint refuses to adhere; the tongue always wagging even when the man is drunk; the shameless eyes, the compromising gestures. Such a face as this, lighted up by the hilarious flames of punch, little befitted a man accustomed to important business. Indeed, only after prolonged and necessary studies in mimicry had Claparon succeeded in adopting a manner not wholly out of keeping with his supposed importance. Du Tillet had assisted personally at Claparon's toilette, anxious as a nervous manager over the first appearance of his principal actor, for he trembled lest the vicious habits of a reckless life should appear through the veneer of the banker.

"Say as little as you can," said his mentor; "a banker never babbles; he acts, thinks, meditates, listens, and ponders. So, to look like a real banker, you must either not speak at all, or say insignificant things. Keep those ribald eyes of yours quiet; look solemn at the risk of looking stupid. In politics, be for the Government, but keep to generalities, such as—'There is a heavy budget; compromise as parties stand is out of the question; Liberalism is dangerous; the Bourbons ought to avoid all collisions; Liberalism is a cloak to hide the schemes of the Coalition; the Bourbons are inaugurating an epoch of prosperity, so let us give them our support, whether we are well affected to them or not; France has had enough of political experiments,' and the like. And don't sprawl over all the tables; remember that you have to sustain the dignity of a millionaire. Don't snort like a pensioner when you take snuff; play with your snuff-box, and look at your boots or at the ceiling before you give an answer; look as wise as you can, in fact. Above all things, rid yourself of your unlucky habit of fingering everything. In society a banker ought to look as if he were glad to let his fingers rest. And look here! you work at night, you are stupid with making calculations, there are so many things to consider in the starting of an enterprise! so much thinking is involved! Grumble, above all things, and say that trade is very bad. Trade is dull, slow, hard to move, perplexing. Keep to that, and let particulars alone. Don't begin to sing drolleries of Béranger's at table, and don't drink too much; you will ruin your prospects if you get tipsy. Roguin will keep an eye on you; you are going among moral people, respectable, steady-going folk, don't frighten them by letting out some of your pot-house principles."

This homily produced on Charles Claparon's mind an effect very similar to the strange sensation of his new suit of clothes. The rollicking prodigal, hail-fellow-well-met with everybody, accustomed to the comfortable, disreputable garments in which his outer man was as much at home as his thoughts in the language that clothed them, held himself upright, stiff as a poker in the new clothes for which the tailor had kept him waiting to the last minute, and was as ill at ease in his movements as in this new phraseology. He put out a hand unthinkingly towards a flask or a box, then, hurriedly recollecting himself, drew it in again, and in the same way he began a sentence and stopped short in the middle, distinguishing himself by a ludicrous incoherence, which did not escape the observant Pillerault. His round face, like the rakish-looking corkscrew ringlets of his wig, were totally out of keeping with his manner, and he seemed to think one thing and say another. But the good folk concluded that his inconsequence was the result of preoccupation.

"He does so much business," said Roguin.

"Business has given him very little breeding," Mme. Ragon said to Césarine.

M. Roguin overheard her, and laid a finger on his lips. "He is rich, clever, and honorable to a fault," he said, bending to Mme. Ragon.

"He may be excused something for such qualities as those," said Pillerault to Ragon.

"Let us read over the papers before dinner," said Roguin. "We are alone."

Mme. Ragon, Césarine, and Constance left the contracting parties, Pillerault, Ragon, César, Roguin, and Claparon, to listen to the reading of the documents by Alexandre Crottat. César signed a mortgage bond for forty thousand francs secured on the land and the factory in the Faubourg du Temple (the money had been lent by one of Roguin's clients); he paid over to Roguin Pillerault's order on the bank, gave (without taking a receipt) twenty thousand francs worth of bills from his portfolio, and drew another bill for the remaining hundred and forty thousand francs on Charles Claparon.

"I have no receipt to give you," said that gentleman. "You are acting for your own side with M. Roguin, as we are doing for our share. Our vendors will receive their money from him in coin; I only undertake to complete your payment by paying a hundred and forty thousand francs for your bills——"

"That is right," said Pillerault.

"Well, then, gentlemen, let us call in the ladies again, for it is cold without them," said Claparon, with a look at Roguin to see whether he had gone too far.

"Ladies! . . . Ah! mademoiselle is your young lady, of course," said Claparon, looking at Birotteau, and straightening himself up. "Well, well, you are not a bungler. Not one of the roses that you have distilled can be compared with her, and perhaps it is because you have distilled roses that——"

"Faith!" said Roguin, interrupting him, "I own that I am hungry."

"Very well, let us have dinner," said Birotteau.

"We are to have dinner in the presence of a notary," said Claparon, with an important air.

"You do a great deal of business, do you not?" said Pillerault, purposely seating himself next to the banker.

"A tremendous amount, wholesale," replied Claparon; "but trade is dull, hard to move—there are canals now. Oh, canals! You have no idea how busy we are with canals. That is comprehensible. The Government wants canals. A canal is a want generally felt. All the trade of a depart-

ment is interested in a canal, you know! A stream, said
Pascal, is a moving highway. The next thing is a market,
and markets depend on embankments, for there are a frightful lot of embankments, and the embankments interest the
poorer classes, and that means a loan, which finally benefits
the poor! Voltaire said, 'Canal, canard, canaille!' But
Government depends for information on its own engineers;
it is difficult to meddle in the matter, at least, it is difficult
to come to an understanding with them; for the Chamber
—— Oh! sir, the Chamber gives us trouble! The Chamber
does not want to grapple with the political question hidden
beneath the financial question. There is bad faith on all
sides. Would you believe this? There are the Kellers—
well, then, François Keller is a public speaker, he attacks
the measures of the Government as to the funds and canals.
He comes home, and then my fine gentleman finds us with
our propositions; they are favorable, and he has to make it
up with the aforesaid Government, which he attacked so
insolently an hour ago. The interests of the public speaker
clash with the interests of the banker; we are between two
fires. Now you understand how thorny affairs become; you
have to satisfy everybody—the clerks, the people in the
chambers, and the people in the ante-chambers, and the
Ministers——"

"The Ministers?" asked Pillerault, who wished to probe
this partner's mind thoroughly.

"Yes, sir, the Ministers."

"Well, then, the newspapers are right," said Pillerault.

"Here is uncle on politics," said Birotteau; "M. Claparon
has set him off."

"Newspapers!" said Claparon, "there are some more con-
founded humbugs! Newspapers throw us all into confusion;
they do us a good turn now and then, but the cruel nights
they make me spend! I would as lief be without them;
they are the ruin of my eyes in fact, poring over them and
working out calculations."

"But to return to the Ministers," said Pillerault, hoping for
revelations.

"Ministers have exigencies which are purely governmental. —But what am I eating; is it ambrosia?" asked Claparon, interrupting himself. "Here is a sort of sauce that you only have in citizens' houses; you never get it at grub-shops——" At that word, the ornaments on Mme. Ragon's cap skipped like rams. Claparon gathered that the expression was low, and tried to retrieve his error.

"That is what the heads of large banking firms call the high-class taverns—Véry, and the Frères Provençaux. Well, neither those vile grub-shops, nor our most accomplished cooks, make you a soft, mellow sauce; some give you water with lemon-juice in it, and others give you chemical concoctions."

The conversation at dinner chiefly consisted in attacks from Pillerault, who tried to plumb his man, and only found emptiness; he looked upon him as a dangerous person.

"It is going on all right," said Roguin in Charles Claparon's ear.

"Oh! I shall get out of my clothes to-night, I suppose," answered Claparon, who was gasping for breath.

"We are obliged to use our dining-room as a sitting-room, sir," said Birotteau, "because we are looking forward to a little gathering of our friends in eighteen days' time, partly to celebrate the liberation of the soil——"

"Right, sir; I myself am also for the Government. My political convictions incline me to the *statu quo* of the great man who guides the destinies of the house of Austria, a fine fellow! Keep what you have, to get more; and, in the first place, get more, to keep what you have.—So now you know the bottom of my opinions, which have the honor to be those of Prince Metternich!"

"Partly on the occasion of my promotion to the Order of the Legion of Honor," César went on.

"Why, yes, I know. Now who was telling me about that? Was it the Kellers, or Nucingen?"

Roguin, amazed at so much presence of mind, signified his admiration.

"Oh, no; it was at the Chamber."

"At the Chamber. Was it M. de la Billardière?" asked César.

"The very man."

"He is charming," said César, addressing his uncle.

"He pours out talk, talk, talk, till you are drowned in talk," said Pillerault.

"It may be," resumed Birotteau, "that I have shown myself worthy of this favor——"

"By your achievements in perfumery; the Bourbons know how to reward merit of every kind. Ah! let us stand by our generous legitimate Princes, to whom we shall owe unheard-of prosperity about to be.—For, you may be sure of it, the Restoration feels that she must enter the lists with the Empire, and the Restoration will make peaceful conquests; you will see conquests! . . ."

"You will no doubt honor us by coming to our ball, sir," said Mme. César.

"To spend an evening with you, madame, I would miss a chance of making millions."

"He certainly is a babbler," said César in his uncle's ear.

While the waning glory of the *Queen of Roses* was about to shed abroad its parting rays, a faint star was rising above the commercial horizon; at that very hour, little Popinot was laying the foundations of his fortune in the Rue des Cinq-Diamants. The Rue des Cinq-Diamants, a short, narrow thoroughfare, where loaded wagons can scarcely pass each other, runs between the Rue des Lombards and the Rue Aubry-le-Boucher, into which it opens just opposite the end of the Rue Quincampoix, that street so famous in the history of France and of old Paris.

In spite of this narrowness, the near neighborhood of the druggists' quarter made the place convenient; and from that point of view, Popinot had not made a bad choice. The house (the second from the end nearest the Rue des Lombards) was so dark, that at times it was necessary to work by artificial light in the daytime. Popinot had taken possession the evening before of all its darkest and most unsavory recesses. His predecessor, a dealer in treacle and raw sugars, had left his mark on the place; the walls, the yard, and the storehouse bore unmistakable traces of his occupation.

Imagine a large and roomy shop, and huge doors barréd with iron and painted dragon-green, the solid iron scroll-work, with bolt heads as large as mushrooms by way of ornament. The shop was adorned and protected, as bakers' shops used to be, by wire-work lattices, which bulged at the bottom, and was paved with great slabs of white stone, cracked for the most part. The walls of a guard-house are not yellower nor barer. Further on came the back-shop and kitchen, which looked out into the yard; and behind these again a second storeroom, which must at one time have been a stable. An inside staircase had been contrived in the back-shop, by which you gained two rooms that looked out upon the street; here Popinot meant to have his counting-house and his ledgers. Above the warehouse there were three small rooms, all backed against the party-wall, and lighted by windows on the side of the yard. It was in these dilapidated rooms that Popinot proposed to live.

The view from the windows was shut in by the high walls that rose about the dingy, crooked yard, walls so damp that even in the driest weather they looked as if they had been newly distempered. The cracks in the paving-stones were choked with black, malodorous filth, deposited there during the tenancy of the dealer in treacle and raw sugars. So much for the outlook. As to the rooms themselves, only one of them boasted a fireplace; the floors were of brick, the walls were unpapered.

Gaudissart and Popinot had been busy there ever since the morning, putting up a cheap wall-paper with their own hands in the ugly room; a journeyman paperhanger whom Gaudissart ferreted out had varnished it for them. The furniture consisted of a student's mattress, a wooden bedstead painted red, a rickety nightstand, a venerable chest of drawers, a table, a couple of armchairs, and half-a-dozen ordinary chairs, a present from Popinot the judge to his nephew. Gaudissart had put a cheap pier-glass over the chimney-piece. It was almost eight o'clock in the evening, and the two friends, sitting before a blazing fire, were about to discuss the remains of their breakfast.

"Away with the cold mutton! It is out of character in a house-warming," cried Gaudissart.

Popinot held up his last twenty-franc piece, which was to pay for the prospectus. "But I——" he began.

"I? . . ." retorted Gaudissart, sticking a forty-franc piece into his eye.

A knock at the street door reverberated through the yard. It was Sunday, the workpeople were taking their holiday away from their workshops, and the idle echoes greeted every sound.

"There is my trusty man from the Rue de la Poterie," Gaudissart went on. "For my own part, it is not simply 'I,' but 'I have.' "

And, in fact, a waiter appeared, followed by two kitchen boys, carrying between them three wicker baskets, containing a dinner, and crowned by six bottles of wine selected with discrimination.

"But how are we to eat such a lot of things?" asked Popinot.

"There is the man of letters," cried Gaudissart. "Finot understands the pomps and vanities. The artless youth will be here directly with a prospectus fit to make your hair stand on end (neat that, eh?), and prospectuses are always dry work. You must water the seeds if you mean to have flowers.—Here, minions," he added, striking an attitude for the benefit of the kitchen-boys, "here's gold for you."

He held out six sous with a gesture worthy of his idol, Napoleon.

"Thank you, M. Gaudissart," said the scullions, more pleased with the joke than with the money.

"As for thee, my son," he continued, turning to the waiter who remained, "there is a portress here. She crouches in the depths of a cave, where at times she does some cooking, as erewhile Nausicaa did the washing, simply by way of relaxation. Hie thee to her, work on her trustful nature; interest her, young man, in the temperature of thy hot dishes. Say to her that she shall be blessed, and above all things respected, highly respected, by Felix Gaudissart, son of Jean-François Gaudissart, and grandson of Gaudissart, vile proletaries of remote lineage, his ancestors. Off with you, and act in such a sort that everything shall be good; for if it isn't, I will make you laugh on the wrong side of your face."

There was another knock at the door.

"That is the ingenious Andoche," said Gaudissart.

A stout young fellow suddenly entered. He had somewhat chubby cheeks, was of middle height, and from head to foot looked like the hatter's son. A certain shrewdness lurked beneath the air of constraint that sat on his rounded features. The habitual dejection of a man who is tired of poverty left him, and a hilarious expression crossed his countenance, at the sight of the preparations on the table and the significant seals on the bottle-corks. At Gaudissart's shout, a twinkle came into the pale-blue eyes, the big head, on which a Kalmuck physiognomy had been carved, rolled from side to side, and he gave Popinot a distant greeting, in which there was neither servility nor respect, like a man who feels out of his element and stands on his dignity.

Finot was just beginning to discover that he had no sort of talent for literature; he did not think of quitting his calling; he meant to exploit literature by raising himself on the shoulders of men who possessed the talent which he lacked. Instead of doing ill-paid work himself, he would turn his business capacities to account. He was just at the turning-point; he had exhausted the expedients of humility;

he had experienced to the full the humiliation of failure; and, like those who take a wide outlook over the financial world, he resolved to change his tactics, and to be insolent in future. He needed capital in the first instance, and Gaudissart had opened out a prospect of making the money by putting Popinot's oil before the public.

"You will make his arrangements with the newspapers," Gaudissart had said, "but don't swindle him; if you do, there will be a duel to the death between us; give him value for his money!"

Popinot looked uneasily at the "author." Your true man of business regards an author with mixed feelings, in which alarm and curiosity are blended with compassion; and though Popinot had been well educated, his relations' attitude of mind and ways of thinking, together with a course of drudgery in a shop, had produced their effect on his intelligence, and he bent beneath the yoke of use and wont. You can see this by noticing the metamorphoses which ten years will effect among a hundred boys, who when they left school or college were almost exactly alike.

Andoche mistook the impression which he had made for admiration.

"Very well. Let us run through the prospectus before dinner, then it will be off our minds, and we can drink," said Gaudissart. "It is uncomfortable to read after dinner; the tongue is digesting too."

"Sir," said Popinot, "a prospectus often means a whole fortune."

"And for nobodies like me," said Andoche, "fortune is nothing but a prospectus."

"Ah! very good," said Gaudissart. "That droll fellow of an Andoche has wit enough for the Forty."

"For a hundred," said Popinot, awestruck with the idea.

Gaudissart snatched up the manuscript, and read aloud, and with emphasis, the first two words—"Cephalic Oil!"

"I like Cesarian Oil better," said Popinot.

"You don't know them in the provinces, my friend," said

Gaudissart. "There is a surgical operation known by that name, and they are so stupid, that they will think your oil is meant to facilitate childbirth; and if they start off with the notion, it would be too hard work to bring them all the way back to hair again."

"Without defending the name," observed the author, "I would call your attention to the fact that Cephalic Oil means oil for the head, and resumes your ideas."

"Go on!" said Popinot impatiently.

And here follows a second historical document, a prospectus, which even at this day is circulating by thousands among retail perfumers.

GOLD MEDAL, PARIS 1824*

CEPHALIC OIL
(Improved Patent).

No cosmetic can make the hair grow; and in the same way, it cannot be dyed by chemical preparations without danger to the seat of the intelligence. Science has recently proclaimed that the hair is not a living substance, and that there is no means of preventing it from blanching or falling out. To prevent xerasia and baldness, the bulb at the roots should be preserved from all atmospheric influences, and the natural temperature of the head evenly maintained. The "Cephalic Oil," based on these principles established by the Royal Academy of Sciences, induces the important result so highly prized by the ancients, the Romans and Greeks, and the nations of the North—a fine head of hair. Learned research has brought to light the fact that the nobles of olden times, who were distinguished by their long, flowing locks, used no other means than these; their recipe, long lost, has been ingeniously rediscovered by A. Popinot, inventor of "Cephalic Oil."

To preserve the glands, and not to provoke an impossible or hurtful stimulation of the dermis which contains them, is, therefore, the

* The next "Quinquennial Exhibition."

function of "Cephalic Oil." This oil, which exhales a delicious fragrance, prevents the exfoliation of the pellicle; while the substances of which it is composed (the essential oil of the hazel-nut being the principal element) counteract the effects of atmospheric air upon the head, thus preventing chills, catarrh, and all unpleasant encephalic affections by maintaining the natural temperature. In this manner the glands, which contain the hair-producing secretions, are never attacked by heat or cold. A fine head of hair —that glorious product so highly valued by either sex—may be retained to extreme old age by the use of "Cephalic Oil," which imparts to the hair the brilliancy, silkiness, and gloss which constitutes the charm of children's heads.

Directions for use are issued on the wrapper of every bottle.

DIRECTIONS FOR USE

It is perfectly useless to apply oil to the hair itself: besides being an absurd superstition, it is an obnoxious practice, for the cosmetic leaves its traces everywhere.

It is only necessary to part the hair with a comb, and to apply the oil to the roots every morning with a small sponge, proceeding thus until the whole surface of the skin has received a slight application, the hair having been previously combed and brushed.

To prevent spurious imitations, each bottle bears the signature of the inventor. Sold at the price of THREE FRANCS by A. POPINOT, Rue des Cinq-Diamants, Quartier des Lombards, Paris.

It is particularly requested that all communications by post should be prepaid.

NOTE.—A. POPINOT also supplies essences and pharmaceutical preparations, such as neroli, oil of spike-lavender, oil of sweet almonds, cacao-butter, cafeine, castor oil, "et cætera."

"My dear fellow," said the Illustrious Gaudissart, addressing Finot, "it is perfectly written! Ye gods, how we plunge into deep science! No shuffling; we go straight to the point! Ah! I congratulate you heartily; there is literature of some practical use!"

"A fine prospectus!" cried Popinot enthusiastically.

"The very first sentence is a deathblow to Macassar," said Gaudissart, rising to his feet with a magisterial air, to proclaim with an oratorical gesture between each word, " 'You—cannot—make—hair—grow.   It—cannot—be—dyed—without—danger!' Aha! success lies in that.   Modern science corroborates the custom of the ancients.   You can suit yourself to old and young.   You have to do with an old man.—Aha, ᵢsir! the Greeks and Romans, the ancients, were in the right; they were not such fools as some would make them out to be! Or if it is a young man.—My dear fellow, another discovery due to the progress of enlightenment; we are progressing.   What must we not expect from steam, and the telegraph, and such like inventions?   This oil is the outcome of M. Vauquelin's investigations!—How if we were to print an extract from M. Vauquelin's paper, eh?   Capital! Come, Finot, draw up your chair! Let us stow the victuals, and tipple down the champagne to our young friend's success!"

"It seemed to me," said the author modestly, "that the time for the light and playful prospectus has gone by; we are entering on an epoch of science, and must talk learnedly and authoritatively to make an impression on the public."

"We will push the oil.   My feet, and my tongue too, are hankering to go.   I have agencies for all the houses that deal in hairdressers' goods, not one of them gives more than thirty per cent of discount; make up your mind to give forty, and I will engage to sell a hundred thousand bottles in six months.   I will make a set on all the druggists, grocers, and hairdressers! And if you will allow them forty per cent on your oil, they will all send their customers wild for it."

The three young men ate like lions, drank like Swiss, and waxed merry over the future success of the Cephalic Oil.

"This oil goes to your head," said Finot, smiling, and Gaudissart exhausted whole series of puns on the words, oil, head, and hair.

In the midst of their Homeric laughter over the dessert, the knocker sounded, and in spite of the toasts and the wishes for luck exchanged among the three friends, they heard it.

"It is my uncle! He is capable of coming to see me," cried Popinot.

"An uncle?" asked Finot, "and we have not a glass!"

"My friend Popinot's uncle is an examining magistrate," said Gaudissart, by way of reply to Finot; "there is no occasion to hoax him, he saved my life. Ah! if you had found yourself in the fix I was in, with the scaffold staring you in the face, where, *kouik,* off goes your hair for good!" (and he imitated the fatal knife by a gesture), "you would be apt to remember the righteous judge to whom you owe ¡the preservation of the channel that the champagne goes down! You would remember him if you were dead drunk. You don't know, Finot, but what you may want M. Popinot one day. *Saquerlotte!* You must make your bow to him, and thirteen to the dozen!"

It was, as a matter of fact, the "righteous judge," who was asking for his nephew of the woman who opened the door. Anselme recognized the voice, and went down, candle in hand, to light his way.

"Good-evening, gentlemen," said the magistrate.

The Illustrious Gaudissart made a profound bow. Finot looked the newcomer over with drunken eyes, and decided that Popinot's uncle was tolerably woodenheaded.

"There is no luxury here," said the judge, ¡gravely looking round the room; "but, my boy, you must begin by being nothing if you are to be something great."

"How profound he is!" said Gaudissart, turning to Finot.

"An idea for an article," said the journalist.

"Oh! is that you, sir?" said the judge, recognizing the commercial traveler. "Eh! what are you doing here?"

"I want to do all my little part, sir, towards making your dear nephew's fortune. We have just been pondering over the prospectus for this oil of his, and this gentleman here is the author of the prospectus, which seems to us to be one of the finest things in the literature of periwigs."

The judge looked at Finot.

"This gentleman is M. Andoche Finot," Gaudissart said,

"one of the most distinguished young men in literature; he does political leaders and the minor theatres for the Government newspapers; he is a Minister who is by way of being an author."

Here Finot tugged at Gaudissart's coat-tails.

"Very well, boys," said the judge, to whom these words explained the appearance of the table covered with the remnants of a feast very excusable under the circumstances.

"As for you, Anselme," he continued, turning to Popinot, "get ready to pay a visit to M. Birotteau; I must go to see him this evening. You will sign your deed of partnership; I have gone through it very carefully. As you are going to manufacture your oil in the Faubourg du Temple, I think that he ought to make over the lease of the workshop to you, and that he has power to sublet; if things are all in order, it will save disputes afterwards. These walls look to me to be very damp, Anselme; bring up trusses of straw, and put them round about where your bed stands."

"Excuse me, sir," said Gaudissart with a courtier's suppleness, "we have just put up the wall-paper ourselves to-day, and—it—is—not quite dry."

"Economy! good!" said the judge.

"Listen," said Gaudissart in Finot's ear; "my friend Popinot is a good young man; he is going off with his uncle, so come along and let us finish the evening with our fair cousins."

The journalist turned out the lining of his waistcoat pocket. Popinot saw the manœuvre, and slipped a twenty-franc piece into the hand of the author of his prospectus. The judge had a cab waiting at the corner of the street, and carried off his nephew to call on Birotteau.

Pillerault, M. and Mme. Ragon, and Roguin were playing at boston, and Césarine was embroidering a fichu, when the elder Popinot and Anselme appeared. Roguin, sitting opposite Mme. Ragon, could watch Césarine, who sat by her side, and saw the happy look on the girl's face when Anselme came in, saw her flush up .red as a pomegranate flower, and called his head-clerk's attention to her by a significant gesture.

"So this is to be a day of deeds, is it?" said the perfumer, when greetings had been exchanged, and the judge explained the reason of the visit.

César, Anselme, and the judge went up to the perfumer's temporary quarters on the second floor to debate the matter of the lease and the deed of partnership drawn up by the elder Popinot. It was arranged that the lease should run for eighteen years, so as to be conterminous with the lease of the house in the Rue des Cinq-Diamants; trifling matter as it appeared at the time, it was destined later to serve Birotteau's interests.

When they returned to the sitting-room, the elder Popinot, surprised by the confusion and the men at work on a Sunday in the house of so devout a man, asked the reason of it all. This was the question for which César was waiting.

"Although you are not worldly, sir, you will not object to our celebrating our deliverance; and that is not all—if we are arranging for a little gathering of our friends, it is partly also to celebrate my promotion to the order of the Legion of Honor."

"Ah!" said the examining magistrate (who had not been decorated).

"It may be that I have shown myself not unworthy of this signal mark of Royal favor by discharging my functions at the Tribunal . . . oh! I mean to say Consular Tribunal, and by fighting for the Royalist cause on the steps——"

"Yes," said the magistrate.

"Steps of Saint-Roch, on the 13th of Vendémiaire, where I was wounded by Napoleon."

"I shall be glad to come," said M. Popinot; "and if my wife is well enough, I will bring her."

"Xandrot," said Roguin, on the doorstep, "give up all

thoughts of marrying Césarine; in six weeks' time you will
see that I have given you sound counsel."

"Why?" asked Crottat.

"My dear fellow, Birotteau is about to spend a hundred
thousand francs over this ball of his, and he is embarking his
whole fortune, against my advice, in this building-land
scheme. In six weeks' time these people will not have bread
to eat. Marry Mlle. Lourdois, the house-painter's daughter; she has three hundred thousand francs to her fortune.
I have planned this shift for you. If you will pay me down
the money, you can have my practice to-morrow for a hundred thousand francs."

The splendors of the perfumer's forthcoming ball, announced to Europe by the newspapers, were very differently
announced in commercial circles by flying rumors of work-
people employed night and day on the perfumer's house.
The rumors took various forms; here is was said that César
had taken the house on either side; there, that his drawing-
ing-rooms were to be gilded; some said that no tradespeople
would be invited, and that the ball was given to Government
officials only; and the perfumer was severely blamed for his
ambition; they scoffed at his political aspirations, they denied
that he had been wounded! More than one scheme was set
on foot, in the second arrondissement, in consequence of the
ball; the friends of the family took things quietly, but the
claims of distant acquaintances were vast.

Those who have favor to bestow, never lack courtiers;
and a goodly number of the guests were at no little pains
to procure their cards of admission. The Birotteaus were
amazed to find so many friends whose existence they had
not suspected. This eagerness on their part alarmed Mme.
Birotteau; she looked more and more gloomy as the days
went by and the solemn festival came nearer. She had
confessed to César from the very first that she should not
know how to act her part as hostess, and the innumerable small
details frightened her. Where was the plate to come from?

How about the glass, the refreshments, the forks and spoons? And who would look after it all?—She begged Birotteau to stand near the door and see that no one came who had not been asked to the ball; she had heard strange things about people who came to dances claiming acquaintance with people whom they did not know by name.

One evening, ten days before the famous Sunday, Messieurs Braschon, Grindot, Lourdois, and Chaffaroux the contractor having given their word that the rooms should be ready for the 17th of December, there had been a laughable conference after dinner in the humble little sitting-room on the mezzanine floor—César and his wife and daughter were making a list of guests and writing the cards of invitation, which had been sent in only that morning, nicely printed in the English fashion on rose-colored paper, in accordance with the precepts laid down in the *Complete Guide to Etiquette.*

"Look here!" said César; "we must not leave anybody out."

"If we forget any one," remarked Constance, "we shall be reminded of it. Mme. Derville, who never called upon us before, sailed in yesterday evening in great state."

"She was very pretty; I liked her," said Césarine.

"Yet before she was married she was even worse off than I," said Constance; "she used to do plain needlework in the Rue Montmartre; she has made shirts for your father."

"Well, let us put the great people down at the top of the list," said César. "Write 'M. le Duc and Mme. la Duchesse de Lenoncourt,' Césarine."

"Goodness! César," cried Constance, "pray don't begin to send invitations to people whom you only know through the business. Are you going to ask the Princesse de Blamont-Chauvry? She is more nearly related to your late godmother, the Marquise d'Uxelles, than even the Duc de Lenoncourt. And shall you ask the two MM. Vandenesse, M. de Marsay, M. de Ronquerolles, M. d'Aiglemont; in short, all your customers? You are mad; honors are turning your head——"

"Yes! but M. le Comte de Fontaine and his family. Eh? He used to come to the *Queen of Roses* under the name of *Grand-Jacques* with the *Gars* (M. le Marquis de Montauran that was) and M. de la Billardière, whom they called the *Nantais* in the days before the great affair of the 13th of Vendémiaire. And they would shake hands with you then, and it was, 'My dear Birotteau, keep your heart up, and give your life, like the rest of us, for the good cause!' We are old fellow-conspirators."

"Put him down," said Constance; "if M. de la Billardière and his son are coming, they must have somebody to speak to."

"Set down his name, Césarine," said Birotteau.—*"Imprimis,* His Worship the Prefect of the Seine; he may or may not come, but he is the head of the municipal corporation, and 'honor to whom honor is due.'—M. de la Billardière, the mayor, and his son. (Write down the number of the people after every name.)—My colleague, M. Granet, and his wife. She is very ugly, but, all the same, we cannot leave her out.—M. Curel, the goldsmith, Colonel of the National Guard, and his wife and two daughters. Those are what I call the authorities. Now for the bigwigs!—M. le Comte and Mme. la Comtesse de Fontaine and their daughter, Mlle. Émilie de Fontaine."

"An insolent girl, who makes me come out of the shop to speak to her at her carriage door in all weathers," said Mme. César. "If she comes at all, it will be to make fun of us."

"In that case, perhaps she will come," said César, who meant to fill his rooms at all costs. "Go on, Césarine—M. le Comte and Mme. la Comtesse de Granville, my landlord, the hardest head in the Court of Appeal, Derville says.—Oh! by the by, M. de la Billardière has arranged for me to be presented to-morrow by M. le Comte de Lacépède himself; it is only polite to ask the Grand Chancellor to dinner and to the ball.—M. Vauquelin. Put him down for the dinner and for the ball too, Césarine. And, while we

remember it, all the Chiffrevilles and the Protez family.
—M. Popinot, judge of the Tribunal of the Seine, and
Mme. Popinot.—M. and Mme. Thirion, he is an usher of
the Privy Chamber, and a friend of the Ragons; it is said
that their daughter is to be married to one of M. Camusot's
sons by his first marriage."

"César, do not forget young Horace Bianchon; he is M.
Popinot's nephew and Anselme's cousin," put in Constance.

"Ah, to be sure! Césarine has put a figure four very
plainly after the Popinots.—M. and Mme. Rabourdin; M.
Rabourdin is at the head of one of the departments in M.
de la Billardière's division.—M. Cochin of the same department, and his wife and son; they are sleeping-part-
ners in M. Matifat's concern; and while we are about it,
put down M. and Mme. and Mlle. Matifat."

"The Matifats have been making overtures for their
friends, M. and Mme. Colleville, M. and Mme. Thuillier,
and the Saillards."

"We shall see," said César. "Our stockbroker, M. Jules
Desmarets and his wife."

"She will be the prettiest woman in the room!" cried
Césarine. "I like her, oh! more than any one!"

"Derville and his wife."

"Just put down M. and Mme. Coquelin, who took over
uncle Pillerault's business," said Constance. "They made
so sure of being asked, that the poor little thing is having
a grand ball-dress made by my dressmaker—a white satin
overskirt covered with tulle, embroidered with blue chicory
flowers. It would not have taken much to persuade her
to have a gold embroidered court-dress. If we left them
out, we should make two bitter enemies."

"Put them down, Césarine; we must show our respect
for trade, for we are tradespeople ourselves.—M. and Mme.
Roguin."

"Mamma, Mme. Roguin will wear her *rivière,* all her
diamonds, and her Mechlin lace gown."

"M. and Mme. Lebas," César continued.—"And next,

the President of the Tribunal of Commerce and his wife
and two daughters (I forgot to put them among the authorities).—M. and Mme. Lourdois and their daughter.—M.
Claparon the banker; M. du Tillet, M. Grindot, M.
Molineux; Pillerault and his landlord; M. and Mme. Camusot, the rich silk mercer, and all their family, the one at the
École polytechnique and the advocate; he will receive an
appointment as judge—he is the one that is engaged to be
married to Mlle. Thirion."

"It will only be a Provincial appointment," said Césarine.

"M. Cardot, Camusot's father-in-law, and all the young
Cardots. Stay! there are the Guillaumes in the Rue du
Colombier, Lebas' wife's people, two old folk who will be
wall-flowers.—Alexandre Crottat,—Célestin——"

"Papa, do not forget M. Andoche Finot and M. Gaudissart, two young men who have been so useful to M. Anselme.",

"Gaudissart? He got himself into trouble. But, never
mind, he is going away in a few days, and will travel for
our oil,—so put him down! As for Master Andoche Finot,
what is he to us?"

"M. Anselme says that he will be a great man; he is
as clever as Voltaire."

"An author is he? They are all of them atheists."

"Put him down, papa; so far there are not so very many
men who dance. Besides, your nice prospectus for the oil
was his doing."

"He believes in our oil, does he?" said César. "Put him
down, dear child."

"So I too have my protégés on the list," commented
Césarine.

"Put M. Mitral, my process-server, and our doctor, M.
Haudry; it is for form's sake, he will not come."

"He will come for his game of cards," said Césarine.

"Ah! by the by, César, I hope that you will ask M. l'Abbé
Loraux to dinner!"

"I have written to him already," said César.

"Oh! we must not forget Lebas' sister-in-law, Mme. Augustine de Sommervieux," said Césarine. "Poor little thing! she is very unwell; Lebas said that she was dying of grief."

"See what comes of marrying an artist," cried the perfumer.—"Just look at your mother; she has fallen asleep," he said, in a low voice, to his daughter. "Bye-bye—sleep softly, Madame César.—Well, now," said César, turning to his daughter, "how about your mother's dress?"

"Yes, papa, everything will be ready. Mamma thinks that she is to have a Canton crape gown like mine, and the dressmaker is sure that there is no need to try it on."

"How many are there altogether?" César went on aloud, as his wife opened her eyes.

"A hundred and nine, with the assistants," said Césarine.

"Where are we going to put all those people?" asked Mme. Birotteau. "And when all is over, after the Sunday comes Monday," she said naïvely.

Nothing can be done simply when people aspire to rise from one social rank to another. Neither Mme. Birotteau, nor César, nor any one else might venture on any pretext whatsoever on to the first floor. César had promised the errand-boy Raguet a new suit of clothes if he kept watch faithfully and carried out his orders properly. Like the Emperor Napoleon at Compiègne, when he had the Château restored for his marriage with Marie-Louise of Austria, Birotteau wanted to see nothing till the whole was finished; he meant to enjoy "the surprise." So all unconsciously the old enemies met, this time not on the field of battle, but on the common ground of bourgeois vanity. M. Grindot was to take César over the new rooms like a cicerone exhibiting a gallery to a tourist.

Every one in the house, moreover, had his or her own "surprise." Césarine, the dear child, had spent a hundred louis, all her little hoard, on books for her father. M. Grindot had confided to her one morning that there were two fitted bookcases in her father's room, which was to be a study; this was the architect's surprise; and Césarine spent all her savings with a bookseller. She had bought the works of Bossuet, Racine, Voltaire, Jean-Jacques Rousseau, Montesquieu, Molière, Buffon, Fénelon, Delille, Bernardin de Saint-Pierre, La Fontaine, Corneille, Pascal, and La Harpe; in short, the ordinary collection of classics to be seen everywhere, books which her father would never read. A terrible bookbinder's bill must of necessity be the result. Thouvenin, that great and unpunctual artist and binder, had undertaken to send the books home on the 18th at midday. Césarine had told her uncle in confidence of her difficulty, and he had undertaken the bill. César's surprise for his wife took the shape of a cherry-colored velvet gown trimmed with lace; it was of this dress that he had just spoken to the daughter, who had been his accomplice. Mme. Birotteau's surprise for the new Chevalier of Honor consisted of a pair of gold buckles and a solitaire pin. Finally, there was the surprise of the new rooms for the whole family, to be followed in a fortnight by the great surprise of the bills to be paid.

After mature reflection, César decided that some of the invitations must be given in person, and some might be delivered by Raguet in the evening. He took a cab and handed his wife into it (his wife, whose beauty suffered a temporary eclipse from a hat and feathers and the last new shawl, the cashmere shawl for which she had longed for fifteen years), and away went the perfumers dressed in their best to acquit themselves of twenty-two calls in a morning.

César spared his wife the difficulties attendant on straining the resources of a bourgeois household to prepare the various confections which the splendor of the occasion demanded. A treaty was arranged between Birotteau and the great Chevet. Chevet would furnish the dinner and the wines; he would provide a splendid service of plate (which brings in as much as an estate to its owner), and a retinue of servants under the command of a sufficiently imposing *maître d'hôtel*, all of them responsible for their sayings and doings. Chevet was to take up his quarters in the kitchen and dining-room on the mezzanine floor, and not to quit possession until he had served up a dinner for twenty persons at six o'clock, and a grand collation an hour after midnight. The ices, to be served in pretty cups with silver-gilt spoons on silver trays, would be supplied by Foy's Café, and the refreshments by Tanrade—an added lustre to the feast.

"Be easy," César said to his wife, who looked somewhat over-anxious on the day before the great day. "Chevet, Tanrade, and the people from Foy's Café will occupy the mezzanine floor, Virginie will be on guard above, and the shop shall be shut up. There is nothing left for us to do but to strut about on the first floor."

On the 16th, at two o'clock, M. de la Billardière came for César. They were to go together to the Chancellerie de la Légion d'honneur, where Birotteau, with some ten others, was to be received as a Chevalier by M. le Comte de Lacépède. The perfumer had tears in his eyes when the mayor came for him; the surprise which Constance had planned had just taken place, and César had been presented with the gold buckles and solitaire.

"It is very sweet to be so loved," said he, as he stepped into the cab; Constance and Césarine standing on the threshold, and the assistants gathered in a group to see him go. All of them gazed at César in his silk stockings and black silk breeches, and the new coat of cornflower blue on which the ribbon was about to blaze—the red ribbon which, according to Molineux, had been steeped in blood.

When César came back at dinner-time, he was pale with joy. He looked at his Cross in every looking-glass, for in his first intoxication he could not be content to wear the ribbon only; there was no tinge of false modesty about his elation.

"The Grand Chancellor is charming, dear," said he; "at a word from M. de la Billardière, he accepted my invitation; he is coming with M. Vauquelin. M. de Lacépède is a great man, yes, as great as M. Vauquelin. He has written forty volumes. And then he is a peer of France as well as an author. We must not forget to say 'Your Lordship,' or 'M. le Comte,' when we address him."

"Do eat your dinner," remarked his wife.—"Your father is worse than a child," Constance added, looking at Césarine.

"How nice that looks at your button-hole!" said Césarine. "They will present arms when you pass; we will go out together!"

"All the sentries will present arms to me."

Grindot and Braschon came downstairs as he spoke. "After dinner, sir, you and madame and mademoiselle may like to look over the rooms; Braschon's foreman is just putting up a few curtain brackets, and three men are lighting the candles."

"You will need a hundred and twenty candles," said Braschon.

"A bill for two hundred francs from Trudon," began Mme. César, but a look from the Chevalier checked her lamentations.

"Your fête will be magnificent, M. le Chevalier," put in Braschon.

"Flatterers already!" César thought within himself. "The Abbé Loraux enjoined it upon me not to fall into their snares, and to remain humble; I will keep my origin in mind."

But César did not understand the drift of the remark let fall by the rich upholsterer of the Rue Saint-Antoine. Braschon had made a dozen futile efforts to secure invitations for himself and his wife, his daughter, aunt, and mother-in-law. And so César made an enemy. On the threshold, Braschon did not call him again "M. le Chevalier."

Then came the private view. César and his wife and Césarine went out through the shop and came in from the street. The door had been reconstructed in a grand style, the two leaves were divided up into square panels, and in the centre of each panel was a cast-iron ornament, duly painted. This kind of door, which is now so common in Paris, was at that time the very newest thing. Beneath the double staircase in the vestibule, opposite the door, in the plinth which had

so disturbed César's mind, a sort of box had been contrived
where an old woman could be ensconced. The vestibule, with
its black-and-white marble floor, and its walls painted to
look like marble, was lighted by a lamp of antique pattern,
with four sockets for the wicks. The architect had combined
a rich effect with apparent simplicity. A narrow crimson
carpet relieved the whiteness of the stone. The first landing
gave access to the mezzanine floor. The door on the staircase,
which gave access to the first-floor rooms, was in the same
style as the street door, but this was a piece of cabinet work.

"How charming!" said Césarine. "And yet there is nothing which catches the eye."

"Exactly, mademoiselle, the effect is produced by the exact
proportions of the stylobates, the plinths, the cornice, and the
ornaments; and then I have not employed gilding anywhere;
the colors are subdued, and there are no glaring tones."

"It is a science," said Césarine.

Then they entered the ante-room; it was simple, spacious,
and tastefully decorated; a parquet floor had been laid down.
The drawing-room was lighted by three windows, which
looked upon the street; here the colors were white and red;
the outlines of the cornices were delicate, so was the paint;
there was nothing to dazzle the eyes. The ornaments on the
mantel-shelf, of white marble supported on white marble columns, had been carefully chosen; there was nothing tawdry
about them, and they were in keeping with the details of the
furniture. In fact, throughout the room a subtle harmony
prevailed, such as none but an artist can establish, by subordi-
nating everything, down to the least accessories, to the general
scheme of decoration; a harmony which strikes the philistine,
though he cannot account for it. The light of twenty-four
wax candles in the chandelier displayed the glories of the
crimson silk curtains; the parquet floor tempted Césarine to
dance. Through a green-and-white boudoir they reached
César's study.

"I have put a bed here," said Grindot, throwing open the
doors of an alcove, cleverly concealed between the two book-

cases. "Either you or Mme. Birotteau may fall ill, and an invalid requires a separate room."

"But the bookcase is full of bound books! . . . Oh! wife, wife!" cried César.

"No, this is Césarine's surprise."

"Pardon a father's emotion," exclaimed Birotteau, embracing his daughter.

"Of course, of course, sir," said Grindot. "You are in your own house."

The prevailing tone of the study was brown, relieved by green; for by skilful modulations all the rooms were brought into harmony with each other. Thus the prevailing color of one room was more sparingly introduced as a subsidiary in another, and *vice versâ*. The print of *Hero and Leander* shone conspicuous from a panel in César's new sanctum.

"And *you* are to pay for all this?" César said merrily.

"That beautiful engraving is M. Anselme's gift to you," said Césarine.

(Anselme, like the others, had managed to afford his surprise.)

"Poor boy! he has done as I did for M. Vauquelin."

Mme. Birotteau's room came next in order. Here the architect had lavished splendors to please the good folk whom he wished to use to his own ends. He had promised to make a study of this redecoration, and he had kept his word. The room was hung with blue silk, but the cords and tassels were white; while the furniture, covered with white cashmere, was relieved with blue. The clock on the white marble chimney-piece took the form of a marble slab, on which Venus reclined. The pretty Wilton carpet, of Eastern design, was the keynote of Césarine's apartment, a dainty little bedroom hung with chintz; there stood her piano, a pretty wardrobe with a mirror in it, a small white bed with plain curtains, and all the little possessions that girls love.

The dining-room lay behind César's study and the blue-and-white bedroom, and was entered by a door on the staircase. Here the decorations were in the style known as Louis XIV.

The sideboards were inlaid with brass and tortoise-shell; there was a Boule clock, and the walls were hung with stuffs and adorned with gilt studs.

No words can describe the joy of these three human beings, which reached its height when Mme. Birotteau, returning to her room, found her new dress lying there on the bed; the cherry-colored velvet gown, trimmed with lace, which her husband had given her. Virginie had stolen in on tiptoe to lay it there.

"The rooms do you great credit, sir," Constance said, addressing Grindot. "More than a hundred people will be here to-morrow evening, and you will be complimented by everybody."

"I shall recommend you," said César. "You will meet all the first-rate people, and you will be better known in a single evening than if you had built a hundred houses."

Constance, touched by what had happened, no longer thought of the expense or of criticising her husband, and for the following reasons. That morning, when Popinot had brought the *Hero and Leander,* he had assured her that the Cephalic Oil would be a success. Constance had always had a high opinion of Popinot's abilities and intelligence, and Popinot was working with unheard-of enthusiasm. The money lavished by Birotteau on these extravagances might amount to a good round sum, but the young lover had promised that, in six months' time, Birotteau's share of the profits on the sales of the oil would cover them. After nineteen years of apprehension, it was so sweet to put doubts aside for a single day; and Constance promised her daughter that she would not spoil her husband's joy by any afterthought, but would give herself up entirely to gladness. So when M. Grindot left them about eleven o'clock, she flung her arms about her husband's neck and shed a few tears of joy.

"Ah, César," she said, "you make me very silly and very happy."

"If it will only last, you mean, do you not?" César asked, smiling.

"It will last; I have no fear now," said Mme. César.

"That is right; you appreciate me at last."

Those who have sufficient greatness of character to know their weaknesses will confess that a poor orphan girl who, eighteen years ago, had been earning her living behind the counter of the *Little Sailor* in the Ile Saint-Louis, and a poor peasant lad who had come on foot from Touraine, stick in hand and with hobnailed shoes on his feet, might well feel gratified and happy to give such a fête on an occasion so much to their credit.

"*Mon Dieu,* I would willingly give a hundred francs for a visitor," cried César.

"M. l'Abbé Loraux," announced Virginie, and the Abbé appeared. The priest was at this time curate of Saint-Sulpice. Never has the power of the soul been more plainly revealed than in this reverend ecclesiastic, who left a profound impression on the minds of all those with whom he came in contact. The exercise of Catholic virtues had given sublimity to a harsh face, almost repellent in its ugliness; it was as if something of the light of heaven shone from it before the time. The influences of a simple and sincere life, passing into the blood, had modified those rugged features, the fires of charity had chastened their uncouth outlines. In Claparon's case, the nature of the man had stamped itself on his face and degraded and brutalized it, but here the grace of the three fair human virtues, Hope, Faith, and Charity, hovered about the wrinkled lines. There was a penetrating power in his words, slowly and gently spoken. He dressed like other priests in Paris, and allowed himself a chestnut-brown overcoat. No trace of ambition had sullied the pure heart, which the angels would surely bear to God in its primitive innocence; it had required all the kindly urgency of the daughter of Louis XVI. to induce the Abbé Loraux to accept a benefice in Paris, and then he had taken one of the poorest.

Just now he looked somewhat disquieted as he surveyed all

these splendors; he smiled at the three before him, and shook his head.

"Children," he said, "it is my part to comfort those that mourn, and not to be present at festivals. I have come to thank M. César and to congratulate you. There is only one festival that will bring me here—the marriage of this pretty maid."

A quarter of an hour later the Abbé took his leave, and neither César nor his wife had dared to show him the new arrangements. The sober apparition threw a few drops of cold water on César's joyous ebullitions.

They slept that night amid the new glories, each taking possession of the little luxuries and pretty furniture for which they had longed. Césarine helped her mother to undress before the mirror of the white marble toilet table; César was fain to use his newly-acquired superfluities at once; and the heads of all the three were filled with visions of the joys of the morrow.

The next day, at four o'clock, they had been to mass, and had read vespers; the mezzanine floor had been delivered over to the secular arm, in the shape of Chevet's people, and Césarine and her mother betook themselves to their toilets. Never was costume more becoming to Mme. César than the cherry-colored velvet gown with the lace about it, the short sleeves adorned with lappets; the rich stuff and the glowing color set off the youthful freshness of her shapely arms, the dazzling whiteness of her skin, the gracious outlines of her neck and shoulders. The naïve happiness felt by every woman when she is conscious that she looks at her best lent a vague sweetness to Mme. Birotteau's Grecian profile; and the outlines of her face, finely cut as a cameo, appeared in all their delicate beauty. Césarine, in her white crape dress, with a wreath of white roses in her hair, and a rose at her waist, her shoulders and the outlines of her bodice modestly covered by a scarf, turned Popinot's head.

"These people are eclipsing us," said Mme. Roguin to her husband, as she went through the rooms.

The notary's wife was furious. A woman can always measure the superiority or inferiority of a rival, and Mme. Roguin felt that she was not as beautiful as Mme. César.

"Pooh, not for long. In a little while the poor thing will be ruined, and your carriage will splash the mud on her as she goes afoot through the streets."

Vauquelin's manner was perfect. He came with M. de Lacépède, who had brought his colleague in his carriage. To Mme. César, in . her radiant beauty, the two learned Academicians paid compliments in scientific language.

"You possess the secret, unknown to chemistry, of retaining youth and beauty, madame."

"You are in your own house, so to speak, M. l'Académicien," said Birotteau.—"Yes, M. le Comte," he went on, turning to the Grand Chancellor of the Legion of Honor, "I owe my success to M. Vauquelin. I have the honor of presenting to your lordship M. le Président (of the Tribunal of Commerce).—That is M. le Comte de Lacépède, a peer of France, and one of the greatest men in France besides; he has written forty volumes," he added, for the benefit of Joseph Lebas, who came with the President.

The guests were punctual. The ordinary tradesman's dinner party followed, abundant in good humor and merriment, and enlivened by the homely jokes that never fail to provoke laughter. Ample justice was done to the excellent dishes, and the wines were thoroughly appreciated. It was half-past nine before they went into the drawing-room for coffee, and cabs had already begun to arrive with impatient dancers. An hour later, the rooms were full, and the dance had become a crush. M. de Lacépède and M. Vauquelin went, in spite of entreaties from César, who followed them despairingly to the staircase. He had better fortune with the elder Popinot and M. de la Billardière, who remained.

With the exception of three women, Mlle. Fontaine, Mme. Jules, and Mme. Rabourdin, who severally represented aristocracy, finance, and official dignities, and by their brilliant beauty, dress, and manner presented a striking contrast to the rest of the assembly, the toilettes of the remainder were of the heavy and substantial order, too suggestive of a well-lined purse, which gives to a crowd of citizens' wives and daughters a certain air of vulgarity, made cruelly prominent in the present case by the daintiness and grace of the three ladies.

The bourgeoisie of the Rue Saint-Denis displayed itself majestically in the full glory of its absurdities carried to the burlesque point. It was that same bourgeoisie, nor more nor less, which tricks its offspring out in the uniform of the Lancers or of the National Guard, that buys *Victories and Conquests, The Old Soldier at the Plough,* and admires *The Pauper's Funeral,* which rejoices to go on Guard, goes on Sundays to the inevitable country house, is at pains to acquire a distinguished air, and dreams of municipal honors; the bourgeoisie that looks on every one with jealous eyes, and yet is kindly, helpful, devoted, warm-hearted, and compassionate, ready to subscribe for the orphan children of a General Foy, for the Greeks (all unwitting of their piracies), for the Champ d'Asile when it no longer exists; a bourgeoisie that falls a victim to its own good qualities, and is flouted by a social superiority which marks a real inferiority, for an ignorance of social conventions fosters that native kindliness of heart; a bourgeoisie which brings up frank-hearted daughters inured to work, full of good qualities, which are lost at once if they mingle with the classes above them; a common-sense, matter-of-fact womankind, from among whom the worthy Chrysale should have taken a wife; that bourgeoisie, in short, so admirably represented by the Matifats, the druggists in the Rue des Lombards, who had supplied the *Queen of Roses* for sixty years.

Mme. Matifat, anxious to appear stately, wore a turban on her head, and was dancing in a heavy poppy-red gown embroidered with gold, a toilette that harmonized with a haughty countenance, a Roman nose, and the splendors of a crimson complexion. Even M. Matifat, so glorious when the National Guard was reviewed, when you might see the chain and bunch of seals blazing on his portly person fifty paces away, was obscured by this Catherine II. of the counting-house; yet her short, stout, spectacled consort, with his shirt collar almost up to his ears, distinguished himself by his deep bass voice and by the richness of his vocabulary.

He never said "Corneille," but "the sublime Corneille." Racine was the "tender Racine"; Voltaire, oh! Voltaire, "takes the second place in every class, more of a wit than a genius, but nevertheless a man of genius!" Rousseau, "a gloomy, suspicious nature, a man over-brimming with pride, who ended by hanging himself." He related tedious stock anecdotes about Piron, who is looked upon as a prodigious personage among the bourgeoisie. There was a slight tendency to obscenity in Matifat's conversation; he was an infatuated admirer of theatrical divinities; and it was even said of him that, in imitation of old Cardot and the wealthy Camusot, he kept a mistress. Now and then Mme. Matifat would hastily interrupt him on the brink of an anecdote by crying, at the top of her voice, "Mind what you are going to tell us, old man!" In familiar conversation she always addressed him as "old man." The voluminous lady of the Rue des Lombards caused Mlle. de Fontaine's aristocratic countenance to lose its repose; the haughty damsel could not help smiling when she overheard Mme. Matifat say to her husband, "Don't make a rush for the ices, old man; it is bad style!"

It is harder to explain the differences which distinguish the great world from the bourgeoisie than it is for the bourgeoisie to efface them. The women, conscious of their toilettes, felt that this was a holiday; they made no attempt to conceal an enjoyment which plainly showed that this ball was a great event in their busy lives; while the three women, each of whom represented a different higher social sphere, were at that moment as they would be on the morrow. They did not seem to be dressed for the occasion, had no desire to behold themselves amid the unaccustomed marvels of their costume, and showed no uneasiness as to its effect, which they had ascertained once and for all as they put the last touches to their ball dresses before the mirror; there was no excitement in their faces; they danced with the grace and ease of movement which the forgotten sculptors of a bygone age caught and recorded in their statues. But the others bore the impress of daily toil, toil showed itself in their attitude, in their exaggerated enjoyment; their glances were naïvely curious, their voices were not subdued to the key of the low murmur which gives such an inimitable piquancy to ballroom conversation; and, above all things, they lacked the impertinent gravity which contains the germ of epigram, the repose of manner which marks those whose self-command is perfect. So Mme. Rabourdin, Mme. Jules, and Mlle. de Fontaine, who had expected infinite amusement from this perfumer's ball, stood out against the background of citizens' wives and daughters, conspicuous by their languid grace, by the exquisite taste displayed in their toilettes, and by their manner of dancing, even as three principal performers at the Opéra are set off by the rank and file of supernumeraries on the stage. Jealous and astonished eyes watched them. Mme. Roguin, Constance, and Césarine formed a link, as it were, between these three aristocratic types and the tradesmen's womankind.

At every ball a moment comes when excitement, or the torrents of light, the gaiety, the music, and the movement of the dance carries away the dancers, and all the shades of difference are drowned in the *crescendo* of the *tutti*. In a little while the ball would become a romp. Mlle. de Fontaine determined to go; but as she sought the venerable Vendean leader's arm, Birotteau and his wife and daughter hastened to prevent the defection of the aristocracy of their assembly.

"There is a perfume of good taste about the rooms which really surprises me; I congratulate you upon it," said the insolent girl, addressing the perfumer.

Birotteau was too much intoxicated by the compliments publicly addressed to him to understand this speech; but his wife flushed up, and did not know what to answer.

"This is a national festival which does you honor," Camusot said.

"I have seldom seen so fine a ball," said M. de la Billardière, an official fib that cost him nothing.

Birotteau took all the congratulations seriously.

"What a charming sight, and how good the band is! Shall you often give us balls?" asked Mme. Lebas.

"What beautiful rooms! Did you plan them yourself?" inquired Mme. Desmarets, and César ventured on a lie, and allowed it to be thought that he was the originator of the scheme of decoration. Césarine, whose list of partners for the quadrilles was of course filled up, learned how much delicacy there was in Anselme's nature.

"If I only listened to my own wishes," he had said in her ear, as they rose from dinner, "I would entreat the favor of a quadrille with you, but my happiness would cost our self-love too dear."

Césarine, who thought all men who walked straight ungraceful in their gait, determined to open the ball with Popinot. Popinot, encouraged by his aunt, who had bade him be bold, dared to speak of his love during the quadrille to the charming girl at his side, but in the roundabout ways that timid lovers take.

"My fortune depends on you, mademoiselle."

"And how?"

"There is but one hope which can give me the power to make it."

"Then hope."

"Do you really know all that you have said in those two words?" asked Popinot.

"Hope for fortune," said Césarine, with a mischievous smile.

As soon as the quadrille was over, Anselme rushed to his friend. "Gaudissart! Gaudissart! succeed, or I shall blow my brains out." He squeezed his friend's arm in a Herculean grasp. "Success means that I shall marry Césarine. She has told me so; and see how beautiful she is!"

"Yes, she is prettily rigged out," said Gaudissart; "and she is rich. We will do her in oil."

The good understanding between Mlle. Lourdois and Alexandre Crottat (Roguin's successor-designate) did not escape Mme. Birotteau, who could not give up without a pang the prospect of seeing her daughter the wife of a Paris notary. Uncle Pillerault, after exchanging a greeting with little Molineux, took up his quarters in an easy-chair near the bookcase. Hence he watched the card-players, listened to the talk about him, and went from time to time to the door to look at the moving flower-garden as the dancers' heads swayed in the figures of the quadrille. He turned a truly philosophical countenance on it all. The men were unspeakable, with the exception of du Tillet, who had already learned something of the manners of the fashionable world; of young Billardière, an incipient dandy; M. Jules Desmarets, and the official personages. But among the faces, all more or less comical, which gave the assembly its character, there was one in particular, worn into meaningless smoothness like the head on a five-franc piece issued by the Republic, but curious by reason of its association with a suit of clothes. This person, it will have been guessed, was none other than the petty tyrant of the Cour Batave, arrayed in fine linen, yellowed with lying by in the press, displaying a shirt frill of venerable lace, secured by a pin with a bluish cameo. Short breeches of black silk treacherously revealed the spindle shanks on which he dared to repose his weight. César triumphantly took him round the four apartments devised by the architect on the first floor of his house.

"Hey! hey! it is your own affair, sir," said Molineux. "My first floor done up in this way will be worth another thousand crowns."

Birotteau turned this off with a joke, but the little old man's words and tone had been like the prick of a needle. "I shall soon have my first floor again; this man is ruining himself!"—that was the underlying sense of that *"will be worth,"* which had been a sudden revelation of Molineux's claws.

The pale, meagre face and cruel eyes struck du Tillet,

whose attention had been called to the landlord in the first instance by the watch-chain from which a pound weight of trinkets hung and jingled, the green coat with white threads in it, and the odd-looking, turned up collar, which gave the old man somewhat the appearance of a rattlesnake. So the banker went over to the little money-lender to learn how he came to be at a merry-making.

"Here, sir," said Molineux, putting a foot into the boudoir, "I am on M. le Comte Granville's property, but here" (he pointed to the other foot) "I am on my own, for this house belongs to me."

And Molineux, more than willing to gratify the only one who had a mind to listen to him, was so charmed with du Tillet's attentive attitude, that he described himself, and gave an account of his habits, together with a complete history of the sauciness of Master Gendrin, and an exact relation of his transactions with the perfumer, without which transaction the ball would not have taken place.

"Ah! so M. César has paid his rent beforehand," said du Tillet; "nothing is more contrary to his habits."

"Oh! I asked him to do so; I am so accommodating with my tenants!"

"If old Birotteau goes bankrupt," thought du Tillet, "that little rogue will certainly make a capital assignee. Such captiousness is not often met with; he must amuse himself at home, like Domitian, by killing flies when he is alone."

Du Tillet betook himself to the card-tables, where Claparon (by his orders) had already taken his post. Du Tillet thought that, screened by a lamp shade, at *bouillotte,* his dummy banker would escape all scrutiny. As they sat opposite one another, they looked such perfect strangers that the most suspicious observer could have discovered no sign of an understanding between them. Gaudissart, who knew that Claparon had risen in the world, did not dare to approach him; the wealthy ex-commercial traveler had given him the portentously cool stare of an upstart who does not care to be claimed by an old acquaintance.

Towards five o'clock in the morning the ball came to an end, like a spent rocket. By that time there only remained some forty cabs out of a hundred or more which had filled the Rue Saint-Honoré; and in the ballroom they were dancing the *boulangère,* which later was succeeded by the cotillon and the English galop. Du Tillet, Roguin, young Cardot, Jules Desmarets, and the Comte de Granville were playing *bouillotte.* Du Tillet had won three thousand francs. The light of the wax-candles was growing pale in the dawn when the card-players rose to join in the last quadrille.

In bourgeois houses this supreme enjoyment never comes to an end without some enormities. Those who imposed awe or restraint on the others are gone; the intoxication of movement, the hot rooms, the spirits that lurk in the most harmless beverages, relax the stiffness of the dowagers, who allow themselves to be drawn into the quadrilles, and yield to the excitement of the moment; men are heated, the lank hair comes down over their faces, and their grotesque appearance provokes laughter; the younger women grow frivolous, flowers have fallen here and there from their hair. Then it is that the bourgeois Momus enters, followed by his antic crew! Laughter breaks out in peals, and every one gives himself up to the merriment, thinking that with morning labor will resume its sway over him. Matifat was dancing with a woman's hat on his head; Célestin was indulging in burlesque movements. A few of the ladies clapped their hands noisily when they changed the figures of the intermidable quadrille.

"How they are enjoying themselves!" said the happy Birotteau.

"If only they break nothing," said Constance, who stood by Uncle Pillerault.

"You have given the most magnificent ball that I have seen, and I have seen many," said du Tillet, with a bow to his late employer.

There is in one of Beethoven's eight symphonies a fantasia like a great poem; it is the culminating point of the *finale*

of the Symphony in C minor. When, after the slow preparation of the mighty magician, so well understood by Habeneck,
the rich curtain rises on this scene; when the bow of the enthusiastic leader of the orchestra calls forth the dazzling
motif, through which the whole gathered force of the music
flows, the poet, as his heart beats fast, will understand that
this ball was in Birotteau's life like this moment when his
own imagination feels the quickening power of the music,
of this *motif,* which in itself perhaps raises the Symphony
in C minor above its glorious sisters. For a radiant fairy
springs up and waves her wand, and you hear the rustling
of the purple silken curtains raised by angels; the golden
doors, carved like the bronze gates of the Baptistery in
Florence, turn upon their hinges of adamant, and your eyes
wander over far-off glories and vistas of fairy palaces. Forms
not of this earth glide among them, the incense of prosperity
rises, the fire is kindled on the altar of fortune, the scented
air circles about it. Beings clad in white blue-bordered tunics
smile divinely as they float before your eyes, shapes delicate
and ethereal beyond expression turn faces of unearthly
beauty upon you. The Loves hover in the air, filling it with
the flames of their torches. You feel that you are loved; you
are glad with a joy that you drink in without comprehending it as you bathe in the floods of a torrent of harmony
which pours out for each the nectar of his choice; for as the
music slides into your inmost soul, its desires are realized for
a moment. Then when you have walked for a while in
heaven, the enchanter plunges you back, by some deep and
mysterious transition of the bass, into the morass of chill
reality, only to draw you thence when he has awakened in you
a thirst for his divine melodies, and your soul cries out to
hear those sounds again. The history of the soul at the most
glorious point in that beautiful *finale* is the history of the
sensations which this festival brought in abundance for Constance and César. But it was no Beethoven, but a Collinet,
who had composed upon his flute the *finale* of their commercial symphony.

The three Birotteaus, tired but happy, slept that morning with the sounds of the festival ringing in their ears. The building, repairs, furniture, banquets, toilettes, and Césarine's library (for the money had been repaid to her) had altogether raised the expense of that entertainment, without César's having a suspicion of it, to sixty thousand francs. So much did that luckless red ribbon, fastened by the King to a perfumer's buttonhole, cost the wearer. If any misfortune should befall César Birotteau, this extravagance of his was like to bring him into serious trouble at the police court; a merchant lays himself open to a term of two years' imprisonment if, on examination, his expenses are considered excessive. It is, perhaps, more unpleasant to go to the Sixth Chamber for simple bad management or for a foolish trifle, than to come before a Court of Assize for a gigantic fraud; and in some people's eyes it is better to be a knave than a fool.

II.

A WEEK after the ball, that final flare of the straw-fire of a prosperity which had lasted for eighteen years, and now was about to die out in darkness, César stood watching the passers-by through his shop window. He was thinking of the wide extent of his business affairs, and found them almost more than he could manage. Hitherto his life had been quite simple; he manufactured and sold his goods, or he bought to sell again. But now there was the speculation in building land, and his own share in the enterprise of A. Popinot & Company, besides a hundred and sixty thousand francs worth of bills to meet. Before long he would be compelled to discount some of his customers' bills (and his wife would not like it), or there must be an unheard-of success on Popinot's part; altogether, the poor man had so many things to think of that he felt as if he had more skeins to wind than he could hold.

How would Anselme steer his course? Birotteau treated Popinot much as a professor of rhetoric treats a student; he felt little confidence in his capacity, and was sorry that he could not be always on hand to look after him. The admonitory kick bestowed on Anselme's shins by way of a recommendation to hold his tongue in Vauquelin's presence will illustrate the fears which the perfumer felt as to the newly-started business. Birotteau was very careful to hide his thoughts from his wife and daughter, and from his assistant; but within himself he felt as a Seine boatman might feel if by some freak of fortune a Minister should give him the command of a frigate. Such thoughts as these, rising like a fog in his brain, were but little favorable to clear thinking, he stood, therefore, trying to see things distinctly in his own mind.

Just at that moment a figure, for which he felt an intense aversion, appeared in the street; he beheld his second landlord, little Molineux. Everybody knows those dreams in which events are so crowded together that we pass through a whole lifetime, dreams in which a fantastical being reappears from time to time, always as the bearer of bad tidings— the villain of the piece. It seemed to Birotteau that fate had sent Molineux to play a similar part in his waking life. That countenance had grinned diabolically at him when the feast was at its height, and had turned an evil eye on the splendor; and now when César saw it again, he remembered the impression which the "little curmudgeon" (to use his own expression) had given him but so much the more vividly, because Molineux had given him a fresh feeling of repulsion by suddenly breaking in upon his musings.

"Sir," said the little man in his vampire voice, "we did this business in such an offhand fashion, that you forgot to approve the additions to this little private covenant of ours."

As Birotteau took up the lease to repair the omission, the architect came in, bowed to the perfumer, and hovered about him with a diplomatic air.

"You know, sir, the difficulties at the outset when you are starting in business," he said at last in Birotteau's ear; "you are satisfied with me; you would oblige me very much by paying my honorarium at once."

Birotteau, who had paid away all his ready money and emptied his portfolio, told Célestin to draw a bill for two thousand francs at three months and a form of receipt.

"It is a very lucky thing for me that you undertook to pay the quarter which your next-door neighbor owed," said Molineux, with malicious cunning in his smile. "My porter has been round to tell me that the authorities have been affixing seals to his property, because Master Cayron had disappeared from the scene."

"If only they don't come down on me for the five thousand francs," thought Birotteau.

"People thought that he was doing very well," said Lourdois, who had just come in to hand his statement to the perfumer.

"No one in business is quite safe from reverses until he retires," remarked little Molineux, folding up his document with punctilious neatness.

The architect watched the little old creature with the pleasure that every artist feels at the sight of a living caricature which confirms his prejudices against the bourgeoisie.

"When you hold an umbrella over your head, you generally suppose that it is sheltered if it rains," he observed.

Molineux looked harder at the architect's moustache and "royale" than at his face, and the contempt that he felt for Grindot quite equaled Grindot's contempt for him. He stayed on to give the architect a parting scratch. By dint of living with his cats, there had come to be something feline in Molineux's ways as well as in his eyes.

Just at that moment, Ragon and Pillerault came in together.

"We have been talking over this business with the judge," Ragon said in César's ear. "He says that in a speculation of this kind we must actually complete the purchase and have a receipt from the vendors if we are really to be severally propriet——"

"Oh! are you in the affair of the Madeleine?" asked Lourdois. "People are talking about it; there will be houses to build!"

The house-painter had come to ask for a prompt settlement, but he found it to his interest not to press the perfumer.

"I have sent in my statement because it is the end of the year," he said in a low voice for César's benefit; "I do not want anything."

"Well, what is it, César?" asked Pillerault, noticing his

nephew's surprise; for César, overcome by the sight of the statement, made no answer to either Ragon or Lourdois.

"Oh! a trifle; I took five thousand francs of bills from a neighbor, the umbrella dealer, who is bankrupt. If he has given me bad paper, I shall be caught like a simpleton."

"Why, I told you so long ago," cried Ragon; "a drowning man will catch hold of his father's leg to save himself, and drag him down with him. I have seen so much of bankruptcies! A man is not exactly a rogue to begin with; but when he gets into trouble, he is forced to become one."

"True," said Pillerault.

"Ah! if I ever get as far as the Chamber of Deputies, or have some influence with Government . . ." said Birotteau, rising on tiptoe, and sinking back again on his heels.

"What will you do?" asked Lourdois. "You are a wise man."

Molineux, always interested by a discussion on law, stayed in the shop to listen; and as the attention paid by others is infectious, Pillerault and Ragon, who knew César's opinions, listened none the less with as much gravity as the three strangers.

"I should have a Tribunal and a permanent bench of judges," said César, "and a public prosecutor for criminal cases. After an examination, made by a judge who should discharge the functions of agents by procuration trustees and registrar, the trader should be declared *temporarily insolvent* or a *fraudulent bankrupt*. In the first case, he should be bound over to pay his creditors in full; to that end, he should be trustee for his own and his wife's property (for everything he had, or might inherit, would belong to his creditors); he should manage his estate for their benefit and under their inspection; in fact, he should carry on the business for them, signing his name, in every case, as 'such a one, in liquidation,' until everybody was paid in full. But if he were made a bankrupt, he should be condemned to stand in the pillory in the Exchange for a couple of hours, as they used to do, with a green cap on his head. His own property and his wife's, and his interest in any other estate, should be forfeit to his creditors, and he should be banished the kingdom."

"Business would be a little safer," said Lourdois; "people would think twice before going into a speculation."

"The law as it stands is never carried out," cried César, lashing himself up; "more than fifty merchants out of a hundred could only pay seventy-five per cent, or they sell goods at twenty-five per cent below invoice price, and spoil trade in that way."

"M. Birotteau is in the right," said Molineux; "the law allows far too much latitude. The entire estate should be made over to the creditors, or the man should be disgraced."

"Bother take it," said César, "at the rate at which things are going, a merchant will become a licensed robber. By signing his name he can dip in any one's purse."

"You are severe, M. Birotteau," said Lourdois.

"He is right," said old Ragon.

"Every man who fails is a suspicious character," César went on, exasperated by the little loss which rang in his ears; it was like the huntsman's first distant halloo to a stag.

As he spoke, Chevet's steward brought his invoice, a pastry-cook's boy from Félix and the Café Foy arrived, together with the clarinet-player of Collinet's band, each with an account.

"The *Quart d'heure de Rabelais,*" smiled Ragon.

"My word, that was a splendid fête of yours," said Lourdois.

"I am busy," César said, and the messengers departed, leaving their invoices.

"M. Grindot," said Lourdois, who noticed that the architect was folding up a bill which bore César's signature, "you will check my account and see that it is all in order; you need do nothing more than run through it, all the prices have been agreed to on M. Birotteau's behalf."

Pillerault looked at Lourdois and Grindot.

"If architect and contractor settle the prices between them, you are being robbed," he said in his nephew's ear.

Grindot went out.   Molineux followed and came up to him with a mysterious expression.

"Sir," he remarked, "you heard what I said, but you did not take my meaning; I wish you an umbrella when it comes on to rain."

Fear seized on Grindot. A man clings all the more tightly to gain which is not lawfully his; such is human nature. As a matter of fact, too, this had been a labor of love for the artist; he had given all his time and his utmost skill to the alterations of the rooms; he had done five times as much as he had been paid for, and had fallen a victim to his own self-love. The contractors had had little difficulty in tempting him. And besides the irresistible argument, there was a menace, understood though not expressed, of doing him an injury by slandering him, and there was a yet more cogent reason for yielding—the remark that Lourdois made as to the building land near the Madeleine. Clearly, Birotteau did not mean to put up a single house; he was only speculating in land.

Architects and contractors are in somewhat the same relative positions as actors and dramatists; they are dependent on each other. Grindot, to whom Birotteau left the settlement of the charges, was for the handicraftsman as against the citizen-householder. So the end of it was that three large contractors—Lourdois, Chaffaroux, and Thorien the carpenter—declared him to be "one of those good fellows for whom it is a pleasure to work." Grindot foresaw that the accounts on which he was to have his share would be paid, like his own fee, by bills; and this little old man had given him doubts as to whether those bills would be met. Grindot was prepared to show no mercy; after the manner of artists, the most ruthless enemies of the bourgeois.

By the end of December, César had invoices for sixty thousand francs. Félix, the Café Foy, Tanrade, and others, to whom small amounts were owing which must be paid in cash, had sent three times for the money. In business these small trifles do more harm than a heavy loss; they set rumors in

circulation. A loss which every one knows is a definite
thing, but panic knows no limits. Birotteau's safe was
empty.

Then fear seized on the perfumer. Such a thing had never
happened before in his business career. Like all people who
have almost forgotten their struggles with poverty, and have
little strength of character, this incident, a daily occurrence
in the lives of most petty shopkeepers in Paris, troubled
César's brain.

He told Célestin to send in invoices to his own customers;
such an unheard-of order had to be repeated twice before
the astonished first assistant understood it. The "clients"
—the grand name that shopkeepers used to apply to their
customers, and retained by César in speaking of them, in
spite of his wife, who had yielded at last with a "Call them
what you like, so long as they pay us"—the "clients" were
wealthy people, who paid when they pleased; in César's business there were no bad debts, though the outstanding accounts
often amounted to fifty or sixty thousand francs. The second
assistant took the invoice-book, and began to copy out the
largest amounts. César stood in fear of his wife. He did
not wish her to see his prostration beneath the simoom of
misfortune, so he determined to go out.

"Good-day, sir," said Grindot, coming in with the careless air that artists assume when they talk of business matters, to which they say they are entirely unaccustomed. "I
cannot obtain ready money of any sort or description for
your paper, so I am compelled to ask you to give me cash instead. It is a most unfortunate thing for me that I must
take this step; but I have not been to the money-lender's
about it; I should not like to hawk your name about; I know
enough of business to know that it would be casting a slur
on it; so it is to your own interest to——"

"Speak lower, sir, if you please," said Birotteau in bewilder-
ment. "I am very much surprised at this."

Lourdois came in.

"Here, Lourdois," said Birotteau with a smile, "do you

know about this?——" he stopped short. With the good faith of a merchant who feels secure, the poor man had been about to ask Lourdois to take Grindot's bill, by way of laughing at the architect; but he saw a cloud on Lourdois' brow, and trembled at his own imprudence. The harmless joke was the death-knell of a credit not above suspicion. In such a case a rich merchant takes back his bill; he does not offer it. Birotteau felt dizzy; it was as if a stroke of a pickaxe had laid open the pit which yawned at his feet.

"My dear M. Birotteau," said Lourdois, retiring with him to the back of the shop, "my account has been checked and passed; I must ask you to have the money ready for me by to-morrow. My daughter is going to be married to young Crottat; he wants money, and notaries will not wait and bargain; besides, no one has ever seen my name on a bill."

"You can send round the day after to-morrow," said Birotteau stiffly (he counted on the payment of the invoices). "And you also, sir,"—he spoke to Grindot.

"Why can I not have it at once?" asked the architect.

"I have my men's wages to pay in the Faubourg," said César, who had never told a lie.

He took up his hat to go with them; but the bricklayer came in with Thorien and Chaffaroux, and stopped him just as he shut the door.

"We really want the money, sir," said Chaffaroux.

"Eh! I haven't the wealth of the Indies," cried César, out of patience; and he quickly put a hundred paces between himself and the three visitors.—"There is something underneath all this. Confound the ball! Everybody takes you for a millionaire. Still, there was something very strange about Lourdois," he thought; "there is some snake in the hedge."

He went along the Rue Saint-Honoré without thinking where he was going, feeling at a very low ebb, when at a corner of the street he ran up against Alexandre Crottat, like a battering-ram, or as one mathematician absorbed in the working of a problem might collide with another.

"Ah! sir," exclaimed the future notary, "one word with you! Did Roguin pay over your four hundred thousand francs to M. Claparon?"

"You were there when the thing was done. M. Claparon gave me no receipt of any kind; my bills were to be negotiated. . . . Roguin ought to have paid them to him . . . my two hundred and forty thousand francs in coin. . . . He was told that the money was to be paid down and the transaction completed. . . . M. Popinot of the Tribunal says. . . . The vendor's receipt! . . . But . . . what makes you ask the question?"

"What makes me ask you such a question? To know whether your two hundred thousand francs are in Claparon's hands or Roguin's. Roguin is such an old acquaintance of yours, that he might have scrupled to take your money, and handed it over to Claparon; if so, you will have had a narrow escape! But how stupid I am! He has made off with them, for he has M. Claparon's money; luckily, Claparon had only paid a hundred thousand francs. Roguin has absconded; I myself paid him a hundred thousand francs for his practice without taking a receipt; I gave it him as I might give my purse to you to keep for me. Your vendors have not been paid a stiver; they have just been round to see me. The money you raised on your land has no existence for you, nor for the man of whom you borrowed it; Roguin had swallowed it like your hundred thousand francs; which—er—he has not had this long while. And he has taken your last payment of a hundred thousand francs with him too; I remember going to the bank for the money."

The pupils of César's eyes dilated so widely that he could see nothing but red flames before him.

"Your draft on the bank for a hundred thousand francs, a hundred thousand francs of mine paid for the practice, and a hundred thousand francs belonging to M. Claparon—three hundred thousand francs gone like smoke, to say nothing of the defalcations that have yet to be found out," the young notary went on. "They feared for Mme. Roguin's

life; M. du Tillet spent the night beside her. Du Tillet himself has had a narrow escape! Roguin has been pestering him
this month past to draw him into the Madeleine speculation,
but, luckily, all his capital was locked up in some project of
the Nucingens'. Roguin wrote his wife a frightful letter.
I have just seen it. For five years he has been gambling with
his clients' money, and why? To spend it on a mistress—*La
belle Hollandaise;* he left her a fortnight before he made
this stroke. She had squandered till she had not a farthing;
her furniture was sold; she had put her name on bills of exchange. Then she hid from her creditors in a house in the
Palais-Royal, and was murdered there last evening by an
officer in the army. Heaven soon dealt the punishment to
her who, beyond a doubt, had run through Roguin's fortune.
There are women to whom nothing is sacred; think of squandering away a notary's practice!

"Mme. Roguin will have nothing except what has been
secured to her by her legal mortgage, and all the scoundrel's
property has been mortgaged beyond its value. The practice
is to be sold for three hundred thousand francs! **and I,**
who thought I was doing a good stroke of business, **must**
begin by paying an extra hundred thousand francs for my
practice; I hold no receipt; and there are defalcations which
will eat up the value of the practice and the deposit of caution money. The creditors will think that I am in it if I say
anything about my hundred thousand francs, and you have to
be very careful of your reputation when you are beginning for
yourself.—You will hardly get thirty per cent. Such a brew
to drink of at my age! That a man of fifty-nine should take
up with a woman. . . . The old rogue! Three weeks ago
he told me not to marry Césarine, and said that before long
you would not have bread to eat, the monster!"

Alexandre might have talked on for a long while; Birotteau stood like a man turned to stone. Each sentence fell
like a stunning blow. He heard nothing in the sounds but his
death-knell; just as when Alexandre first began to speak, he
had seemed to see his own house in flames. He looked so

white, and stood so motionless, that Alexandre Crottat, who had taken the worthy perfumer for a clear-headed, capable man of business, was frightened at last. Roguin's successor did not know that this stroke had swept away César's whole fortune. A swift thought of suicide flashed through the brain of the merchant, so profoundly religious by nature. In such a case suicide is a way of escape from a thousand deaths, and it seems logical to accept but one. Alexandre Crottat lent his arm, and tried to walk with him, but it was impossible —César tottered as if he had been drunk.

"Why, what is the matter with you?" asked Crottat. "My good M. César, pluck up heart a little! It takes more than this to kill a man! Besides, you will recover forty thousand francs; the man who lent you the money had not the money to lend, and did not pay it over to you; you might plead that the contract was void."

"My ball.—My Cross.—Two hundred thousand francs' worth of my paper on the market, and nothing in the safe. . . . The Ragons, Pillerault. . . . And my wife, who saw it all!"

A shower of confused words, which called up ideas that overwhelmed him and caused unbearable pangs, fell like hail laying waste the flower beds of the *Queen of Roses*.

"If only my head were cut off," Birotteau cried at last; "it is so heavy that it weighs me down, and it is good for nothing in this . . ."

"Poor old Birotteau!" said Alexandre; "then are you in difficulties?"

"Difficulties!"

"Very well; keep up your heart and struggle with them."

"Struggle!" echoed the perfumer.

"Du Tillet used to be your assistant; he has a level head, he will help you."

"Du Tillet?"

"Come along!"

"Good heavens! I don't like to go home like this," cried Birotteau. "You that are my friend, if friends there are, you who have dined with me, you in whom I have taken an interest, call a cab for me, for my wife's sake; and come with me, Xandrot . . ."

With no little difficulty Crottat put the inert mechanism, called César, into a cab.

"Xandrot," he said, in a voice broken with tears, for the tears had begun to fall, and the iron band about his head seemed to be loosened a little, "let us call at the shop. Speak to Célestin for me. My friend, tell him that it is a matter of life and death for me and for my wife. And let no one prattle about Roguin's disappearance on any pretext whatever. Ask Césarine to come down, and beg her to allow no one to say anything about it to her mother. You must beware of your best friends, Pillerault, the Ragons, everybody——"

The change in Birotteau's voice made a deep impression on Crottat, who understood the importance of the request. On their way to the magistrate, they stopped at the house in the Rue Saint-Honoré. Célestin and Césarine were horrified to see Birotteau lying back in white and speechless hebetude, as it were, in the cab.

"Keep the affair a secret for me," said the perfumer.

"Ah!" said Xandrot to himself, "he is coming round; I thought it was all over with him."

The conference between Alexandre and the magistrate lasted long. The President of the Chamber of Notaries was sent for; César was taken hither and thither like a parcel; he did not stir, he did not utter a word. Towards seven o'clock in the evening Alexandre Crottat took the perfumer home again, and the thought of appearing before his wife had a bracing effect on him. The young notary had the charity to precede him, to tell Mme. Birotteau that her husband had had a sort of fit.

"His ideas are confused," he said, making a gesture to describe a bewildered state of the brain; "perhaps he should be bled, or leeches ought to be put on him."

"I knew how it would be," said Constance—nothing was further from her thoughts than the actual disaster—"he did not take his medicine as usual at the beginning of winter, and for these two months he has been working like a galley slave, as if he had to earn his daily bread."

So César's wife and daughter begged him to go to bed, and Dr. Haudry, Birotteau's doctor, was sent for. Old Haudry was a doctor of the school of Molière; he had a large practice, and adhered to old-fashioned methods and out-of-date formulæ; consulting physician though he was, he drugged his patients like any quack doctor. He came, made his diagnosis, and ordered the immediate application of a sinapism to the soles of César's feet; he detected symptoms of cerebral congestion.

"What can have brought it on?" asked Constance.

"The damp weather," said the doctor. Césarine had given him a hint.

A doctor is often obliged professionally to talk nonsense with a learned air, to save the honor or the life of persons in health who stand about the patient's bed. The old physician had seen so much, that half a word sufficed for him. Césarine went out on to the stairs to ask about the treatment.

"Rest and quiet; then when there is less pressure on the head, we will venture on tonics."

For two days Mme. César sat by her husband's bedside. Often she thought that he was delirious. As he lay in his wife's pretty blue chamber, he said many things, which were enigmas for Constance, at the sight of the hangings, the furniture, and the costly magnificence of the room.

"He is light-headed," she said to Césarine, when César sat upright in bed and began solemnly to repeat scraps of the Code. "If the personal or household expenses are considered excessive. . . . Take away those curtains!" he cried.

After three dreadful days of anxiety for César's reason, the Tourangeau's strong peasant constitution triumphed, the pressure on the brain ceased. M. Haudry ordered cordials and a strengthening diet, and after a cup of coffee seasonably administered, César was on his feet again. Constance, worn out, took her husband's place.

"Poor thing!" said César, when he saw her sleeping.

"Come, papa, take courage! You have so much talent, that you will triumph over this. Never mind. M. Anselme will help you," and Césarine murmured the sweet, vague words, made still sweeter by tenderness, which put courage into the most sorely defeated, as a mother's crooning songs soothe the pain of a teething infant.

"Yes, child, I will struggle. But not a word of this to any one whatever; not to Popinot, who loves us, nor to your uncle. In the first place, I will write to my brother; he is a canon, I believe, a priest attached to a cathedral. He spends nothing, so he must have saved something. Five thousand francs put by every year for twenty years—he ought to have a hundred thousand francs. Priests have credit in country places."

Césarine, in her hurry to set a little table and the necessaries for writing a letter before her father, brought the remainder of the rose-colored cards for the ball.

"Burn them all!" cried the merchant. "The devil alone could have put the notion of that ball into my head. If I fail, it will look as if I were a rogue. Come, let us go straight to the point."

César's letter to François Birotteau.

"MY DEAR BROTHER,—My business is passing through a crisis so difficult that I implore you to send me all the money at your disposal, even if you are obliged to borrow.—Yours truly,   CÉSAR.

"Your niece Césarine, who is with me as I write this letter, while my poor wife is asleep, desires to be remembered to you, and sends her love."

This postscript was added at Césarine's instance. She gave the letter to Raguet.

"Father," said she, when she came up again, "here is M. Lebas, who wants to speak to you."

"M. Lebas!" cried César, starting as though misfortune had made a criminal of him, "a judge!"

"Dear M. Birotteau," said the stout merchant-draper as he came in, "I take too deep an interest in you—knowing each other so long as we have, and being elected judges together, as we were, for the first time—not to let you know that one Bidault, otherwise Gigonnet, has bills of yours made payable to his order, *without guarantee,* by the firm of Claparon. Those two words are not merely an insult; they give a fatal shake to your credit."

"M. Claparon would like to speak to you," said Célestin, putting in his head; "am I to show him up?"

"We shall soon hear the why and wherefore of this affront," remarked Lebas.

"This is M. Lebas, sir," said César, as Claparon came in; "he is a judge of the Tribunal of Commerce, and my friend——"

"Oh! the gentleman is M. Lebas, is he?" said Claparon, interrupting César, "delighted to make his acquaintance; M. Lebas of the tribunal, there are so many Lebas, to say nothing of the *hauts* and the *bas*——"

"He has seen the bills which I gave to you, and which (so you told me) should not be negotiated," Birotteau went on, interrupting the rattle in his turn; "he has seen them with the words 'without guarantee' written upon them."

"Well," said Claparon, "and as a matter of fact they will not be negotiated; they are in the hands of a man with whom I do a great deal of business—old Bidault. That is why I put 'without guarantee' on them. If the bills had been meant to be put in circulation, you would have made them to his order in the first place. M. Lebas, as a judge, will understand my position. What do the bills represent? The price of some landed property. To be paid by whom? By Birotteau. Why would you have me guarantee Birotteau by my signature? We must, each of us, pay our share of the aforesaid price. Now, isn't it enough to be jointly and severally responsible to the vendors? I have made an inflexible rule in business: I no more give my signature for nothing than I give a receipt for money that is still to be paid. I assume the worst. Who signs, pays. I don't want to be laid open to pay three times over."

"Three times," said César.

"Yes, sir," said Claparon. "I have already guaranteed Birotteau to the vendors; why should I guarantee him again to the bill-discounter? Our case is a hard one; Roguin goes off with a hundred thousand francs of mine; so, even now, my half of the land is costing me five hundred thousand instead of four. Roguin has taken two hundred and forty thousand francs belonging to Birotteau. What would you do in my place, M. Lebas? Put yourself in my shoes. I have not the honor of being known to you, any more than I know M. Birotteau. Do you take me? We go halves in a business speculation. You pay down all your share of the money in cash; and as for me, I give bills for my share. I offer you the bills, and out of excessive benevolence you take them and give money for them. You learn that Claparon the rich banker, looked up to by everyone—I accept all the virtues in the world—that the virtuous Claparon is in difficulties for a matter of six millions; would you select that moment to give your name as a guarantee for mine? You would be mad! Well, now, M. Lebas, Birotteau is in the position in which I imagined Claparon to be. Don't you see that in that case, being jointly and severally responsible, I may be made to pay the purchasers; that I can be called upon to pay a second time for Birotteau's share to the extent of his bills, that is, if I back them, without having——"

"Pay whom?" interrupted the perfumer.

"Without having his half of the land," pursued Claparon, heedless of the interruption, "for I should have no hold on him; so I should have to buy it over again. So—I might pay three times over."

"Repay whom?" insisted Birotteau.

"Why, the holder of the bills; if I endorsed them, and you came to grief."

"I shall not fail, sir," said Birotteau.

"All right," said Claparon. "You have been a judge, you are a clever man of business, you know that we ought to provide for all contingencies, so do not be astonished is I act in a business-like way."

"M. Claparon is right," said Joseph Lebas.

"I am right," continued Claparon, "right from a business point of view. But this is a question of landed property. Now, what ought I myself to receive?—Money, for the vendors must be paid in coin. Let us set aside the two hundred and forty thousand francs, which M. Birotteau will find, I am sure," said Claparon, looking at Lebas. "I came to ask you for the trifling sum of twenty-five thousand francs," he added, looking at Birotteau.

"Twenty-five thousand francs!" cried César, and it seemed to him that the blood turned to ice in his veins. "But, sir, what for?"

"Eh! my dear sir, we are bound to sign, seal, and deliver the deeds in the presence of a notary. Now, as to paying for the land, we may arrange that among ourselves, but when the Treasury comes in—your humble servant! The Treasury does not amuse itself with idle words; it allows you credit from your hand to your pocket, and we shall have to come down with the money—forty-four thousand francs this week in law expenses. I was far from expecting reproaches when I came here; for, thinking that you might find it inconvenient to pay twenty-five thousand francs, I was going to tell you that by the merest chance I had saved for you——"

"What?" asked Birotteau, giving in that word that cry of distress which no man can mistake.

"A trifle! Twenty-five thousand francs in bills given to you by one and another, which Roguin gave me to discount. I have credited you with the amount as against the registration and other expenses; I will send you the account; there is a little matter to deduct for discounting them, and six or seven thousand francs will still be owing to me."

"This all seems to me to be perfectly fair," said Lebas. "In the place of this gentleman, who appears to me to understand business very well, I should act the same towards a stranger."

"This will not be the death of M. Birotteau," said Claparon; "it takes more than one blow to kill an old wolf; I have seen wolves with bullets in their heads running about like—Lord, yes, like wolves."

"Who could have foreseen such rascality on Roguin's part?" asked Lebas, as much alarmed by César's dumbness as by so vast a speculation outside the perfumery trade.

"A little more, and I should have given this gentleman a receipt for four hundred thousand francs," said Claparon, "and I was in a stew. I had paid over a hundred thousand francs to Roguin the night before. Our mutual confidence saved me. It would have seemed to us all a matter of indifference whether the money should be lying at his office or in my possession till the day when the contracts were completed."

"It would have been much better if each had deposited his money with the Bank of France till the time came for paying it over," said Lebas.

"Roguin was as good as the Bank, I thought," said César. "But he too is in this business," he added, looking at Claparon.

"Yes, for a fourth, and in name only," answered Claparon. "After the imbecility of allowing him to go off with my money, there is but one thing more out-and-out idiotic—and that would be to make him a present of some more. If he sends me back my hundred thousand francs, and two hundred thousand more on his own account, then we will see! But he will take good care not to put the money into an affair that must simmer for four years before you have a spoonful of soup. If he has only gone off with three hundred thousand francs, as they say, he will want quite fifty thousand livres a year to live decently abroad."

"The bandit!"

"Eh! goodness! An infatuation for a woman brought Roguin to that pass," said Claparon. "What man at his age can answer for it that he will not be mastered and carried away by a last fancy? Not one of us, sober as we are, can tell where it will end. A last love is the most violent. Look at Cardot, and Camusot, and Matifat—every one of them has a mistress! And if all of us are gulled, is it not our own fault? How was it that we did not suspect a notary who speculated on his own account? Any notary, any bill-broker, or stockbroker who does business on his own account, is not to be trusted. Failure for them is fraudulent bankruptcy; they are sent up to the Court of Assize for trial; so, of course, they prefer a foreign court. I shall not make that blunder again. Well, well, we are all too weak to pass judgment by default on a man with whom we have dined, who has given grand balls, a man in society, in fact! Nobody complains; it is wrong."

"Very wrong," said Birotteau. "The provisions of the law with regard to liquidations and insolvency ought to be revised throughout."

"If you should happen to need me," said Lebas, addressing Birotteau, "I am quite at your service."

"M. Birotteau has need of no one," said the indefatigable prattler (du Tillet had opened the sluices after pouring in the water, and Claparon was repeating a lesson which du Tillet had very skilfully taught him). "His position is clear. Roguin's estate will pay a dividend of fifty per cent, from what young Crottat tells me. Besides the dividend, M. César will come by the forty thousand francs which the lender on the mortgage did not pay over; he can raise more money on his property; and we have four months in which to pay two hundred thousand francs to the vendors. Between now and then M. Birotteau will meet his bills (for he ought not to reckon on meeting them with the money which Roguin made off with). But if M. Birotteau should find himself a little pinched . . . well, with one or two accommodation bills, he will pull through."

The perfumer took heart as he listened. Claparon analyzed the business, summed it up, and traced out a plan of action, as it were, for him. Gradually his expression grew decided and resolute, and he conceived a great respect for the ex-commercial traveler's business capacity. Du Tillet had thought it expedient to make Claparon believe that he was one of Roguin's victims. He had given Claparon a hundred thousand francs to give to Roguin, who returned them to du Tillet. Claparon, being uneasy, played his part to the life; he told anybody who cared to listen to him that Roguin had mulcted him of a hundred thousand francs. Du Tillet doubted Claparon's strength of mind; he fancied that principles of honesty and conscientious scruples still lingered in his puppet, and would not confide the whole of his plans to him; he knew, moreover, that his instrument was incapable of guessing at them.

A day came when his commercial go-between reproached him. "If our first friend is not our first dupe, we should never find a second," said du Tillet, and he broke in pieces the tool which was no longer useful.

M. Lebas and Claparon went out together, and Birotteau was left alone.

"I can pull through," he said to himself. "My liabilities, in the shape of bills to be met, amount to two hundred and thirty-five thousand francs. That is to say—seventy-five thousand francs for the house, and a hundred and seventy-five thousand francs for the building-land. Now, to cover this, I have Roguin's dividend, which will amount may be to a hundred thousand francs; and I can cancel the loan on my land, that is a hundred and forty thousand francs in all. The thing to be done is to make a hundred thousand francs by the Cephalic Oil; and a few accommodation bills, or a loan from a banker, will tide me over until I can make good the loss, and the building-land reaches its enhanced value."

When a man in misfortune once can weave a romance of hope out of the more or less solid reasonings with which he fills the pillow on which he lays his head, he is often saved. Many a one has taken the confidence given by an illusion for energy.—Perhaps the half of courage is really hope, and the Catholic religion reckons hope among the virtues. Has not hope buoyed up many a weakling, giving him time to await the chances which life brings?

Birotteau made up his mind to apply, in the first place, to his wife's uncle, and to disclose his position to his relative before going elsewhere. He went down the Rue Saint-Honoré and reached the Rue Bourdonnais, not without experiencing inward pangs, which caused such violent internal disturbance that he thought his health was deranged. There was a fire in his vitals. As a matter of fact, those whose sentience is keenest in the diaphragm suffer in that region; just as those whose faculty of perception resides in the brain suffer in the head. In the grave crises, the system is attacked at the point where the temperament locates the seat of life in the individual; weaklings have the colic, a Napoleon grows drowsy.

Before a man of honor can storm a confidence and overleap the barriers of pride, he must have felt the prick of the spur of Necessity, that hard rider, more than once. So for two days Birotteau had borne that spurring before he went to see Pillerault, and then family reasons decided him—however things might go, he must explain the position to the stern ironmonger. Yet, for all that, when he reached the door, he felt in his inmost soul as a child feels on a visit to the dentist, that his courage was sinking away; and Birotteau was not about to face a momentary pang, he quailed before a whole lifetime to come. Slowly he went up the stairs, and found the old man reading the *Constitutionnel* by the fireside; on a little round table his frugal breakfast was set— a roll, butter, Brie cheese, and a cup of coffee.

"There is real wisdom," said Birotteau to himself, and he envied his uncle's life.

"Well," said Pillerault, laying down his spectacles, "I heard about Roguin's affair yesterday at the Café David; so his mistress, *La belle Hollandaise,* is murdered! I hope that, warned by us who want to be actual proprietors, you have been to Claparon and taken a receipt?"

"Alas! uncle, that is just it; vou have laid your finger on the spot. No."

"Oh, bother! you are ruined," said Pillerault, dropping his paper; and Birotteau picked it up, although it was the *Constitutionnel.*

This thought was such a shock, that Pillerault's stern features, always like a profile on a coin, grew hard as if they had been struck in bronze. He stared with steady eyes that saw nothing, through the windows, at the opposite wall, and listened while Birotteau poured out a long discourse. Evidently while he heard he deliberated; he was pondering the case with the inflexibility of a Minos who crossed the Styx of commerce, when he left the Quai des Morfondus for his little third-floor dwelling.

"Well, uncle," asked Birotteau at last, expecting some answer to a final entreaty to sell *rentes* worth six thousand francs a year.

"Well, my poor nephew, I cannot do it. Things have gone too far. We, the Ragons and I, shall both lose fifty thousand francs. It was by my advice that the good folk sold their shares in the Wortschin Mines. I feel myself bound, if they lose the money, not to replace their capital, but to give them a helping hand, and to help my niece and Césarine. You might perhaps all of you want bread, and you must come to me——"

"Bread, uncle?"

"Well, yes, bread. Just look the facts in the face: *you will not pull through!* Out of five thousand six hundred francs a year, I will set aside four thousand to divide between you and the Ragons. When your disaster comes, I know Constance, she will slave and deny herself everything—and so will you, César!"

"There is hope yet, uncle."

"I do not see it as you do."

"I will prove the contrary."

"Nothing would please me better."

Birotteau went without an answer for Pillerault. He had come to find comfort and encouragement, he had received a second blow; a blow less heavy than the first one, it is true;

but whereas the first had been dealt at his head, this thrust had gone to his heart, and the poor man's life lay in his affections. He had gone down part of the way, and then he turned and went up again.

"Sir," he said, in a constrained. voice, "Constance knows nothing of this, keep the secret for me at least; and beg the Ragons not to disturb the peace that I need if I am to fight against misfortune."

Pillerault made a sign of assent.

"Take courage, César," he said. "I see that you are angry with me, but some day you will acknowledge that I am right, when you think of your wife and daughter."

Discouraged by this opinion given by his uncle, whose clear-headedness he acknowledged, César suddenly dropped from the heights of hope into the miry slough of uncertainty. When a man's affairs take an ugly turn like this, he is apt to become the plaything of circumstances, unless he is of Pillerault's temper; he follows other people's ideas, or his own, much as a wayfarer pursues a will-o'-the-wisp. He allows himself to be swept away by the whirlwind when he should either lie prostrate with his eyes shut, and let it pass over him, or rise and watch the direction that it takes, to escape the blast. In the midst of his anguish, Birotteau bethought himself of the necessary steps to be taken with regard to his loan. He went to see Derville, a consulting barrister in the Rue Vivienne, so as to set about it the sooner, if Derville should see any chance of cancelling the contract. Him he found sitting, wrapped in his white flannel dressing-gown, by the fireside, staid and self-possessed, as is the wont of men of law, accustomed as they are to the most harrowing disclosures. Birotteau felt, as a new thing in his experience, this necessary coolness; it was like ice to an excited man like Birotteau, telling the story of his misfortunes, smarting from the wounds that he had received, stricken with the fever induced by the risks his fortunes were running, and cruelly beset, since honor and life and wife and child were all imperiled.

"If it is proved," said Derville, when he had heard him out, "that the lender no longer had in Roguin's keeping the sum of money which Roguin induced you to borrow of him, as there has been no transfer of the actual money, the contract might be annulled, and the lender will have his remedy (as you also will have for your hundred thousand francs) in Roguin's caution-money. In that case, I will answer for your lawsuit, so far as it is possible to answer for any action at law, for no action is a foregone conclusion."

The opinion of so learned an expert put a little heart into Birotteau. He begged Derville to obtain a judgment within a fortnight. The advocate answered to the effect that Birotteau might be obliged to wait three months before the contract would be annulled.

"Three months!" cried Birotteau, who thought that he had found an expedient for raising money at once.

"Well, if you yourself succeed in gaining a prompt hearing for your case, we cannot hurry your opponent to suit your pace; he will take advantage of the delays of procedure; advocates are not always at the Palais; who knows but that the other party will let judgment go against him by default? And he will appeal. You can't set your own pace, my dear sir!" said Derville, smiling.

"But at the Tribunal of Commerce——"

"Oh!" said the advocate, "the Consular Tribunal is one thing, and the Tribunal of First Instance is another. You do things in a slashing way over yonder. Now, at the Palais de Justice there are formalities to be gone through. These formalities are the bulwarks of Justice. How would you like it if a demand for forty thousand francs was suddenly fired off at you? Well, your opponent, who will see that amount compromised, will dispute it. Delays are the *chevaux-de-frise* of the law."

"You are right," said Birotteau, and he took leave of Derville with a deadly chill at his heart.—"They are all right. Money! Money!" cried the perfumer, out in the street, talking

to himself, as is the wont of busy men in this turbulent seething Paris, which a modern poet calls "a vat."

As he came into his shop, one of the assistants, who had
been out delivering invoices to the customers, told him that
as the New Year was at hand, every one had torn off the re-
ceipt-form at the foot and kept the invoices.

"Then there is no money anywhere!" Birotteau exclaimed
aloud in the shop. All the assistants looked up at this, and he
bit his lips.

In this way five days went by; and during those five days
Braschon, Lourdois, Thorien, Grindot, Chaffaroux, and all
the creditors whose bills remained unpaid, passed through
the chameleon's intermediate transitions of tone, from the
serene hues of confidence to the wrathful red of the commercial Bellona. In Paris, in such crises, suspicion is as quick
to reach the panic stage as confidence is slow to show expan-
sive symptoms; and when a creditor once adopts the restrin-
gent system of doubts and precautions in business relations, he
is apt to descend to underhand villainies that put him below
his debtor's level. From cringing civility, the creditors passed
successively through the inflammatory phase, the red of impatience, the lurid coruscations of importunity, to outbursts
of disappointment, and from the cold-blue stage of making
up their minds to the black insolence of threatening to serve
a writ.

Braschon, the rich furniture-dealer of the Faubourg Saint-
Antoine, who had not been included in the invitations to the
ball, sounded to arms in his quality of the creditor whose self-
love has been wounded. Paid he meant to be, and within
twenty-four hours; he required security, not deposits of furniture, but a second mortgage, the mortgage for forty thousand francs on the property in the Faubourg du Temple. In
spite of their furious recriminations, these gentry still left
César occasional intervals of peace, when he might breathe;
but instead of bringing a resolute will to carry these outworks
cf an awkward position, and so putting an end to them, Birotteau was taxing all his wits to keep the state of things from

the knowledge of his wife, and the one person who could give him counsel knew nothing of his difficulties. He stood sentinel on the threshold of his shop. He confided his momentary inconvenience to Célestin, who watched his employer with curious and astonished eyes; already César had fallen somewhat in his esteem, as men accustomed to prosperity are apt to dwindle when evil days discover that all their power consists in the increased facility of dealing with matters of every-day experience, acquired by an ordinary intelligence.

But if César lacked the mental energy required for defending himself when attacked at so many points at once, he had sufficient courage to face his position. Before the 15th of January he required the sum of sixty thousand francs, and thirty thousand of these were due on the 31st of December. Part of this sum was owing for the house, part for rent and accounts to be paid in ready money, part of it in bills to be met; with all his efforts he could only collect twenty thousand francs, so that there was a deficit of ten thousand, to be made up by the end of the month. Nothing seemed hopeless to him, for he had already ceased to look beyond the present moment, and, like an adventurer, had begun to live from day to day. At length he resolved to make what for him was a bold stroke. Before it was known that he was in difficulties, he would apply to François Keller, banker, orator, and philanthropist, widely known for his beneficence, and for his desire to stand well with the mercantile world of Paris, always with a view to representing their interests one day as a deputy in the Chamber. In politics the banker was a Liberal, and César was a Royalist; but the perfumer decided that the capitalist was a man after his own heart, and that a difference of opinion in politics was but one reason the more for opening an account. If paper should be necessary, he did not doubt Popinot's devotion, and counted upon obtaining from him some thirty bills of a thousand francs each; with these he might hold out until he gained his lawsuit, the forty thousand francs involved in it being offered as security to the most urgent creditors.

The effusive soul, who was wont to confide to the pillow of

his dear Constance the least emotions of his existence, who drew his courage from her, and was wont to seek of her the light thrown by contradiction on all topics, was cut off from all exchange of ideas with his first assistant, his uncle, and his wife, and found that the weight of his cares was thereby doubled. Yet this self-sacrificing martyr preferred suffering alone to the alternative of casting his wife's soul into the fiery furnace; he would tell her about the danger when it was past. Perhaps, too, he shrank from telling her the hideous secret; he stood in some fear of his wife, and this fear lent him courage. He went every morning to low mass at Saint-Roch, and told his troubles to God.

"If I do not meet a soldier on my way back from Saint-Roch, I will take it as a sign that my prayer is heard. It shall be God's answer to me," he said to himself, after he had prayed for deliverance.

And, for his happiness, he did not meet a soldier. Yet, nevertheless, his heart was over-full, and he needed another human heart to whom he could make moan. Césarine, to whom he had already told the fatal news, learned the whole truth, and stolen glances were exchanged between them, glances fraught with despair or repressed hope, passionate invocations, appeals, and sympathetic responses, answering gleams of intelligence between soul and soul. For his wife César put on high spirits and mirth. If Constance asked any question—"Pshaw, everything was all right. Popinot" (to whom César gave not a thought) "was doing well! The Oil was selling! Claparon's bills would be met; there was nothing to fear." The hollow merriment was ghastly. When his wife lay sleeping amid the splendors, Birotteau would rise, and fall to thinking over his misfortune; and more than once Césarine came in, in her night-shift, barefooted, with a shawl about her white shoulders.

"Papa, you are crying; I can hear you," she would say, and she would cry herself as she spoke.

When César had written to ask the great François Keller to make an appointment with him, he fell into such a state of torpor that Césarine persuaded him to walk out with her. In the streets of Paris he saw nothing but huge red placards, and the words CEPHALIC OIL in staring letters everywhere met his eyes.

While the glory of the *Queen of Roses* was thus waning in disastrous gloom, the firm of A. Popinot was dawning radiant with the sunrise splendors of success. Anselme had taken counsel of Gaudissart and Finot, and had launched his oil boldly. During the past three days two thousand placards had been posted in the most conspicuous situations in Paris. Every one in the streets was confronted with the Cephalic Oil, and willy-nilly must read the pithy remarks from Finot's pen as to the impossibility of stimulating the growth of the hair, and the perils attendant on dyeing it, together with an extract from a paper read before the Académie des Sciences by Vauquelin. It was as good as a certificate of existence for dead hair, thus held out to those who should use the Cephalic Oil. The shop-doors of every perfumer, hair-dresser, and wig-maker in Paris were made glorious with gilded frames, containing a beautiful design, printed on vellum paper, with a reduced facsimile of the picture of *Hero and Leander* at the top, and beneath it ran the motto, *The ancient peoples of antiquity preserved their hair by the use of* CEPHALIC OIL.

"He has thought of permanent frames; he has found an advertisement that will last for ever!" said Birotteau to himself, as he stood staring in dull amazement at the shop-front of the *Silver Bell*.

"Then you did not see a frame on your own door?" asked his daughter. "M. Anselme brought it himself, and left three hundred bottles of the oil with Célestin."

"No, I did not see it," he answered.

"And Célestin has already sold fifty to chance comers, and sixty to our own customers."

"Oh!" said César.

The sound of myriad bells that misery sets ringing in the ears of her victims had made the perfumer dizzy; his head seemed to spin round and round in those days. Popinot had waited a whole hour to speak with him on the day before, and had gone away after chatting with Constance and Césarine; the women told him that César was very busy over his great scheme.

"Oh yes, the building-land!" Popinot had said.

Luckily, Popinot had not left the Rue des Cinq-Diamants for a month; he had worked day and night at his business, and had seen neither Ragon, nor Pillerault, nor his uncle. _The poor lad was never in bed before two o'clock in the morning; he had only two assistants, and at the rate at which things were going he would soon have work enough for four.   Opportunity is everything in business; success is a horse which, if caught by the mane and ridden by a bold rider, will carry him on to fortune.   Popinot told himself that he should receive a welcome when, at the end of six months, he could carry the news to his aunt and uncle—"I am saved; my fortune is made!"—a welcome, too, from Birotteau when, at the end of the first half year, he should bring him his share of the profits—thirty or forty thousand francs! He had not heard of Roguin's disappearance, nor of César's consequent disasters and difficulties; so that he could not let fall any indiscreet remarks in Madame Birotteau's presence.

Popinot had promised Finot five hundred francs for each of the leading newspapers (ten in all), and three hundred francs for each second-rate paper (and of these, too, there were ten), if the Cephalic Oil was mentioned three times a month in each. Of those eight thousand francs, Finot beheld three thousand as his own, his first stake to lay on the vast green table of speculation. So he had sprung like a lion upon his friends and acquaintances; he haunted newspaper offices; writers of newspaper articles awoke from slumber to find him sitting by their pillows; and the evening found him pacing the lobbies of all the theatres. "Remember my oil, my dear fellow; it is nothing to me; a matter of good fellowship, you know; Gaudissart, a jolly dog." With this formula, his harangues always began and ended. He filled up spaces at the foot of the last columns in the papers, and left the money to those upon the staff. He was as cunning as any super who is minded to transform himself into an actor, and as active as an errand boy on sixty francs a month; he wrote insinuating letters, he worked on the vanity of all and sundry, he did dirty work for editors, to the end that his paragraphs might be inserted in their papers. His enthusiastic energy left no means untried—money, dinners, platitudes. By means of tickets for the play he corrupted the men who finish off the columns towards midnight with short paragraphs of small news items already set up; hanging about the printing-office for that purpose, as if he had proofs to revise.

So by dint of making every one his friend, Finot secured the triumph of the Cephalic Oil over the *Pâte de Regnault* and the *Mixture Brésilienne,* over all the inventions, in fact, whose promoters had the wit to comprehend the influence of journalism and the effect produced upon the public mind by the piston stroke of the reiterated paragraph. In that age of innocence, journalists, like draught-oxen, were unaware of their strength; their heads ran on actresses—Mesdemoiselles Florine, Tullia, Mariette—they lorded it over all creation, and made no practical use of their powers. In Andoche's propositions there was no actress to be applauded, no drama to be put upon the stage; he did not ask them to make a success of his vaudevilles, nor to pay him for his paragraphs; on the contrary, he offered money in season and opportune breakfasts; so there was not a newspaper that did not mention the Cephalic Oil, and how that it was in accordance with Vauquelin's investigations; not a journal that did not scoff at the superstition that the hair could be induced to grow, and proclaim the danger of dyeing it.

These paragraphs rejoiced Gaudissart's heart. He laid in a supply of papers wherewith to demolish prejudice in the provinces, and accomplished the manœuvre known among speculators since his time as "taking the public by storm." In those days newspapers from Paris exercised a great influence in the departments, the hapless country districts being still "without organs." The Paris newspaper, therefore, was taken up as a serious study, and read through from the heading to the printer's name on the last line of the last page, where the irony of persecuted opinion might be supposed to lurk.

Gaudissart, thus supported by the press, had a brilliant success from the very first in every town where his tongue had play. Every provincial shopkeeper was anxious for a frame and copies of *Hero and Leander*. Finot devised that charming joke against Macassar Oil, which drew such laughter at the Funambules, when Pierrot takes up an old house-brush, visibly worn down to the holes, and rubs it with Macassar Oil, and lo the stump becomes a mop, a piece of irony which brought down the house. In later days Finot would gaily relate how that but for those three thousand francs he must have died of want and misery. For him three thousand francs was a fortune. In this campaign he discovered the power of advertising, which he was to wield so wisely and so much to his own profit. Three months later this pioneer was the editor of a small paper, of which after a time he became the proprietor, and so laid the foundation of his fortune. Even as the Illustrious Gaudissart, that Murat among commercial travelers, "took the public by storm," and gained brilliant victories along the frontiers and in the provinces for the house of Popinot, so did the cause gain ground in public opinion in Paris, thanks to the desperate assault upon the newspapers, which gave it the prompt publicity likewise secured by the *Mixture Brésilienne* and the *Pâte de Regnault*. Three fortunes were made by this means, and then began the descent of the thousands of ambitious tradesmen who have since gone down by battalions into the arena of journalism, and there called advertising into being. A mighty revolution was wrought.

At that moment the words "Popinot & Company" were flaunting on every wall and shop door; and Birotteau, unable to measure the enormous area over which these announcements were displayed, contented himself with saying to Césarine, "Little Popinot is following in my footsteps," without comprehending the difference of the times, without appreciation of the new methods and improved means of communication which spread intelligence much more rapidly than heretofore.

Birotteau had not set foot in his factory since the ball; he did not know how busy and energetic Popinot had been. Anselme had set all Birotteau's operatives on the work, and slept in the place. He saw Césarine sitting on every packing-case and reclining on every package; her face looked at him from each new invoice. "She will be my wife!" he said to himself, as with coat thrown off, and shirt-sleeves rolled above the elbows, he hammered in the nails with all his might, while his assistants were sent out on business.

The next day, after spending the whole night in pondering what to say and what not to say to the great banker, César reached the Rue du Houssaye, and entered, with a heart that beat painfully fast, the mansion of the Liberal financier, the adherent of a political party accused, and not unjustly, of desiring the downfall of the Bourbons. To Birotteau, as to most small merchants in Paris, the manners and customs and the personality of those who move in high financial circles were quite unknown; for the smaller traders usually deal with lesser houses, which form a sort of intermediate term, a highly satisfactory arrangement for the great capitalists, who find in them one guarantee the more.

Constance and Birotteau, who had never overdrawn their balance, who had never known what it was to have no money in the safe, and no bills in the portfolio, had not had recourse to these banks of the second order; and, for the best of reasons, were entirely unknown in the higher financial world. Perhaps it is a mistaken policy sedulously to abstain from borrowing even though you may not require the money; opinions differ on this head; but be that as it may, Birotteau at that moment deeply regretted that he had never put his signature to a piece of paper. Yet, as he was known as a deputy-mayor and a shrewd man of business, he imagined that he would only have to mention his name, and he should

see the banker at once; he did not know that men flocked to
the Kellers' audiences as to the court of a king. In the ante-
chamber of the study occupied by the man with so many
claims to greatness, Birotteau found himself among a crowd
composed of deputies, writers, journalists, stockbrokers, great
merchants, men of business, engineers, and, above all, of fa-
miliars, who made their way through the groups of speakers
and knocked in a particular manner at the door of the study,
where they had the privilege of entry.

"What am I in the middle of this machinery?" Birotteau
asked himself, quite bewildered by the stir and bustle in this
factory, where so much brain-power was at work furnishing
daily bread for the camp of the Opposition; this theatre where
rehearsals of the grand tragi-comedy played by the Left were
wont to take place.

On one hand he heard a discussion relative to a loan that
was being negotiated to complete the construction of the
principal lines of canal recommended by the Department of
Roads and Bridges; a question of millions! On the other,
journalists, the bankers' jackals, were talking of yesterday's
sitting and of their patron's *extempore* speech. During the
two hours while he waited, he saw the banker-politician thrice
emerge from his cabinet, accompanying some visitor of importance for a few paces through the ante-chamber. Keller
went as far as the door with the last—General Foy.

"It is all over with me!" Birotteau said to himself, and
something clutched at his heart.

As the great banker returned to his cabinet, the whole troop
of courtiers, friends, and followers crowded after him, like
the canine race about some attractive female of the species.
One or two bolder curs slipped in spite of him into the audience chamber. The conferences lasted for five minutes, ten
minutes, a quarter of an hour. Some went away visibly chop-
fallen; some with a satisfied look; some assumed important
airs. Time went by, and Birotteau looked anxiously at the
clock. No one paid the slightest attention to the man with a
secret care, sighing restlessly in the gilded chair by the

hearth, at the very door of the closet that contained that panacea for all troubles—credit.

Dolefully César thought how that he too in his own house, and for a little while, had been a king, as this man was, morning after morning; and he fathomed the depths of the abyss into which he was falling. He had bitter thoughts! How many unshed tears were crowded into those two hours! How many petitions he put up that this man might incline a favorable ear; for beneath the husk of popularity-seeking goodnature, Birotteau instinctively felt that there lurked in Keller an insolent, tyrannous, and violent temper, a brutal craving to domineer, which alarmed his meek nature. At length, when but ten or a dozen people were left, Birotteau determined to start up when the outer door of the audience chamber creaked on its hinges, and to put himself on a level with the great public speaker with the remark, "I am Birotteau!" The first grenadier who flung himself into the redoubt at Borodino did not display more courage than the perfumer when he made up his mind to carry out this manœuvre.

"After all," said he to himself, "I am his deputy-mayor," and he rose to give his name.

François Keller's countenance took on an amiable expression; clearly he meant to be civil; he glanced at Birotteau's red ribbon, turned, opened the door of his cabinet, and indicated the way; but stayed behind himself for a while to speak with two newcomers who sprang up the staircase with tempestuous speed.

"Decazes would like to speak with you," said one of these two.

"It is a question of making an end of the Pavillon Marsan! The King sees clearly. He is coming over to us!" cried the other.

"We will all go to the Chambers," returned the banker, and he entered his cabinet with the air of the frog that would fain be an ox.

"How can he think of his own affairs?" thought César, overwhelmed.

The radiance of the sun of superiority dazzled the perfumer, as the light blinds those insects which can only exist in the shade or in the dusk of a summer night. Birotteau saw a copy of the Budget lying on a vast table, among piles of pamphlets and volumes of the *Moniteur,* which lay open, displaying marked passages, past utterances of a Minister, which were shortly to be hurled at his head; he was to be made to eat his words amid the plaudits of a crowd of dunces, incapable of comprehending that events modify everything. On another table stood a collection of boxes full of papers, a heap of memorials and projects, the thousand and one reports confided to a man in whose exchequer every nascent industry endeavors to dip.

The regal splendor of the cabinet, filled with pictures and statues and works of art; the litter on the chimney-piece; the accumulations of documents relating to business concerns at home and abroad, heaped up like bales of goods,—all these things impressed Birotteau; he dwindled in his own eyes, his nervousness increased, the blood ran cold in his veins.

On François Keller's desk there lay some bundles of bills, letters of exchange, and circular-letters. To these the great man addressed himself; and as he swiftly put his signature to those that required no examination, "To what do I owe the honor of your visit, sir?" asked he.

At these words addressed to him alone, by the voice that spoke to all Europe, while the restless hand never ceased to traverse the paper, the poor perfumer felt as if a red-hot iron had been thrust through his vitals. His face forthwith assumed that ingratiating expression with which the banker had grown familiar during ten years of experience; the expression always meant that the wearers desired to involve the house of Keller in some affair of great importance to the would-be borrowers and to no one else, an expression which shuts the banker's doors upon them at once. So François Keller shot a glance at César, a Napoleonic glance, which seemed to go through the perfumer's head. This imitation of their Emperor was a slight piece of affectation which certain parvenus permitted themselves, though the false coin was scarcely a passable copy of the true. For César, of the extreme Right in politics, the fanatical partisan of the Government, the factor in the monarchical election, that glance was like the stamp which a custom-house officer sets on a bale of goods.

"I do not want to take up your minutes unduly, sir; I will be brief. I have come on a simple matter of private business, to know if you will open a loan account with me. As an ex-judge of the Tribunal of Commerce, and a man well known at the Bank of France, you can understand that if I had bills to discount I should only have to apply to the Bank where you are a Governor. I have had the honor of being associated in my functions at the Tribunal with M. le Baron Thibon, the head of the bill-discounting department, and he certainly would not refuse me. But as I have never tried to borrow money nor accepted a bill, my signature is unknown, and you know how many difficulties lie in the way of negotiating a loan in such a case——"

Keller moved his head; and Birotteau, construing this as a sign of impatience, continued:

"The fact is, sir, that I have engaged in a speculation in land, outside my own line of business——"

François Keller, still signing and reading, and, to all appearance, paying no attention to César's remarks, turned at this, with a sign that he was following what was said. Birotteau took heart; his affair was in a promising way, he thought; he breathed more freely.

"Go on; I understand," said Keller good-humoredly.

"I am the purchaser of one-half of the building-land near the Madeleine."

"Yes. I heard from Nucingen of the big affair that the firm of Claparon is negotiating."

"Well," the perfumer went on, "a loan of a hundred thousand francs, secured on my share of the land, or on my business, would suffice to tide me over until I can touch the profits which must shortly accrue from a venture in my own way of business. If necessary, I would cover the amount by bills drawn on a new firm—Popinot & Company, a young house which——"

Keller seemed to be very little interested in this description of the firm of Popinot, and Birotteau gathered that he had somehow taken a wrong turn; he stopped; then, in dismay at the pause, he went on again.

"As for the interest, we——"

"Yes, yes," said the banker; "the thing may be arranged, and do not doubt my desire to meet you in the matter. Occupied as I am, I have all the finances of Europe on my hands, and the Chamber absorbs every moment of my time, so you will not be surprised to hear that I leave the investigation of a vast amount of regular business to my managers. Go downstairs, and see my brother Adolphe; explain the nature of your guarantees to him; and if he assents, return here with him to-morrow or the day after, at the time when I look into affairs of this kind, at five o'clock in the morning. We shall be proud and happy to receive your confidence; you are one of the consistent Royalists; and your esteem is the more flattering, since that politically we may find ourselves at enmity."

"Sir," said the perfumer, elated by this oratorical flourish, "I am as deserving of the honor you do me as of the signal mark of Royal favor . . . not unmerited by the discharge of my functions at the Consular Tribunal, and by fighting for——"

"Yes," continued the banker, "the reputation which you enjoy is a passport, M. Birotteau. You are sure to propose nothing that is not feasible, and you can reckon upon our co-operation."

A door, which Birotteau had not noticed, was opened, and a woman entered; it was Mme. Keller, one of the two daughters of the Comte de Gondreville, a peer of France.

"I hope I shall see you, dear, before you go to the Chamber," said she.

"It is two o'clock," exclaimed the banker; "the battle has begun. Excuse me, sir,—the question is one of upsetting a ministry——" he went as far as the door of the salon with the perfumer, and bade a man in livery, "Take this gentleman to M. Adolphe."

Birotteau traversed a labyrinth of staircases on the way to a private office, less sumptuous than the cabinet of the head of the firm, but more business-like in appearance; he was borne along by an *if,* that easiest pacing mount that hope can furnish; he stroked his chin, and thought that the great man's compliments augured excellently well for his plans. It was regrettable that a man so amiable, so capable, so great an orator, should be inimical to the Bourbons.

Still full of these illusions, he entered M. Adolphe Keller's sanctum, a bare, chilly-looking room. Dingy curtains hung in the windows, the floor was covered with a much-worn carpet, and the furniture consisted of a couple of cylinder desks and one or two office chairs. This cabinet was to the first as the kitchen to the dining-room, as the factory to the shop. Here matters of business were penetrated to the core, here enterprises were analyzed, and preliminary charges levied by the bank on all promising undertakings. Here originated all those bold strokes for which the Kellers were so well known in the highest commercial regions, when they would secure and rapidly exploit a monopoly in a few days. Here, too, omissions on the part of the legislature received careful attention, and unblushing demands were made for "sops in the pan" (in the language of the Stock Exchange), that is to say, for money paid in consideration for small indefinable services, for standing godfather to an infant enterprise, and so accrediting it. Here were woven those tissues of fraud after a legal pattern, which consist in investing money as a sleeping-partner in some concern in temporary difficulties, with a view to slaughtering the affair as soon as it succeeds; the brothers would lie in wait, call in their capital at a critical moment, an ugly manœuvre that put the whole thing in their own hands, and involved the hapless active partner in their toils.

The two brothers adopted separate *rôles.* On high stood

François, the politician, the man of brilliant parts; he bore himself like a king, he distributed favors and promises, he made himself agreeable to every one. Everything was easy when you spoke with him; he did business royally; he poured out the heady wine of fair words, which intoxicated inexperienced speculators and promoters of new schemes; he developed their own ideas for them. But Adolphe below absolved his brother on the score of political preoccupations, and cleverly raked in the winnings; he was the responsible brother, the one who was hard to persuade; so that there were two words to every bargain concluded with that treacherous house, and not seldom the gracious Yes of the sumptuous cabinet was transmuted into a dry No in Adolphe's office.

This manœuvre of delay gained time for reflection, and often served to amuse less skilful competitors.

Adolphe Keller was chatting with the famous Palma, the trusted counselor of the house, who withdrew as Birotteau came in. The perfumer explained his errand; and Adolphe, the more cunning of the two brothers, lynx-natured, keen-eyed, thin-lipped, hard-favored, listened to him with lowered head, watching the app'icant over his spectacles, eyeing him the while with what must be called the banker's gaze, in which there is something of the vulture, something of the attorney; a gaze at once covetous and cold, clear and inscrutable, sombre and ablaze with light.

"Will you be so good as to send me the documents relative to this Madeleine affair," said he, "since therein lies the guarantee of the account; they must be examined into before we begin to discuss the case on its merits. If the affair is satisfactory, we might possibly, to avoid encumbering you, be content to take part of the profits instead of discount."

"Come," said Birotteau to himself, as he went home again, "I see his drift. Like the hunted beaver, I must part with some of my skin. It is better to loose your fleece than to lose your life."

He went upstairs in high spirits, and his mirth had a genuine ring.

"I am saved," he told Césarine; "Keller will open a loan account with me."

But not until the 29th of December could Birotteau gain admittance a second time to Adolphe Keller's office. On the occasion of his first call, Adolphe was six leagues away from Paris, looking at some property which the great orator had a mind to buy. The next time both the Kellers were closeted together, and could see no one that morning; it was a question of a tender for a loan proposed by the Chambers, and they begged M. Birotteau to return on the following Friday. These delays were heartbreaking to the perfumer; but Friday came at last, and Birotteau sat by the fire in the office, with the daylight falling full on his face, and Adolphe Keller, sitting opposite, was saying, as he held up the notarial deeds, "These are all right, sir; but what proportion of the purchase-money have you paid?"

"A hundred and forty thousand francs."

"In money?"

"In bills.

"Have they been met?"

"They have not fallen due."

"But suppose that you have given more for the land than it is actually worth (taking it at its present value), where is our guarantee? We should have no security but the good opinion which you inspire and the esteem in which you are held. Business is not based on sentiment. If you had paid two hundred thousand francs, supposing that you have given too much by a hundred thousand francs to get possession of the land, we should in that case have at any rate a guarantee of a hundred thousand francs for the hundred thousand you want to borrow. The result for us would be that we should be owners of the land in your place, by paying your share; in that case we must know if it is a good piece of business. For if we are to wait five years to double our capital, it would be better to put the money out to interest through the bank. So many things may happen. You want to draw an accommodation bill to meet your bills when they fall due? It is a risky thing to do! You go back to take a leap better. This is not in our way of business."

For Birotteau, it was as if the executioner had touched his shoulder with the branding-iron. He lost his head.

"Let us see," said Adolphe, "my brother takes a warm interest in you; he spoke of you to me. Let us look into your affairs," he added, and he glanced at the perfumer with the expression of a courtesan pressed for a quarter's rent.

Birotteau became a Molineux, and acted the part of the man at whom he had laughed so loftily. Kept in play by the banker, who took a pleasure in unwinding the skein of the poor man's thoughts, and showed himself as expert in the art of examining a merchant as the elder Popinot was skilled in unloosing a criminal's tongue, César told the story of his business career; he brought the Pâte des Sultanes and the Toilet Lotion upon the scene; he gave a complete account of his dealings with Roguin, and, finally, of the lawsuit with regard to that mortgage from which he had reaped no benefit. He saw Keller's musing smile and jerk of the head from time to time, and said to himself, "He is giving an ear to me! He is interested; I shall have my loan!" and Adolphe Keller was laughing at Birotteau, as Birotteau himself had laughed at Molineux. Carried away by the impulse of loquacity peculiar to those people on whom misfortune has an intoxicating effect, César showed himself as he really was; he helped the banker to take his measure when he suggested as his final expedient the Cephalic Oil and the firm of Popinot by way of a guarantee. Led away by a delusive hope, he allowed Adolphe Keller to fathom him and examine into his affairs, until Adolphe Keller saw in the man before him a Royalist blockhead on the brink of bankruptcy. Then, delighted at the prospect of this failure of the deputy-mayor of his arrondissement, of a man whose party was in power, who had been but lately decorated, Adolphe told Birotteau plainly that he could neither open a loan account with him, nor speak on his behalf to the orator brother, the great François. If François were inclined to extend an imbecile generosity to a political adversary, and to come to the aid of a man who held opinions diametrically opposed to his own, he, Adolphe, had no mind that his brother should be a dupe; he would do all that in him lay to prevent his brother from holding out a helping hand to one of Napoleon's old antagonists, to a man who was wounded at Saint-Roch. Birotteau, exasperated at this, tried to say something about covetousness in the high places of the financial world, of hard-heartedness and sham philanthropy; but he was overcome with such terrible distress, that he could scarcely stammer out a few words about the institution of the Bank of France, to which the Kellers had recourse.

"But the Bank of France will never make an advance which a private bank declines," said Adolphe Keller.

"It has always seemed to me," said Birotteau, "that the Bank was not fulfilling the purpose for which it was established, when the governors congratulate themselves on a oalance-sheet in which they have only lost one or two hundred thousand francs in transactions with the mercantile world of Paris; it is the province of the Bank to watch over and foster trade."

Adolphe began to smile, and rose to his feet like a man who is bored.

"If the Bank began to finance all the men in difficulties on 'Change, where rascality congregates in the slipperiest places of the financial world, the Bank would file her schedule before a year was out. The Bank is hard put to it as it is to guard against accommodation bills and fraudulent letters of exchange, and how would it be possible to examine into the affairs of every one who should be minded to apply for assistance?"

"I want ten thousand francs for to-morrow, Saturday the 30th; and where are they to come from?" Birotteau asked himself, as he crossed the court.

When the 31st is a holiday, payment is due on the 30th, according to custom. César's eyes were so full of tears that, as he reached the great gateway, he scarcely saw a handsome

English horse, covered with foam, that pulled up sharply at the gate, and one of the neatest cabriolets to be seen in the streets of Paris. He would fain have been run over by the cabriolet; it would be an accidental death, and the confusion in his affairs would have been set down to the suddenness of the catastrophe. He did not recognize du Tillet's slender figure in faultless morning dress, or see him fling the reins to his servant and put a rug over the back of the thoroughbred.

"What brings *you* here?" asked du Tillet, addressing his old master.

Du Tillet knew quite well why Birotteau had come. The Kellers had made inquiries of Claparon, and Claparon, taking his cue from du Tillet, had blighted the perfumer's old-established business reputation. The tears in the unlucky merchant's eyes told the tale sufficiently plainly, in spite of his sudden effort to keep them back.

"Perhaps you have been asking these Turks to oblige you in some way," said du Tillet, "cut-throats of commerce that they are, who have played many a mean trick; they will make a corner in indigo, for instance; they lower rice, forcing holders to sell cheap, so that they can get the game into their own hands and control the market; they are inhuman pirates, who know neither law, nor faith, nor conscience. You cannot know what things they are capable of doing. They will open a loan account with you if you have some promising bit of business; and as soon as you have gone too far to draw back, they will pull you up and put pressure upon you till you make the whole affair over to them for next to nothing. Pretty stories they could tell you at Havre and Bordeaux and Marseilles about the Kellers! Politics are a cloak that cover a lot of dirty doings, I can tell you! So I make them useful without scruple. Let us take a turn or two, my dear Birotteau. —Joseph, walk the horse up and down, he is overheated, and a thousand crowns is a big investment in horse-flesh."

He turned towards the Boulevard.

"Now, my dear master (for you used to be my master), is it money that you need? And they have asked you for secur-

ity, the wretches! Well, for my own part, I know you; and I
can offer to give you cash against your bills. I have made my
money honorably, and with unheard-of toil. I went in quest
of fortune to Germany! At this time of day, I may tell you
this—that I bought up the King's debts there for forty per
cent of their value; your guarantee was very useful to me
then, and I am grateful. If you want ten thousand francs,
they are at your service."

"What! du Tillet," cried César, "do you really mean it?
Are you not making game of me? Yes, I am a little pressed
for money, just for the moment——"

"I know; Roguin's affair," returned du Tillet. "Eh! yes.
I myself have been let in there for ten thousand francs, which
the old rogue borrowed of me to run away with; but Mme.
Roguin will repay the money out of her claims on his estate.
I advised her, poor thing, not to be so foolish as to give up her
fortune to pay debts contracted for a mistress; it would be
very well if she could pay them all, but how is she to make
distinctions in favor of this or that creditor, to the prejudice
of others? You are no Roguin; I know you," continued du
Tillet; "you would rather blow your brains out than cause
me to lose a sou. Here we are in the Rue de la Chaussée-
d'Antin; come up and see me."

It pleased the young upstart to take his old employer, not
through the offices, but by way of the private entry, and to
walk deliberately, so as to give him a full view of a handsome
and luxuriously furnished dining-room, adorned with pictures bought in Germany; through two drawing-rooms, more
splendid and elegant than any rooms that Birotteau had yet
seen save in the Duc de Lenoncourt's house. The good citizen was dazzled by the gilding, the works of art, the costly
knickknacks, precious vases, and countless little details. All
the glories of Constance's rooms paled before this display,
and knowing, as he did, the cost of his own extravagance—
"Where can he have found all these millions?" said he to
himself.

Then they entered a bedroom, which as much surpassed his

wife's as the mansion of a great singer at the Opéra sur-
passes the third-floor dwelling of some supernumerary. The
ceiling was covered with violet satin relieved with silken folds
of white, and the white fur of an ermine rug beside the bed
brought out in contrast all the violet tints of a carpet from
the Levant. The furniture and the accessories were novel in
form, and exhibited the very refinement of extravagance.
Birotteau stopped in front of an exquisite timepiece, with a
Cupid and Psyche upon it, a replica of one which had just
been made for a celebrated banker. At length master and
assistant reached a cabinet, the dainty sanctum of a fashionable dandy, redolent rather of love than of finance. It was
Mme. Roguin, doubtless, who, in her gratitude for the care
and thought given to her fortune, had bestowed, by way of a
thank-offering, the paper-cutter of wrought gold, the carved
malachite paper-weights, and all the costly gewgaws of un-
bridled luxury. The carpet, one of the richest products of
the Belgian loom, was as great a surprise to the eyes as its
soft, thick pile to the tread. Du Tillet drew a chair to the
fire for the poor dazzled and bewildered perfumer.

"Will you breakfast with me?" He rang the bell; it was
answered by a servant, who was better dressed than the visitor.

"Ask M. Legras to come up, and then tell Joseph to return, you will find him at the door of Keller's bank; and you
can go to Adolphe. Keller's house, and say that instead of
seeing him now, I shall wait till he goes on 'Change. Send
up breakfast, and be quick about it."

This talk dazed the perfumer.

"So he, du Tillet, makes that formidable Adolphe Keller
come to him at his whistle, as if he were a dog!"

A hop-o'-my-thumb of a page came in and spread a table
so slender, that it had escaped Birotteau's notice, setting
thereon a Strasbourg pie, a bottle of Bordeaux wine, and
various luxuries which did not appear on Birotteau's table
twice in a quarter, on high days and holidays. Du Tillet was
enjoying himself. His feeling of hatred for the one man who

had a right to despise him diffused itself like a warm glow
through his veins, till the sight of Birotteau stirred in the
depths of his nature the same sensations that the spectacle of
a sheep struggling for its life against a tiger might give. A
generous thought flashed across him; he asked himself
whether he had not carried his vengeance far enough; he
hesitated between the counsels of a newly-awakened pity and
those of a hate grown drowsy.

"Commercially speaking, I can annihilate the man," he
thought; "I have power of life and death over him, over his
wife, who kept me on the rack, and his daughter, whose hand
once seemed to me to grasp a whole fortune. I have his
money as it is, so let us be content to let the poor simpleton
swim to the end of his tether, which I shall hold."

But honest folk are wanting in tact; they do what seems
good to them without calculating its effect on others, because
they themselves are straightforward, and have no after-
thoughts. So Birotteau filled up the measure of his own misfortune; he irritated the tiger; all unwittingly he sent a shaft
home, and made an implacable enemy of him at a word, by his
praise, by giving expression to his honest thoughts, by the
sheer light-heartedness which is the gift of a blameless conscience. The cashier came in; and du Tillet said, looking
towards César, "M. Legras, bring me ten thousand francs in
cash, and a bill for the amount payable to my order in ninety
days by this gentleman, who is M. Birotteau, as you know."

Du Tillet waited on his guest, and poured out a glass of
Bordeaux wine for him; and Birotteau, who thought himself
saved, laughed convulsively, fingered his watch-chain, and did
not touch the food until his ex-assistant said, "You do not
eat." In this way he laid bare the depths of the gulf into
which du Tillet's hand had plunged him, while the hand
which had drawn him out was still stretched over him, and
might yet plunge him back again. When the cashier returned,
and the bill had been accepted, and César felt the ten banknotes in his pocket, he could no longer contain his joy. But a
moment ago the news that he could not meet his engagements

seemed to be about to be published abroad through his Quarter, the Bank must know it, he must confess that he was ruined to his wife; now everything was safe! The joy of his deliverance was as keen as the torture of impending bankruptcy had been. Tears filled the poor man's eyes in spite of himself.

"What can be the matter, my dear master?" asked du Tillet. "Would you not do to-morrow for me what I am doing to-day for you? Isn't is as simple as saying good-day?"

"Du Tillet," said the worthy man, with solemn emphasis, as he rose and took his ex-assistant by the hand, "I restore you to your old place in my esteem."

"What! had I forfeited it?" asked du Tillet; and, for all his prosperity, he felt this rude home-thrust, and his color rose.

"Forfeited . . . not exactly that," said Birotteau, thunderstruck by his folly; "people talked about you and Mme. Roguin. The devil! another man's wife . . ."

"You are beating about the bush, old boy," thought du Tillet, in an old phrase learned in his earlier days.

And even as that thought crossed his mind, he returned to his old design. He would lay this virtue low, he would trample it under foot; all Paris should point the finger of scorn at the honest and honorable man who had caught him, du Tillet, with his hand in the till. Every hatred of every kind, political or private, between woman and woman, or between man and man, dates from some similar detection. There is no cause for hate in compromised interests, in a wound, nor even in a box on the ear; such injuries as these are not irreparable. But to be found out in some base piece of iniquity, to be caught in the act! . . . The duel that ensues between the criminal and the discoverer of the crime cannot but be to the death.

"Oh! Mme. Roguin," said du Tillet laughingly, "but isn't that rather a feather in a young man's cap? I understand you, my dear master, they must have told you that she lent me money. Well, on the contrary, it is I who have re-established her finances, which were curiously involved in her husband's affairs. My fortune has been honestly made, as I have just told you. I had nothing, as you know. Young men sometimes find themselves in terrible straits, and in dire need one may strain a point; but if, like the Republic, one has made a forced loan now and again, why, one returns it afterwards, and is as honest as France herself."

"Just so," said César. "My boy—God—Isn't it Voltaire who says:

> " He made of repentance the virtue of mortals?''

"So long as one does not take his neighbor's money in a base and cowardly way," du Tillet continued, smarting once more under this application of verse; "as if you, for instance, were to fail before the three months are out, and it would be all up with my ten thousand francs——"

"I fail?" cried Birotteau (he had taken three glasses of wine, and happiness had gone to his head). "My opinions of bankruptcy are well known. A failure is commercial death. I should die."

"Long life to you!" said du Tillet.

"To your prosperity!" returned the perfumer. "Why do you not come to me for your perfumery?"

"Upon my word," said du Tillet, "I confess that I am afraid to meet Mme. César, she always made an impression upon me; and if you were not my master, faith, I——"

"Oh! you are not the first who has thought her handsome, and wanted her, but she loves me! Well, du Tillet, my friend, do not do things by halves."

"What!"

Birotteau explained the affair of the building-land, and du Tillet opened his eyes, complimented César upon his acumen and foresight, and spoke highly of the prospects.

"Oh, well, I am much pleased to have your approbation; you are supposed to have one of the longest heads in the banking line, du Tillet! You can negotiate a loan from the Bank of France for me until the Cephalic Oil has made its way."

"I can send you to the firm of Nucingen," answered du
Tillet, inwardly vowing that his victim should dance the whole
mazy round of bankruptcy. He sat down to his desk to write
the following letter to the Baron de Nucingen:

"MY DEAR BARON,—The bearer of this letter is M. César
Birotteau, deputy-mayor of the second arrondissement, and
one of the best known manufacturing perfumers in Paris. He
desires to be put in communication with you; you need not
hesitate to do anything that he asks of you, and by obliging
him you oblige your friend,

"F. DU TILLET."

Du Tillet put no dot over the *i* in his name. Among his
business associates this clerical error was a sign which they all
understood, and it was always made of set purpose; it annulled
the heartiest recommendations, the warmest praise and instance in the body of the letter. On receiving such a note as
this, where the very exclamation-marks breathed entreaty, in
which du Tillet, figuratively speaking, went down on his
knees, his associates knew that the writer had been unable to
refuse the letter which was to be regarded as null and void.
At sight of that undotted *i*, the receiver of the letter forthwith
dismissed the applicant with empty compliments and vain
promises. Not a few men of considerable reputation in the
world are put off like children by this trick; for men of business, bankers, bill-discounters, and advocates have one and
all two methods of signing their names; one is a dead letter,
the other living. The shrewdest are deceived by it. You
must have felt the double effect of a cold communication and
a warm one to discover the stratagem.

"You are saving me, du Tillet," said César, as he read the
present specimen.

"Oh dear me," said du Tillet, "just ask Nucingen for the
money, and when he has read my letter he will let you have
all that you want. Unluckily, my own capital is locked up
at present, or I would not send you to the prince of bankers,

for the Kellers are dwarfs compared with Nucingen. He is a second Law. With my bill of exchange, you will be ready for the 15th, and after that we will see. Nucingen and I are the best friends in the world; he would not disoblige me for a million."

"It is as good as a guarantee," said Birotteau to himself, and as he went away his heart thrilled with gratitude for du Tillet. "Ah, well," he thought, "a good deed never loses its reward," and he fell incontinently to moralizing. Yet there was one bitter drop in his cup of happiness. He had, it is true, prevented his wife from looking into the ledgers for several days. Célestin must undertake the bookkeeping in addition to his work, with some help from his master; he could have wished his wife and daughter to remain upstairs in possession of the beautiful rooms which he had arranged and furnished for them; but when the first little glow of enjoyment was over, Mme. César would have died sooner than renounce the personal supervision of the details of the business, "the handle of the frying-pan," to use her own expression.

Birotteau was at his wits' end; he had done everything that he could think of to conceal the symptoms of his embarrassment from her eyes. Constance had strongly disapproved of sending in the accounts; she had scolded the assistants, and asked Célestin if he meant to ruin the house, believing that the idea was Célestin's own. And Célestin meekly bore the blame by Birotteau's orders. In the assistant's opinion, Mme. César governed the perfumer; and though it is possible to deceive the public, those of the household always know who is the real power in it. The confession was bound to come, and that soon, for du Tillet's loan would appear in the books, and must be accounted for.

As Birotteau came in at the door he saw, not without a shudder, that Constance was at her post, going through the amounts due to be paid, and doubtless balancing the books.

"How will you pay these to-morrow?" she asked in his ear, when he took his place beside her.

"With money," he replied, drawing the banknotes from his pocket, with a sign to Célestin to take them.

"But where do those notes come from?"

"I will tell you the whole story to-night.—Célestin, enter in the bill-book a bill for ten thousand francs due at the end of March, to order of du Tillet."

"Du Tillet!" echoed Constance, terror-stricken.

"I am just going to Popinot," said César. "It is too bad of me; I have not been round to see him yet. Is his oil selling?"

"The three hundred bottles which he brought are all sold out."

"Birotteau, do not go out again; I have something to say to you," said Constance. She caught her husband's arm, and drew him to her room in a hurry, which, under any other circumstances, would have been ludicrous.—"Du Tillet!" she exclaimed, when the husband and wife were together, and she had made sure that there was no one but Césarine present; "Du Tillet robbed us of three thousand francs! And you are doing business with du Tillet! A monster who—who tried to seduce me," she said in his ear.

"A bit of boyish folly," said Birotteau, suddenly transformed into a free thinker.

"Listen to me, Birotteau; you are falling out of your old ways; you never go to the factory now. There is something, I can feel it. Tell me about it; I want to know everything."

"Well, then," said Birotteau, "we have nearly been ruined; we were ruined, in fact, this very morning, but everything is set straight again," and he told the dreadful story of the past two weeks.

"So that was the cause of your illness!" exclaimed Constance.

"Yes, mamma," cried Césarine. "Father has been very brave, I am sure. If I were loved as he loves you, I would not wish more. He thought of nothing but your trouble."

"My dream has come true," said the poor wife, and pale, haggard, and terror-stricken, she sank down upon the sofa by the fireside. "I foresaw all this. I told you so that fatal night, in the old room which you have pulled down; we shall have nothing left but our eyes to cry over our losses. Poor Césarine, I——"

"Come, now; so that is what you say!" cried Birotteau. "I stand in need of courage, and are you damping it!"

"Forgive me, dear," said Constance, grasping César's hand in hers, with a tender pressure that went to the poor man's heart. "I was wrong; the misfortune has befallen us, I will be dumb, resigned, and strong to bear it. No, César, you shall never hear a complaint from me."

She sprang into César's arms, and said, while her tears fell fast, "Take courage, dear. I should have courage enough for two, if it were needed."

"There is the Oil, dear wife; the Oil will save us."

"May God protect us!" cried Constance.

"Will not Anselme come to father's assistance?" asked Césarine.

"I will go to him now," exclaimed César, his wife's heart-breaking tone had been too much for his feelings; it seemed that he did not know her yet, after nineteen years of married life. "Do not be afraid, Constance; there is no fear now. Here, read M. du Tillet's letter to M. de Nucingen; he is sure to lend us the money. Between then and now I shall have gained my lawsuit. Besides," he added (a lying hope to fit the circumstances), "there is your uncle Pillerault. Courage is all that is wanted."

"If that were all!" said Constance, smiling.

Birotteau, with the great weight taken off his mind, walked like a man set free from prison; but within himself he felt the indefinable exhaustion consequent on mental exertion which has made heavy demands upon the nervous system, and required more than the daily allowance of will-power; he was conscious of the deficit when a man has drawn, as it were, on the capital of his vitality. Birotteau was growing old already.

Popinot's shop in the Rue des Cinq-Diamants had under-

gone great changes in the last two months. It had been re-
painted. The rows of bottles ensconced in the pigeon-hole
shelves, touched up with paint, rejoiced the eyes of every
merchant who knows the signs of prosperity. The floor of the
shop was covered with packing-paper. The warehouse contained certain casks of oil, for which the devoted Gaudissart
had procured an agency for Popinot. The books were kept
upstairs in the counting-house. An old servant had been installed as housekeeper to Popinot and his three assistants.

Popinot himself, penned in a cash-desk in the corner of
the shop screened off by a glass partition, was usually arrayed
in a green baize apron and a pair of green-cloth over-sleeves,
when he was not buried, as at this moment, in a pile of papers. The post had just come in, and Popinot, with a pen
behind his ear, was taking in handfuls of business letters and
orders, when at the words, "Well, my boy?" he raised his
head, saw his late employer, locked his cash-desk, and came
forward joyously. The tip of the young man's nose was red,
for there was no fire in the shop, and the door stood open.

"I began to fear that you were never coming to see me,"
he answered respectfully.

The assistants hurried in, eager to see the great man of
the perfumery trade, their own master's partner, the deputy-
mayor who wore the red ribbon. César was flattered by this
mute homage, and he who had felt so small in the Kellers'
bank must needs imitate the Kellers. He stroked his chin,
raised himself on tiptoe once or twice with an air, and poured
forth his commonplaces.

"Well, my dear fellow, are you up early in the mornings?"
asked he.

"No, we don't always go to bed," said Popinot; "one must
succeed by hook or by crook."

"Well, what did I tell you? My Oil is a fortune."

"Yes, sir; but the method of selling it counts for something; I have given your diamond a worthy setting."

"As a matter of fact," said the perfumer, "how are we getting on? Have any profits been made?"

"At the end of a month!" cried Popinot. "Did you expect it? My friend Gaudissart has not been gone much more than three weeks. He took a post-chaise without telling me about it. Oh! he has thrown himself into this. We shall owe a good deal to my uncle! The newspapers will cost us twelve thousand francs," he added in Birotteau's ear.

"The newspapers . . .!" cried the deputy-mayor.

"Have you not seen them?"

"No."

"Then you know nothing of this," said Popinot. "Twenty thousand francs in placards, frames, and prints! . . . A hundred thousand bottles paid for! . . . Oh! it is nothing but sacrifice at this moment. We are bringing out the Oil on a large scale. If you had stepped over to the Faubourg, where I have often been at work all night, you would have seen a little contrivance of mine for cracking the nuts, which is not to be sneezed at. For my own part, during the last five days I have made three thousand francs in commission on the druggists' oils."

"What a good head!" said Birotteau, laying his hand on little Popinot's hair, and stroking it as if the young man had been a little child, "I foresaw how it would be."

Several people came into the shop.

"Good-bye till Sunday; we are going to dine then with your aunt, Mme. Ragon," said Birotteau, and he left Popinot to his own affairs. Evidently the roast which he had scented was not yet ready to carve.—"How extraordinary it is! An assistant becomes a merchant in twenty-four hours," he thought, and Birotteau was as much taken aback by Popinot's prosperity and self-possession as by du Tillet's luxurious rooms. "Here is Anselme drawing himself up a bit when I put my hand on his head, as if he were a François Keller already."

It did not occur to Birotteau that the assistants were looking on, and that the head of an establishment must preserve his dignity in his own house. Here, as in du Tillet's case the good man had made a blunder in the kindness of his heart, and the real feeling expressed in that homely familiar way would have mortified any one but Anselme.

The Sunday dinner-party at the Ragons' house was destined to be the last festivity in the nineteen years of César's married life, the life which had been so completely happy. The Ragons lived on the second floor of a quaint and rather stately old house in the Rue du Petit-Bourbon-Saint-Sulpice. Over the paneled walls of their rooms danced eighteenth century shepherdesses in hooped petticoats, amid browsing eighteenth century sheep; and the old people themselves belonged to the bourgeoisie of that bygone eighteenth century, with its solemn gravity, its quaint habits and customs, its respectful attitude to the noblesse, its loyal devotion to Church and King.

The timepieces, the linen, the plates and dishes, all the furniture in fact had such an old-world air, that by very reason of its antiquity it seemed new. The sitting-room, hung with brocatelle damask curtains, contained a collection of "duchesse" chairs and what-nots; and from the wall a superb Popinot, Mme. Ragon's father, the alderman of Sancerre, painted by Latour, smiled down upon the room like a parvenu in all his glory. Mme. Ragon at home was incomplete without her tiny King Charles, who reposed with marvelous effect on her hard little *roccco* sofa, a piece of furniture which certainly had never played the part of Crébillon's sofa.

Among the Ragons' many virtues, the possession of old wines arrived at perfect maturity was by no means the least endearing; to say nothing of certain liqueurs of Mme. Anfoux's, brought from the West Indies by the lovely Mme. Ragon's admirers, sufficiently dogged to love on without hope (so it was said). Wherefore the Ragons' little dinners were highly appreciated. Jeannette, the old cook, served the two old folk with a blind devotion; for them she would have stolen fruit to make preserves; and so far from investing her money in the savings-bank, she prudently put it in the lottery, hoping one day to carry home the great prize to her master and mistress. In spite of her sixty years, Jeannette, on Sundays when they had company, superintended the dishes in the kitchen, and waited at table with a deft quickness which would have given hints to Mlle. Contat as Suzanne in the *Marriage of Figaro.*

This time the guests were ten in number—the elder Popinot, Uncle Pillerault, Anselme, César and his wife and daughter, the three Matifats, and the Abbé Loraux. Mme. Matifat, first introduced arrayed for the dance in her turban, now wore a gown of blue velvet, thick cotton stockings, kid slippers, green-fringed chamois leather gloves, and a hat lined with pink, and adorned with blossoming auriculas.

Every one had arrived by five o'clock. The Ragons used to beg their guests to be punctual; and when the good folk themselves were asked out to dinner, their friends were careful to dine at the same hour, for at the age of seventy the digestion does not take kindly to the new-fangled times and seasons ordained by fashionable society.

Césarine knew that Mme. Ragon would seat Anselme beside her; all women, even devotees, or the feeblest feminine intellects, understand each other in the matter of a love affair. The toilette of the perfumer's daughter was designed to turn young Popinot's head. Constance, who had given up, not without a pang, the idea of the notary, who for her was an heir-presumptive to a throne, had helped Césarine to dress, certain bitter reflections mingling with her thoughts the while. Foreseeing the future, she lowered the modest gauze kerchief somewhat on Césarine's shoulders, so as to display rather more of their outline, as well as the throat on which the young girl's head was set with striking grace. The bodice *à la Grecque,* four or five folds, crossing from left to right, gave short glimpses of delicately rounded contours beneath; and the leaden-gray merino gown, with its flounces trimmed with green ornaments, clearly defined a shape which had never seemed so slender and so lissome. Gold filagree earrings hung from her ears. Her hair, dressed high *à la Chinoise,* was drawn back from her face, so that the delicate freshness of its surface and the dim tracery of the veins which suffused the white velvet with the purest glow of life, was apparent at a glance. Indeed, Césarine was so coquettishly lovely, that Mme. Matifat could not help saying so, without perceiving that the mother and daughter had felt the necessity of bewitching young Popinot.

Neither Birotteau, nor his wife, nor Mme. Matifat, nor any one else, broke in upon the delicious talk between the two young people; love glowed within them as they spoke with lowered voices in the draughty window-seat, where the cold made a miniature northeaster. Moreover, the conversation of their seniors grew animated when the elder Popinot let something drop concerning Roguin's flight, saying that this was the second notary-defaulter, and that hitherto such a thing had been unknown. Mme. Ragon had touched her brother's foot at the mention of Roguin, Pillerault had spoken aloud to cover the judge's remark, and both looked significantly from him to Mme. Birotteau.

"I know all," Constance said, and in her gentle voice there was a note of pain.

"Oh, well then," said Mme. Matifat, addressing herself to Birotteau, who humbly bent his head, "how much of your money did he run away with? To listen to the gossip, you might be ruined."

"He had two hundred thousand francs of mine. As for the forty thousand which he pretended to borrow for me from one of his clients whose money he had squandered, we are going to law about it."

"You will see that settled this coming week," said the elder Popinot. "I thought that you would not mind my explaining your position to M. le Président; he has ordered Roguin's papers to be brought into the *Chambre de Conseil;* on examination it will be discovered when the lender's capital was embezzled, and Derville's allegations can be proved or disproved. Derville is pleading in person, to save expense to you."

"Shall we gain the day?" asked Mme. Birotteau.

"I do not know," Popinot answered. "Although I belong to the Chamber before which the case will come, I shall re-

frain from deliberating upon it, even if I should be called
upon to do so."

"But can there be any doubt about such a straightforward
case?" asked Pillerault. "Ought not the deed to state that
the money was actually paid down, and must not the notaries
declare that they have seen it handed over? Roguin would go
to the galleys if he fell into the hands of justice."

"In my opinion," the judge answered, "the lender should
look to Roguin's caution-money and the amount paid for
the practice for his remedy; but sometimes, in still simpler
cases than this, the Councillors at the Court-Royal have been
divided six against six."

"What is this, mademoiselle; has M. Roguin run away?"
asked Popinot, overhearing at last what was being said. "M.
César said nothing about it to me—to me who would give my
life for him . . ."

Césarine felt that the whole family was included in that
"for him"; for if the girl's inexperience had not understood
the tone, she could not mistake the look that wrapped her
in a rosy flame.

"I was sure of it; I told him so, but he hid it all from
mother, and told his secret to no one but me."

"You spoke to him of me in this matter," said Popinot;
"you read my heart, but do you read all that is there?"

"Perhaps."

"Oh! I am very happy," said Popinot. "If you will re-
move all my fears, in a year's time I shall be so rich that your
father will not receive me so badly when I shall speak to him
then of our marriage. Five hours of sleep shall be enough
for me now of a night . . ."

"Do not make yourself ill," said Césarine, and no words
can reproduce the tones of her voice as she gave Popinot a
glance wherein all her thoughts might be read.

"Wife," said César, as they rose from table, "I think those
young people are in love."

"Oh, well, so much the better," said Constance gravely; "my
daughter will be the wife of a man who has a head on his

shoulders and plenty of energy. Brains are the best endowment in a marriage."

She hurried away into Mme. Ragon's room. During dinner, César had let fall several remarks which had drawn a smile from Pillerault and the judge, so plainly did they exhibit the speaker's ignorance; and it was borne in upon the unfortunate woman how little fitted her husband was to struggle with misfortune. Constance's heart was heavy with unshed tears. Instinctively she mistrusted du Tillet, for all mothers understand *timeo Danaos et dona ferentes* without learning Latin. She wept, and her daughter and Mme. Ragon, with their arms about her, could not learn the cause of her trouble.

"It is the nerves," said she.

The rest of the evening was spent over the card-table by the old people, and the younger ones played the blithe childish games styled "innocent amusements," because they cover the innocent mischief of bourgeois lovers. The Matifats joined the young people.

"César," said Constance, as they went home again, "go to M. le Baron de Nucingen some time about the 8th, so as to be sure some days beforehand that you can meet your engagements on the 15th. If there should be any hitch in your arrangements, would you raise a loan one day to pay your debts between one day and the next?"

"I will go, wife," César answered, and he grasped her hand and Césarine's in his as he added, "My darlings, I have given you bitter New Year's gifts!" And in the darkness inside the cab the two women, who could not see the poor perfumer, felt hot tears falling on their hands.

"Hope, dear," said Constance.

"Everything will go well, papa; M. Popinot told me that he would give his life for you."

"For me—and for my family; that is it, is it not?" answered César, trying to speak gaily.

Césarine pressed her father's hand in a way which told him that Anselme was her betrothed.

Two hundred cards arrived for Birotteau on New Year's Day and the two following days. This influx of tokens of favor and of false friendship is a painful thing for people who are being swept away by the current of misfortune. Three times César presented himself at the Baron de Nucingen's hôtel, and each time in vain. The New Year's festivities sufficiently excused the banker's absence. But on the last visit Birotteau went as far as the banker's private office, and learned from a German, the head clerk, that M. de Nucingen had only returned from a ball given by the Kellers at five o'clock that morning, and that he would not be visible until half-past nine. Birotteau chatted with this man for nearly half an hour, and contrived to interest the German in his affairs. So, during the day, this cabinet minister of the house of Nucingen wrote to tell César that the Baron would see him at twelve o'clock the following morning, January the 3d. Although every hour brought its drop of bitterness, that day went by with dreadful swiftness. The perfumer took a cab and drove to the hôtel; the courtyard was already blocked with carriages, and the poor honest man's heart was oppressed by the splendors of that celebrated house.

"Yet he has failed twice," he said to himself, as he went up the handsome staircase, with flowers on either side, and through the luxuriously furnished rooms by which the Baroness, Delphine de Nucingen, had made a name for herself. The Baroness strove to rival the most splendid houses in the Faubourg Saint-Germain—the houses of a circle into which as yet she had no right of entry.

The Baron and his wife were at breakfast. In spite of the number of those who were waiting in his offices for him, he said that he would see du Tillet's friends at any hour. Birotteau trembled with hope at the change which the Baron's message produced on the lackey's insolent face.

"Bardon me, my tear," said the Baron, addressing his wife, as he rose to his feet and bowed slightly to Birotteau, "dees shentleman ees ein goot Royaleest, and de indimate frient of du Dillet. Meinnesir Pirôdôt is teputy-mayor of de Second

Arrontussement, and gifs palls of Asiatic magnificence; you vill make, no doubt, his agquaintance mit bleasure."

"I should be delighted to take lessons of Mme. Birotteau, for Ferdinand——" ("Come," thought the perfumer, "she calls him Ferdinand, plump and plain")—"Ferdinand spoke of the ball to us with an admiration which says the more, because Ferdinand is very critical; everything must have been perfect. Shall you soon give another?" asked Mme. de Nucingen, with a most amiable expression.

"Madame, poor folk like us seldom amuse ourselves," answered the perfumer, doubtful whether the Baroness was laughing at him, or if her words were simply an empty compliment.

"Meinnesir Crintod suberindended de alderations in your house," said the Baron.

"Oh! Grindot! is he that nice young architect who has just come back from Rome?" asked Delphine de Nucingen. "I am quite wild about him; he is making lovely sketches for my album."

No conspirator in the hands of the executioner in the torture chamber of the Venetian Republic could have felt less at his ease in the boots than Birotteau in his ordinary clothes at that moment. Every word had for him an ironical sound.

"Ve too gif liddle palls here," the Baron continued, giving the visitor a searching glance. "Eferypody does it, you see!"

"Will M. Birotteau join us at breakfast?" asked Delphine, and indicated the luxuriously-furnished table.

"I am here on business, Mme. la Baronne, and——"

"Yes!" said the Baron, "matame, vill you bermit us to talk pizness?"

Delphine made a little gesture of assent. "Are you about to buy some perfumery?" she asked of the Baron, who shrugged his shoulders, and turned in despair to César.

"Du Dillet take de greatest inderest in you," said he.

"At last we are coming to the point," thought the hapless merchant.

"Mit his ledder, your gretid mit my house is only limited py de pounds of my own fortune . . ."

The life-giving draught which the angel bore to Hagar in the wilderness must surely have been like the dew which these outlandish words effused through Birotteau's veins. The cunning Baron clung of set purpose to the horrible accent of the German Jew, who flatters himself that he has mastered an alien tongue; for this system led to misapprehensions highly useful to him in the way of business.

"And you shall have ein gurrent aggount, dat is how we vill do it," remarked the good, the great, and venerable financier, with Alsatian geniality.

Birotteau's doubts were all laid to rest; he had had experience of business, and he knew that a man never goes into details unless he is disposed to oblige you and to carry out a plan.

"I neet not say to you that the Pank demands dree zignatures off eferypody, gif de amount is large or small. So you shall make all your pills to de order off our friend du Dillet, who vill send dem de same day to de Pank mit my zignature, and py four o'glock you shall have de amount of de pills dat you haf accept in de morning, and at Pank rate. I do not vant gommission nor discount—nor nossing; for I shall haf de bleasure of peing agreeable to you. . . . But I make one gondition!" he added, touching his nose with the forefinger of his left hand, and putting an indescribable cunning into the gesture.

"It is granted before you ask it, M. le Baron," said Birotteau, imagining that the banker meant to stipulate for a share in the profits.

"Ein gondition to vich I addach de greatest price, because I should like Montame de Nichinguenne to take, as she has said, some lessons of Montame Pirôdôt."

"M. le Baron, do not laugh at me, I beg."

"Meinnesir Pirôdôt," said the financier seriously, "it is an agreement; you are to infite us to your next pall. My wife is chealous; she would like to see your house, of vich eferypody says such great dings."

"M. le Baron!"

"Oh! if you refuse me, no loan aggount! You are in great favor. Yes! I know dat de Brefect of de Seine was go to you."

"M. le Baron!"

"You had La Pillartière, ein shentleman-in-ordinary to de King; and de goot Fentéheine, for you were wounded—at Sainte——"

"On the 13th of Vendémiaire, M. le Baron."

"You had Meinnesir de Lassebette, Meinnesir Fauqueleine of de Agademie——"

"M. le Baron!"

"Eh! *der teufel,* do not be so modest, Meester Teputy-Mayor; I haf heard dat de King said dat your pall——"

"The King?" asked Birotteau, destined to learn no more, for at this moment a young man came into the room; the sound of his footsteps, heard at a distance, had brought a bright color into Delphine de Nucingen's fair face.

"Goot-tay, my tear de Marsay," said the Baron. "Take my blace; dere are a lot of beoples in my office, dey say. Who knows why? De Mines off Wortschinne are baying two hunderd ber cent! Yes. I have receifed de aggounts. You haf a hunderd tousand francs more of ingom. dis year, Montame de Nichinguenne; you could buy girdles and kew-kaws to make yourself pretty, as if you neeted dem!"

"Good heavens!" exclaimed Birotteau. "The Ragons have sold their shares!"

"Who may these gentlemen be?" asked the young dandy with a smile.

"Dere!" said Nucingen, who had gone as far as the door already, "it looks to me as if dose bersons. . . . Te Marsay, dis is Meinnesir Pirôdôt, your berfumer, who gifs palls mit Asiatic magnificence, and has been degoraded py de King——"

De Marsay, taking up his eyeglass, remarked, "Ah! to be sure. I thought that the face was familiar. Then are you about to perfume your affairs with some efficacious oil, to make them run smoothly?"

"Ach! vell, dose Rakkons had an aggount mit me," the
Baron went on. "I put dem in de vay of ein fortune, and
dey could not vait one more day for it."

"M. le Baron!" cried Birotteau.

The worthy perfumer found himself very much in the dark
about his affairs, and fled after the banker without taking
leave of the Baroness or of de Marsay. M. de Nucingen was
on the lowest step of the stairs, but even as he reached the
door of his office, Birotteau was beside him. As he turned the
handle, he saw the despairing gesture of the poor creature,
for whom the gulf was yawning, and said:

"Eh! it is understood, is it not? See du Dillet, and ar-
ranche it all mit him."

It occurred to Birotteau that de Marsay might have some
influence with the Baron; he darted upstairs with the speed
of a swallow, and slipped into the dining-room where, by
rights, the Baroness and de Marsay should have been, for
he had left Delphine waiting for her coffee and cream. The
coffee indeed was now waiting, but the Baroness and the
young dandy had vanished; the servant looked amused at
Birotteau's astonishment, and there was nothing for it but to
go more leisurely downstairs again. From the Nucingens'
hôtel he went at once to du Tillet, only to hear that he was at
Mme. Roguin's house in the country. He took a cab, and
paid an extra fare to be driven to Nogent-sur-Marne as
quickly as if he had traveled post. But at Nogent-sur-
Marne the porter told him that *Monsieur and Madame* had set
out for Paris, and Birotteau returned quite tired out.

When he told his wife and daughter the story of his excursion, he was amazed to receive the sweetest consolation
and assurances that all would go well from Constance, who
had always taken all the little ups and downs of business as
occasions on which to utter her boding cries.

At seven o'clock the next morning, Birotteau took up his
position before du Tillet's door in the dim light. He begged
the porter to put him into communication with du Tillet's
man, and, by dint of slipping ten francs into the porter's

hands, obtained the favor of an interview with du Tillet's man; of him he asked to give him an interview with du Tillet as soon as du Tillet should be visible, and to that end a couple of gold pieces found their way into the possession of du Tillet's man. By way of these little sacrifices and great humiliations, common to courtiers and petitioners, he attained his end. At half-past eight, when his ex-assistant had slipped on a dressing-gown and shaken off the confused ideas of a man awakened from sleep, had yawned, stretched himself, and asked pardon of his old master, Birotteau found himself face to face with the tiger thirsting for revenge, the man whom he was fain to consider as his one friend in the world.

."Do not mind me," said Birotteau, replying to the apology.

"What do you want, *my good César?*" asked du Tillet; and César, not without terrible palpitations, gave the Baron de Nucingen's answer and demands to an inattentive listener, who looked about for the bellows, and scolded his man-servant for taking so long over lighting the fire.

César did not notice at first that if the master was not heedful, the man was interested; but seeing this at last, he grew confused and broke off, to begin again, spurred on by a "Go on, go on; I am listening," from the abstracted banker.

The good man's shirt was soaked with perspiration, which turned icy cold when du Tillet looked full and steadily at him, and he could see those eyes of silver streaked with a few gold threads; there was a diabolical light in them which pierced him to the heart.

"My dear master, the Bank refused your paper, passed on to Gigonnet *without guarantee* by the firm of Claparon; is that my fault? What! you have been a judge at the Consular Tribunal, how could you make such blunders? I am, before all things, a banker. I will give you my money, but I could not expose my signature to a refusal from the Bank. I live by credit. So do we all. Do you want money?"

"Can you let me have all that I need in cash?"

"That depends upon the amount to be paid. How much do you want?"

"Thirty thousand francs."

"Plenty of chimney-pots tumbling about my ears!" exclaimed du Tillet, and he burst into a laugh.

The perfumer, misled by the splendor of du Tillet's surroundings, chose to regard that laugh as a sign that the sum was a mere trifle. He breathed again. Du Tillet rang the bell.

"Tell the cashier to come up."

"He is not here yet, sir," the servant answered.

"Those rogues are laughing at me! It is half-past eight; they ought to have done a million francs' worth of business by now."

Five minutes later, M. Legras came upstairs.

"How much have we in the safe?"

"Only twenty thousand francs. Your orders were to buy thirty thousand livres per annum in *rentes,* at present price, payable on the 15th."

"That is right; I am still asleep."

The cashier gave Birotteau a sly glance, and went.

"If truth were banished from the earth, she would leave her last word with a cashier," said du Tillet. "But have you not an interest in little Popinot's business, now that he has just set up for himself?" he added, after a horrible pause, in which the sweat gathered in drops on Birotteau's forehead.

"Yes," said César innocently. "Do you think you could discount his signature for a fair amount?"

"Bring me fifty thousand francs' worth of his acceptances, and I will get them negotiated for you at a reasonable rate by one Gobseck; very easy to do business with when he has plenty of capital on his hands, and he has a good deal just now."

Birotteau went home again heartbroken. He did not see that bankers and bill-discounters were sending him backwards and forwards in a game of battledore and shuttlecock; but Constance guessed even then that it would be impossible to obtain a loan of any sort. If three bankers had already refused credit to a man as well known as the deputy-mayor, every one would hear of it, and the Bank of France was no longer to be thought of.

"Try to renew" (this was Constance's advice). "Go to your co-associate, M. Claparon, to every one, in fact, whose bills fall due on the 15th, and ask them to renew. There will be time enough then to go to bill-discounters with Popinot's bills."

"To-morrow will be the 13th!" exclaimed Birotteau, worn out with anxiety.

He was "endowed with a sanguine temperament," to quote his own prospectus; a temperament upon which the wear and tear of emotion and of thought tells so enormously, that sleep is imperatively needed to repair the waste. Césarine brought her father into the drawing-room, and played *Rousseau's Dream,* that charming composition of Hérold's, while Constance was sewing by her husband's side. The poor man lay back on the ottoman couch. Every time his eyes rested on his wife he saw a sweet smile on her lips, and so he fell asleep.

"Poor man," said Constance. "What torture is in store for him! . . . If only he can endure it!"

"Oh, mamma, what is it?" asked Césarine, seeing her mother in tears.

"I see bankruptcy ahead, darling. If your father is obliged to file his schedule, there must be no asking for pity of any one. You must be prepared to be an ordinary shop-girl, my dear. If I see you doing your part bravely, I shall have strength to begin life again. I know your father; he will not keep back one farthing; I shall give up my claims, all that we have will be sold. Take your clothes and trinkets to-morrow to Uncle Pillerault; you are not bound to lose anything, my child."

At these words, spoken with such devout sincerity, Césarine's terror knew no bounds. She thought of going to Anselme, but a feeling of delicacy withheld her.

The next morning found Birotteau in the Rue de Provence

at nine o'clock. He had fallen a victim to fresh anxieties of a totally different kind. To borrow money is not necessarily a complicated process in business; it is a matter of daily occurrence, for capital must always be found wherever a new enterprise is started; but to ask a man to renew a bill is in commercial circles what the Police Court is to the Court of Assize; it is a first step to bankruptcy, even as a misdemeanor is half-way to a crime. The secret of your weakness and your embarrassment passes out of your own keeping. A merchant delivers himself up, bound hand and foot, to another merchant, and charity is not a virtue much practised on the Stock Exchange.

The perfumer, who hitherto had walked the streets of Paris with bright confident eyes, now cast down by doubts, hesitated to go to Claparon; he was beginning to understand that with bankers the heart is merely a portion of the internal economy. Claparon had seemed to him so brutal in his coarse hilarity, and he had felt so much vulgarity in the man, that he shrank from approaching this creditor.

"He is nearer the people, perhaps he will have more soul!" This was the first word of accusation which the anguish of his position wrung from him.

César glanced up at the windows, and at the green curtains yellowed by the sun; then he drew the last of his stock of courage up from the depths of his soul, and climbed the stairs that led to a shabby mezzanine floor. He read the word *Office*, engraven in black letters on an oval brass-plate upon the door, and knocked. No one answered, so he went in.

The whole place was something more than humble; it savored of dire poverty, avarice, or neglect. No clerk showed his face behind a barrier of unpainted deal, surmounted at elbow height by a brass wire lattice, an arrangement which screened off an inner space occupied by tables and desks of blackened wood. Scattered about the deserted offices lay inkstands, in which mold was growing, quill-pens touzled like a street urchin's head, twisted up into suns with rays; the rooms were littered with cardboard cases, papers, and circulars, useless no doubt. The floor of the lobby was as worn, as damp and gritty as the floor of a lodging-house parlor. Through a door on which the word *Counting-house* was inscribed, the visitor entered a second room, where everything was in keeping with the sinister waggery displayed in the first. In one corner stood a large cage of oak with a grill of copper-wire, and a cashier's sliding window. An enormous iron letter-box had doubtless been abandoned to the rats for a playground. The open door of this cage gave a view of yet another of these whimsical offices, and of a shabby and worm-eaten green chair, a mass of horsehair escaping through a hole underneath this piece of furniture in countless corkscrew curls that called its owner's wig to mind. Evidently this room had been the drawing-room of the house before it had been converted into offices, but the only attempt at ornamental furniture was a round table covered with a green cloth, and some old chairs covered with black leather and adorned with gilt nail-heads which stood about it. The chimney-piece had some pretensions to elegance, the hearthstone was unblackened, and there were no visible signs that a fire had been lighted there. The pier-glass above it, tarnished with fly-spots, had a mean look, so had a mahogany clock-case bought at the sale of some departed notary's office furniture, a dreary object which enhanced the depressing effect of the pair of empty candle-sticks and the all-pervading sticky grime. The dinginess of the paper on the walls, drab with a rose-colored border, spoke plainly of the habitual presence of smokers and absence of ventilation. The whole stale-looking room resembled nothing so much as a newspaper editor's office. Birotteau, afraid of intruding on the banker's privacy, gave three sharp taps on the door opposite the one by which he had entered.

"Come in !" cried Claparon, and the sound of his voice evidently came from a room beyond. The perfumer could hear a good fire crackling on the hearth, but the banker was not there. This apartment did duty, as a matter of fact, for a private office. François Keller's elegantly furnished sanctum differed from the grotesque neglect of this sham capitalist's surroundings as widely as Versailles differs from the wigwam of a Huron chief; and Birotteau, who had beheld the glories of the banking world, was about to be introduced to its blackguardism.

In a sort of oblong den, contrived behind the private office, where the whole of the furniture, scarcely elegant in its prime, had been battered, broken, covered with grease, slit to rags, soiled and spoiled by the slovenly habits of the occupier, reclined Claparon, who, at sight of Birotteau, flung on a filthy dressing-gown, laid down his pipe, and drew the bed-curtains with a haste that seemed suspicious even to the innocent perfumer.

"Take a seat, sir," said du Tillet's banker puppet.

Claparon without his wig, his head tied up in a bandana handkerchief all awry, was to Birotteau's thinking the more repulsive in that his loose dressing-gown gave glimpses of a nondescript knitted woolen garment, once white, but now a dingy brown, from indefinitely prolonged wear.

"Will you breakfast with me?" asked Claparon, bethinking himself of the ball, and prompted partly by a wish to turn the tables on his host, partly by anxiety to put Birotteau off the scent. And, in point of fact, a round table, hastily cleared of papers, was suspiciously suggestive; for it displayed a pâté, oysters, white wine, and a dish of vulgar kidneys, *sautés au vin de Champagne,* cooling in their gravy, while an omelette with truffles was browning before the sea-coal fire. The table was set for two persons; two table-napkins, soiled at supper on the previous evening, would have enlightened the purest innocence. Claparon, in the character of a man who has a belief in his own adroitness, insisted in spite of Birotteau's refusals.

"I should by rights have had somebody to breakfast, but that somebody has not kept the appointment," cried the cunning commercial traveler, speaking loud, so that the words might reach the ears of an auditor hiding under the blankets.

"I have come on business pure and simple, sir," said Birotteau, " and I shall not detain you long."

"I am overwhelmed with business," returned Claparon, pointing to a cylinder desk and to the tables, which were heaped up with papers, "not a poor little minute may I have to myself. I never see people except on Saturdays; but for you, my dear sir, I am always at home. I have no time left nowadays for love-affairs or lounging about; I am losing the business instinct, which takes intervals of carefully-timed idleness, if it is to keep its freshness. Nobody sees me busy doing nothing in the boulevards. Pshaw! business bores me, I don't care to hear any more about business at present; I have money enough, and I shall never have pleasure enough. My word, I have a mind to turn tourist and see Italy. Ah! beloved Italy! fair even amid her adversity, adorable land, where, doubtless, I shall find some magnificent, indolent Italian beauty; I have always admired Italian women! Have you ever had an Italian mistress? No? Oh, well, come to Italy with me. We will see Venice, the city of the Doges, fallen, more's the pity, into the hands of those philistines the Austrians, who know nothing of art. Pooh! let us leave business, and canals, and loans, and governments in peace. I am a prince when my pockets are well lined. Let us travel, by Jove!"

"Just one word, sir, and I will go," said Birotteau. "You passed my bills on to M. Bidault."

"Gigonnet, you mean; nice little fellow, Gigonnet; a man as easy-going as a—as a slip-knot."

"Yes," said César. "I should be glad—and in this matter I am relying on your integrity and honor—(Claparon bowed) —I should be glad if I could renew——"

"Impossible," said the banker roundly—"impossible. I am not the only man in the affair. We are all in council, 'tis a regular Chamber; but that we are all on good terms among ourselves, like rashers in a pan. Oh, we deliberate, that we do! The building land by the Madeleine is nothing; we are doing other things elsewhere. Eh! my good sir, if we were not busy in the Champs-Élysées, near the new Exchange which has just been finished, in the Quartier Saint-

Lazare and about the Tivoli, we should not be *vinanciers,* as old Nucingen says. So what is the Madeleine? A little speck of a business. Prrr! we do not dabble, my good sir," he said, tapping Birotteau's chest, and giving him a hug. "There, come and have your breakfast, and we will have a talk," Claparon continued, by way of softening his refusal.

"By all means," said Birotteau.—"So much the worse for the other," thought he. He would wait till the wine went to Claparon's head, and find out then who his partners really were in this affair, which began to have a very shady look.

"That is right!—Victoire!" shouted the banker, and at the call appeared a genuine Leonarda, tricked out like a fish-wife.

"Tell the clerks that I cannot see anybody, not even Nucingen, Keller, Gigonnet, and the rest of them!"

"There is no one here but M. Lempereur."

"He can receive the fashionables," said Claparon, "and the small fry need not go beyond the public office. They can be told that I am meditating how to get a pull—at a bottle of champagne."

To make an old commercial traveler tipsy is to achieve the impossible. César had mistaken his boon companion's symptoms, and thought his boisterous vulgarity was due to intoxication, when he tried to shrive him.

"There is that rascal Roguin still in it with you," said Birotteau; "ought you not to write and tell him to help out a friend whom he has left in the lurch, a friend with whom he dined every Sunday, and whom he has known for twenty years?"

"Roguin? A fool; we have his share. Don't be down-hearted, my good friend, it will be all right. Pay on the 15th, and that done, we shall see! I say, 'we shall see'—(a glass of wine!)—but the capital is no concern of mine whatever. Oh! if you should not pay at all, *I* should not give you black looks; my share in the affair is limited to a percentage on the pur-chase-money, and something down on the completion of the contract, in consideration of which ᵞ brought round the

vendors. . . . Do you understand? Your associates are
good men, so I am not afraid, my dear sir. Business is so
divided up nowadays. Every business requires the co-operation of so many' specialists! Do you join the rest of us?
Then do not dabble in combs and pomade pots—a paltry way
of doing business; fleece the public, and go in for the speculation."

"A speculation?" asked the perfumer; "what sort of business is it?"

"It is commerce in the abstract," replied Claparon, "an
affair which will only come to light in ten years' time at the
bidding of the great Nucingen, the Napoleon of finance, a
scheme by which a man embraces sum-totals, and skims the
cream of profits yet to be made; a gigantic conception, a
method of marking expectations like timber for annual fell-
ing; it is a new cabal, in short. There are but ten or twelve of
us as yet, long-headed men, all initiated into the cabalistic secrets of these magnificent combinations."

César opened his eyes and ears, trying to comprehend these
mixed metaphors.

"Listen to me," Claparon continued, after a pause; "such
strokes as these need capable men. Now, there is the man
who has ideas, but has not a penny, like all men with ideas.
That sort of man spends and is spent, and cares for nothing. Imagine a pig roaming about a wood for truffles, and
a knowing fellow on his tracks; that is the man with the
money, who waits till he hears a grunt over a find. When
the man with the ideas has hit upon a good notion, the man
with the money taps him on the shoulder with a 'What is
this? You are putting yourself in the furnace-mouth, my
good friend; your back is not strong enough to carry this;
here are a thousand francs for you, and let *me* put this affair
in working order.' Good! Then the banker summons the
manufacturers—'Set to work, my friends! Out with your
prospectuses! Blarney to the death!' Out come the hunt-
ing-horns, and they pipe up with 'A hundred thousand francs
for five sous!'—or five sous for a hundred thousand francs,

gold-mines, coal-mines; all the flourishes and alarums of commerce, in short. Art and science are paid to give their opinion, the affair is paraded about, the public rushes into it, and receives paper for its money, and our takings are in our hands. The pig is safe in his sty with his potatoes, and the rest of them are wallowing in bills of exchange. That is how it is done, my dear sir. Go in for speculation. What do you want to be? A pig or a gull, a clown or a millionaire? Think it over. I have summed up the modern theory of loans for you. Come to see me; you will find a good fellow, always jolly. French joviality, at once grave and gay, does no harm in business, quite the contrary! Men who can drink are made to understand each other. Come! another glass of champagne? It is choice wine, eh? It was sent me by a man at Épernay, for whom I have sold a good deal of it, and at good prices too (I used to be in the wine trade). He shows his gratitude, and remembers me in my prosperity. A rare trait."

Birotteau, bewildered by this flippancy and careless tone in a man whom everybody credited with such astonishing profundity and breadth, did not dare to question him any further. But in spite of the confusion and excitement induced by unwonted potations of champagne, a name let fall by du Tillet came up in his mind, and he asked for the address of a bill-discounter named Gobseck.

"Is that what you are after, my dear sir?" asked Claparon. "Gobseck is a bill-discounter in the same sense that the hangman is a doctor. The first thing that he says to you is 'Fifty per cent.' He belongs to the school of Harpagon; he will supply you with canary birds, and stuffed boa-constrictors, with furs in summer and nankin in winter. And whose bills are you going to offer him? He will want you to deposit your wife, your daughter, your umbrella, and everything that is yours, down to your hat-box, your clogs (do you wear hinged clogs?), poker and tongs, and the firewood in your cellar, before he will take your bills with your bare name to them! . . . Gobseck! Gobseck! In the name of misfortune, who sent you to the guillotine of commerce?"

"M. du Tillet."

"Oh! the rogue; just like him. We used to be friends once upon a time; and if the quarrel has gone so far that we do not speak to each other now, I have good reason for disliking him, believe me! He let me see the bottom of his soul of mud, and he made me uncomfortable at that fine ball you gave. I cannot bear him, with the coxcomb airs he gives himself, because he has the good graces of a *notaresse!* I could have marquises myself if I had a mind; he will never have my esteem, I know. Ah! my esteem is a princess who will never take up too much room on his pillow. I say though, old man, you are a funny one to give us a ball, and then come and ask us to renew two months afterwards! You are likely to go far. Let us go into speculation together. You have a character; it would be useful to me. Oh! du Tillet was born to understand Gobseck. Du Tillet will come to a bad end in the Place de Grève. If, as they say, he is one of Gobseck's lambs, he will soon come to the length of his tether. Gobseck squats in a corner of his web like an old spider who has seen the world. Sooner or later, *zut!* and the money-lender sucks in his man like a glass of wine. So much the better! Du Tillet played me a trick—oh! a scurvy trick!"

After an hour and a half spent in listening to meaningless prate, Birotteau determined to go, for the commercial traveler was preparing to relate the adventure of a representative of the people at Marseilles, who had fallen in love with an actress who played the part of *La Belle Arsène.* The Royalist pit hissed the lady.

"Up he gets," said Claparon, "and stands bolt upright in his box. *'Arté qui l'a siblée?'* says he; *'eu!* . . . *Si c'est oune femme, je l'amprise; si c'est oune homme, nous se verrons; si c'est ni l'un ni l'autte, que le troun di Diou le cure!'* . . . How do you think the adventure ended?"

"Good-day, sir," said Birotteau.

"You will have to come and see me," said Claparon at this.

"Cayron's first bill has come back protested, and I am the in-
dorser; I have reimbursed the money, and I shall send it
on to you, for business is business."

Birotteau felt this cool affectation of a readiness to oblige,
as he had already felt Keller's hardness and Nucingen's Teu-
tonic banter, in his very heart. The man's familiarity, his
grotesque confidences made in the generous glow of champagne, had been like a blight to the perfumer; he felt as if he
were leaving some evil haunt in the world financial.

He walked downstairs; he found himself in the streets and
went, not knowing whither he went. He followed the boulevard till he reached the Rue Saint-Denis, then he bethought
himself of Molineux, and turned to go towards the Cour
Batave. He mounted the same dirty tortuous staircase which
he had ascended but lately in the pride of his glory. He remembered Molineux's peevish meanness, and winced at the
thought of asking a favor of him. As on the occasion of his
previous visit, he found the owner of house property by the
fireside, but this time he had eaten his breakfast. Birotteau
formulated his demand.

"Renew a bill for twelve hundred francs?" said Molineux,
with an incredulous smile. "You do not mean it, sir. If you
have not twelve hundred francs on the 15th to meet my bill,
will you please to send me back my receipt for rent that has
not been paid? Ah! I should be angry; I do not use the
slightest ceremony in money matters; my rents are my income. If I acted otherwise, how should I pay my way? A
man in business will not disapprove of that wholesome rule.
Money knows nobody; money has no ears; money has no
heart. It is a cold winter, and here is firewood dearer again.
If you do not pay on the 15th, you will receive a little summons by noon on the 16th. Pshaw! old Mitral, who serves
your processes, acts for me too; he will send you your summons in an envelope, with due regard for your high position."

"A writ has never been served on me, sir," said Birotteau.

"Everything must have a beginning," retorted Molineux. The perfumer was taken aback by the little old man's frank ferocity; the knell of credit rang in his ears; and every fresh stroke awoke memories of his own sayings as to bankruptcies, prompted by his remorseless jurisprudence. Those opinions of his seemed to be traced in letters of fire on the soft substance of his brain.

"By the by," Molineux was saying, "you forget to write 'For value received in rent' across your bills; that might give me a preferential claim."

"My position forbids me to do anything to the prejudice of my creditors," said Birotteau, dazed by that glimpse into the gulf before him.

"Good, sir, very good. I thought that I had nothing left to learn in my dealings with messieurs my tenants. You have taught me never to take bills in payment. Oh! I will take the thing into Court, for your answer as good as tells me that you will not meet your engagements. The case touches every landlord in Paris."

Birotteau went out, sick of life. Feeble and tender natures lose heart at the first rebuff, just as a first success puts courage into them. César's only hope now lay in little Popinot's devotion; his thoughts naturally turned to him as he passed the Marché des Innocents.

"Poor boy! who would have told me this when I started him six weeks ago at the Tuileries."

It was nearly four o'clock, the time when the magistrates leave the Palais. As it fell out, the elder Popinot had gone to see his nephew. The examining magistrate, who in moral questions had a kind of second-sight which laid bare the secret motives of others, who discerned the underlying significance of the most commonplace actions of daily life, the germs of crime, the roots of a misdemeanor, was watching Birotteau, though Birotteau did not suspect it. Birotteau seemed to be put out by finding the uncle with the nephew; the perfumer's manner was constrained, he was preoccupied and thoughtful. Little Popinot, busy as usual with his pen behind his ear, always fell flat, figuratively speaking, before Césarine's father. César's meaningless remarks to his partner, to the judge's thinking, were merely screens, some important demand was about to be made. Instead of leaving the shop, therefore, the shrewd man of law stayed with his nephew, for he thought that César would try to get rid of him by making a move himself. And so it was. When Birotteau had gone, the judge followed, but he noticed César lounging along the Rue des Cinq-Diamants in the direction of the Rue Aubry-le-Boucher. This infinitely small matter bred suspicion in the mind of Popinot the elder; he mistrusted César's intentions, went along the Rue des Lombards, watched the perfumer go back to Anselme's shop, and promptly repaired thither.

"My dear Popinot," César had begun, "I have come to ask you to do me a service."

"What is there to be done?" asked Popinot, with generous eagerness.

"Ah! you give me life!" cried the good man, rejoicing in this warmth from the heart that sent a glow through him after those twenty-five days of glacial cold. "It is this, to allow me to draw a bill on you on account of my share of the profits; we will settle between ourselves."

Popinot looked steadily at César; César lowered his eyes. Just at that moment the magistrate reappeared.

"My boy—Oh! I beg your pardon, M. Birotteau—my boy, I forgot to say . . ." and with the imperative gesture learned in the exercise of his profession, the elder Popinot drew his nephew out into the street, and marched him, bareheaded and in shirt-sleeves as he was, in the direction of the Rue des Lombards.

"Your old master will very likely find himself in such straits, that he may be forced to file his schedule, nephew. Before a man comes to that, a man who, may be, has a record of forty years of upright dealing, nay the very best of men, in his anxiety to save his honor, will behave like the most frantic gambler. Men in that predicament will do anything.

They will sell their wives and traffic in their daughters; they will bring their best friends into the scrape, and pawn property which is not theirs; they will go to the gaming-table, turn actors—nay, liars; they will shed tears at need.   In short, I have known them do the most extraordinary things. You yourself know how good-natured Roguin was, a man who looked as though butter would not melt in his mouth. I do not press these conclusions home in M. Birotteau's case; I believe that he is honest; but if he should ask you to do anything at all irregular, no matter what it is; if he should want you, for instance, to accept accommodation bills, and so start you in a system which, to my way of thinking, is the beginning of all sorts of rascality (for it is counterfeit paper-money), promise me that you will sign nothing without first consulting me.   You must remember that if you love his daughter, even for your own sake and hers, you must not spoil your future.   If M. Birotteau must come to grief, what is the use of going with him?   What is it but cutting yourselves off from all chance of escape through your business, which will be his refuge?"

"Thank you, uncle; a word to the wise is sufficient," said Anselme; his uncle's words explained that heartrending cry from his master.

The merchant who dealt in druggists' oils and sundries looked thoughtful as he entered his dark shop.   Birotteau saw the change.

"Will you honor me by coming up to my room? we can talk more at our ease there than here.   The assistants, busy as they are, might overhear us."

Birotteau followed Popinot, a victim to such cruel suspense as the condemned man knows, while he waits for a reprieve or the rejection of his appeal.

"My dear benefactor," Anselme began, "you do not doubt my devotion; it is blind.   Permit me to ask but one thing, will this sum of money save you once and for all?   Or will it merely put off some catastrophe? in which case, what is the use of carrying me with you?   You want bills at ninety days. Very well, but I am sure that I myself shall not be able to meet them in three months' time."

Birotteau, white and grave, rose to his feet, and looked into Popinot's face.

Popinot, in alarm, cried, "I will do it if you wish it."

"Ungrateful boy!" cried the perfumer, gathering all his strength to hurl at Anselme the words which should brand him as infamous.

Birotteau walked to the door and went. Popinot, recovering from the sensation which the terrible words had produced in him, darted downstairs and rushed into the street, but saw no sign of the perfumer. The dreadful words of doom rang in the ears of Césarine's lover, poor César's face of anguish was always before his eyes; he lived, indeed, like Hamlet, haunted by a ghastly spectre.

Birotteau staggered along the streets like a drunken man. He found himself at last on the Quai, and followed its course to Sèvres, where he spent the night in an inn, stupefied with sorrow; and his frightened wife dared not make any inquiries for him. Under such circumstances, it is fatal to give the alarm rashly. Constance wisely immolated her anxiety to her husband's business reputation; she sat up all night for him, mingling prayers with her fears. Was César dead? Had he left Paris in the pursuit of some last hope? When morning came, she behaved as though she knew the cause of his absence; but when at five o'clock César had not returned, she sent word to her uncle and begged him to go to the Morgue. All through that day the brave woman sat at her desk, her daughter doing her embroidery by her side, and, neither sad nor smiling, both confronted the public with quiet faces.

When Pillerault came, he brought César with him; he had met his niece's husband after 'Change in the Palais Royal, hesitating to enter a gaming-house. That day was the 14th.

César could eat nothing at dinner. His stomach, too violently contracted, rejected food; it was a miserable meal; but it was not so bad as the evening that came after it. For the hundredth time, the merchant experienced one of the hideous alternations of despair and hope which wear out weak natures, when the soul passes through the whole scale of sensations, from the highest pitch of joy to the lowest depths of despair. Derville, the consulting barrister, rushed into the splendid drawing-room. Mme. César had done everything in her power to keep her poor husband there; he had wanted to sleep in the attic, "so as not to see the monuments of my folly," he said.

"We have gained the day," cried Derville.

At these words the lines in César's face were smoothed out, but his joy alarmed Pillerault and Derville. The two frightened women went away to cry in Césarine's room.

"Now I can borrow on the property!" exclaimed the perfumer.

"It would not be wise to do so," said Derville; "they have given notice of appeal, the Court-Royal may reverse the decision, but we shall know in a month's time."

"A month!"

César sank into a lethargy, from which no one attempted to rouse him. This species of intermittent catalepsy, during which the body lives and suffers while the action of the mind is suspended, this fortuitous respite from mental anguish, was regarded as a godsend by Constance, Césarine, Pillerault, and Derville—and they were right. In this way Birotteau was able to recover from the wear and tear of the night's emotions. He lay in a low chair by the fireside; over against him sat his wife, who watched him closely, with a sweet smile on her lips—one of those smiles which prove that women are nearer to the angels than men, in that they can blend infinite tenderness with the most sincere compassion, a secret known only to the angels whose presence is revealed to us in the dreams providentially scattered at long intervals in the course of human life. Césarine, sitting on a footstool at her mother's feet, now and again bent her head over her father's hands and brushed them lightly with her hair, as if by this caress she would fain communicate through the sense of touch the thoughts which at such a time are importunate when rendered by articulate speech.

Pillerault, that philosopher prepared for every emergency, sat in his armchair, like the statue of the Chancellor of the Hôpital in the peristyle of the Chamber of Deputies, wearing the same look of intelligence which is stamped on the features of an Egyptian sphinx, and talked in a low voice with Derville. Constance had recommended that the lawyer, whose discretion was above suspicion, should be consulted. With the schedule already drafted in her mind, she laid the situation before Derville; and after an hour's consultation or thereabouts, held in the presence of the dozing performer, Derville looked at Pillerault and shook his head.

"Madame," said he, with the pitiless coolness of a man of business, "you must file your petition. Suppose that by some means or other you should contrive to meet your bills to-morrow, you must eventually pay at least three thousand francs before you can borrow on the whole of your landed property. To your liabilities, amounting to five hundred and fifty thousand francs, you oppose assets consisting of a very valuable and very promising piece of property which cannot be realized—you must give up in a given time, and it is better, in my opinion, to jump from the window than to roll down the stairs."

"I am of that opinion, too, my child," said Pillerault.

Mme. César and Pillerault both went to the door with Derville.

"Poor father!" said Césarine, rising softly to put a kiss on César's forehead.—"Then could Anselme do nothing?" she asked, when her mother and uncle came in again.

"The ungrateful boy!" cried César. The name had touched the one sensitive spot in his memory, like the string of a piano resonant to the stroke of the hammer.

Little Popinot, meanwhile, since those words had been hurled at him like an anathema, had not had a moment's peace or a wink of sleep. The hapless youth called down maledictions on his uncle, and went in search of him. To induce experience and legal acumen to capitulate, young Popinot poured forth all a lover's eloquence, hoping to work on the feelings of a judge, but his words slid over the man of law like water over oilcloth.

"Commercial usage," pleaded Anselme, "permits a sleeping partner to draw to a certain extent upon his co-associate on account of profits; and in our partnership we ought to put it in practice. After looking into my business all round, I feel sure that I am good to pay forty thousand francs in three months' time. M. César's honesty permits me to feel confident that he will use the forty thousand francs to meet his bills. So, if he fails, the creditors will have no reason to complain of this action on our part. And besides, uncle, I would rather lose forty thousand francs than give up Césarine. At this moment, while I am speaking, she will have heard of my refusal, and I shall be lowered in her eyes. I said that I would give my life for my benefactor! I am in the case of the young sailor who must go to the bottom with his captain, or the soldier who is bound to perish with his general."

"A good heart and a bad man of business; you will not be lowered in *my* eyes," said the judge, grasping his nephew's hand. "I have thought a good deal about this," he continued; "I know that you love Césarine to distraction; I think that you can obey the laws of your heart without breaking the laws of commerce."

"Oh! uncle, if you have found out a way, you will save my honor."

"Lend Birotteau fifty thousand francs on his proprietary interest in your Oil; it has become, as it were, a piece of property; I will draw up the document for you."

Anselme embraced his uncle, went home, made out bills for fifty thousand francs, and ran all the way from the Rue des Cinq-Diamants to the Place Vendôme; so that at the very moment when Césarine, her mother, and Pillerault were gazing at the perfumer, amazed by the sepulchral tone in which the words "Ungrateful boy!" were uttered in answer to the girl's question, the drawing-room door opened, and Popinot appeared.

"My dearly beloved master," he said, wiping the perspiration from his forehead, "here is the thing for which you asked me."

He held out the bills.

"Yes. I have thought carefully over my position; I shall meet them, never fear! Save your honor!"

"I was quite sure of him," cried Césarine, grasping Popinot's hand convulsively.

Mme. César embraced Popinot. The perfumer rose out of his chair, like the righteous at the sound of the last trump; he too was issuing from a tomb. Then with frenzied eagerness he clutched the fifty stamped papers.

"One moment!" cried the stern Uncle Pillerault, snatching up Popinot's bills. "One moment!"

The four persons composing this family group—César and his wife, Césarine and Popinot—bewildered by their uncle's interposition, and by the tone in which he spoke, looked on in terror while he tore the bills to pieces and flung them into the fire, where they blazed up before any one of them could stop him.

"Uncle!"

"Uncle!"

"Uncle!"

"Sir!"

There were four voices, and four hearts in one, a formidable unanimity. Uncle Pillerault put an arm round little Popinot, held him tightly to his heart, and put a kiss on his forehead.

"You deserve to be adored by any one who has a heart at all," said he. "If you loved my daughter, and she had a million, and you had nothing but *that*" (he pointed to the blackened scraps of paper), "you should marry her in a fortnight if she loved you. Your master," indicating César, "is mad.—Now, nephew," Pillerault began gravely, addressing the perfumer, "no more illusions! Business must be carried on with hard coin, and not with sentiments. This is sublime, but it is useless. I have been on 'Change for a couple of hours. No one will give you credit for two farthings; everybody is talking about your disaster; everybody knows that you could not get renewals, that you went to more than one banker, and that they would have nothing to say to you, and all your other follies; it is known that you climbed six pair of stairs to ask the landlord who chatters like a jackdaw to renew a bill for twelve hundred francs; everybody says that you gave a ball to hide your embarrassment. . . . They will say directly that you had no money deposited with Roguin. Roguin is a blind, according to your enemies. One of my friends, commissioned to report everything, has brought confirmation of my suspicions. Every one expects that you will try to put Popinot's bills on the market; in fact, you set him up on purpose to tide you over your difficulties. In short, all the gossip and slander usually set in motion by any man who tries to mount a step in the social scale is going the round of business circles at this moment. You would spend a week in hawking Popinot's bills from place to place, you would meet with humiliating refusals, and nobody would have anything to do with them. There is nothing to show how many of them you are issuing, and people look to see you sacrificing this poor boy to save yourself. You would ruin Popinot's credit in pure waste. Do you know how much the most sanguine bill-discounter would give you for your fifty thousand francs? Twenty thousand; *twenty thousand,* do you understand? There are times in business when you must contrive to hold out for three days without food, as if you had the indigestion, and the fourth brings admission to the pantry of credit. You cannot hold out for the three days, and therein lies the whole position. Take heart, my poor nephew, you must file your schedule. Here is Popinot, and here am I; as soon as your assistants have gone to bed we will set to work to spare you the misery of it."

"Uncle! . . ." cried the perfumer, clasping his hands.

"César, do you really mean to arrive at a fraudulent bankruptcy with assets *nil?* Your interest in Popinot's business saves your honor."

This last fatal light thrown on his position made it clear to César; he saw the full extent of the hideous truth; he sank down into his low chair, and then on to his knees; his mind wandered, he became a child again. His wife thought the shock had killed him, and knelt to raise him, but she clung close to him when she saw him clasp his hands and raise his eyes; and in spite of the presence of his uncle, his daughter, and Popinot, he began with remorseful resignation to repeat the sublime prayer of the Church on earth:

"Our Father which art in Heaven, Hallowed be Thy name. Thy kingdom come. Thy will be done in earth, as it is in Heaven. *Give us this day our daily bread.* And forgive us our trespasses, as we forgive them that trespass against us. And lead us not into temptation, but deliver us from evil. Amen."

Tears filled Pillerault's stoical eyes, and Césarine stood, white and rigid as marble, with her tear-stained face hidden on Anselme's shoulder. Then the old merchant took the young man's arm, "Let us go downstairs," he said.

At half-past eleven they left César in the care of his wife and daughter. Just at that moment Célestin, who had looked after the business during this storm, came upstairs and opened the drawing-room door. Césarine heard his footsteps, and hurried forward to place herself so as to screen the prostrate master of the house.

"Among this evening's letters," he said, "there was one from Tours, the direction was not clear, it has been delayed. I thought it might be from the master's brother, so I did not open it."

"Father," cried Césarine, "there is a letter from uncle at Tours."

"Ah! I am saved!" exclaimed César. "My brother! my brother!" and he kissed the letter, which ran thus:

François Birotteau to César Birotteau.

"MY BELOVED BROTHER,—Your letter has given me the keenest distress; and so when I had read it, I offered up to God on your behalf the holy sacrifice of the mass, praying Him, by the blood shed for us by our Divine Redeemer, to look mercifully upon you in your affliction. And now that I have put up my prayer *pro meo fratre Cæsare,* my eyes are filled with tears to think that by misfortune I am separated from you at a time when you must need the support of a brother's affection. But then I bethought me that the worthy and venerated M. Pillerault will doubtless fill my place. My dear César, in the midst of your troubles, do not forget that this life of ours is a life of trial and a transition state; that one day we shall be rewarded if we have suffered for the holy name of God, for His holy Church, for putting in practice the doctrines of the Gospel, or for leading a virtuous life; if it were not so, the things of this present world would be unintelligible. I repeat these words, though I know how good and pious you are, because it may happen to those who, like you, are tossed by the tempests of this world, and launched upon the perilous seas of human concerns, to be led to blaspheme in their distresses, distracted as they are by pain. Do not curse the men who will wound you, nor God, who mingles bitterness with your life at His will. Look not on the earth, but rather keep your eyes lifted to Heaven; thence comes comfort for the weak, the riches of the poor are there, and the fears of the rich . . ."

"Oh, Birotteau," interrupted his wife, "just miss that out, and see if he is sending us anything."

"We will often read it over," said her husband, drying his eyes. He opened the letter, and a draft on the Treasury fell out. "I was quite sure of him, poor brother," said Birotteau, picking up the draft.

". . . I went to see Mme. de Listomère," he continued, reading in a voice choked with tears, "and without giving a reason for my request, I begged her to lend me all that she could spare, so as to swell the amount of my savings. Her generosity enables me to make up the sum of a thousand francs, which I send you in the form of a draft by the Receiver-General of Tours upon the Treasury."

"A handsome advance!" said Constance, looking at Césarine.

"By retrenching some superfluities in my way of living, I shall be able to repay Mme. de Listomère the money I have borrowed of her in three years' time; so do not trouble about it, my dear César. I am sending you all that I have in the world, with the wish that the sum may assist you to bring your difficulties to a happy termination; doubtless they are but momentary. I know your delicacy, and wish to anticipate your scruples. Do not dream of paying any interest on the amount, nor of returning it in the day of prosperity, which will dawn for you before long, if God deigns to grant the petitions which I make daily for you. After your last letter, received two years ago, I thought that you were rich, and that I might give my savings to the poor; but now all that I have belongs to you. When you have weathered this passing squall, keep the money for my niece Césarine, so that when she is established in life she may spend it on some trifle which will remind her of an old uncle, whose hands are always raised to Heaven to implore God's blessing upon her, and for all those who shall be dear to her. Bear in mind, in fact, dear César, that I am a poor priest, living by the grace of God, as the wild-birds live in the fields, walking quietly in my own path, striving to keep the commandments of our divine Saviour, and consequently needing but little. So do not have the least hesitation in your difficult position, and think of me as one who loves you tenderly. Our excellent Abbé Chapeloud (to whom I have not said a word about your strait) knows that I am writing to you, and wishes me to send the most kindly messages to all your family, with wishes for your continued prosperity. May God vouchsafe to preserve you and your wife and daughter in good health; and I pray for patience to you all, and courage in the day of adversity.   "FRANÇOIS BIROTTEAU.

"Priest of the Cathedral Church of Tours, and Vicar of the Parish Church of Saint-Gatien."

"A thousand francs!" cried Mme. Birotteau, in vehement anger.

"Lock it up," César said gravely; "it is all he has. Besides, it belongs to our Césarine, and should enable us to live without asking anything of our creditors."

"And then they will believe that you have taken away large sums."

"I shall show them his letter."

"They will say that it is a fraud."

"*Oh! mon Dieu! mon Dieu!*" cried César, appalled at this; "I have often thought that very thing of poor folk who, no doubt, were just in my position."

Mother and daughter were both too anxious about César to leave him, and they sewed on by his side. There was a deep silence. At two o'clock in the morning the drawing-room door was softly opened, and Popinot beckoned to Mme. César to come downstairs. At the sight of his niece, Uncle Pillerault took off his spectacles.

"There is hope yet, my child," he said; "all is not over; but your husband could not stand the strain of the ups and downs of this business, so Popinot and I will try to arrange it. Do not leave the shop to-morrow, and take down the names of all the holders of the bills; we have all the day till four o'clock. This is my idea. There is nothing to fear from M. Ragon or from me. Suppose now that Roguin had paid over to the vendors the hundred thousand francs you deposited with him —in that case, you would no more have them than you have them to-day. You have to meet bills to the amount of a hundred and forty thousand francs, payable to Claparon's order;

you must pay them anyhow, so it is not Roguin's bankruptcy which is ruining you. Now, to meet your liabilities, I see forty thousand francs to be borrowed sooner or later on your factory, and sixty thousand francs in Popinot's bills. So you may struggle through; for once through, you can raise money on that building-land by the Madeleine. If your principal creditor agrees to help you, I shall not consider my fortune; I will sell my *rentes;* I shall be without bread; Popinot will be between life and death; and, as for you, you will be at the mercy of the smallest events. But the Oil will give a good return, no doubt. Popinot and I have been consulting together; we will support you in this struggle. Oh, I will eat my dry bread gaily, if success dawns on the horizon. But everything depends on Gigonnet and on Claparon and his associates. We are going to see Gigonnet between seven and eight, Popinot and I, and then we shall know what to make of their intentions."

Constance, carried away by her feelings, put her arms about her uncle, and could not speak for tears and sobs. Neither Popinot nor Pillerault could know that Bidault, *alias* Gigonnet, and Claparon were but two of du Tillet's doubles, and that du Tillet had set his heart upon reading this terrible paragraph in the *Gazette:*

"Decree of the Tribunal of Commerce. M. César Birotteau, wholesale perfumer, of 397 Rue Saint-Honoré, Paris, declared a bankrupt, date provisionally fixed, 16th of January 1819. Registrar: M. Gobenheim-Keller. Agent: M. Molineux."

Anselme and Pillerault studied César's affairs till daylight came, and at eight o'clock that morning the two heroic comrades, the old veteran and the subaltern of yesterday, neither of whom was destined to experience on his own account the dreadful agony of mind endured by those who go up and down the stairs of Bidault, otherwise Gigonnet, betook themselves without a word to the Rue Grenétat. It was a

painful time for both of them.   More than once Pillerault
passed his hand over his forehead.

In the Rue Grenétat multifarious small trades are carried
on in every overcrowded house.   Every building has a repulsive aspect.   The hideousness of these houses has a distinct
quality of its own, in which the mean squalor of a poor in-
dustrial neighborhood predominates.

Old Gigonnet inhabited the third floor in one of these
houses.   All the windows, with their dirty square panes of
glass, were secured to the frames by pivots, and tilted to admit the air; you walked straight up the staircase from the
street, and the porter lived in the box on the mezzanine floor
lighted from the staircase.   Every one in the house, except
Gigonnet, plied some handicraft; workmen came and went
all day long.   Every step on the stairs, where filth was allowed
to accumulate, was plastered over with a coating of mud,
hard or soft, according to the state of the weather.   Each
landing on this fetid stair displayed the name of some crafts-
man painted in gilt letters on a sheet of iron, which was
painted red and varnished, and some sample of the man's
achievements in his trade.   The doors, for the most part, stood
ajar, affording glimpses of grotesque combinations of industry and domestic life; the sounds which issued thence,
snatches of song, yells, whistlings, and uncouth growls recalled the noises heard at the Jardin des Plantes towards
four o'clock.   The smartest braces for the trade in the *article
Paris* were being made in a loathsome den on the first floor; on
the second, among heaps of the most unsavory litter, the
manufacture of the daintiest cardboard boxes, displayed at
the New Year in shop windows, was carried on.   Gigonnet,
who was worth eighteen hundred thousand francs, lived and
died on the third floor in this house.   Nothing would induce
him to leave it, although his niece, Mme. Saillard, offered him
rooms in a mansion in the Place Royale.

"Courage!" said Pillerault, as he jerked the cord of the
lever bell-pull that hung by Gigonnet's neat gray-painted
door.

Gigonnet himself opened it, and the perfumer's two champions in the lists of bankruptcy went through a formal, chilly-looking room, with curtainless windows, and entered a second, where all three seated themselves.

The bill-discounter took up his position before a grate full of ashes, in which the wood maintained a stubborn resistance to the flames. The sight of his green cardboard cases, and the monastic austerity of the office, windy as a cave, sent a cold chill through Popinot. His dazed eyes wandered over the pattern of the cheap wall-paper—tricolor flowers on a bluish background—which had been hung some five-and-twenty years back; and turned from that depressing sight to the ornaments on the chimney-piece, a lyre-shaped clock and oval vases, blue Sèvres ware, handsomely mounted in gilt copper. This bit of flotsam, recovered by Gigonnet from the wreck of Versailles, when the palace was sacked by the populace, came from a queen's boudoir, but the magnificent-looking ornaments were flanked by a couple of wrought-iron candlesticks of the commonest description, a harsh contrast which continually reminded the beholder of the manner in which their owner had come by those royal splendors.

"I know that you cannot come on your own account," said Gigonnet, "but for the great Birotteau. Well, what is it, my friends?"

"I know that you have nothing to learn, so we will be brief," said Pillerault. "Have you his bills payable to Claparon?"

"Yes."

"Will you exchange the first fifty thousand francs that will fall due for bills accepted by M. Popinot here, less the discount, of course?"

Gigonnet lifted the terrible green cap, which seemed to have been born with him, and displayed a bald butter-colored pate, then with a Voltairean grin:

"You want to pay me in oil for hair," he remarked, "and what should I do with it?"

"When you joke, it is time for us to take ourselves off," said Pillerault.

"You speak like the sensible man that you are," said Gigonnet, with a flattering smile.

"Very well, and how if I back M. Popinot's bills?" asked Pillerault, making a final effort.

"You are as good as gold ingots, M. Pillerault; but I have no use for gold ingots, all that I want is current coin."

Pillerault and Popinot took their leave and went. Even at the foot of the staircase Popinot's knees still shook under him.

"Is he a man?" he asked of Pillerault.

"People say so," answered the older man. "Keep this little interview always in mind, Anselme! You have seen what money-lending is, stripped of its masquerade and palaver. Some unforeseen event turns the screw upon us, and we are the grapes, and bill-discounters the barrels. This speculation in building-land is a good piece of business no doubt; Gigonnet, or somebody behind him, has a mind to cut César's throat and to step into his shoes. That is all; there is no help for it now. And this is what comes of borrowing money; never resort to it."

It had been a dreadful morning for Mme. Birotteau. For the first time she had taken the addresses of those who came for money, and had sent away the Bank collector without paying him; yet the brave woman was glad to spare her husband these humiliations. Towards eleven o'clock she saw Pillerault and Anselme returning; she had been expecting them with ever-increasing anxiety, and now she read her doom in their faces. There was no help for it, the schedule must be filed.

"He will die of grief," said the poor wife.

"I could wish that he might," said Pillerault gravely; "but he is so devout, that as things stand his director the Abbé Loraux alone can save him."

Pillerault, Popinot, and Constance remained below, while one of the assistants went for the Abbé Loraux. The Abbé should prepare Birotteau for the schedule which Célestin was copying out fair for his master's signature. The assistants

were in despair; they loved their employer. At four o'clock
the good priest came. Constance told him all the details of
the calamity which had befallen them, and the Abbé went upstairs like a soldier mounting to the breach.

"I know why you have come," César exclaimed.

"My son," said the priest, "your sentiments of submission
to the Divine will have long been known to me, now you are
called upon to put them in practice. Keep your eyes fixed
ever upon the Cross, contemplate the Cross without ceasing,
and think of the cup of humiliation of which the Saviour
of men was compelled to drink, think of the anguish of His
Passion, and thus you may endure the mortifications sent to
you by God——"

"My brother the Abbé has already prepared me," said César,
holding out the letter, which he read over again, to his confessor.

"You have a good brother," said M. Loraux, "a virtuous
and sweet-natured wife, and a loving daughter, two real
friends in your uncle and dear Anselme, two indulgent creditors in the Ragons. All these kind hearts will pour balm into
your wounds continually, and will help you to carry your
cross. Promise me to bear yourself with a martyr's courage, and to take the blow without wincing."

The Abbé coughed, a signal to Pillerault in the next room.

"My submission is unlimited," said César calmly. "Disgrace has come upon me; I ought only to think of making
reparation."

Césarine and the priest were both surprised by poor Birotteau's tone and look. And yet nothing was more natural.
Every man bears a definitely known misfortune better than
suspense and constant alternations of excessive joy at one moment, followed on the next by the last extremity of anguish.

"I have been dreaming for twenty-two years," he said, "and
to-day I wake to find myself staff in hand again." César had
once more become the Tourangeau peasant.

At these words Pillerault held his nephew tightly in his
arms. César looked up and saw his wife and Célestin, the

latter with significant documents in his hands; then he glanced calmly round the group; all the eyes that met his were sad but friendly.

"One moment!" he said, and unfastening his Cross of the Legion of Honor, which he gave to the Abbé Loraux, "you will give that back to me when I can wear it without a blush. —Célestin," he continued, turning to his assistant, "send in my resignation; I am no longer deputy-mayor. M. l'Abbé will dictate the letter to you, date it January 14th, and send Raguet with it to M. de la Billardière."

Célestin and the Abbé Loraux went downstairs. For nearly a quarter of an hour perfect silence prevailed in César's study. Such firmness took the family by surprise. Célestin and the Abbé came back again, and César signed the letter of resignation; but when Pillerault laid the schedule before him, poor Birotteau could not repress a dreadful nervous tremor.

"Oh, God! have mercy upon us!" he said, as he signed the terrible instrument and handed it to Célestin.

Then Anselme Popinot spoke, and a gleam of light crossed his clouded brow. "Monsieur and madame," he said, "will you grant me the honor of mademoiselle's hand?"

This speech brought tears into the eyes of all who heard it; César alone rose to his feet, took Anselme's hand, and said in a hollow voice, but with dry eyes, "My boy, you shall never marry a bankrupt's daughter."

Anselme looked Birotteau steadily in the face.

"Will you promise, sir, in the presence of your whole family, to consent to our marriage, if mademoiselle will take me for her husband, on the day when you shall have paid all your creditors in full?"

There was a moment's pause. Every one felt the influence of the emotion recorded in the perfumer's weary face.

"Yes," he said at last.

Anselme stretched out his hand to Césarine with an indescribable gesture; she gave him hers, and he kissed it.

"Do you also consent?" he asked her.

"Yes," she said.

"So I am really one of the family. I have a right to interest myself in your affairs," was his comment, with an enigmatical look.

Anselme hurried away lest he should betray a joy in too great contrast with his master's trouble. Anselme was not exactly delighted with the bankruptcy; but so absolute, so egoistical is love, that Césarine herself in her inmost heart felt a glow of happiness strangely at variance with her bitter distress of mind.

"While we are about it, let us strike every blow at once," said Pillerault, and in Constance's ear.

An involuntary gesture, a sign not of assent, but of sorrow, was Mme. Birotteau's answer.

"What do you mean to do, nephew?" said Pillerault, turning to César.

"To continue the business."

"I am not of that opinion," said Pillerault. "Go into liquidation, let your assets go to your creditors in the shape of dividend, and go out of business altogether. I have often thought what I should do if I were placed in a similar position. (Oh! you must be prepared for everything! The merchant who does not contemplate possible insolvency is like a general who does not lay his account with a defeat; he is only half a merchant.) I myself should never have gone on again. What! Be compelled to blush before men whom I should have wronged, to endure their suspicious looks and unspoken reproaches? I can think of the guillotine—in one instant all is over; but to carry a head on your shoulders to have it cut off daily, is a kind of torture from which I should escape. Plenty of men begin again as though nothing had happened; so much the better for them!—they are braver than Claude-Joseph Pillerault. If you pay your way (and pay ready-money you must), people will say that you managed to save something for yourself; and if you have not a half-penny, you will never recover. 'Tis good-evening to you. Surrender your assets, let them sell you up, and do something else."

"But what?" asked César.

"Eh! try for a place under the Government," said Pillerault; "you have influence, have you not? There are the
Duc and Duchesse de Lenoncourt, Mme. de Mortsauf, M. de
Vandenesse! Write to them, go to see them, they will
find you some post in the Household, with a thousand crowns
or so hanging to it; your wife will earn as much again; your
daughter, perhaps, may do the same. The case is not desperate. You three among you will earn something like ten
thousand francs a year. In ten years' time, you will be in a
position to pay a hundred thousand francs, for you will have
no expenses meanwhile; your womankind shall have fifteen
hundred francs from me; and, as for you, we shall see."

It was Constance, and not César, who pondered these wise
words, and Pillerault went on 'Change. At that time stockbrokers used to congregate in a provisional structure of planks
and scaffolding, a large circular room, with an entrance
in the Rue Feydeau. The perfumer's failure was already
known, and had created a sensation in high commercial
circles, for their prevailing politics were Constitutional at
that time. Birotteau was a conspicuous personage, and envied
by many. Merchants, on the other hand, who leaned towards
Liberalism, regarded Birotteau's too celebrated ball as an au-
dacious attempt to trade on their sentiments, for the Opposition were fain to monopolize patriotism. Royalists were allowed to love the King, but the love of their country was
the exclusive privilege of the Left, the Left was for the people; and those in power had no right to rejoice thus vi-
cariously through the administration, in a national event
which the Liberals meant to exploit for their own benefit.
For which reasons the fall of a Ministerialist in favor at
Court, of an incorrigible Royalist who had insulted Liberty
by fighting against the glorious French Revolution on Vendémiaire 13th, set all tongues wagging on 'Change, and was
received with applause.

Pillerault wanted to know what was being said, and to
study public opinion. He went up to one of the most eager

groups; du Tillet, Gobenheim-Keller, Nucingen, old Guillaume and his son-in-law Joseph Lebas, Claparon, Gigonnet, Mongenod, Camusot, Gobseck, Adolphe Keller, Palma, Chiffreville, Matifat, Grindot, and Lourdois were discussing the news.

"Well, well, how careful one had need to be!" said Gobenheim, addressing du Tillet; "my brothers-in-law all but opened an account with Birotteau, it was a near thing."

"I am let in for ten thousand francs myself," said du Tillet; "he came to me a fortnight ago, and I let him have the money on his bare signature. But he obliged me once, and I shall lose it without regret."

"Your nephew is like the rest," said Lourdois, addressing Pillerault. "Gave entertainments. I can imagine that a rogue might try to throw dust in your eyes to induce confidence; but how could a man who passed for the cream of honest folk descend to the stale mountebank's trickery that never fails to catch us?"

"Like leeches," commented Gobseck.

"Only trust a man if he lives in a den like Claparon," said Gigonnet.

"Vell," said the stout Baron Nucingen, for du Tillet's benefit, "you haf dried to blay me a nice drick, sending Pirôdôt to me. I do not know," he went on, turning to Gobenheim the manufacturer, "why he did not send roundt to me for vifty tousend vrancs; I should haf led him haf dem."

"Oh! not you, M. le Baron," said Joseph Lebas. "You must have known quite well that the Bank had refused his paper; you were on the Discount Committee which declined it. This poor man, for whom I still feel a very great respect, fails under singular circumstances——"

Pillerault grasped Joseph Lebas' hand.

"It is, in fact, impossible to explain how the thing has happened," said Mongenod, "except by the theory that there is some one behind Gigonnet, some banker whose intention it is to spoil the Madeleine speculation."

"The thing which has happened to him always happens to people who go out of their own line," said Claparon, interrupting Mongenod. "If he had brought out his Cephalic Oil himself, instead of sending up the price of building lots in Paris by rushing into land speculation, he would have lost his hundred thousand francs through Roguin, but he would not have gone bankrupt. He will start afresh under the name of Popinot."

"Keep an eye on Popinot," said Gigonnet.

According to this crowd of merchants, Roguin was "poor Roguin"; the perfumer was "that unlucky Birotteau." A great passion seemed to excuse the one, the other appeared the more to blame on account of his pretensions. Gigonnet left the Exchange, and took the Rue Perrin-Gasselin on his way home to the Rue Grenétat. He looked in on Mme. Madou, the dry fruit saleswoman.

"Well, old lady," said he, with his cruel good-humor, "and how are we getting on in our way of business?"

"Middling," said Mme. Madou respectfully, and she offered the money-lender her only armchair with a friendly officiousness which she had never shown to any one else but the dear departed.

Mother Madou, who would fell a carman with a blow if he were refractory or carried a joke too far, who had not feared to assist at the storming of the Tuileries on the 10th of October, who railed at her best customers (for that matter, she was capable of heading a deputation of the Dames de la Halle, and speaking to the King himself without a tremor)—Angélique Madou received Gigonnet with the utmost respect. She was helpless in his presence; she winced under his hard eyes. It will be a long while yet before the executioner ceases to be a terror to the people, and Gigonnet was the executioner of the small traders. The man who sets money in circulation is more looked up to in the Great Market than any other power; all other human institutions are as nought compared with him. For them the Commissaire is Justice personified, and with the Commissaire they of the

Market become familiar. But the sight of the money-lender entrenched behind his green cardboard cases, of the usurer whom they implore with fear in their hearts, dries up the sources of wit, parches the throat, and abashes the bold eyes; the people grew respectful in his presence.

"Have you come to ask something of me?" said she.

"A mere trifle; be prepared to refund the amount of Birotteau's bills, the old man has gone bankrupt, so all outstanding claims must be sent in; I shall send you in a statement to-morrow."

The pupils of Mme. Madou's eyes first contracted like the eyes of a cat, then flames leapt forth from them.

"O the beggar! O the scamp! and he came here himself to tell me that he was deputy-mayor, piling on his lies! The Lord ha' mercy! That's just the way with business; there is no trusting mayors nowadays; the Government cheats us! You wait, I will have the money out of them, I will——"

"Eh! everyone comes out of this sort of thing the best way he can, my little dear!" said Gigonnet, lifting one leg with the precise little gesture of a cat picking its way among puddles, a trick to which he owed his nickname.* "Some swells have been let in who mean to get themselves out of the scrape——"

"Good! good! I will get my hazel-nuts out.—Marie Jeanne! my clogs and my lamb's-wool shawl. Quick! or I will lend you a clout that will warm your cheeks."

"That will make it hot for them yonder up the street," said Gigonnet to himself, as he rubbed his hands. "Du Tillet will be satisfied; there will be a scandal in the Quarter. What that poor devil of a perfumer can have done to him, I don't know; for my own part, I am as sorry for the man as for a dog with a broken paw. He isn't a man; he has no fight in him."

Mme. Madou broke out like an insurrection in the Faubourg Saint-Antoine towards seven o'clock that evening, and swept to the luckless Birotteau's door, which she opened with unnecessary violence, for her walk had had an exciting effect.

---

* Gigonnet, from *Gigotter*, to kick the legs about.

"Brood of vermin, I must have my money, I want my money! You give me my money! or I will have sachets and satin gimcracks and fans till I have the worth of my two thousand francs! A mayor robbing the people! Did any one ever see the like! If you don't pay me, I will send him to jail; I will go for the public prosecutor; I will put the whole posse of them on his tracks! I do not stir from here without my money, in fact."

She looked as if she would open the glass door of a cupboard in which expensive goods were kept.

"The Madou is helping herself," said Célestin, speaking in a low voice to his neighbor. The lady overheard the remark, for during a paroxysm of rage the senses are either deadened, or preternaturally alert, according to the temperament. She bestowed on Célestin the most vigorous box on the ear ever given and received in a perfumer's shop.

"Learn to respect women, my cherub," quoth she, "and not to bedraggle the names of the people you rob."

Mme. Birotteau came forward from the back shop. Her husband by chance was also there; in spite of Pillerault, he chose to remain, carrying his humility and obedience to the law so far as to be ready to submit to be put in prison. "Madame," said Constance, "for Heaven's sake, do not bring a crowd together in the street."

"Eh! let them come in," cried the saleswoman; "I will tell them about it; it will make them laugh! Yes, my goods and the francs I made by the sweat of my brow go for you to give balls. You go dressed like a Queen of France, forsooth, and fleece poor lambs like me for the wool! *Jésus!* stolen goods would burn *my* shoulders, I know! I have nothing but shoddy on my carcase, but it is my own! Bandits and thieves! my money, or——"

She pounced upon a pretty inlaid case full of costly perfumery.

"Leave it alone, madame," said César, appearing on the scene; "nothing here belongs to me, it is all the property of my creditors; I have nothing left but myself; and if you have a mind to seize me and put me in jail, I give you my word of honor" (a tear overflowed his eyes at this) "that I will wait here for your process-server, police-officer, and bailiff's men."

From his tone and gesture, he evidently meant to do as he said; Mme. Madou's anger died down.

"A notary has absconded with my money, and the disasters which I cause come through no fault of mine," César went on; "but in time you shall be paid, if I have to work myself to death and earn the money by my hands as a market porter."

"Come, you are a good man," said the market woman. "Excuse my speaking, madame; but I shall have to fling myself into the river, for Gigonnet will be down upon me, and I have nothing but bills at ten months to give for your cursed paper."

"Come round and see me to-morrow morning," said Pillerault, coming forward; "I will arrange the business for you at five per cent with a friend of mine."

"*Quien!* that is good Father Pillerault!—Why, yes, he is your uncle," she went on, turning to Constance. "Come, now, you are honest folk; I shall not lose anything, shall I? —Good-bye till to-morrow, old Brutus," she added, for the benefit of the retired ironmonger.

César insisted on remaining amid the ruins of his glory, and would hear of no other course; he said that by so doing he could explain his position to all his creditors. In this determination, Uncle Pillerault upheld César in spite of the entreaties of his niece. César was persuaded to go upstairs, and then the wily old man hurried to M. Haudry, put César's case before him, obtained a prescription for a sleeping-draught, had it made up, and went back to spend the evening in his nephew's house. With Césarine's assistance, he constrained César to drink as they did; the narcotic did its work; and fourteen hours later Birotteau awoke to find himself in Pillerault's own bedroom in the Rue des Bourdonnais, a prisoner in the house of his uncle, who slept on a camp bedstead put up in the sitting-room.

When Pillerault had put César into the cab, and Constance had heard it roll away, then her courage failed her. Our strength is often called forth by the necessity of sustaining some one weaker than ourselves; and the poor woman, now that she was left alone with her daughter, wept as she would have wept for César if he had been lying dead.

"Mamma," said Césarine, seating herself on her mother's knee, with the gracious kitten-like ways that women only display for each other, "you said that if I bore my part bravely, you would be able to face adversity. So do not cry, mother dear. I am ready to work in a shop; I will forget what we have been; I will be a forewoman, as you were when you were a girl; you shall never hear a regret or a complaint from me. And I have a hope. Did you not hear M. Popinot?"

"Dear boy! he shall not be my son-in-law."

"Oh! mamma——"

"He will be my own son."

"There is this one good thing about trouble, it teaches us to know our real friends," said Césarine; and, changing places with her mother, she at last comforted her, and soothed the poor woman's grief.

The next morning Constance left a note for the Duc de Lenoncourt, one of the first Gentlemen of the Bedchamber. She asked for an interview at a certain hour. Meanwhile, she went to M. de la Billardière, told him of the predicament in which César found himself in consequence of Roguin's flight from the country, and begged the mayor to give her his support with the Duke, and to speak for her, for she feared that she might express herself ill. She wanted some post for Birotteau. Birotteau would be the most honest of cashiers, if there are degrees in the quality of honesty.

"The King has just appointed the Comte de Fontaine as Comptroller-General of the Royal Household; there is no time to be lost."

At two o'clock La Billardière and Mme. César ascended the great staircase of the Hôtel de Lenoncourt in the Rue Saint-Dominique, and were brought into the presence of

one of the nobles highest in the King's favor, in so far as
Louis XVIII. could be said to have preferences. The gracious
reception accorded to her by a great noble, one of the little
group who formed a connecting link between the eighteenth-
century noblesse and those of the nineteenth, put hope into
Mme. César. The perfumer's wife was great and simple in
her sorrow; sorrow ennobles the most commonplace natures,
for it has a grandeur of its own, but only those who are true
and sincere can take its polish. Constance was essentially
sincere. It was a question of prompt application to the King.

In the midst of the discussion, M. de Vandenesse was announced.

"Here is your deliverer," exclaimed the Duke.

Mme. Birotteau was not unknown to the young man, who
had been once or twice to the perfumer's shop for those trifles
which are often of as much importance as great things. The
Duke explained La Billardière's views; and when Vandenesse
learned the disasters, he went immediately with La Billardière
to see the Comte de Fontaine on behalf of the Marquise
d'Uxelles' godson. Mme. Birotteau was asked to await the
result.

M. le Comte de Fontaine, like La Billardière, was one of
the provincial noblesse, the almost unknown heroes of La
Vendée. Birotteau was no stranger to him, for he had seen
the perfumer at the *Queen of Roses* in former days. At that
time, those who had shed their blood for the Royalist cause
enjoyed privileges, which the King kept secret for fear of
hurting Liberal susceptibilities, and M. de Fontaine, one of
the King's favorites, was supposed to be in the confidence
of Louis XVIII. Not only did this influential person
definitely promise to obtain a post for the perfumer, but he
went to the Duc de Lenoncourt, then in attendance, to ask
him for a moment's speech with the King that evening, and
to entreat for La Billardière an audience with Monsieur
the King's brother, who had a particular regard for the old
Vendean.

That very evening M. le Comte de Fontaine came from

the Tuileries to inform Mme. Birotteau that as soon as her husband had received his discharge, he would be appointed to a post worth two thousand five hundred francs per annum in the Sinking Fund Department, all places in the Household being at that time filled with noble supernumeraries to whom the Royalist family were bound.

This success was but a part of the task undertaken by Mme. Birotteau. The poor woman went to Joseph Lebas at the sign of the *Cat and Racket* in the Rue Saint-Denis. On the way thither she met Mme. Roguin in her showy carriage, doubtless on a shopping expedition. Their eyes met, and the visible confusion on the beautiful face of the notary's wife, at this meeting with the woman who had been brought to ruin, gave Constance courage.

"Never will I drive in a carriage paid for with other people's money," said she to herself.

Welcomed by Joseph Lebas, she asked him to look for a situation for her daughter in some respectable house of business. Lebas made no promises, but a week later it was arranged that Césarine should be placed in a branch of one of the largest drapery establishments in Paris, which had just been opened in the Quartier des Italiens. She was to live in the house, and to take charge of the shop and counting-house, with a salary of three thousand francs. She would represent the master and mistress, and the forewoman was to act under her orders.

As for Mme. César herself, she went on the same day to ask Popinot to allow her to take charge of the books, the correspondence, and the household. Popinot knew well that this was the one commercial house in which the perfumer's wife might take a subordinate position and still receive the respect due to her. The noble-hearted boy installed her in his house, gave her a salary of three thousand francs, arranged to give his own room to her, and went up into the attic. And so it came to pass that the beautiful woman, after one short month spent amid novel splendors, was compelled to take up her abode in the poor room where Gaudissart, Anselme, and Finot had inaugurated the Cephalic Oil.

The Tribunal of Commerce had appointed Molineux as agent, and he came to take formal possession of César's property. Constance, with Célestin's help, went through the inventory with him; and then mother and daughter went to stay with Pillerault. They went out on foot, and simply dressed, and without turning their heads, and this was their leave-taking of the house in which they had spent the third part of a lifetime. Silently they walked to the Rue des Bourdonnais, and dined with César, for the first time since their separation. It was a melancholy dinner. They had each had time to think over the position, to weigh the burden laid upon them, to estimate their courage. All three were like sailors, prepared to face the coming tempest without blinking the danger. Birotteau took heart again when he heard that great personages had interested themselves for him and provided for his future; but he broke down when he heard of the arrangement which had been made for his daughter. Then hearing how bravely his wife had begun to work again, he held out his hand to her.

Tears filled Pillerault's eyes for the last time in his life at the sight of this pathetic picture of the father, mother, and daughter united in one embrace; while Birotteau, the most helpless and downcast of the three, held up his hand and cried, "We must hope!"

"To save expense, you must live here with me; you shall have my room, and share my bread. For a long time past I have been tired of living alone; you will take the place of that poor boy I lost. And it will only be a step from here to your office in the Rue d'Oratoire."

"Merciful God!" cried Birotteau. "There is a star to guide me when the storm is at its height."

By resignation to his fate, the victim of a misfortune consumes his misfortune. Birotteau could fall no further; he had accepted the position; he became strong again.

In France when a merchant has filed his petition, the only thing he need trouble himself to do is to retreat to some oasis at home or abroad where he may passively exist like the child that he is in the eye of the law; theoretically he is a minor, and incapable of acting in any capacity as a citizen.* Practically, however, he is by no means a nullity. He does not, indeed, show his face until he receives a "certificate of immunity from arrest" (which no registrar nor creditor has been known to refuse), for if he is found at large without it he is liable to be put in prison; but once provided with his safe conduct, his flag of truce, he can take a stroll through the enemy's camp, not from idle curiosity, but to counteract and thwart the evil intentions of the law with regard to bankrupts.

A prodigious development of perverse ingenuity is the direct result of any law which touches private interests. The one thought of a bankrupt, as of everybody else who finds his purposes crossed in any way by the law of the land, is how to evade it. The period of civil death, during which time a bankrupt must be considered as a kind of commercial chrysalis, lasts for three months or thereabouts, the interval required for the formalities which must be gone through before creditors and debtor sign a treaty of peace, otherwise known as a *concordat,* a word which indicates sufficiently clearly that concord reigns after the storm raised by the clashing of various interests which run counter to one another.

Directly the schedule is deposited, the Tribunal of Commerce appoints a registrar to watch over the interests of the throng of unascertained creditors on the one hand, and on the other to protect the bankrupt from the vexatious importunities and inroads of infuriated creditors, a double part which presents magnificent possibilities if registrars had but time to develop them. The registrar authorizes an agent by procuration, to take formal possession of the bankrupt's property, bills, and effects, and the agent checks the statement of assets in the schedule; lastly, the clerk of the court convenes a meeting of creditors, by tuck of drum, that is to say, by ad-

---

*In France a bankrupt loses his civil and political status ; he recovers the right of administering his own affairs after his discharge ; but the disabilities are only removed by Rehabilitation. This is an order granted by the Court when it is proved that the bankrupt has paid debts and costs in full.

vertisements in the newspapers. The creditors, genuine or otherwise, are called upon to assemble and agree among themselves to appoint provisional trustees, who shall replace the agent, step into the bankrupt's shoes, and, by a legal fiction, become indeed the bankrupt himself. These have power to realize everything, to make compromises, or to sell outright; in short, to wind up the whole business for the benefit of the creditors, provided that the bankrupt makes no opposition. As a rule, in Paris the bankruptcy is not carried beyond the stage of the provisional trustees, and for the following reasons:

The nomination of trustees is a proceeding calculated to stir up more angry feeling than any other resolution which can be passed by an assembly of men, deluded, baffled, befooled, ensnared, bamboozled, robbed, cheated, and thirsting for vengeance; and albeit, as a general thing, the creditor is cheated, robbed, bamboozled, ensnared, befooled, baffled, and deluded, in Paris no commercial crisis, no feeling, however high, can last for three mortal months. Nothing in commerce but a bill of exchange is capable of starting up clamorous for payment at the expiration of ninety days. Before the three months are out, all the creditors, exhausted by the wear and tear, and worn out by the marches and counter-marches of the liquidation, sleep soundly by the side of their excellent little wives. These facts may enable those who are not Frenchmen to understand how it comes to pass that the appointment of provisional trustees is usually final; out of a thousand provisional trustees, there are not five who are appointed to carry the thing further. The reasons of the swift abjuration of commercial enmity which has its source in a failure may be imagined; but for those who have not the good fortune to be merchants, some explanation of the drama known as a bankruptcy is necessary if they are to comprehend how it constitutes the most monstrous legal farce in Paris, and understand the ordinary rule to which César's case was to be so marked an exception.

A failure in business is a thrilling drama in three distinct acts. Act the first may be called The Agent; act the second, The Trustees; and act the third, The *Concordat,* or payment of composition. The spectacle is twofold, as is the case with plays performed on the stage; for there is the spectacular effect intended for the public, and the more or less invisible mechanism by which the effects are produced, and the same play if seen before and behind the scenes looks quite different from different points of view. In the wings stand the bankrupt and his attorney (one of the advocates who practise at the Tribunal of Commerce), and the trustees and agent and the registrar complete the list.

Nobody outside Paris knows what no Parisian can fail to know, that a registrar is the most extraordinary kind of magistrate which the freaks of civilization have devised. In the first place, he is a judge who, at every moment of his official life, may go in fear that his own measure may be dealt to him again. Paris has even seen the President of her Tribunal of Commerce compelled to file his petition; and the ordinary judge, who is called upon to act as a registrar, is no venerable merchant retired from business, whose magistracy is a tribute to a stainless career; but the active senior partner of some great house, a man burdened with the responsibility of vast enterprises. It is a *sine qua non* that a judge who is bound to give decisions on the torrents of commercial disputes which pour incessantly upon the capital shall have as much, or more, business of his own than he can manage.

Thus the Tribunal of Commerce, which might have been a useful transition stage and half-way house between the trading community and the regions of the *noblesse,* is composed of busy merchants, who may one day be made to suffer for unpopular awards, and a Birotteau among them may find a du Tillet.

The judge or registrar, therefore, is of necessity a personage in whose presence a great deal is said to which perforce he lends an ear, thinking the while of his private concerns. He is very apt to leave public business in the hands of the trustees and the attorneys who practise at the Tribunal of

Commerce, unless some odd and unusual case turns up; some instance of theft under curious circumstances, to draw from him the remark that either the creditor or the debtor must be a clever fellow. This personage, set on high above the scene, like the portrait of a king in an audience-chamber, is to be seen of a morning from five to seven o'clock in his yard, if he is a timber merchant; in his shop, if, like Birotteau, he is a perfumer; and again, in the evening at dessert after dinner, but always and in any case terribly busy. For these reasons this functionary is usually dumb.

Let us do justice to the law; the registrar's hands are tied by the hasty legislation which provided for these matters; and many a time he sanctions frauds which he is powerless to hinder, as will shortly be seen.

The agent, instead of being the creditors' man, may play into the debtor's hands. Each creditor hopes to swell his share, and in some way to make better terms for himself with the bankrupt, whom every one suspects of a secret hoard. The agent can make something out of both sides, by dealing leniently with the bankrupt on the one hand, or on the other by securing something for the more influential creditors, and in this way can hold with the hare and run with the hounds. Not unfrequently a crafty agent has annulled a judgment by buying out the creditors and releasing the merchant, who springs up again at a rebound like an india-rubber ball.

The agent turns to the best furnished crib; he will, if necessary, cover the largest creditors and let the debtor go bare, or he will sacrifice the creditors to the merchant's future, as suits him best. So the whole drama turns on the first act; and the agent, like the attorney of the Tribunal, is the utility-man in a piece in which neither will play unless he is sure of his fees beforehand. In nine hundred and ninety-nine cases out of a thousand, the agent is for the debtor.

At the time when this story took place, it was the practice of attorneys at the Tribunal of Commerce to go to the judge who was to act as registrar and nominate a man of their own, some one who knew something of the debtor's affairs and could manage to reconcile the interests of the many and of the one—the honorable trader who had fallen into misfortune. Of late years it has been the practice of shrewd judges to wait till this has been done so as to avoid the nominee, and to make an effort to appoint a man of passable integrity.

During this first act the creditors, genuine or presumed, present themselves to select the provisional trustees, an appointment which, as has been said, is practically final. In this electoral assembly every creditor has a voice, whether his claim is for fifty sous or fifty thousand francs, and the votes are reckoned by count and not by weight. The names of the trustees are proposed at the meeting, packed by the debtor with sham creditors (the only ones who never fail to put in an appearance); and from the names thus sent in, the registrar, the powerless president, is *bound* to choose those who shall act. Naturally, therefore, the registrar takes the trustees from the debtor's hands, another abuse which turns this catastrophe into one of the most burlesque dramas sanctioned by a court of justice. The "honorable trader fallen into misfortune" is master of the situation, and proceeds to carry out a premeditated robbery with the law at his back. In Paris, as a rule, the petty tradesmen are blameless. Before a shopkeeper files his schedule, the poor honest fellow has left no stone unturned; he has sold his wife's shawl, and pawned his spoons and forks; and when he gives in at last, it is with empty hands, he is utterly ruined, and has not even money to pay the attorney, who troubles himself very little about his client.

The law demands that the *concordat,* which remits a part of the debt and restores the debtor to the management of his affairs, should be put to the vote and carried by a sufficient majority, with due regard to the amounts claimed by the voters. To secure the majority is a great feat which demands the most skilful diplomacy on the part of the debtor, his attorney, and the trustees amid the clash of conflicting interests. The ordinary commonplace stratagem consists in offering to such a body of the creditors as will represent the majority required by the law, a premium to be paid over and above the dividend which the meeting of creditors is to consent to accept. For this gigantic swindle there is no remedy. Successive Tribunals of Commerce, familiar with it by dint of practice in non-official capacity, and grown wise by experience, have decided of late that all claims are made void where there is a suspicion of fraud; thus it is to the debtor's interest to complain of the "extortion," and the judges of the Tribunal hope in this way to raise the moral tone of proceedings in liquidation. But they will only succeed in making matters worse; creditors will exercise their ingenuity to invent still more rascally devices which the judges will brand as registrars, and profit by as merchants.

Another extremely popular expedient, which gave rise to the expression "serious and legitimate creditor," consists in creating creditors, much as du Tillet created a firm of bankers. By introducing a sufficient number of Claparons into the meeting, the debtor, in these diverse manifestations, receives a share of the spoils, and sensibly diminishes the dividends of the real creditors. This plan has a double advantage. The debtor obtains resources for the future, and at the same time secures the proper number of votes representing (to all appearance) a sufficient proportion of the claims upon the estate, the majority necessary for his discharge. These "gay bogus creditors" are like sham electors in the electoral college. What help has the "serious *bonâ-fide* creditor" against his "gay, bogus" compeer? He can rid himself of him by attacking him! Very good. But if the "serious and *bonâ-fide*" creditor means to oust the intruder, he must leave his own business to take care of itself, and he must employ an attorney; and as the said attorney makes little or nothing out of the case, he prefers to "conduct" bankruptcies, and does not take a bit of pettifogging business too seriously. Then, at the outset, before the "gay and bogus" one can be unearthed, a labyrinth of procedure must be entered upon, the bankrupt's books must be gone through to some remote epoch, and application must be made to the Court to require that the books of the pretended creditor shall be likewise produced; the improbability of the fiction must be set forth and clearly proved to the satisfaction of the judges of the Tribunal, and the serious creditor must come and go and plead and arouse interest in the indifferent. This Quixotic performance, moreover, must be gone through afresh in each separate case; and each gay and bogus creditor, if fairly convicted of "gaiety," makes his bow to the court with an "Excuse me, there is some mistake; I am very serious indeed." All this is done without prejudice to the rights of the debtor, who may appeal and bring Don Quixote into the Court-Royal. And in the meantime Don Quixote's own affairs go askew, and he too may be compelled to file his schedule.

Moral: Let the debtor choose his trustees, verify the claims, and arrange the amount of composition himself.

Given these conditions, who cannot imagine the underhand schemes, the tricks worthy of Sganarelle, stratagems that a Frontin might have devised, the lies that would do credit to a Mascarille, the empty wallets of a Scapin, and all the results of these two systems? Any bankruptcy since insolvency came into fashion would supply a writer with material sufficient to fill the fourteen volumes of *Clarissa Harlowe*. A single example shall suffice.

The illustrious Gobseck, the master at whose feet the Palmas, Gigonnets, Werbrusts, Kellers, and Nucingens of Paris have sat, once found himself among the creditors of a bankrupt who had managed to swindle him, and whom, on that account, he proposed to handle roughly. Of this person he received bills to fall due *after the discharge* for a sum which (taken together with the dividends received at the time) should pay the amount owing to him (Gobseck) in full. Gobseck, in consequence, recommended that a final dividend of twenty-five per cent be paid. Behold the creditors swindled for Gobseck's benefit! But the merchant had signed the illegal bills in the name of the insolvent firm; and when the time came, a dividend of twenty-five per cent was all that he could be made to pay upon them, and Gobseck, the great Gobseck, received a bare fifty per cent. He always took off his hat with ironical respect when he met that debtor.

As all transactions which take place within ten days before the time when a man files his schedule are open to question, certain prudent prospective bankrupts are careful to break ground early, and to approach some of their creditors, whose interest it is, not less than their own, to arrive at a prompt settlement. Then the more astute creditors will go in search of the simple or of the very busy, paint the failure in the darkest colors, and finally buy up their claims for half their value. When the estate is liquidated, these shrewd folk come by the dividend on their own share, and make fifty, thirty, or twenty-five per cent on the liabilities which they have purchased, and in this way contrive to lose nothing.

After the failure is declared, the house in which a few bags of money yet remain from the pillage is more or less hermetically sealed. Happy the merchant who can effect an entrance by the window, the roof, the cellar, or a hole in the wall, and secure a bag to swell his share! When things have come to this pass, this Beresina, where the cry of "Each for himself" has been raised, it is hard to say what is illegal or legal, false or true, honest or dishonest. A creditor is thought a clever fellow if he "covers himself"; that is to say, if he secures himself at the expense of the rest. All France once rang with discussion of a prodigious failure, which took place in a certain city where there was a Court-Royal; the magistrates therein being all personally interested in the case, arrayed their shoulders in waterproof cloaks so heavy, that the mantle of justice was worn into holes, on which grounds it was necessary to transfer the affair into another court. There was no registrar, no agent, no final judgment possible in the bankrupt's own district.

In Paris these commercial quicksands are so thoroughly well appreciated, that every merchant, however much time he may have on his hands, accepts the loss as an uninsured accident; and, unless he is involved for some very large sum, passes the matter to the wrong side of his profit and loss account. He is not so foolish as to waste time over wasted money; he prefers to keep his own pot boiling. As for the little trader, hard put to it to pay his monthly accounts, and tied to the narrow round of his own business, tedious law proceedings, involving a heavy initial outlay, scare him; he gives up the attempt to see through the matter, follows the example of the great merchant, and makes up his mind to his loss. Wholesale merchants do not file their schedule in these days; they liquidate by private arrangement; their creditors take what is offered them, and give a receipt in full; a plan which saves publicity, and the delays of the law, and solicitors' fees, and depreciation of stock consequent on a sudden realization. It is a common belief that it pays better to have a private arrangement than to force the estate into bankruptcy, so private arrangements are more frequent than failures in Paris.

The second act of the drama is intended to prove that a trustee is incorruptible; that there is not the slightest attempt at collusion between them and the debtor. The audience, who have most of them been at some time cast for the part of trustees themselves, know that a trustee is another name for a creditor whose claims are "covered." He listens, and believes as much as he pleases, till, after three months spent in investigating liabilities and assets, the day comes when composition is offered and accepted. Then the provisional trustees read a little report for the assembled creditors. The following is a general formula:

"GENTLEMEN,—The total amount owing to us was one million. We have dismantled our man like a stranded frigate. The sale of old iron, timber, and copper has brought in three hundred thousand francs, the assets therefore amount to thirty per cent of the liabilities. In our joy at finding this sum, when our debtor might have left us a bare hundred thousand francs, we proclaim him to be an Aristides. We vote him crowns and a premium by way of encouragement! We propose to leave him his assets, and to give him ten or a dozen years in which to pay us the dividend of fifty per cent, which

he condescends to promise us.   Here is the *concordat,* walk
up to the desk, and put your names to it!'"

At these words the happy creditors fall on each other's
necks and congratulate one another.   When the *concordat*
has been ratified by the Tribunal, the merchant's assets are
put at his disposition, and he begins business again as if
nothing had happened.   He is at liberty to fail once more over
the payment of the promised dividends—a sort of great-
grandchild of a failure, which not seldom appears like an infant borne by a mother nine months after she has married her
daughter.

If the *concordat* is not accepted, the creditors forthwith
make a final appointment of trustees.   They resort to extreme
measures, and band themselves together to exploit the debtor's
property and business; they lay their hands on everything
he has or may have, his reversionary rights in the property
of father and mother, uncles and aunts, and the like.   This
is a desperate remedy found by a "union of the creditors."

If a man fails in business, therefore, there are two ways
open to him; by the first method, he takes things into his
own hands, and means to recover himself; in the second,
having fallen into the water, he is content to go to the bottom.
Pillerault knew the difference well.   He was of Ragon's opinion, that it was as hard to issue from the first experience with
clean hands as to emerge from the second a wealthy man.
He counseled surrender at discretion, and betook himself to
the most upright attorney on 'Change, asking him to conduct
the liquidation, and to put the proceeds at the disposition of
the creditors.   The law requires that the creditors should
make an allowance for the support of the debtor and his family while the drama is in progress.   Pillerault gave notice to
the registrar that he himself would maintain his niece and
nephew.

Du Tillet had planned everything with a view to prolong-
ing the agony of his old master's failure, and in the following manner.   Time is so valuable in Paris, that, though there

are usually two trustees appointed, one only acts in the case; the other is nominated for form's sake; he approves the proceedings, like the second notary in a notarial deed; and the active trustee as often as not leaves the work to the attorney employed by the bankrupt. By these means a failure of the first kind is conducted so vigorously that everything is patched up, fixed, settled, and arranged during the minimum time required by the legal procedure. In a hundred days the registrar might repeat the cold-blooded epigram of the Minister who announced that "Order reigns in Warsaw."

Du Tillet meant to make an end of César, commercially speaking. So the names of the trustees appointed through his influence had an ominous sound for Pillerault. M. Bidault, otherwise Gigonnet, the principal creditor, was to do nothing. Molineux, the fidgety little old person who had lost nothing, was to do everything. Du Tillet had thrown this noble corpse of a business to the little jackal to worry before he devoured it.

Little Molineux went home after the meeting of creditors at which the trustees were appointed, "honored" (so he put it) "by the suffrages of his fellow-citizens," and as happy in the prospect of domineering over Birotteau as an urchin who has an insect to torment. The owner of house-property, being a stickler for the law, bought a copy of the *Code of Commerce,* and asked du Tillet to give him the benefit of his lights. Luckily, Joseph Lebas, forewarned by Pillerault, had, at the outset, obtained a sagacious and benevolent registrar, and Gobenheim-Keller (on whom du Tillet had fixed his choice) was replaced by M. Camusot, an assistant judge, and Pillerault's landlord, a Liberal, and a rich silk merchant, spoken of as an honorable man.

One of the most dreadful scenes in César's life was his enforced conference with little Molineux; the creature whom he had looked upon as such a nullity was now, by legal fiction, become César Birotteau. There was no help for it; so, accompanied by his uncle, he climbed the six pair of stairs in the Cour Batave, reached the old man's dismal room, and confronted his guardian, his *quasi* judge, the man who represented the body of his creditors.

"What is the matter?" Pillerault asked on the stairs, hearing a groan from César.

"Oh! uncle, you do not know what kind of a man this Molineux is."

"I have seen him at the Café David these fifteen years; he plays a game of dominoes there of an evening now and then. That is why I came with you."

Molineux was prodigiously civil to Pillerault, and his manner towards the bankrupt was contemptuously patronizing. The little old man had thought out his course, studied his behavior down to the minutest details, and his ideas were ready prepared.

"What information do you want?" asked Pillerault. "None of the claims are disputed."

"Oh! the claims are all in order," said little Molineux; "they are all verified. The creditors are serious and *bonâfide!* But there's the law, sir; there's the law! The bankrupt's expenditure is out of proportion to his means. It appears that the ball——"

"At which you were an invited guest," put in Pillerault.

"Cost nearly sixty thousand francs! At any rate, that amount was spent on the occasion, and the debtor's capital at that time only amounted to a hundred and some odd thousand francs! There is warrant sufficient for bringing the matter before a registrar-extraordinary, as a case of bankruptcy caused by serious mismanagement."

"Is that your opinion?" asked Pillerault, who noticed Birotteau's despondency at those words.

"Sir, the said Birotteau was a municipal officer, that makes a difference——"

"You did not send for us, I suppose, to tell us that the case was to be transferred to a criminal court," said Pillerault. "The whole Café David would laugh this evening at your conduct."

The little old man seemed to stand in some awe of the

opinion of the Café David; he gave Pillerault a scared look. He had reckoned upon dealing with Birotteau alone, and had promised himself that he would pose as sovereign lord and Jupiter.   He had meant to strike terror into Birotteau's soul by the thunderbolts of a formal indictment, to brandish the axe above his head, to enjoy the spectacle of his anguish and alarm, and then to relent at the prayer of his victim, and send him away with eternal gratitude in his soul.   But instead of the insect, he was confronted with this business-like old sphinx.

"There is nothing whatever to laugh at, sir!" said he.

"I beg your pardon," returned Pillerault.   "You are consulting M. Claparon pretty freely; you are neglecting the interests of the other creditors to obtain a decision that you have preferential claims.   Now I, as a creditor, can intervene.   The registrar is there."

"Sir," said Molineux, "I am incorruptible."

"I know you are," said Pillerault; "you are only getting yourself out of the scrape, as the saying is.   You are shrewd; you have done as you did in the case of that tenant of yours——"

"Oh! sir, my lawsuit in the matter of the Rue Montorgueil is not decided yet!" cried the trustee, slipping back into the landlord at the word, just as the cat who became a woman pounced upon the mouse.   "A new issue, as they say, has been raised.   It is not a sub-tenancy; he holds direct, and the scamp says now that as he paid his rent a year in advance, and there is only a year to run" (at this point Pillerault gave César a glance which recommended the closest attention to what should follow), "and the year's rent being prepaid, he might clear his furniture out of the premises.   So there is a new lawsuit.   As a matter of fact, I ought to look after my guarantees until I am paid in full; there may be repairs which the tenant ought to pay for."

"But you cannot distrain except for rent," remarked Pillerault.

"And accessories!" cried Molineux, attacked in the centre.

"The article in the Code is interpreted by the light of decisions; there are precedents. The law, however, certainly wants mending in this respect. At this moment I am drafting a petition to his lordship the Keeper of the Seals concerning the hiatus. It would become the Government to consider the interests of owners of property. The State depends upon us, for we bear the brunt of the taxes."

"You are well qualified to enlighten the Government," said Pillerault; "but on what point in this business of ours can we throw any light for you?"

"I want to know," said Molineux with imperious emphasis, "whether M. Birotteau has received any money from M. Popinot."

"No, sir," answered Birotteau. A discussion followed as to Birotteau's interest in the firm of Popinot, in the course of which it was decided that Popinot had a right to demand the repayment of his advances in full without putting in his claim under the bankruptcy as one of Birotteau's creditors for the half of the expenses of starting his business, which Birotteau ought to have paid. Gradually, under Pillerault's handling, Molineux became more and more civil, a symptom which proved that he set no little store on the opinion of the frequenters of the Café David. Before the interview ended he was condoling with Birotteau, and asked him no less than Pillerault to share his humble dinner. If the ex-perfumer had gone by himself, he would perhaps have exasperated Molineux, and brought rancor into the business; and now, as at some other times, old Pillerault played the part of guardian angel.

One horrible form of torture the law inflicts upon bankrupts; they are bound to appear in person with the provisional trustees and the registrar at the meeting of creditors which decides their fate. For a man who can rise above it, as for the merchant who is seeking his *revanche,* the dismal ceremony is not very formidable; but for any one like César the whole thing is an agony only paralleled by the last day in the condemned cell. Pillerault did all in his power to make that day endurable to his nephew.

Molineux's proceedings, sanctioned by the bankrupt, had been on this wise. The lawsuit concerning the mortgage on the property in the Faubourg du Temple had been gained in the Court of Appeal. The trustees decided to sell the land, and César made no objections. Du Tillet, knowing that the Government meant to construct a canal to open communication between Saint-Denis and the Upper Seine, and that the canal would pass through the Faubourg du Temple, bought César's property for seventy thousand francs. César's rights in the Madeleine building-land were abandoned to M. Claparon, on condition that he on his side should make no demand for half the registration fees, which César should have paid on the completion of the contract; it was arranged that Claparon should take over the land and pay for it, and receive the dividend in the bankruptcy which was due to the vendors.

The perfumer's interest in the firm of Popinot & Company was sold to the said Popinot for forty-eight thousand francs. Célestin Crevel bought the business as a going concern for fifty-seven thousand francs, together with the lease of the premises, the stock, the fittings, the proprietary rights in the Pâte des Sultanes and Carminative Toilet Lotion, a twelve years' lease of the factory and the plant being included in the sale.

The liquid assets reached a total of one hundred and ninety-five thousand francs, to which the trustees added seventy thousand francs from the liquidation of "that unlucky fellow Roguin." Two hundred and sixty-five thousand francs in all. The liabilities amounted to about four hundred and forty thousand francs, so that there would be a dividend of more than fifty per cent.

A liquidation is something like a chemical process, from which the clever insolvent merchant endeavors to emerge as a saturated solution. Birotteau, distilled entirely in this retort, yielded a result which infuriated du Tillet. Du Tillet thought that there would be a dishonoring bankruptcy, and behold a liquidation highly creditable to his man. He cared very little about the pecuniary gain, for he would have the building-land by the Madeleine without opening his purse; he wished to see the poor merchant disgraced, ruined, and humbled in the dust. The meeting of creditors would doubtless carry out the perfumer in triumph on their shoulders.

As Birotteau's courage returned, his uncle, like a wise physician, gradually told him the details of the proceedings in bankruptcy. These rigorous measures were so many heavy blows. A merchant cannot but feel depressed when the things on which he has spent so much money and so much thought are sold for so little. He was petrified with astonishment at the tidings which Pillerault brought.

"Fifty-seven thousand francs for the *Queen of Roses!* Why, the stock is worth ten thousand francs! We spent forty thousand francs on the rooms, and the fittings, the plant, the moulds and boilers over at the factory cost thirty thousand francs! Why, if the things are sold for half their value, there is the worth of ten thousand francs in the shop, and the Pâte des Sultanes and the Lotion are as good as a farm!"

Poor ruined César's jeremiads did not alarm Pillerault very much. The old merchant took them much as a horse takes a shower of rain; but when he came to talk of the meeting of creditors, César's gloomy silence frightened him. Those who understand the weakness and vanity of human nature in every social sphere, will understand that for an ex-judge a return as a bankrupt to the Palais where he had sat was a ghastly form of torture. He must receive his enemies in the very place where he had been so often thanked for his services; he, Birotteau, whose views as to bankruptcy were so well known in Paris, he who had said, "A man who files his schedule is an honest man still, but by the time he comes out of a meeting of creditors he is a rogue." His uncle watched for favorable opportunities, and tried to accustom him to the idea of appearing before his creditors assembled, as the law requires. This condition was killing Birotteau.

His dumb resignation made a deep impression on Pillerault, who, through the thin partition wall, used to hear him cry at night. "Never! never! I will die sooner."

Pillerault, so strong himself by reason of his simple life, understood weakness. He made up his mind to spare Birotteau the anguish to which his nephew might succumb, the dreadful and inevitable meeting with his creditors! The law is precise, positive, and unflinching in this respect; the debtor who refuses to appear is liable on these grounds alone to have his case transferred out of the commercial into the criminal court. But if the law compels the appearance of the debtor, it exercises no such constraint upon the creditors.

A meeting of creditors is a mere formality except in certain cases; when, for example, a rogue is to be ousted, or the creditors unite to refuse the dividend offered, or cannot agree among themselves because some of their number are privileged to the prejudice of the rest, or the dividend offered is outrageously small, and the bankrupt is doubtful of obtaining a majority to carry the resolution. But when the estate has been honestly liquidated, or when a rascally debtor has squared everybody, the meeting is only a matter of form. So Pillerault went round to the creditors one after another, and asked each to empower his attorney to represent him on that occasion. Every creditor, du Tillet excepted, was sorry for Birotteau now that he had been brought low. All of them knew how he had behaved, how well his books had been kept, and how straightforward he had been in the matter. They were well pleased to find not one "gay" creditor among their number. Molineux, as agent in the first place, and afterwards as trustee, had found all that the poor man possessed, down to the print of *Hero and Leander* which Popinot had given him. Birotteau had not taken away such small matters as his gold-buckles, his pin, and the two watches, which even an honest man might not have scrupled to keep. This touching obedience to the law made a great sensation in commercial circles. Birotteau's enemies represented these things as conclusive signs of the man's stupidity;

but sensible people saw them in their true light, as a magnificent excess of honesty. In two months a change had been brought about in opinion on 'Change. The most indifferent admitted that this failure was one of the greatest curiosities of commerce ever heard of. So when the creditors knew that they were to receive sixty per cent, they agreed to do all that Pillerault asked of them. There are but few attorneys practising at the Tribunal; so several of the creditors deputed the same man to represent them, and the whole formidable assemblage was reduced to three attorneys, Ragon, the two trustees, and the registrar.

"César, you can go without fear to your meeting to-day; you will find nobody there," Pillerault said on the morning of that memorable day.

M. Ragon wished to go with his debtor. At the sound of the thin elderly voice of the previous owner of the *Queen of Roses,* all the color left his successor's face; but the kind little old man held out his arms, and Birotteau went to him like a child to his father, and both shed tears. This indulgent goodness put fresh heart into César, and he followed his uncle to the cab.

Punctually at half-past three they arrived in the Cloître Saint-Merri, where the Tribunal of Commerce then held its sessions. The Salle des Faillites was deserted. The day and the hour had been fixed to that end with the approbation of the trustees and the registrar. The attorneys were there on behalf of their clients; there was nothing to fill César's soul with dread; and yet the poor man could not enter M. Camusot's room (which had once been his) without deep emotion, and he shuddered as he went through the Salle des Faillites.

"It is cold," said M. Camusot, turning to Birotteau; "these gentlemen will not be sorry to stay here instead of being frozen in the Salle." (He would not say the Salle des Faillites.) "Seat yourselves, gentlemen."

Every one sat down; the registrar put César, still confused, into his own armchair. Then trustees and attorneys signed their names.

"In consideration of the abandonment of your estate," said Camusot, again addressing Birotteau, "your creditors unanimously agree to forego the remainder of their claims; your *concordat* is couched in language which may soften your regrets; your attorney will have it confirmed by the Tribunal at once. So you are discharged. All the judges of the Tribunal have felt sorry that you should be placed in such a position, dear M. Birotteau, without being surprised by your courage," Camusot went on, taking Birotteau's hands, "and there is no one but appreciates your integrity. Through your disasters you have shown yourself worthy of the position which you held here. I have been in business these twenty years, and this is the second time that I have seen a merchant rise in public esteem 'after his failure.' "

Birotteau grasped the registrar's hand and squeezed it. There were tears in his eyes. Camusot asked him what he meant to do, and Birotteau answered that he was going to work, and that he intended to pay his creditors in full.

"If you should be in want of a few thousand francs to carry out your noble design you will always find them if you come to me," said Camusot; "I would give them with great pleasure to see a thing not often seen in Paris."

Pillerault, Ragon, and Birotteau left the Tribunal.

"Well, was it so bad after all?" said Pillerault, when they stood outside.

"I can see your hand in it, uncle," said César, deeply touched.

"And now that you are on your feet again, come and see my nephew," said Ragon; "it is only a step to the Rue des Cinq-Diamants."

It was with a cruel pang that César looked up and saw Constance sitting at her desk in a room on the low dark floor above the shop; dark, for a signboard outside, on which the name "A. Popinot" was painted, cut off one-third of the light from the window.

"Here is one of Alexander's lieutenants," said Birotteau, pointing to the sign with the forced mirth of misfortune.

This constrained gaiety, the naïve expression of Birotteau's old belief in his superior talents, made Ragon shudder, despite his seventy years. But César's cheerfulness broke down when his wife brought down letters for Popinot to sign, and his face turned white in spite of himself.

"Good-evening, dear," she said, smiling at him.

"I need not ask whether you are comfortable here," César said, and he looked at Popinot.

"I might be in my own son's house," she said, and her husband was struck by the tender expression which crossed her face.

Birotteau embraced Popinot, saying, "I have just lost for ever the right to call you my son."

"Let us hope," said Popinot. *"Your* Oil is going well, thanks to our efforts in the newspapers, and thanks to Gaudissart, who has been all over, and flooded France with placards and prospectuses. He is having prospectuses in German printed at Strasbourg, and is just about to descend on Germany like an invasion. We have orders for three thousand gross."

"Three thousand gross!" echoed César.

"And I have bought some land in the Faubourg Saint-Marceau, not badly; a factory is to be built there. I shall keep on at the other place in the Faubourg du Temple."

"With a little help, wife," Birotteau said in Constance's ear, "we shall pull through."

From that memorable day César and his wife and daughter understood one another. Poor clerk, as he was, he had set himself a task which, if not impossible, was gigantic; he would pay his creditors in full! The three, united by a common bond of fierce independence, grew miserly, and denied themselves everything; every farthing was consecrated to this end. Césarine, with one object in her mind, threw herself into her work with a young girl's devotion. She spent her nights in devising schemes for increasing the prosperity of the house; she invented designs for materials, and brought her inborn business faculties into play. Her employers were obliged to check her ardor for work, and rewarded her with presents, but she declined the ornaments and trinkets which they offered; it was money that she preferred. Every month she took her salary, her little earnings, to her Uncle Pillerault, and César and Mme. Birotteau did the same. All three of them recognized their lack of ability, and shrank from assuming the responsible task of investing their savings. So the uncle went into business again, and studied the money market. At a later time it was known that Jules Desmarets and Joseph Lebas had helped him with their counsel; both had zealously looked for safe investments.

· Birotteau, living in his uncle's house, did not even dare to ask any questions about the uses to which the family savings were put. He went through the streets with a bent head, shrinking from all eyes, downcast, nervous, blind to all that passed. It vexed him that he must wear fine cloth.

"At any rate, I am not eating my creditors' bread," he said, with an angelic glance at the kind old man. "Your bread is sweet" (he went on), "although you give it me out of pity, when I think that, thanks to this sacred charity, I am not robbing my creditors of my earnings."

The merchants who met the Birotteau of those days could not see a trace of the Birotteau whom they used to know. Vast thoughts were awakened in indifferent beholders at sight of that face so dark with the blackest misery, of the man who had never been thoughtful so bowed down beneath the weight of a thought; it was a revelation of the depths, in that this being, dwelling on so ordinary a human level, could have had so far to fall. To the man who would fain be wiped out comes no extinction. Shallow natures who lack a conscience, and are incapable of much feeling, can never furnish forth the tragedy of man and fate. Religion alone sets its peculiar seal on those who have sounded these depths; they believe in a future and in a Providence; a certain light shines in them, a look of holy resignation, blended with hope, which touches those who behold it; they know all that they have lost, like the exiled angel weeping at the gates of Heaven.

A bankrupt cannot show his face on 'Change; and César, thrust out from the society of honest men, was like the angel sighing for pardon.

For fourteen months César refused all amusements; his mind was full of religious thoughts, inspired by his fall. Sure though he was of the Ragons' friendship, it was impossible to induce him to dine with them; nor would he visit the Lebas, nor the Matifats, the Protez and Chiffrevilles, nor even M. Vauquelin, though all were anxious to show their admiration for César's behavior. He would rather be alone in his own room, where he could not meet the eyes of any one to whom he owed money; and the most cordial kindness on the part of his friends recalled him to a sense of the bitterness of his position.

Constance and Césarine went nowhere. On Sundays and holidays, the only times when they were free, the two women went first to Mass, and then home with César after the service. Pillerault used to ask the Abbé Loraux to come—the Abbé Loraux who had sustained César in his trouble—and they made a family party. The old ironmonger could not but approve his nephew's scruples, his own sense of commercial honor was too keen; and therefore his mind was bent upon increasing the number of people whom the bankrupt might look in the face with a clear brow.

In May 1821 the efforts of the family thus struggling with adversity were rewarded by a holiday, contrived by the arbiter of their destinies. The first Sunday in that month was the anniversary of the betrothal of César and Constance. Pillerault and the Ragons had taken a little house in the country at Sceaux, and the old ironmonger wanted to make a festival of the house-warming.

On the Saturday evening he spoke to his nephew. "We are going into the country to-morrow, César," he said, "and you must come too."

César, who wrote a beautiful hand, copied documents for Derville and several other lawyers in the evenings, and on Sundays (with a dispensation from the curé) he worked like a negro.

"No," he answered; "M. Derville is waiting for an account of a guardianship."

"Your wife and daughter deserve a holiday, and there will be no one but our friends—the Abbé Loraux, the Ragons, and Popinot and his uncle. Besides, I want you to come."

César and his wife, carried away by the daily round of their busy lives, had never gone back to Sceaux, though from time to time they both had wished to see the garden again, and the lime-tree beneath which César had almost swooned with joy, in the days when he was still an assistant at the *Queen of Roses*. To-day, when Popinot drove them, and Birotteau sat with Constance and their daughter, his wife's eyes turned to his from time to time, but the look of intelligence in them drew no answering smile from his lips. She whispered a few words in his ear, but a shake of the head was the only response. The sweet expressions of tenderness, unalterable, but now forced somewhat, brought no light into César's eyes; his face grew gloomier, the tears which he had kept back began to fill his eyes. Twenty years ago he had been along this very road, when he was young and prosperous and full of hope, the lover of a girl as lovely as Césarine, who was with them now. Then he had dreamed of happiness to come; to-day he saw his noble child's face, pale with long hours of work, and his brave wife, of whose great beauty there remained such traces as are left to a beautiful city after the lava flood has poured over it. Of all that had been, love alone was left. César's attitude repressed the joy in the girl's heart and in Anselme, the two who now represented the lovers of that bygone day.

"Be happy, children; you deserve to be happy," said the poor father, in heartrending tones. "You can love each other with no after-thoughts," added he; and as he spoke, he took both his wife's hands in his and kissed them with a reverent, admiring affection which touched her more than the brightest cheerfulness. Pillerault, the Ragons, the Abbé Loraux, and Popinot the elder were all waiting for them at the house; there was an understanding among those five kindly souls, and their manner, and looks, and words put César at his ease, for it went to their hearts to see him always as if on the morrow of his failure.

"Take a walk in the Bois d'Aulnay," said Pillerault, putting César's hand into his wife's hand. "Go and take Anselme and Césarine with you, and come back again at four o'clock."

"Poor things, we are in the way," said Mme. Ragon, touched by her debtor's unfeigned misery; "he will be very happy before long."

"It is a repentance without the sin," said the Abbé Loraux.

"He could only have grown great through misfortune," said the judge.

The power of forgetting is the great secret of strong and creative natures; they forget after the manner of nature, who knows nothing of a past; with every hour she begins afresh the constant mysterious workings of fertility. But weak natures, like Birotteau, take their sorrows into their lives instead of transmuting them into the axioms of experience; and, steeping themselves in their troubles, wear themselves out by reverting daily to the old unhappiness.

When the two couples had found the footpath which leads to the Bois d'Aulnay, set like a crown on one of the loveliest of the low hills about Paris; when the Vallée-aux-Loups lay below them in its enchanting beauty, the bright day, the charm of the view, the fresh green leaves about them, and delicious memories of that fairest day of their youth, relaxed the chords which grief had strung to resonance in César's soul; he held his wife's arm tightly against his beating heart; his eyes were glazed no longer, a glad light shone in them.

"At last I see you again, my dear César," Constance said. "It seems to me that we are behaving well enough to allow ourselves a little pleasure from time to time."

"How can I?" poor Birotteau answered. "Oh! Constance, your love is the one good left to me. I have lost everything, even the confidence that I used to have in myself. I have no heart left in me; I want to live long enough to pay my dues on earth before I die, and that is all. You, dear, who have been wisdom and prudence for me, who saw things clearly, you who are not to blame, may be glad. Among us three, I am the only guilty one. Eighteen months ago, at that unlucky ball, I saw this Constance of mine, the only woman whom I have loved, more beautiful perhaps than the young girl with whom I wandered along this path twenty years ago, as our children are wandering together now. . . . In less than two years I have blighted that beauty, my pride, and I had a right to be proud of it. I love you more as I know you better. . . . Oh! dearest!" and his tone gave the word an eloquence that went to his wife's heart, "if only I might hear you scold me, instead of soothing my distress."

"I did not think it possible," she said, "that a woman could love her husband more after twenty years of life together."

For a moment César forgot all his troubles at the words that brought such a wealth of happiness to a heart like his. It was with something like joy in his soul that he went towards *their* tree, which by some chance had not been cut down. Husband and wife sat down beneath it and watched Anselme and Césarine, who walked to and fro, on the same plot of grass, unconscious of their movements, fancying perhaps that they were still walking on and on.

"Mademoiselle," Anselme was saying, "do you think me so base and so greedy as to take advantage of the fact that I own your father's interest in the Cephalic Oil? I have carefully set aside his share of the profits; I am keeping them for him. I am adding interest to the money; if there are any doubtful debts, I pass them to my own account. We can only belong to each other when your father has been rehabilitated; I am trying with all the strength that love gives me to bring that day soon."

He had carefully kept his secret from Césarine's mother; but the simplest lover is always anxious to be great in his love's eyes.

"And will it come soon?" she asked.

"Very soon," said Popinot.

The tone in which the answer was given was so penetrating, that the innocent and pure-hearted girl held up her forehead for her lover's kiss, fervent and respectful, for Césarine's noble nature had spoken so plainly in the impulse.

"Everything is going well, papa," she said, with the air of one who knows a great deal. "Be nice, and talk, and don't look so sad any longer."

When these four people, so closely bound together, returned to Pillerault's new house, César, unobservant though he was, felt from the Ragons' altered manner that something was impending. Mme. Ragon was peculiarly gracious; her look and tone said plainly to César, "We are paid."

After dinner the notary of Sceaux appeared. Pillerault asked him to be seated, and glanced at Birotteau, who began to suspect some surprise, though he did not imagine how great it would be. Pillerault began:

"Your savings for eighteen months, nephew, and those of your wife and daughter amount to twenty thousand francs. I received thirty thousand francs in the shape of dividend, so we have fifty thousand francs to divide among your creditors. M. Ragon has received thirty thousand francs as dividend; so this gentleman, who is the notary of Sceaux, is about to hand you a receipt in full for principal and interest, paid to your friends. The rest of the money is with Crottat for Lourdois, old Mme. Madou, the builder, and the carpenter, and the more pressing of your creditors. Next year we shall see. One can go a long way with time and patience."

Birotteau's joy cannot be described; he embraced his uncle, and shed tears.

"Let him wear his Cross to-day," said Ragon, addressing the Abbé Loraux, and the confessor fastened the red ribbon to César's buttonhole. A score of times that evening he looked at himself in the mirrors on the walls of the sitting-room with a delight which people who believe themselves to be superior would laugh at; but these good-hearted citizens saw nothing

unnatural in it. The next day Birotteau went to see Mme.
Madou.

"Oh! is that you!" she cried; "I did not know you, old man,
you have grown so gray. Still, the like of you don't come
to grief; there are places under Government for you. I myself am working as hard as a poodle that turns a spit, and deserves to be christened."

"But, madame——"

"Oh, I'm not blaming you," she said; "you had your discharge."

"I have come to tell you that I will pay you the balance
to-day, at Maître Crottat's office, and interest also——"

"Really?"

"You must be there at half-past eleven."

"There's honesty for you! good measure, and thirteen to
the dozen," cried she, in outspoken admiration. "Stop, sir, I
do a good trade with that red-haired youngster of yours; he is
a nice young fellow; he lets me make my profit without hag-
gling over the price, so as to make up to me for the loss. Well,
then, I will give you the receipt; keep your money, poor old
soul! La Madou fires up like tinder, she hollers out, but she
has something here," and she tapped the most ample cushion
of live flesh ever known in the Great Market.

"Never!" said Birotteau, "the law is explicit; I mean to
pay you in full."

"Then there is no need to keep on begging and praying
of me. And to-morrow at the Market I will sound your
praises; they shall all know about you. Oh! it is a rare joke!"

The worthy man went through the same scene again with
the house-painter, Crottat's father-in-law, but with some va-
riations. It was raining. César left his umbrella in a corner
by the door, and the well-to-do house painter, sitting at breakfast with his wife in a handsomely furnished room, saw the
stream of water trickle across the floor, and was not too con-
siderate.

"Hallo, poor old Birotteau, what do you want?" he asked,
in the hard tone which people use to a tiresome beggar.

"Has not your son-in-law asked you, sir——"

"What?" Lourdois broke in impatiently. Some request was to follow, he thought.

"To go to his office this morning at half-past eleven, to give me a receipt in full for the balance of your claim."

"Oh! that is another thing! Just sit you down, M. Birotteau, and take a bite with us——"

"Do us the honor of breakfasting with us," said Mme. Lourdois.

"Doing pretty well?" asked her burly spouse.

"No, sir. I have had to lunch off a roll in my office to get some money together, but I hope in time to repair the wrong done to my neighbors."

"Really, you are a man of honor," remarked the house-painter, as he swallowed a mouthful of bread and butter and Strasbourg pie.

"And what is Mme. Birotteau doing?" asked Mme. Lourdois.

"She is keeping the books in M. Anselme Popinot's counting-house."

"Poor things!" said Mme. Lourdois, in a low voice.

"If you should want me, come and see me, my dear M. Birotteau," began Lourdois; "I might be of use——"

"I want you at eleven o'clock, sir," said Birotteau, and with that he went.

This first result gave Birotteau fresh courage, but it did not give him peace of mind. The desire to redeem his character perturbed him beyond all measure. He completely lost the bloom which used to appear in his face, his eyes grew dull, his cheeks hollow. Old acquaintances who met him at eight o'clock in the morning, or after four in the afternoon on his way to and from the Rue de l'Oratoire, saw a pale-faced, nervous, white-haired man, wearing the same overcoat which he had had at the time of the bankruptcy (for he was as careful of it as a poor sub-lieutenant who economizes his uniform). Sometimes they would stop him in spite of himself, for he was quick-sighted, slinking home, keeping close to the wall like a thief.

"People know how you have behaved, my friend," they
would say. "Everybody is sorry to see how hardly you live,
you and your wife and daughter."

"Take a little more time about it," others would suggest.
"A wound in the purse is not mortal."

"No, but a wound in the soul is deadly indeed," the poor
feeble César said one day in answer to Matifat.

At the beginning of the year 1823 the Canal Saint-Martin
was decided upon, and land in the Faubourg du Temple
fetched fabulous prices. The canal would actually pass
through the property once César's, now du Tillet's. The company who had purchased the concession were prepared to pay
du Tillet an exorbitant sum for the land if he would put them
in possession within a given time, and Popinot's lease was
the one obstacle in the way. So du Tillet went to see the
druggist in the Rue des Cinq-Diamants.

If Popinot himself regarded du Tillet with indifference,
as Césarine's lover he felt an instinctive hatred of the man.
He knew nothing of the theft, nor of the disgraceful machina-
tions of the lucky banker, but a voice within him said, "This
is a thief who goes unpunished." Popinot had not had the
slightest transaction with du Tillet, whose presence was hateful to him, and particularly hateful at that moment when
he beheld du Tillet enriched with the spoils of his employer's
property, for the building-land at the Madeleine was beginning to command prices which presaged the exorbitant sums
which were asked for them in 1827. So when the banker
explained the reason of his visit, Popinot looked at him with
concentrated indignation.

"I do not mean to refuse outright to surrender my lease,
but I must have sixty thousand francs for it, and I will not
bate a farthing."

"Sixty thousand francs!" cried du Tillet, making as though
he would go.

"The lease has fifteen years to run, and it will take another three thousand francs per annum to replace the factory.

So, sixty thousand francs, or we will say no more about it,"
said Popinot, turning into the shop, whither du Tillet followed him.

The discussion waxed warm, when Mme. Birotteau, hearing her husband's name pronounced, came downstairs, and
saw du Tillet for the first time since the famous ball. He,
on his side, could not avoid making a startled gesture at the
sight of the change wrought in her face; he was frightened
at his work, and lowered his eyes.

"This gentleman is receiving three hundred thousand
francs for *your* land," said Popinot, addressing Mme. César,
"and he declines to pay *us* sixty thousand francs by way of indemnity for *our* lease——"

"Three thousand francs per annum," said du Tillet, laying stress on the words.

"Three thousand francs!" Madame César repeated the
words quietly and significantly.

Du Tillet turned pale; Popinot looked at Mme. Birotteau.
There was a pause and a deep silence, which made the scene
still more inexplicable to Anselme.

"Sign your surrender," said du Tillet; "I have had the
document drafted by Crottat," and he drew a stamped agreement from a side-pocket. "I will give you a draft on the
Bank for sixty thousand francs."

Popinot stared at Mme. César with great and unfeigned
astonishment; he thought that he was dreaming. While du
Tillet was making out his draft at a desk, Mme. César vanished upstairs again. The druggist and the banker exchanged papers, and du Tillet went out with a frigid bow to
Popinot.

"At last!" cried Popinot. "Only a few months now, and
I shall have my Césarine, thanks to this queer business," and
he watched du Tillet turn into the Rue des Lombards, where
his cab was waiting for him. "My dear little wife shall not
wear herself to death at her work. What! was a look from
Mme. César enough? What is there between her and that
brigand? It is a very extraordinary thing."

Popinot sent the draft to be cashed at the Bank, and went up to speak to Mme. Birotteau; but she was not in the counting-house, doubtless she had gone to her room. Anselme and Constance lived like a mother-in-law and son-in-law when these are on good terms with each other, so he went to Constance's room in all the haste natural in a lover who sees happiness within his grasp.

Great was his astonishment to find his mother-in-law (whom he surprised by springing into the room) reading a letter from du Tillet, for Anselme recognized the handwriting at once. The sight of a lighted candle and black phantom scraps of burnt paper on the floor sent a shudder through Popinot, whose long-sighted eyes had involuntarily read the words with which the letter began, "I adore you! You know it, angel of my life, and why——"

"What hold have you on du Tillet to make him conclude such a bargain as this?" he asked, with the jerky laugh of repressed suspicion.

"Let us not talk of it," she said, and he saw that she was painfully agitated.

"Yes," answered Popinot, quite taken aback, "we must talk of the end of your troubles." Anselme swung round on his heels and drummed on the window-pane, staring out into the yard. "Very well," said he to himself, "and suppose that she loved du Tillet, is that any reason why I should not behave like a man of honor?"

"What is it, my boy?" the poor woman asked.

"The net profits on the Cephalic Oil amount to two hundred and forty-two thousand francs, and the half of two hundred and forty-two is one hundred and twenty-one," said Popinot abruptly. "If I deduct from that sum the forty-eight thousand francs already paid to M. Birotteau, there still remain seventy-three thousand; add to it the sixty thousand just paid for the surrender of the lease, and *you* will have one hundred and thirty-three thousand francs."

Mme. César listened in such glad excitement, that Popinot could hear the beating of her heart.

"Well, I have always looked on M. Birotteau as my partner," he continued; "we can employ the money in repaying his creditors. Your savings, twenty-eight thousand francs, in Uncle Pillerault's keeping, will raise the sum to a hundred and sixty-one thousand francs. Uncle will not refuse to give us a receipt for his twenty-five thousand francs. No power on earth can prevent my lending to my father-in-law, on account of next year's profits, enough to pay off the remainder of his creditors. . . . And—he will—be—re-habilitated——"

"Rehabilitated!" cried Mme. César, kneeling before her chair, and, clasping her hands, she repeated a prayer. The letter had slipped from her fingers. She crossed herself. "Dear Anselme!" she said, "dear boy!" She took his face in her hands, kissed him on the forehead, and held him tightly in her arms. "Césarine is yours indeed," she cried. "My daughter will be very happy. She will leave the house where she is working herself to death."

"Through love," said Anselme.

"Yes," smiled the mother.

"Listen to a little secret," said Anselme, looking out of the corner of his eye at the unlucky letter. "I obliged Célestin when he wanted capital to buy your business, but it was on one condition. Your rooms are just as you left them. I had my own idea, but I did not think then that fortune would favor us so greatly. Célestin has undertaken to sublet your old rooms to you; he has not set foot in them, and all the furniture there is yours. I am reserving the second story, so that Césarine and I may live there; she shall never leave you. After we are married, I will spend the day here from eight o'clock in the morning till six in the evening. Then I will buy out M. César's interest in the business for a hundred thousand francs, so that, with his post, you will have ten thousand livres a year. Will you not be happy?"

"Do not say any more, Anselme, or I shall go mad with joy."

Mme. César's angelic bearing, her pure eyes, the innocence

on her fair brow, gave the lie so magnificently to the countless thoughts which surged up in the young lover's brain,
that he made up his mind to slay the chimeras of his fancy.
The sin was irreconcilable with the life and the sentiments
of Pillerault's niece.

"My dear adored mother," he began, "a horrible doubt has
just crossed my mind. If you would see me happy, you will
set it at rest."

Popinot held out his hand as he spoke, and took possession
of the letter.

"Unintentionally I read the first words in du Tillet's handwriting," he said, alarmed at the consternation in her face.
"The words coincide so oddly with the effect you just produced
upon the man, who complied at once with my extravagant
demands, that anybody would find the explanation which the
devil suggests to me in spite of myself. A glance from you,
and three words were enough——"

"Stop," said Mme. César, and taking back the letter, she
burned it under Anselme's eyes. "I am cruelly punished
for a trifling fault, my child. And now you must know all,
Anselme. The suspicion attaching to the mother must not
do her daughter an injury, and besides, I may speak without
a blush; I could tell my husband this that I am about to tell
you. Du Tillet tried to seduce me, my husband was warned
at once, and Du Tillet was to be dismissed. The very day
that my husband was to discharge him du Tillet took three
thousand francs."

"I suspected it," said Popinot, with all his hatred of the
man in his tone.

"Anselme, your future and your happiness required this
confidence, but it must die in your own breast, as it had died
in César's and mine. You surely remember the fuss my husband made about the mistake in the books. M. Birotteau, no
doubt, put three thousand francs into the safe (the price of
the shawl, which was not given to me for three years), so
as to avoid ruining the young man by bringing him into a
police court. So there you have the explanation of my cry
of surprise. Alas, my dear boy, I will confess my childish

conduct. Du Tillet had written three love letters to me, letters which showed his nature so plainly that I kept them— as a curiosity. I only read them once; but, after all, it was not wise to keep them. When I saw du Tillet, I thought of them, and went up to my room to burn them. When you came in, I was looking at the last one. That is all, my dear."

Anselme knelt and kissed Mme. César's hand. The expression in his eyes drew tears of admiring affection from hers. Constance raised her son-in-law, and clasped him to her heart.

That day was destined to be a day of joy for César. The King's private secretary, M. de Vandenesse, came to the office to speak with him. They went out together into the little courtyard of the Sinking-Fund Department.

"M. Birotteau," said the Vicomte, "the story of your struggle to pay your creditors came by chance to the King's knowledge. His Majesty was touched by such unusual conduct; and learning that, from motives of humility, you were not wearing the Order of the Legion of Honor, has sent me to command you to resume it. His Majesty also wishes to assist you to discharge your obligations, and has ordered me to pay this amount to you out of his own privy purse, with regrets that he can do no more for you. Let the matter remain a profound secret, for His Majesty thinks it little becomes a King to make official proclamation of his good actions," and the private secretary paid over six thousand francs to the employé, who heard these words with indescribable emotions.

Birotteau could only stammer inarticulate thanks. Vandenesse smiled, and waved his hand. César's principles are so rarely seen in practice in Paris, that by degrees his life had won admiration. Joseph Lebas, Popinot the elder, Camusot, Ragon, the Abbé Loraux, the head partner of the firm which employed Césarine, Lourdois, and M. de la Billardière had spoken of it. The scale of opinion had already turned in his favor, and people praised him to the skies.

"There goes a man of honor!" The words had reached César's ears several times in the street; he heard them with the sensations of an author who hears his name pronounced. This fair renown disgusted du Tillet. César's first thought on receiving the King's banknotes was of repayment to his ex-assistant. The good man betook himself to the Rue de la Chaussée-d'Antin, and it so fell out that the banker, returning home from business, met him upon the staircase.

"Well, my poor Birotteau," said he, in a caressing tone.

"Poor?" the other cried proudly. "I am very rich. I shall lay my head on the pillow to-night with the satisfaction of knowing that I have paid you."

The words, so full of honesty, put du Tillet for a moment on the rack. Every one respected him, but he had lost his self-respect; a voice which could not be stifled cried within him, "This man is heroic!" But he spoke:

"Pay me! What business can you be in?"

Birotteau felt quite sure that du Tillet would not repeat the story.

"I shall never start in business again, sir. No human power could foresee the thing that befell me. Who knows but that I might be the victim of another Roguin? But my conduct has been put before the King, his heart has deigned to compassionate my struggles, and he has encouraged them by sending me at once a fairly large sum, which——"

"Do you want a receipt in full?" du Tillet cut him short. "Are you paying——"

"In full, and interest besides. So I must beg you to come to M. Crottat's office, a step or two away."

"In the presence of a notary!"

"Why, sir, there is nothing to prevent me from thinking of my rehabilitation, and a document so authenticated is legal evidence——"

"Come, let us go," said du Tillet, and he went out with Birotteau; "it is only a step. But who will find you so much money?" he went on.

"No one finds it for me," said César. "I am earning it by the sweat of my brow."

"You owe an enormous amount to Claparon."

"Alas! yes, that is the heaviest of my debts; I am afraid the effort will be too much for me."

"Oh! you will never be able to pay it all," said du Tillet harshly.

"He is right," thought Birotteau.

He went home again by way of the Rue Saint-Honoré, a piece of inadvertence, for he always went round some other way, that he might not see his shop, nor the windows of his old home. For the first time since his fall, he saw the house where he had spent eighteen happy years, and three months of anguish that effaced those memories.

"I used to count on ending my days there," he said to himself; and he quickened his pace at the sight of a new name on the shop front:

CÉLESTIN CREVEL

Late César Birotteau.

"My eyes dazzle. . . . Is that Césarine?" he cried, thinking that he had seen a golden head at the window.

It was really Césarine whom he saw, and his wife was there, and so was Popinot. The two lovers knew that Birotteau never went past his old home; and it was impossible that they should imagine the great event in the Rue de l'Oratoire, so they had gone to make arrangements for the fête they were planning to give in Birotteau's honor. The strange apparition astonished César so much that he stood stockstill.

"There is M. Birotteau looking at his old house," said M. Molineux to a shopkeeper who lived over against the *Queen of Roses.*

"Poor man!" returned Birotteau's old neighbor, "he gave one of the grandest balls there—there were two hundred carriages in the street."

"I went to it; he went bankrupt three months afterwards, and I was trustee," said Molineux.

Birotteau fled, his legs trembling beneath him, and reached Pillerault's house.

Pillerault knew what was passing in the Rue des Cinq-Diamants, and it seemed to him that his nephew was scarcely fit to bear the shock of a joy so great as his rehabilitation. He had been a daily witness of César's mental sufferings, knew that Birotteau's own stern doctrine as to bankrupts was always in his thoughts, and that he was living up to the very limit of his strength. Dead honor might have its Easter Day for him; and it was this hope that gave him no respite from pain. Pillerault undertook to prepare César for the good news; so when he came in, his uncle was thinking how to attain his end. César began to tell the news of the interest that the King had taken in him, his joy seemed to Pillerault to be auspicious, and his amazement that Césarine should be at the window at the sign of the *Queen of Roses* afforded an excellent opening.

"Well, César," Pillerault began, "do you know what brought it about? Popinot is impatient to marry Césarine. He will not and ought not to be bound any longer by your extravagant ideas of honor, to spend his youth in eating dry bread and smelling a good dinner. Popinot is determined to pay off your creditors in full."

"He is going to buy his wife."

"Isn't it to his credit that he wants to rehabilitate his father-in-law?"

"But questions might be raised, and besides——"

"And besides," cried Uncle Pillerault in feigned anger, "you may sacrifice yourself if you like, but you have no right to sacrifice your daughter."

A lively discussion began, and Pillerault worked himself up.

"Eh! If Popinot lent you nothing," cried he; "if he had looked upon you as his partner; if he chose to consider the money that he paid over to your creditors for your interest in the Oil as an advance on account of the profits, so that you should not be robbed——"

"It would look as though I had arranged with him to cheat my creditors."

Pillerault pretended to be defeated by this logic. He knew enough of human nature to guess that during the night the good man would argue out the case with himself; and those private reflections of his would accustom him to the idea of rehabilitation.

"But how came my wife and daughter to be in our old house?" he asked at dinner.

"Anselme means to take one of the floors, and he and Césarine will set up housekeeping there. Your wife is on his side. They have had the banns put up without telling you, so as to compel you to give your consent. Popinot says that there will be less merit in marrying Césarine after you are rehabilitated. You accept the King's six thousand francs, and yet you will take nothing from your relatives! Now, for my own part, I am quite justified in giving you a receipt in full; would you refuse it?"

"No," said César. "But it would not hinder me from saving the money to pay you, receipt or no."

"All this is splitting hairs," said Pillerault, "and when honesty is in question, I ought to be allowed to know what is right. What folly were you talking just now? When your creditors are all paid in full, will you still persist that you have cheated them?"

César looked full at Pillerault as he spoke, and it touched the older man to see a bright smile on his nephew's face after three years of dejection.

"You are right," he said, "they would be paid.—But it is like selling my daughter!"

"And I wish to be bought," cried Césarine, who came in with Popinot.

The lovers stealing on tiptoe through the lobby had overheard the words. Mme. Birotteau was just behind them. The three had made a round in a cab, asking all the creditors to meet in Crottat's office that evening; Popinot's lover's logic bore down César's scruples; but he still persisted in calling himself a debtor, and would have it that he was outflanking the law by a substitution. Conscience yielded to an outburst from Popinot:

"So you mean to kill your daughter, do you?"

"Kill my daughter!" echoed César, bewildered.

"Well, now," said Popinot, "what is there to prevent me from making a deed of gift in your favor of a sum which on my conscience I believe to be yours? Can you refuse?"

"No," said César.

"Good. Then let us go to Alexandre Crottat this evening, so that there shall be no going back upon it, and our marriage contract can be decided at the same time."

An application for reinstatement and all the necessary certificates were duly deposited by Derville at the office of the Procureur-Général of the Court of Appeal.

During the month which elapsed between the putting up of the banns and the marriage, and during the progress of the formalities, César lived in a state of constant nervous excitement. He was ill at ease. He feared that he might not live to see the great day when his disabilities should be formally removed. His pulse throbbed unaccountably, he said, and he complained of a dull pain about his heart. He had been exhausted by painful emotion, and this supreme joy was wearing him out. Decrees of rehabilitation are rare in Paris; there is scarcely one in ten years.

There is something indescribably solemn and imposing in the ceremony of justice for those who take society seriously. An institution is to men as they consider it, and is invested with dignity and grandeur by their thoughts. When a nation has ceased, not to feel the religious instinct, but to believe; when primary education relaxes the bonds of union by teaching children a habit of merciless analysis, a nation is dissolved; for the only ties that are left to bind men together and make of them one body are the ignoble ties of material interest, and the dictates of the selfish cult created by egoism well carried out. Birotteau, sustained by religion, saw Justice as Justice ought to be regarded among men, as the expression of society itself; beneath the forms he saw the sovereign **will,** the laws by which men have agreed to live. If the magistrate is old, feeble, and white-haired, so much the more solemn does his priestly office appear, an office which demands so profound a study of human nature and of things, an office to which the heart is immolated, for of necessity it becomes callous in a guardian of so many palpitating interests.

In these days the men who cannot ascend the staircase of the Court of Appeal in the old Palais de Justice in Paris, without feeling deeply stirred, are growing rare; but Birotteau was one of these men. There are not many who notice the majestic grandeur of that staircase, so magnificently planned to produce an effect. It rises at the further end of the peristyle which adorns the Cour du Palais. The doorway opens on the centre of the gallery which leads from the vast Salle des Pas Perdus at its one end to the Sainte-Chapelle at the other, two monuments which may well dwarf everything about them into insignificance. The Church of St. Louis is in itself one of the grandest buildings in Paris, and there is an indescribable dim atmosphere of romance about it when approached by way of this gallery; while the vast Salle des Pas Perdus is flooded with daylight, and it is hard to forget the memories of the history of France that cling about its walls. So the staircase must have a grandeur of its own if it is not utterly overshadowed by the glories of those two famous buildings. Perhaps there is something to stir the soul at the sight of the place where decrees are executed, beheld through the rich scroll-work of the screen of the Palais. The staircase gives entrance to a vast room, the Salle des Pas Perdus of this court, beyond which lies the Hall of Audience. Imagine the feeling with which Birotteau (always so much impressed by the circumstance of justice) mounted the staircase among a little crowd of his friends— Lebas, at that time President of the Tribunal of Commerce; Camusot, who had acted as registrar; Ragon, his old master; and the Abbé Loraux, his confessor. The presence of the good priest enhanced these earthly honors by a reflection from heaven, which gave them yet more value in César's eyes.

Pillerault, that practical philosopher, had bethought him of the expedient of dwelling upon and exaggerating the joy of the release, so that the actual experience might not overwhelm César. Just as he finished dressing, he found himself surrounded by faithful friends, all anxious for the honor of accompanying him to the bar of the Court. The delight which suffused the good man's soul at the sight of this group raised him to a pitch of happiness necessary for him if he was to endure the alarming ordeal. He found others of his friends standing in the Great Hall of Audience, where a dozen Councillors were sitting.

After the cases had been called, Birotteau's attorney made application in a brief formula. At a sign from the President, the Attorney-General rose to give his opinion. In the name of the Court, the Attorney-General, the public accuser, was about to make demand that the merchant's honor, which had been pledged, should be vindicated; a proceeding unique in law, for a condemned man can only be pardoned. Those who have hearts that feel can imagine Birotteau's feelings when M. de Granville spoke somewhat as follows:

"Gentlemen," said the great lawyer, "on the 16th of January 1820, Birotteau was declared a bankrupt by the Tribunal of Commerce of the Seine. The insolvency was not occasioned by imprudence on the part of the merchant, nor by dishonest speculation, nor any other cause which could stain his honor. We feel that it is necessary to state it publicly— the calamity was brought about by one of those disasters which occur from time to time, to the great affliction of Justice and of the city of Paris. It was reserved for this present century, in which the evil leaven of subverted morals and revolutionary ideas will long ferment, to behold the Parisian notariat depart from the honorable traditions of its past; there have been more cases of insolvency in that body during the last few years than in two preceding centuries under the ancient monarchy. The greed of gold rapidly acquired has seized upon officials, those guardians of the public welfare and intermediary authorities."

Then followed a tirade based on this text, in the course of which M. le Comte de Granville (speaking in character) took occasion to incriminate Liberals, Bonapartists, and all and sundry who were disaffected, as in duty bound. Events have shown that there was good ground for the Councillor's apprehensions.

"The immediate cause of the plaintiff's ruin was the action of a Paris notary, who absconded with the money which Birotteau deposited with him. The sentence passed by the Court in Roguin's case shows how shamefully he had betrayed his client's trust. A *concordat* followed. We will observe, for the honor of the applicant, that the proceedings were characterized by honesty not to be met with in the scandalous failures which daily occur in Paris. Birotteau's creditors, gentlemen, found every trifle that he possessed, down to trinkets and articles of wearing apparel belonging not only to him, but to his wife, who, to swell the assets, gave up all that she had. Birotteau at this juncture showed himself worthy of the respect which he had won by the discharge of his municipal functions; for he was at that time deputy-mayor of the second arrondissement, and had just received the Cross of the Legion of Honor accorded to the devoted Royalist, who shed his blood for the cause on the steps of Saint-Roch in Vendémiaire; and, no less, to the Consular judge, who had won respect by his ability, and popularity by his conciliatory spirit; to the modest municipal officer, who declined the honors of the mayoralty for himself, and put forward the name of another as more worthy—the honorable Baron de la Billardière, one of the noble Vendeans whom he had learned to esteem in evil days."

"He put that better than I did," said César in his uncle's ear.

"The creditors, therefore, receiving sixty per cent of their claims, thanks to the upright merchant and his wife and daughter, who surrendered everything that they possessed, gave expression to their respect in the *concordat,* by which they forewent the remainder of their claims in consideration

of the dividend.   The attention of the Court is called to the
manner in which this record is worded."—Here the Attorney-
General read the *concordat*—"After such expressions of goodwill, gentlemen, many a trader would have considered himself free, and would have walked with head erect in public; but so far from considering his liabilities to be discharged, Birotteau would not give way to despair, but made
an inward resolution to hasten the coming of a glorious day
which here and now dawns for him.   Nothing turned him
aside from his purpose.   Our beloved sovereign gave a post to
the man who was wounded at Saint-Roch, and the bankrupt
merchant set by the whole of his salary for the benefit of his
creditors, for the devotion of his family did not fail him——"

Tears came into Birotteau's eyes as he squeezed his uncle's
hand.

"His wife and daughter poured their earnings into the
common treasury; they too had embraced Birotteau's loyal
purpose.   They descended from their position to take a
subordinate place.   Such sacrifices as these, gentlemen, deserve all honor, for they are the hardest of all.   This was the
task which Birotteau laid upon himself."

The Attorney read an abbreviated version of the schedule,
giving the names of the creditors and the balances due to
them.

"Every one of these amounts, gentlemen, has been paid (interest included).   The receipts have not been given by notes
of hand which demand investigation, but by certificates of
payment made in the presence of a notary, documents which
do not abuse the good faith of the Court, though, nevertheless,
the inquiries required by the law have been duly made.   You,
therefore, restore to Birotteau not his honor, but the civil and
political privileges of which he has been deprived, and in so
doing you do justice.   Such cases come so seldom before you,
that we cannot refrain from giving expression to our admiration of the conduct of the applicant, who has already
received the encouragement of august patronage."

With that, he read the formal application.   The Court deliberated without retiring, and the President rose to pronounce the decree.

"The Court charges me to inform M. Birotteau of the satisfaction with which the decree, granted under such circumstances, is passed.—Call the next case."

Birotteau, already invested with a caftan of honor by the Attorney-General's speech, was struck dumb with joy when he heard these solemn words from the President of the Highest Court of Appeal in France, words which made those who heard them feel that the impassive Themis had a heart. He could not move from his place, he seemed to be glued to the floor, and gazed with bewildered eyes at the Councillors, who seemed to him like angels who had opened the gates which admitted him to life among his fellows. His uncle took him by the arm and drew him away. Then César, who had not obeyed the desire of Louis XVIII., fastened the red ribbon at his buttonhole, like a man in a dream, and went down in triumph with his friends about him to the hackney cab.

"Where are you taking me?" he asked of Joseph Lebas, Pillerault, and Ragon.

"Home."

"No. It is three o'clock; I want to go on 'Change again, now that I have the right."

"To the Exchange," Pillerault gave the order, and looked significantly at Lebas, for there were symptoms which made him uneasy; he feared for Birotteau's reason.

So Birotteau went back on 'Change between his uncle and Joseph Lebas; the two merchants whom every one respected linked their arms in his. The news of his rehabilitation was abroad. Du Tillet was the first to see the three and old Ragon, who followed behind.

"Ah! my dear master! Delighted to hear that you have pulled through your difficulties. Perhaps I contributed to bring about this happy termination by allowing little Popinot to pluck me so easily. I am as glad of your happiness as if it were my own."

"It is the only way open to you," said Pillerault, "for you will never experience it yourself."

"What do you mean, sir?" asked du Tillet.

"A good dig in the ribs, by George," said Lebas, smiling at Pillerault's malicious revenge. He knew nothing of the part that du Tillet had played, but he looked on him as a scoundrel.

Matifat saw César, and immediately all the most respected merchants crowded about the perfumer; he received an ovation on 'Change, the most flattering congratulations and handshakes, which caused here and there some heart-burnings, and here and there a pang of remorse, for fifty out of every hundred present had been insolvent at some time or other.

Gigonnet and Gobseck, chatting in a corner, stared at César as the learned must have stared when the first electric eel was brought for their inspection, and they beheld that strange curiosity, a living Leyden jar.

Then, still breathing the incense of triumph, César went out to the cab, and drove home to his house, where the marriage-contract between his dear child Césarine and the devoted Popinot was to be signed that evening. He laughed nervously, in a way that alarmed his three old friends.

It is one of the mistakes of youth to imagine that every one has the vitality of youth, a defect nearly akin to its best endowment; for youth does not behold life through a pair of spectacles, but through the radiant hues of a reflected glow, and age itself is credited with its own exuberant life. Popinot, like César and Constance, cherished memories of the pomp and splendor of the ball, the strains of Collinet's orchestra had often rung in his ears; he had seen the gay throng of dancers, and tasted the joy so cruelly punished, as Adam and Eve might have thought of the forbidden fruit which banished them from the Garden, and brought Death and Birth into the world, for it seems that the multiplication of the angels is one of the mysteries of the Paradise above.

Popinot, however, could think of that night's festivity not only without remorse, but with joy in his heart, for then it was that Césarine in all her glory had given her promise to him in his poverty. That evening he had known beyond all doubt that he was loved for himself alone. So when he paid Célestin for the rooms which Grindot had restored, and stipulated that everything should be left untouched; when he had carefully seen that the merest trifles belonging to César and Constance were in their place, he had dreamed of giving a ball there on the day of his wedding. The preparations for the fête had been a work of love. It should be exactly like the previous one, except in the extravagances. Extravagance was over and done with. Still, the dinner was to be served by Chevet, and the guests were almost the same. The Abbé Loraux took the place of the Grand-Chancellor; and Lebas, the President of the Tribunal of Commerce, was to be there. Popinot added M. Camusot's name to the list, as an acknowledgment of the kindness he had shown to Birotteau in so many ways. M. de Vandenesse and M. de Fontaine took the place of M. and Mme. Roguin.

Césarine and Popinot had exercised their discretion in the matter of invitations to the ball. They both shrank from making a festival of their wedding, and had avoided the publicity which jars on pure and tender hearts by giving the dance on the occasion of the signing of the contract. Constance had found the cherry-colored velvet dress in which she had shone for the brief space of a single day; and Césarine had pleased herself by surprising Popinot in. the ball-dress of which he had talked times out of mind. So the house was to wear the same air of an enchanted festival, and neither Constance, nor Césarine, nor Anselme thought that there was any danger for César in this joyful surprise. They waited till four o'clock, and grew almost childish in their happiness.

After the hero of the hour had passed through the indescribable emotions of returning to the Exchange, a fresh shock awaited him in the Rue Saint-Honoré. As he came up the stairs, which still looked new, he saw his wife in the cherry-colored velvet dress; he saw Césarine, the Comte de Fontaine, the Vicomte de Vandenesse, the Baron de la Billardière, and the great Vauquelin; a light film spread over his eyes, and

Uncle Pillerault, on whose arm he leaned, felt the shudder that ran through his nephew.

"It is too much for him," the old philosopher said to the enamored Anselme; "he will not stand all the wine which you have poured out for him."

But all hearts beat so high with joy, that César's emotion and tottering steps were ascribed to an intoxication, very natural, as they thought—but not seldom fatal. When he looked round the drawing-room, and saw it filled with guests and women in ball toilets, the sublime rhythm of the *finale* of Beethoven's great symphony beat in his pulses and flooded his brain. That imaginary music streamed in on him like rays of light, sparkling from modulation to modulation; it was to be indeed the *finale* that rang clear and high through the recesses of the tired brain. Overcome by the harmony that swept through him, he laid his hand on his wife's arm, and in tones, rendered almost inaudible by the effort to keep back the flowing blood which filled his mouth:

"I am not well," he said.

Constance, in alarm, led her husband to her room; he was barely able to reach the armchair, into which he sank, exclaiming, "M. Haudry! M. Loraux!"

The Abbé came in, followed by the guests and women in evening dress, who stood in consternation. César in the midst of this brightly-colored throng grasped his confessor's hand, and laid his head on the breast of the wife who knelt beside him. A blood-vessel had been ruptured in the lungs, and the resulting aneurism was stopping his last breath.

"Behold the death of the righteous!" the Abbé Loraux said solemnly, as he stretched his hand towards César with one of those Divine gestures which Rembrandt's inspiration beheld and recorded in his picture of Christ raising Lazarus from the dead.

Christ bade Earth surrender her prey; the good priest sped a soul to heaven, where the martyr to commercial integrity should receive an unfading palm.

FINE WORKS OF FICTION
AVAILABLE IN QUALITY
PAPERBACK EDITIONS FROM
CARROLL & GRAF

☐ Appel, Allen/TIME AFTER TIME	Cloth $17.95
☐ Asch, Sholem/THE APOSTLE	$10.95
☐ Asch, Sholem/MARY	$10.95
☐ Asch, Sholem/THE NAZARENE	$10.95
☐ Asch, Sholem/THREE CITIES	$10.50
☐ Ashley, Mike (ed.)/THE MAMMOTH BOOK OF SHORT HORROR NOVELS	$8.95
☐ Asimov, Isaac/THE MAMMOTH BOOK OF CLASSIC SCIENCE FICTION	$8.95
☐ Babel, Isaac/YOU MUST KNOW EVERYTHING	$8.95
☐ Balzac, Honoré de/CESAR BIROTTEAU	$8.95
☐ Bellaman, Henry/KINGS ROW	$8.95
☐ Bernanos, George/DIARY OF A COUNTRY PRIEST	$7.95
☐ Céline, Louis-Ferdinand/CASTLE TO CASTLE	$8.95
☐ Chekov, Anton/LATE BLOOMING FLOWERS	$8.95
☐ Conrad, Joseph/SEA STORIES	$8.95
☐ Conrad, Joseph & Ford Madox Ford/ THE INHERITORS	$7.95
☐ Conrad, Joseph & Ford Madox Ford/ROMANCE	$8.95
☐ Coward, Noel/A WITHERED NOSEGAY	$8.95
☐ Cozzens James Gould/THE LAST ADAM	$8.95
☐ de Montherlant, Henry/THE GIRLS	$11.95
☐ Dos Passos, John/THREE SOLDIERS	$9.95
☐ Feuchtwanger, Lion/JEW SUSS	$8.95 Cloth $18.95
☐ Feuchtwanger, Lion/THE OPPERMANS	$8.95
☐ Fisher, R.L./THE PRINCE OF WHALES	Cloth $12.95
☐ Flaubert, Gustave/NOVEMBER	$7.95
☐ Fonseca, Rubem/HIGH ART	$7.95
☐ Ford Madox Ford/see CONRAD, JOSEPH	
☐ Fuchs, Daniel/SUMMER IN WILLIAMSBURG	$8.95
☐ Gold, Michael/JEWS WITHOUT MONEY	$7.95
☐ Greenberg & Waugh (eds.)/THE NEW ADVENTURES OF SHERLOCK HOLMES	$8.95

- [ ] Greene, Graham & Hugh/THE SPY'S BEDSIDE BOOK $7.95
- [ ] Hamsun, Knut/MYSTERIES $8.95
- [ ] Hardinge, George (ed.)/THE MAMMOTH BOOK OF MODERN CRIME STORIES $8.95
- [ ] Hawkes, John/VIRGINIE: HER TWO LIVES $7.95
- [ ] Hugo, Victor/NINETY-THREE $8.95
- [ ] Ibañez, Vincente Blasco/THE FOUR HORSEMEN OF THE APOCALYPSE $8.95
- [ ] Jackson, Charles/THE LOST WEEKEND $7.95
- [ ] James, Henry/GREAT SHORT NOVELS $11.95
- [ ] Lewis, Norman/DAY OF THE FOX $8.95
- [ ] Linder, Mark/THERE CAME A PROUD BEGGAR   Cloth $18.95
- [ ] Lowry, Malcolm/HEAR US O LORD FROM HEAVEN THY DWELLING PLACE $9.95
- [ ] Lowry, Malcolm/ULTRAMARINE $7.95
- [ ] Macaulay, Rose/CREWE TRAIN $8.95
- [ ] Macaulay, Rose/KEEPING UP APPEARANCES $8.95
- [ ] Macaulay, Rose/DANGEROUS AGES $8.95
- [ ] Macaulay, Rose/THE TOWERS OF TREBIZOND $8.95
- [ ] Mailer, Norman/BARBARY SHORE $9.95
- [ ] Mauriac, François/WOMAN OF THE PHARISEES $8.95
- [ ] Mauriac, François/VIPER'S TANGLE $8.95
- [ ] McElroy, Joseph/LOOKOUT CARTRIDGE $9.95
- [ ] McElroy, Joseph/PLUS $8.95
- [ ] McElroy, Joseph/A SMUGGLER'S BIBLE $9.50
- [ ] Moorcock, Michael/THE BROTHEL IN ROSENSTRASSE $6.95
- [ ] Munro, H.H./THE NOVELS AND PLAYS OF SAKI $8.95
- [ ] O'Faolain, Julia/THE OBEDIENT WIFE $8.95
- [ ] O'Faolain, Julia/NO COUNTRY FOR YOUNG MEN $8.95
- [ ] O'Faolain, Julia/WOMEN IN THE WALL $8.95
- [ ] Olinto, Antonio/THE WATER HOUSE   Cloth $18.95
- [ ] Plievier, Theodore/STALINGRAD $8.95
- [ ] Pronzini & Greenberg (eds.)/THE MAMMOTH BOOK OF PRIVATE EYE NOVELS $8.95
- [ ] Rechy, John/BODIES AND SOULS $8.95
- [ ] Scott, Evelyn/THE WAVE $9.95
- [ ] Sigal, Clancy/GOING AWAY $9.95
- [ ] Singer, I.J./THE BROTHERS ASHKENAZI $9.95

☐ Taylor, Peter/IN THE MIRO DISTRICT $7.95
☐ Tolstoy, Leo/TALES OF COURAGE AND
   CONFLICT $11.95
☐ Wassermann, Jacob/CASPAR HAUSER $9.95
☐ Wassermann, Jacob/THE MAURIZIUS CASE $9.95
☐ Werfel, Franz/THE FORTY DAYS OF
   MUSA DAGH $9.95

Available from fine bookstores everywhere or use this coupon for ordering:

Caroll & Graf Publishers, Inc., 260 Fifth Avenue, N.Y., N.Y. 10001

Please send me the books I have checked above. I am enclosing $_____ (please add $1.75 per title to cover postage and handling.) Send check or money order—no cash or C.O.D.'s please. N.Y. residents please add 8¼% sales tax.

Mr/Mrs/Miss _____

Address _____

City _____ State/Zip _____
Please allow four to six weeks for delivery.